BALDR
AND
BEATRICE

By

Mark Seinfelt

All persons and places in this book are either
fictitious or are used fictitiously.

ISBN: 1453847308
ISBN-13: 9781453847305
LCCN: 2010914471

ALSO BY MARK SEINFELT

FICTION

Henry Boulanger of Mushannon Town
Symphonie Fantastique

NONFICTION

Final Drafts: Suicides of World-Famous Authors

MADE BY MARK FOR MELINDA IN
CELEBRATION OF HER BIRTHDAY

Forgetful heart that is like a shadow walking in my brain....

Bob Dylan

Perhaps, I thought, while her words still hung in the air between us like a wisp of tobacco smoke—a thought to fade and vanish like smoke without a trace—perhaps all our loves are merely hints and symbols; a hill of many invisible crests; doors that open as in a dream to reveal only a further stretch of carpet and another door; perhaps you and I are types and this sadness which sometimes falls between us springs from disappointments in our search, each straining through and beyond the other, snatching a glimpse now and then of the shadow which turns the corner always a pace or two ahead of us.

Evelyn Waugh

Contents

waikan

worak

waikan

Two plunge downward

It must have been as if he had come from where dreams are born! The first words he spoke to her: "And I, Princess, consign myself to your ear and find that nest sufficient." Ah, if truth be told, they both came from the same magic realm, the land of eternal ideas of which everything here below presents but a transient image, a pale copy or reflection. Yet this chaotic, shifting realm beneath always attracts souls of light, who forgetting their higher home for a time voluntarily take on fleshly garb and enter the world of form and death out of an independent and spontaneous—yet potent, oh-so potent— desire, a longing to mingle with matter in order to experience the opposite of the timeless and eternal, to know the sensual and passional, the mutable and transient, and come to understand the one through the other. Thus diverse souls continually and routinely make the happy fall out of the fixed and higher realm and, caught up in the whirr and churning of the primal-passional, assist and partake directly in the All Highest's continuous act of kaleidoscopic creation, and perform as agents of that creation—lesser deities perhaps—indeed mortal deities—yet did not the All Highest Himself once become mortal? —but nonetheless still wrestling with refractory matter, shaping and giving it form, and thereby gratifying their desire to be at one with the All Highest, to share and take part in his ceaseless procreative toil if only in a time-bound way and for a span of three score and ten.

Baldr aimed and aspired to compose beautiful *Minnelieder* and Beatrice to embroider huge tapestries, vivid explosions of color, to express their love, but the two together also wanted to jointly create in higher and loftier fashion. Why did the two souls of light fall? Simply put, Baldr and his beloved Beatrice decided to cross the threshold between the worlds for Beatrice to bear Baldr's children. They decided to experience the eternal in the now, because together in the upper reaches and highest circles they had dreamed the dream of Titurel and Britomart, their potential offspring. And did not the Highest also become flesh precisely for the sake of his offspring Man, to redeem his child from error and point the way back home? He too shared in the sin. He too in his own person experienced the fall—the descent into hell—because he loved his offspring even in their perishable, pupal state. He understood that He lived in them and they in Him and what seemed sin truly wasn't, for his children the name givers were his co-creators. Only through these agent-witnesses of his puissant creation did He attain his Godhead, for it was just these poor fallen yet free agents of the divine will who provided the means for Him to ceaselessly toil and divert himself in the world of forms. For it was precisely God's highest task and function to dream both the eternal and mutable worlds, to strive and create forever. He shaped the eternal realm first and initially found all pure and perfect. Yet somehow Perfection itself came in time to seem flawed. God saw the need for the insufficient and limited, of which the eternal world did not yet have sufficient knowledge, so he brought into being the material realm and once again began creating and did not stop but found himself engaged and caught up in ongoing explosive genesis. All the souls in the Upper Circles felt to their core the new urge, the sudden desire for the ever shifting. Baldr and Beatrice could experience each other's essence perfectly, knew Milton's communion of Angels. Not restrained by the exclusive bars of membrane, joint or limb, they could mix their irradiance. Easier than air with air their spirits could embrace; they could merge and comprehend each other utterly but nothing new, independent or separate would come to be out of their communion and perfect knowing of each other. No restrained conveyance, as of flesh to flesh, needed they to commune soul to soul but their interpenetration remained sterile. Nonetheless they saw a vision— scales fell from their eyes—of the children that could be, sensed their potentiality, their almost quickness, but the only place those children could come into existence they quickly realized—now understood—was in the sublunary world, where they would underpin the flux with something sound solid eternal. So the two decided to depart from their garden high in the sky, the land of eternal forms and ideas, and to discover the herebefore and the hereafter in the here.

Intent on reifying her love, a tigress already licking the faces of her little offspring with their shut and unseeing eyes and snarling at the male to keep off, Beatrice leapt first. She had the greater strength and desire, quickly developed mother's nerve. The weaker, hesitating Baldr followed on her heels immediately however, whispering, "I'll come, I'll pursue you from behind" into her ear just as she disappeared. Swooning, his heart amputated from his breast at the moment she absented herself, he too, willed to cross over and seconds after her, found himself plunging downward through the void headed toward the glorious and immemorial Deutsche, or, according to the harder or softer pronunciation, Teutsche Lands during the reign of the greatest Holy Roman Emperor after Charlemagne Carolus Augustus the Caesar Emperor of the West, Friedrich Barbarossa whose coming to the throne because of his Hohenstauffen father and Bavarian dam healed the breach between Welf and Waibling, that brave keen generous man proud violent self-willed with sparkling blue eyes fair hair and beard with red tinge, for which the Italians famously fondly denominated him, the king destined to sleep under the mountain until his country would most need him, who as an old man his beard all white after the capture of Jerusalem by Saladin, before the other two kings Richard of England and Philip of France embarked and set sail, ventured out first on the Third Crusade, who at Iconium with his war cry of Christ reigns Christ conquers overcame the enemy but only a few days later a chill struck him as he bathed in the cold, swift river Kalykadmus and he sank into the rapid current his body later found and buried at Antioch though his loyal Germans swore he had not died but sat turned to stone with all his loyalist knights round a great table, his once red now white beard growing through the fissures in the rock, asleep till ravens ceased far in the future to fly through the gray mists and clouds wreathing the top and sides of his enchanted mountain.

For before willing themselves outside of the eternal realm Baldr and Beatrice both agreed as to the time and place of their incarnation in the fallen world and had selected their respective fathers and mothers. Of the many locations she had looked at and examined she had fallen in love with and had therefore chosen the pleasant if tiny, in comparison to kingdoms elsewhere, Landgraviate of Thuringia through which ran that stretch of ancient rounded mountains covered by forests of fir and pine the *Thüringer Wald* with its ancient path the *Rennsteig*, following the summits of the main ridges and marking the shift in terrain from green rolling hills to the more towering Alps of the South, her father-to-be a Prince and Imperial Elector. She entered the vale of woe in the year of our lord 1174. Baldr had determined to begin life in the flesh as a son to educated commoners in an adjoining little state but who nonetheless would rise to the rank of Minnesinger and because of his prowess at song writing become a knight and vassal of a great German lord, but, as they had not leapt simultaneously, he would fall to earth a full seven years after she, he calculated the instant before his venture down, his flight and precipitation through utter middle darkness, chaos and eternal night. Still he vowed that his hesitation would not thwart him. He made up his mind to reunite with her.

However, a spiteful shadow-being and thief of others' shadows to darken his own—a horrid angel of the gloom and murk and the stonily unconscious who hated creation and light and longed for the universe to stretch out and keep stretching until the night sky became dark but for the nearby moons and planets of the solar system, for space to expand and the stars one by one like the lights in a Tenebrae service to wink out, who in his deepest inmost heart became a servile, groveling creature a devoted servant of negation and naught, waylaid Baldr as his soul descended to take birth. Arms stretched aloft, talons at the ready to catch the fluttering flibbet as it flew by him, the Black Prince snatched in his loathsome claws Baldr's mote of light and diverted it elsewhere, far away from its intended destination. Wherever there is love, these monsters come by inimical attraction. Because the heavens remain propitious to true lovers, the beasts of the abysses band to destroy them, stimulated by innumerable sad victories. Every love tale involves an epic war of the upper and lower powers.

Where Baldr found himself

Far below: two ranges of metamorphosed sandstone rise upward, together forming an oval ring of hills. Baldr, as he falls, sees both—the southern range wider, the hills all adjoining and adjacent, whereas the rises and mounts curving northward stand farther apart. He hears a voice he knows not wherefrom telling of the dawn of time and the first and most ancient of days: of how, during the period of mountain sculpting, when the world stood newborn and the fires of creation still seethed, the Earthmaker compressed and folded the rock of these ranges like bread dough and subjected it to great heat and great pressure which fused the quartz sand with the quartz silica and made the resultant stone with its fine laminations and ripples resistant to wind and water. A swathe of hummocky moraine drapes both ranges, bisecting each down its middle from north to south. Isolated, small, flatcapped buttes of younger less durable rock than the sandstone dot the surrounding landscape. Such layers of rock once overlaid and buried the quartzite or "metamorphosed sandstone" itself but eroded away with the passage of time whereas the quartzite withstood all the ravages of weathering and climate change. For after the folding and transmutation of the earth and centuries upon centuries of erosion, the Earthmaker caused the waters to rise and a great inland sea submerged the region and the tops of the hills of both ranges became islands until after another seemingly immeasurable span of time the waters receded and laid bare the rocks to the elements once more. From somewhere below the spirit voice intones that the strip of low mounds and hillocks of sediment and debris covering and cutting across each of these two ranges marked the final advance of two great floes of ice that the Earthmaker thrust and drove into the region with his two all-powerful hands at some later but still ancient and remote time. These floes had long since melted leaving the debris and transported rock behind in their wake.

The voice seems to emanate from a cobalt-blue pupil surrounded and ringed by conifer and deciduous hardwood forest still far below but coming closer and closer with each passing second. The lake-eye gleams from an elongate gorge, a basin plugged on both sides by terminal moraine, in the southern range. Gleaming talus mantles the gorge's sides varying in color from pink to maroon to darkish purple. The new entity the being once known as Baldr blinks suddenly within the descending orb. When his eyes reopen he has lost sight of the feature the target he has increasingly fixed on while plunging downward from the sky— the circle of blue water. He looks up and down the southern range two or three times before again finding it. The eye formerly clear and piercingly blue has since cataracted and clouded, a white nimbus of fog stealing in across the rippling waves with the approach of twilight. An otherworldly lake, the child being once called Baldr thinks to himself. *Limbo Lake.* Honing in on the target once again, the mote of light hurtles downward at increased speed. The child being sees sweeping views of lake with bluffs shooting upward from its shores high into the air with fantastical outcroppings and great cragged lopsided formations of rocks at their tops, huge stone blocks stacked in haphazard fashion one atop the other by a race of giants, and on the eastern bluff a great field of purple, cascading boulders coming down to the shore itself. The ball of light falling so fast for most of its journey begins decreasing its speed. It floats downward through the drizzle until it comes to rest along the lakeshore at the foot of the eastern bluff. As it touches down directly in front of four or five cat o' nine tails whipping in the wind it looks like an iridescent bubble as a ray of sun catches and glances it. As a fresh wind rises off the lake the bubble pops and a little boy materializes. He looks glassy and transparent yet clearly has a freckled face, blue eyes and the whitest of blond hair. He peers across the waves and a stone's throw from the shore makes out a lone white water lily as it bobs up and down on the bosom of the darkling water. His eyes slant shut with the sunset.

When he next opens them it is morning. With the new day the haze has begun to lift, and he sees minnows darting in the shallow water at his feet. He hears a gentle rustle of tree limbs and looks at the reflection of the thick-foliaged forest in the water then across the lake at the opposite majestic five hundred-foot bluff. He hears the spirit voice in the water murmuring and intoning the syllables *da-wa-kah-char-gra da-wa-kah-char-gra* over and over again. Soon his eyes droop, as the voice makes him drowse, and years, many years, pass as the wheel keeps turning about in its same repetitive annual circuit. The transparent ageless boy, a soul without a body, a changeling and homunculus most visible in the early dawn, sleeps his suspect only marginally realized existence away closing his tired, irritated eyes suddenly drained of their former blue hue to become gray and virtually colorless and keeping them tightly clamped shut both through the nights and through the days his glassy outline all but fading away and disappearing completely from the spot where he sits on a great pink rock. Many lifetimes of quick and living things go by and generation follows after generation before he opens his eyes once again. He always hibernates during the cold, cruel winters, and in time starts dropping down between two red boulders into a tiny den where he curls up in a fetal position as the snow begins to fall and accumulate, burying the world under a deep and heavy mantle of white for the long months the earth lies dormant and inactive. During brief spells of awareness, mostly in the early spring, when flute-like sounds seem to emanate from the lake and flowers fill with the hum of bees, tempted by the dulcet sound he hears coming from the water, the boy enters the shallows and feels either sharp stones or scratchy water plants under his feet or else the squish of sand between his toes until he steps out of his depths and has to begin paddling wildly with his hands and feet, at last swimming vigorously in the direction of the lone water lily, or in the autumn with its brilliant foliage and irruption of scintillating color he explores the many acres of pristine forests round the lake and observes all the different animal and bird tracks in the silt loam soil. He leaves no prints for the eagle-eyed hunter to follow but sees marks made by others with ten toes among those of the myriad species and creatures of the lake. He also sees the effigies of lynxes and other animals now familiar to him from his explorations traced on small mounds, chiseled there by unknown hands. In the summer he climbs the multiple cliffs, scales great chimneys and high ramparts scuttling over the beautiful but smooth and slick red and purple quartzite and looking down from his high perch at the lake below and dreaming that he is again dropping in a freefall from somewhere high in the sky. He often follows a favorite route that ascends and descends the spectacular East

Bluff twice. He sets his face to the tallest and most precipitate of the rock formations that rise highest into the blue, riven, jagged crags where the nimblest hands and feet would be rendered useless and only wings would avail the power and means to reach the topmost summits, but with the morning sun his glassy form casts no shadow from where he stands to the base of the first cliff such as on another dawn he witnesses a bear standing erect on its hind legs cast from the very same spot. He who has once hurtled downwards from above does not fear to scale the heights but easily finds toe and finger slots. He loves to ascend the gorgeous large buttresses until the winter snows drive him to his den underneath the red and purple boulders. He has no fear the rock will slide and shift during his long winter slumbers, that in the early spring he will awaken to a loud crack as of thunder as the boulders begin tumbling down the slope and come crashing into the water of the lake for long ago he has taken note of the angle of repose of the talus and how tight and snug the quartzite blocks all lie. Usually flute tones herald the stir and rerousing of the world after the long dead time of winter but one year the drowsy child is awakened by high-pitched shrieks of young girls, of both prepubescent maidens and those who have this month just become women, mingled with the dulcet flute tones. An animal cry he has not yet heard and suddenly open eyed, every fiber of his being pulsing with adrenalin rushes to investigate, emerging from his gap in the rock like a mouse that has mistakenly entered a snake hole and whipped about his tiny heart throbbing in fear at the first scent of copperhead. As he careens over the scree, launches in the air and comes tumbling down on hands and knees in the white sand of the beach his eyes turn almost as blue as the cobalt-blue lake itself when drenched in summer sun at midday when he first catches sight of fellow ten-toes these same crying young girls who appear to him to be a kind or species of deer on two legs. He sees these black-haired, olivefaced creatures with slightly flattened nose bridges in their sleeveless dresses made of two deerskins joined together at the shoulders which he can't tell yet is not their own hide, with their brown almond eyes, pupils, suddenly grown large and wide as a fawn's upon encountering a panther, as they run toward and at last leap up over him, displaying their leggings also of deerskin which reach from their knees down to their ankles and are tied on by a thong just below the knee, onto the purple and red boulders above, and then on across the boulder field bounding across alternating huge stones of purple and red, as they make for the trailhead in the pine trees on the far side, their squared chins pointed high, the wings of their flat, round noses flaring as they look back over their shoulders to see if they are being pursued. Soon they all disappear and the air round him no longer rings with their screams and wailing. Maybe their time will come next year; in twelve months they will perhaps overcome their fear. Again he hears flute tones intermixed with a wonderful new ten-toe sound that reminded him of the purling of a stream. Baldr heard for the first time the laughter of young women in first bud: bright, bubbly and babbling as any brook or rill, and, turning his head again toward the lakeshore, he saw them, their hair wound in long single braids which descended half way down their backs, the older sisters of the affrighted and fleeing barefooted maids who had almost trampled him to death, as at water's margin they took their bead necklaces and medicine bags from around their necks and kicked off their soft squaretoed footgear whose upper front reminded Baldr of the split upper lip and dark nose of a doe and then began divesting themselves of all their garments first their waist sashes then their long tanned deerskin shirts with their bead and quill designs and finally their underclothes of woven nettle fiber and the fingerwoven garters which held in place their leggings, and afterward in their true skins fearlessly plunging into the lake and swimming out toward the fluteplayer standing in the shallows in profile in a breechclout of deerskin which passed between his legs and up over a waist thong leaving flaps in the front and back. Thousands and thousands of waterbeads little transparent globes or eggs glistened on his great humpback and atop his head he wore an otterskin turban fringed with turkey beards, the otter's snout brought round in a circle so it could clasp its tail in its teeth. Above the turban rose a great crest or roach of animal hair which descended in alternating short-long rows of tail hairs of deer dyed red and white guard hairs of porcupines all the way down to the fluteplayer's shoulders, a bone roach spreader running through the headdress' top center lifting the stiff hair upward and outwards, three or four antenna-like protrusions of upraised porcupine quills trimmed with eagle feathers projecting from the very top. Across the water doe of the familiar four-legged kind emerged from the forest and also plunged into the water and swam in *kokopelli's* direction, for Baldr at once abruptly knew the humpbacked flautist's name and he realized—it dawned within him with sure and ringing certainty— that it was the god's flute playing that chased away winter and ushered in the spring. An army of tiny lizards began to scuttle from out of the grass fringing the white sand. They too made for the water. Snakes also slither out from their winter lairs to bathe themselves in the sun. To all these living things Baldr remains invisible. *Kokopelli* himself, however, suddenly becomes aware of his presence for he stops making music, ceases playing the flute and says quite clearly to Baldr though he does not open his mouth, does not part his lips *lost little child you don't belong to the sturgeon people you are not one of the fishy stinkards.* He slips the thong bound to his flute round his neck and plunges both his hands into the cold water to catch a wriggling great eel of a fish. The eel struggles to slip out of the God's clutch and back into the water where the two- and four-legged does bathe. The hump-back at last succeeds in forcing the coiling and protesting creature under the front flap of his breechclout, and by tightening his waist thong securing it there where it still writhes and squirms and makes a prominent bulge. *Kokopelli* has not forgotten Baldr. Although sunshiny but seconds before, it starts to rain when the God steps out of the water. As he bends over, his giant face looms down at Baldr, who only now sees the swarm of midges and mosquitoes that circle and buzz about the God's headdress. *You must have fallen off my back or I caught hold of you accidentally when I grabbed the flower seeds to toss and sow, which I also carry on my hump with the souls of all the humans and animals destined to find mothers in the springtime and take their births after their kind later in the year.*

The God invited Baldr to remount, but now the little spirit quaked and trembled and felt a fear akin to that of the prepubescent girls who had just now fled into the pines. *Kokopelli* stared and stared at him. He marveled at the transparent thing's strange countenance. *I bathe and play my flute in all the rivers and lakes of the Earthmaker's land. You do not belong to the Hocągara or any of the other peoples. None have eyes or hair the color of yours. Come anyway. I will find you a friendly home. Occasionally a rabbit or deer is born snowy white though its parents' skins are of the customary brown color.*

Baldr spoke up: *Great* kokopelli *I fell from on high but my journey's end was not this world. The Black spirit intercepted me and with his great claw knocked me off course.*

Kokopelli bid the sprite to mount anyway, saying the child could choose another life to live now that he had come here, but as the God spoke Baldr remembered his Beatrice and darted under a boulder and ran down the trail to his den. *Kokopelli* took pity on the little lost one and called to him sweetly. He even played a few bars on his flute in an attempt to bring him forth into the open air, but after a time, he sadly shook his head and moved on as he had many more streams, rivers and lakes to visit. Nine months later Baldr would again encounter the Ho-Chunk ten-toes. Many of the women in first bud whom he had previously seen swimming in the lake would then be clasping nursing babes to their breasts.

Beatrice stares into Oma's cauldron

Beatrice (whatever new name she bore in her Thuringian incarnation) did not glance into her grandmother's great iron kettle at the same moment the fertility god *kokopelli* espied the not-yet-born transparent wraithlike entity, the potentially quick child who in the fullness of his being had once been the unfallen Baldr and who could rise to that same fullness once again if he could only somehow, some way, find his way home to his beloved Beatrice-Beatrix-Beatris. She who makes happy by disclosing beauty and conferring benefaction. At least not linearly speaking. What happened to Baldr happened on an altogether different timeline. In another present as eternal and abiding as Beatrice's, separated from it by a great span. Six hundred and more rotations of the Wheel of The Year with its eight spokes indicating the solstices and equinoxes, the four greater and the four lesser Sabbats. If not by a whole vista of time-coulisses opening out infinitely, as if in mockery of the human mind's puny ability to even begin to comprehend the complexity and interconnectedness of all creation. Nor did Beatrice's young eyes have the power and discernment to make out either the fluteplayer in his breechclout and shaggy mosquito-and-tick-breeding headdress or the glassy young boy standing on the sandy beach. She merely saw, as she leaned over and looked into the great basin, a lake in springtime, the newly green branches of the encircling trees fluttering in the wind as the wavelets undulated in the sunshine and came lapping into the shore. Her eyes peered as through an open door nonetheless. Baldr felt her force and presence. Even though she was just a slip of a girl and not her majestic, heavenly self he felt her power radiating out to him through the conduit supplied by the ancient ones—the spirits of water. The thought of her arose in his mind for the first time since he fell to earth at Spirit Lake and for an instant he perceived her vast child's face with her green eyes and curly corkscrew curls and her toothy smile of wonder and enchantment. The elongate basin of quartzite bluffs surrounding the lake became the rim of a great cauldron, down into which the outsize face peered. The lake itself became the water in the cauldron. The sandy beach and the ring of trees appeared in miniature on the surface of the water. The boy felt he should be on the outside looking down into the bowl standing hand-in-hand with the girl he saw with bent head and eyes open in wonderment. He had to escape out of one reality into the other. So he set his heart against the sweet solicitations of *kokopelli* and shut out the bell-like, silvery tones of his flute and darted back in his tunnel underneath the red and purple rocks.

Though her surprise and stupefaction never bated or let up, Beatrice, however, was used to seeing all sorts of apparitions and mental pictures when she peered into her mirror. Oma's kettle often divulged strange things unbidden and spontaneous. Visions of other worlds as well as other eras and epochs of this same world, and Oma's familiar voice at the same time the voice of the ancient and all-powerful World-Mother herself, manifested to Beatrice out of the air: All that can be is. Everything that can possibly happen does happen. Simultaneously and all at once. And indeed Beatrice often beheld multiple reflections of herself: saw the events, say, of the previous week or a few

days again play themselves out but with subtle differences: on
her birthday her father, Oma's son, the Landgrave, gave her a
kitten instead of a mastiff whelp with broad skull, beady eyes,
drooping ears and pendulous lips. Or she still received the same
soulful, sad-eyed dog but Father wore slightly different attire.
While he donned the same hat trimmed with peacock's feathers, the same surcoat of linsey-woolsey without sleeves and a
black silk cloak open at the chest, reddish brown breeches and
long hoses the same color as the breeches and kept up by the
lower part of the latter, he wore felt slippers instead of his
customary high shoes with Polish points, or instead of the cap
with peacock feathers, he wore a red velvet one, or, yet again,
he had no hat on at all, his long, flowing flaxen or light brown
hair tied above his forehead into a kind of tuft and then made
to fall behind his head like a horse's tail. Beatrice had to look
carefully: sometimes she saw ten or eleven little discrepancies
from the old picture lodged in her young memory: sometimes
she challenged herself to find so many disparities and diver-
gences but could not for the short time the image remained in
focus before another likeness or representation appeared. Her
eyes ranged up and down the length and breadth of the fluc-
tuating, watery picture and flicked back and forth and from
side to side. She looked at the ermine or martin trim of the
surcoat to see if its color had switched from brown to red.
Sometimes to her surprise she saw no trim at all. It had vanished, and she registered another change. She counted the capa-
cious, generous buttons going down the linsey-woolsey to make
sure that their number remained as she remembered. She mea-
sured the long sleeves of the cloak to see if the slits up the sides
where the arms went through remained of equal length or had
magically shortened. Mostly the changes she witnessed were

minute. Yet other times she squinted and instead of just one image she saw the same, single image multiplied as if she saw out of an insect's eyes instead of her own: each of the different versions had small, subtle alterations from one another or even key, major ones: in one of the many beads her mother, for instance, stood alongside her smiling, laughing father as he presented Beatrice with the puppy: her mother who died in childbirth as she was delivered of Beatrice's poor little stillborn brother a month before Beatrice's own fifth birthday, twelve months before, one rotation of the great Wheel having taken place in the interim. There she stood nonetheless, her blonde braids flowing down from her white linen cap fringed all round with tiny bells and pink and blue lappets. In another bead Beatrice's mother sat nursing the living pink wrinkle-faced little manikin as Beatrice sat next to her imitating what she saw with the yellow-eyed white-and-gray kitten, the little living breathing thing which she pretended to likewise love and mother. Also, sometimes the multiple Beatrices she beheld did not all share the same face and features. She didn't just see parallels. The lips might be less thin or more full, and the color of hair and eye would differ as would the girls' often bewilderingly odd and variegated apparel: nonetheless Beatrice felt herself alive in each of the girls (the many cups, the many daughters, you will pour yourself into, Oma's voice, which at the same time was also the Earth Mother's great voice, called out, the descent of the essential you through many embodiments and manifestations BOTH PARALLEL AND SKEW) and briefly, for the shortest of instances, Beatrice could even see out their eyes and glimpse into all their separate and far-flung worlds so at variance from her own, and she not only knew that she was still herself but she understood the strange things of that world;

understood that she held, just drawn from each of their rawhide holsters bestudded with blue, red, and green rhinestones her two gold-sighted, silver cap guns firing them high above her head BANG-BANG-BANG as she flashed her most toothsome happy smile as on cue Pap-pap snapped the photograph: his prize shot of his little curly haired sweet-pea in her miniature, child's ten-gallon hat, tied onto her sweet little noodle head by a tiny braided string right under her chinny-chin-chin by her Grammy June: Shirley Temple better look out! In yet another bead she recognized herself as the brunette-plainjane-Lancaster-Quaker girl wooed by the tubby, yellow-haired Dutch boy who trafficked in charms and medicinal herbs and unbeknownst to his good, pious, no-nonsense progenitors went into the woods to attend the Indian pow-wows and who said he sold his soul to the Black man of the Forest one moonlit night as he danced round the heathens' fires and gulped firewater so as to win her love on this side of the great divide: he cared not what befell his immortal part on the other. Yet the beads bubbled so quickly, multiplied and popped now in such a seething ferment she forgot the thread of each life as they all bled over into one another as her attention and concentration diverted from one forming bead to countless other forming beads. She beheld a great tapestry made by all the Beatrices and forgot the single destinies of each. Oma's voice would call her back into the real world of the *Landgrafshaft*, now a state of the Holy Roman Empire, but formerly a Frankish duchy and a Pagan kingdom. She had peered long enough into the great kettle. One can't dream the whole day away. Oma had in her turn stared into the very self-same kettle: her Oma's and her Oma's before that. Each, under the guidance of her predecessor in the great chain, would develop the second sight of the Mothers of the Thuringii.

But Beatrice's particular own Oma had to proceed with her granddaughter's education with great secrecy and caution. Each time granddaughter herself became grandmother, she found the mission of passing on the old ways a more difficult task than had her own grandmother, but although the late Landgraf had chosen a daughter of the people when he took Beatrice's Oma for his bride yet he had particularly insisted she give up the old practices and follow the Cross, and indeed Beatrice's Oma loved the crucified one but she perceived with the wisdom of all the mothers in the chain before her, some of whom had known the pain of a Mary upon losing a child, that each and every day the supposed people of the faith, the very ones who professed that the Christ had died for them, crucified him anew, put him back up on the tree in their fear, nailed his hands and feet once more to the wood with the spikes of their intolerance and the unbending nails of their dogma, whereas the Christ himself was incarnate love and forgiveness. The Lord Jesus had the soul of a woman. He belonged as much to Mary as the stern Patriarch. He would never countenance the killing of those who did not think and believe exactly as he. Oma's own son quickly took to his father's creed, espousing and embracing it unhesitatingly, steadfastly keeping his eyes and mind shut to all other influence, and in his capacity as Landgraf doing all he could to stamp out the old beliefs and persecute their practitioners. So Oma had to hush her granddaughter whenever in her son's company they strolled through the winding corridors and the great Romanesque rooms which comprised the magnificent edifice of the Wartburg, the great feudal castle and seat of the Thuringian landgraves, constructed round the square, crenellated watchtower built by Ludwig der Springer count of Schauenburg, which sits so majestically on its hillside overlooking Eisenach. According to legend, Ludwig when he first saw the little mountain, enchanted by the site, shouted: *"Warte, Berg, du sollst mir eine Burg werde."* He toted clay from the neighboring land, which he indeed owned, to the top of the little *Berg*, so he could truthfully avow that the fortress or *Burg* that he would erect there, though he was destined to only complete the *Warte* or tower, stood on Ludwig's soil. Yes, Oma would have to look down at the little girl and squeeze her hand, their agreed upon signal, when Beatrice began to prate in front of her father about events she saw happening around her in the chapel, the *Palas* and *Landgrafenhaus* (though none but she and Oma witnessed them: for only those two did they seem real and actual): how she saw a great *Sängersaal* or Hall of Minstrels arise beside the chapel (she minutely described frescoes celebrating the triumph of Christianity and her father believed in this instance she was rapt in beatific vision), a place of courtly culture where the minstrels would gather to engage in their great contest or *Sängerkrieg* in order to determine who of the guild paid greatest homage to Frau Minne or Dame Venus (Oma sharply squeezed her granddaughter's hand at the mention of the old goddess), or how the black old Teufel got ink thrown in his face when he jeered at and tried to distract and hamstring in his work that sensitive emotionally overwrought always testy and nervous monk Junker Jörg (Oma positively blanched when Beatrice said she saw the ink-covered face of the red-eyed Tempter). When the two again stood alone, Oma clasped the coiled buns on each side of Beatrice's head and scolded and upbraided the little girl unmercifully, threatening to never allow her to stare into her kettle again. But later when she was again her kind old Oma self, she admitted that she also experienced visions of things to come, how she too had seen the saintly woman from Hungary dispensing gifts who would be brought to the castle at the age of four and would be sent to Marburg a widow (*Witwe*) and exile (*Verbännte*) at twenty-one by her scheming and conniving brother-in-law, but also centuries later the students of the newly formed German *Burschenschaften* marching to the Wartburg to celebrate the German victory over the first of the three great Antichrists, the French son of the Devil, who burnt books in effigy on the castle hill—substituting scraps of parchment bearing the titles of the conservative volumes for the costly books themselves, though one of their number would assassinate the author of one of the tomes but two years after, as they gathered round the bonfire and called for a unified German nation and finally, even farther hence, the days of the land's occupation by the great Power to the East when armoured dragons with red stars on their sides, traveling upon two tracks of endlessly rotating rectangular iron belts, traversed the land and roving and rolling over the terrain plunged through all manner of muck and mud. Again and again the old woman cautioned her granddaughter to keep quiet about her visions. Although when the two were alone, she admitted that she herself beheld the shadows of things to come—that she, too, shared in the second sight. Beatrice obstinately refused to listen to her Oma and childishly prattled about all she saw. No one, however, paid her any heed. Oma feared needlessly, for Beatrice saw, prattled, and then forgot.

Red Horn

The spirit voice in the water murmured and intoned the syllables *da-wa-kah-char-gra da-wa-kah-char-gra*. The morning star shone resplendently in the eastern sky. Its reflection blazed in the lake and the words *da-wa-kah-char-gra da-wa-kah-char-gra* seemed to emanate from the reflected jewel. Before dawn, the entire tribe of ten-toes from the reverend elders in their ceremonial garbs with special designs and feathers woven in the cloth, their faces, arms and chests painted, and copper long-nosed and short-nosed god maskettes suspended from their pierced ears to the old and young women in their long full deerskin dresses, their necklaces of fawns' hooves, and their three styles of headdress to the countless children all naked and some splashing into the water, the entire Hocąk nation had gathered on the beach to watch and listen, and Baldr crouched among them unperceived and unnoticed by any, so intent were the Hocąk people, even the great shamans and medicine men who under normal circumstance might have made out and discerned the sprite or little child's spirit, to witness the great miracle then taking place. Silver beam after silver beam of bi-lobed arrow flights came streaming down to the lake from the sky at the pre-dawn rising of the sun's harbinger in the east. The reflected jewel brightened until it gleamed blue-white in the dull waters, and the voice of Morning Star, *mą'ųna's* or Earthmaker's son—the great spirit created by the deity's own

hands who periodically took birth among the two-legged walkers, the puniest and most helpless of Earthmaker's children, in
order to drive off and defeat their foes and adversaries, who
from the very first of days had constantly plagued and tried to
kill off the two-legged children of *mą'ųna*, all the wicked spirits
from the Beneath World, the cold dank realm of the Underwater
Panther that hybrid cougar-rattlesnake-deer-and-hawk, as well
as the multi-headed green-and-red horned serpents, the especial
antagonists and foemen of the Thunderers, the Birdmen and
Falcon Beings of the Overworld with whom they forever stand
in fierce, mutual opposition, as well as the ancient Corn Mother
or Woman Who Never Dies herself—spoke, spoke from the
waters of the lake. The old raconteur, the Father of all raconteurs, launched into yet another of his endless, extended, meandering, braggadocious stories (the star-deity of the Overworld
a *waika* or an immortal became his familiar funny old human
self a *worak* when he crossed over to the lake and again stood
among his people. Few could see his spectral form which was
transparent as Baldr's own, but while he walked on the shore
in his human skin as a god he shot the swift, silver arrows carrying his golden flow of words, as dexterous in his marksman-
ship as Venus' own son. From the bright star, his heavenly home,
they came down at the cobalt-blue lake below, whizzing at
incredible speed across all that great distance, and those who
had their ears open could hear Red Horn's jocular laughing
voice) most of which long and mighty narratives concerned his
own exalted bumptious self—how he led war parties to contest
both the giants and the water spirits—and his two splendid
enterprising sons, the eldest *hejąkiga* (One Horn) the child of
the orphan girl She Who Wears A White Beaver Skin Wrap,
and his near twin the much longer-nosed *herok'aga* (Without

26

Horns) the son of a giantess with a long nose and even longer red hair, one of the tribe of *wąge-rucge* or man-eaters who stacked and piled the boulders and rocks atop one another round about Spirit Lake and at all the precipitate edges and dropoffs of the surrounding cliffs and bluffs, She who challenged Morning Star (or rather Red Horn) to a game of *kisik* or chunkey, the best of all the *wąge-rucge* players, She who could whack the chunkey stones furthest over the low hills and make them fall to earth miles and miles away with either the striped or even the broken chunkey sticks. Their contest took place after Red Horn again arrived in the Middle World and again been born into an ordinary family of two-legged walkers and after Red Horn had already won the great footrace he ran along with his nine older brothers, the oldest of whom *kunu* had four arms, and some of whom, but not *kunu*, would out of jealousy attempt to send him down forever to the underworld by persuading a beautiful *wakcexi* or female water spirit to spring a trap door to the Beneath World, where she enticed him to stand at the back of her lodge. Otter and Loon however would befriend him in the underworld and help him return to earth where he would avenge himself on his disloyal brothers by hitting them with a club and turning them all into foxes and coyotes just as he earlier turned himself into a winged arrow and shot himself ahead of all the other competitors to win the big race—the red-skinned boy red from head to foot who always feasted on the deer lungs and trachea which the bi-lobed arrows resembled as well as the ceremonial calumet of the Hocągara adoption ritual—he who after winning his great victory received the two names *įco-horúšika* and *he-šucka*, the former for the two little human faces on the lobes of his ears which came alive when he attached the earbobs he had won in the race to the bottoms of his ears

and which so resembled the visages of his two future sons and
the latter for winding his hair into a long red braid or horn.
Indeed Red Horn and his two friends and fellow spirits from
the Overworld Turtle and Storms-as-he-walks engaged in a
whole series of contests with the *wąge-rucge* at the behest of their
human suppliants whom the giants were eating to extinction.
In fact, the giantess lost the game and had to give herself in
marriage to Red Horn and bear his second son because the two
little faces on Red Horn's ears made funny faces and stuck their
tongues out at her during the epic contest and caused her to
laugh and not keep her eye on the flying chunkey stones. Those
two blessed boys She Who Wears A White Beaver Skin Wrap's
and the red-haired giantess' sons (whom the two human faces
on his earlobes so resembled and eerily prefigured) the first
with identical facial features as his father and with the same
flaming red hair and even the same identical two human heads
hanging from his ears, the second a red-haired boy also but
with the living faces where his nipples should have been, always
found some way, the different versions of the endlessly shifting
and changing story all varied significantly from telling to telling—each raconteur added something new of his own devising—to reattach Red Horn's, Turtle's, and Storms-as-he-walk's
heads to their bodies and thereby reanimate them so they could
participate in the final battle with the bad and wicked spirits,
for the trio would forfeit their heads to the giants after losing
a wrestling match subsequent to Red Horn's victory over the
giantess. After his revived friends in gratitude gave short-nosed
hejąkiga and long-nosed *herok'aga* each a wonder weapon, Red
Horn spoke to them, "My sons, I have nothing to give you, for
I am not your equal and, besides, you are already just like me."
Father and sons stood as one. A man lives on in his children,

even in his long-nosed adopted ones whose noses could all be pared down to size with a sharp stone or seashell. In one raconteur's version of the final battle between Good and Evil, Red Horn led a select war party of Turtle, Wolf, Sleets-as-he-walks, Bladder, Trickster, Black Hawk, Otter, Loon and the Twins Flesh and Stump against all the evil spirits plaguing the Hocąk. As the world-transforming fight came to its climax the great chief cut off the single, very red horn from off his forehead tossing the braid into the water whereupon it ignited and immolated all the evil beings which called the water home. The leader cried, "Henceforth no man shall call me *he-šucka*. I have burnt my braid to save humanity. Hereafter all shall call me *herok'aga* or Without Horns because I have caused myself to be without any. Father and son have now in truth become one." In practically all of his human incarnations *wąkšucka* (Red Man) somehow or the other lost his head. In one of his lives, his granddaughter in that particular life (or oral narrative) had married a Forked Man who had two bodies attached at the waist and who had proved his worthiness to wed her by surviving an ordeal of her father *herok'aga's* devising, and she had set up home with him and his grandfather. One day she looked into the fire and saw a head made red by the heat, tears streaming down its grieving face. The head explained to the girl their blood relation and explained that the Forked Man's grandfather had just beheaded him and had thrown the skull in the fire while the headless body ran up and down Red Hill in its confusion and consternation. The girl retrieved the bloated head from the fire and wrapped a white deerskin around it. She went straight to the Forked Man her husband with his two heads and two torsos and told him all that had happened. The two found the headless body and brought it back to their cave where they made a sweat bath in which they reattached the swollen and burnt head to the body. Restored and made whole, the chief of the *herok'a he-šucka* cursed the evil spirit who stole the appearance of the Forked Man's grandfather and with a wave of the hand changed its face back to that of an owl, the spirit's true features.

Morning Star-Red Horn did not relate only his own exploits. Indeed, at first—for Baldr came to the lake many times when the tribe had all gathered on the lake's rim in the early morning before dawn—Baldr heard only the music of his voice, heard only the spirit voice chanting those same mysterious words *da-wa-kah-char-gra da-wa-kah-char-gra*. Then he suddenly understood the sense of what the spirit said, the meaning of his words, and at the same time for the first time perceived his red-ochre face with its spatulate nose and slits for mouth and eyes in the center of the lake where the star also shone—his hair in an occipital bun with a long red braid dropping over his left shoulder, the two smiling and winking faces depending and bobbing from his earlobes, a triple-strand necklace of wampum beads covering his bare throat and chest, his only body clothing a cape with a spade or feather design draped over his back, and his right hand spatulate as his nose lifted high in the air, a human eye gazing out from the palm—Morning Star's human incarnation was telling the story of how the Hocąk made the great migration from the Spirit World to Red Banks. How they materialized as the Menominee chief, whose spirit animal was the *kaǧi*, the raven or northern crow, foresaw they would. In advance of their coming, the *kaǧi* chief decreed that the Menominee, the destined future friendship tribe of the Hocąk nation, cart all sorts of goods, materials, stores and provisions down to the white sand beach of *te-rok*, the western arm or as the Hocąk called it "the within lake" of *te-šišik* or the lake of the bad waters, which was a hundred miles long and ten to twenty miles wide and separated from the greater lake by the Door Peninsula. When all the supplies lay arranged on the white sand and the sun reached its height at noon a single black cloud appeared in the sky far to the east and bore down on the beach. The Menominee as the cloud approached could see that it was composed of hundreds of individual ravens or *kaǧi* spirit birds. They had rainbow plumage and their wings shone brightly with color unlike ordinary ravens. Baldr wondered if it might be the spirit of the great Barbarossa speaking from the lake for he remembered that his King was to have hair with a reddish tinge and that the raven tribe built their nests atop his mist-wreathed enchanted mountain. Red Horn, however, wore no great bushy beard. His cheeks remained clean-shaven and without bristle. Red Horn continued to narrate his story. The first bird landed and transformed into a naked, kneeling man. The Menominee chief commanded that his people bring him clothing and proclaimed the postulant chieftain of the Hocąk nation. The other birds also one by one came to ground and likewise changed into men upon landing. The Menominee showed them great hospitality and bade them all welcome to Red Banks. Another time Baldr heard him tell of the first days and how Earthmaker shaped and folded the world with his two hands, how he brought into being the great Cedar Tree the trunk of which connected the Above World, the home of the Thunderers, Sun, Moon, and Morning Star with the Middle World of the two-legged walkers and the roots of which plunged deep in the dark, watery chaos that was the home of the Underwater Panther and the Corn Mother. And on yet another occasion, Baldr witnessed Red Horn acting the lawgiver. As the Father of all raconteurs he was setting down the rules for all future Hocąk bards, explaining how the stories of the Hocąk were divided into two distinct types, the first called what-is-sacred *waikan* and the second what-is-related-and-told *worak*. The first dealt with the unchangeable, eternal Overworld and spirits or *waika* such as Morning Star and demi-deities such as Red Horn, Morning Star's semi-divine self, who could also from a certain light be considered a *worak*, a mere human being or at best a fallen divine who has thrown his lot in with man. *Waikan* did not end tragically as the heroes lived eternally and therefore could never die except temporarily as when the giants beheaded Red Horn, Turtle, and Storms-as-he-walks. A *worak* always ended in a warrior's death. A *worak* could be related all year round. No *waikan*, however, could be told while the snakes remained above the ground. The rules, of course, did not apply to the lawgiver himself. The Father of all raconteurs violated all the commandments with blithe unconcern if not positive glee. He, as the first and greatest storyteller and also a *waika*, could get away with it, but no two-legged walker dare try, no *worak* raconteur son of his, whether a normal-nosed domesticated brother and native son or a long-nosed wild Twin war captive undergoing assimilation into the Hocąk tribe whose adoption into the nation would become complete with the calumet ceremony when after several symbolic trimmings of his beak the elders adjudged him taken in and accepted into the tribe, a true son of Red Horn-Morning Star. At each stage of the process the headman gave the captive a new set of copper long-nosed and short-nosed god maskettes to pin to his nipples. On each subsequent maskette *herok'aga's* nose was trimmed shorter and shorter until at last it was the same size as *hejąkiga's*. While *he-šucka* was chief of the great spirits with horns and of the *herok'a*, the spirits without horns, his adopted son *herok'aga* was chief of the little children or fawns' spirits (those as yet without horns) who shared the same power of the *herok'a*.

In the end however far afield they traveled, Red Horn's stories which he narrated to the gathered Hocąk people just before dawn at Spirit Lake when Morning Star blazed in the sky of the Overworld and at the same time also from out of the waters where his light vanquished and consumed in its fire all the evil spirits from the dark realm of chaos where the Underwater Panther threateningly and stealthily swam—Red Horn existed simultaneously in Over, Middle, and Beneath Worlds—he himself constituted the *axis mundi* the Cedar Tree the red-and-white Striped-Center-Pole which ran through all three of Earthmaker's realms—however far off his narratives drifted away from himself and his adventures they eventually returned back to them with a vigor and a vengeance and once more he would begin relating how he could recognize a spirit from the underworld posing as a two-legged walker because of the designs woven on his clothing: swastikas or crosses in circles or ogee motifs which resembled the mouths of caves or female genitalia or the human eye: portals to the underworld all. *He-šucka*, *hejąkiga*, and *herok'aga* as well as all the two-legged Hocąk warriors, the Birdmen of the Overworld and the greatest of the Hocąk chunkey players, all wore bi-lobed arrows in their headdresses, bi-lobed arrows which so resembled the deer lungs hanging in *kunu's* lodge which Four-arms threw to his younger brother who subsisted on a steady diet of deer lungs so he would develop air sacks as robust as a deer's so as to be able to run just as fast as the antlered buck through the woods and forests of Red Banks and win the race for the chief's daughter, receive the victor's earbobs, and reveal himself to be Red Horn,

Morning Star's *worak* incarnation. The arrow also bore a marked similarity to both an atlatl, a shaft or stick with a cup at one end in which darts are tightly fitted to be flung at the enemy, and to the long-stemmed calumet of the Hocqk adoption ceremony. The celestial beings also had anthropomorphic heads, petaloids, feathers and tri-lobes—the last indicated their ability to travel to and from all three worlds—woven on their clothes.

Morning Star, the spirit voice in the water, murmurs the syllables *da-wa-kah-char-gra*. All those gathered at the beach including Baldr can hear the voice of the god, but the god addresses each one individually and in private. The raconteur has a special story tailored for each according to the ability of each to perceive and comprehend. He chose for Baldr a story about *herok'aga*, the chief of the little children or fawns' spirits, Red Horn's foster son who became his blood son by puffing on the long-stemmed calumet and shortening and rounding down his Pinocchio nose. *The woman would not listen to the man. She sprang each and every one of his deer traps. Got herself caught in all of them and none would attract a deer after she fouled it. The magic departed from the snare. The small son and daughter of the man and woman grew wan and emaciated. They would have starved had not the father shot the mother with an arrow from his bow. The father then packed the young children off to his sons from his first marriage. The brothers of the murdered wife would eventually find and slay him. After many adventures the boy married a beautiful woman whose mother set fantastic task after fantastic task for her son-in-law to perform. Eventually she challenged him to a game of* wegodiwa. *He and his spirit friends had to stand at the edge of the bluff above the lake here. The old woman and several of her daughters walked off the edge but instead of plummeting down and smashing themselves off the purple boulders below they hung suspended in the air. The old woman shrieked and suddenly a black funnel cloud appeared. Her demon sons together expelled all the air from* their collected lungs and tried four times to blow the young husband and his spirit friends to their deaths on the rocks below. The blinds fell off the young man's eyes. He realized only then who he was: herok'aga son of Red Horn he-šucka. He understood that his brother-in-laws caused the tornadoes and made the black clouds and the lightning; herok'aga, however, shared his father's prowess with the bow. Moreover like he-šucka he did not need arrows to kill. He merely had to breathe correctly in the correct herok'a manner and utter the word ahahe twice and let fly the empty bowstring and all his foes would fall over dead. He slew all his brother-in-laws and took over their village. His wife would bear him a daughter, the girl who would later marry the Forked Man and find he-šucka's head in the fire, take it out, and wrap it in the white deerskin. Red Horn addressed the little sprite directly. Little speckled fawn without nubs. Let me adopt you. Herok'aga and I are one and the same. When I wear my herok'aga guise I am still he-šucka. Thus it is I the great horned one who is the true protector of all the little fawns.

Baldr spoke up: Great Morning Star I fell from on high but my journey's end was not this world. The Black spirit intercepted me and with his great claw knocked me off course, so now I am divided from my heart, from my sweet Bea. Morning Star scratched his head. I seem to recall, he said, that in one version of the Red Horn cycle, I believe in the traditional eighth episode, the younger of Red Horn's sons long-nosed herok'aga pursues an elusive woman and is demeaned by a black spirit. Perhaps in this version of the tale which together we will enact, my son, the tale about to now unfold, this Beatrice you speak of will be that woman. I will trim your nose and raise a horn on your head—you and I shall join—my son.

Then you shall help me find Beatrice, Father Barbarossa? She is not of this world.

Morning Star can pass from world to world. He shoots his arrows down from the Overworld to this very lake so all the Hocąk hear his song from the sky. I will teach you to shoot the bow and turn your words into arrows that can pass from any one of Earthmaker's worlds to all the endless others in his infinite creation. Can you sing little Fawn?

I was born to sing to Beatrice. A Minnesänger in the Wartburg, I would have joined all the others in the Sängersaal, where I would have bested all opponents in the great Sängerkrieg. No one would have sung her praises like I. I would have won both her hand and heart!

Then sing my son. She may yet hear you even though she is far, far away.

Beatrice enters the circle

The feasts and high holidays of the two faiths almost always coincided. The adherents of the two religions celebrated their solemn rites and festively banqueted at the same times and season. Sometimes their sacraments even fell on the very same day. Oma explained that the Christians had decreed new festivals to overlap and correspond with the feast days of the old practices to make the process of conversion to Christianity easier. The crafty priests deliberately placed the birth of the son god near Solstice Night or Yula—each day after which the sun climbs a little higher in the sky as the dark half of the year declines and gives way to the growing light—the long night during which the Thuringii awaited the rebirth of the Sun King, the newborn solstice sun, the giver of life and child of promise who warmed the frozen earth, the white goddess who gave him birth and whom in the months to come he will refertilize with his rays making her bear forth from the seeds protected through the fall and winter in her womb.

Which ritual Beatrice observed and to some small childish degree participated in (the two blended seamlessly in her mind) depended on whether she accompanied her grandmother to her ancestral castle high in the mountains on the ancient path of the *Rennsteig* deep in the forests of fir and pine or whether instead of traveling cross country with her grandmother's train of servitors, she remained with her father at the Wartburg. Garlands and wreathes hung in the windows and on the walls of both castles. The vassals in their conical hats and tight waistcoats fastened by tags and their tight, close-fitting breeches decorated all the rooms of the castles with boughs of evergreen, ivy, and red-berried holly and bright banners and tapestries of green and red fluttered in all the halls with their long tables on which the servers arranged a great many dishes, silver tureens of soup on the whitest cloths, multitudes of fresh meats, fare of the noblest sort as well as mugs of foamy beer and decanters of sparkling red and golden wine. The leathery green leaves and waxy white berries of the mistletoe hung from the doorways. Had the Landgraf like Oma known that, according to the old ways, the white berries of the mistletoe stems, which purportedly possessed great healing power and gave mortal men access to divine realms and a sense of immortality as did the evergreen boughs which bestrewed the castles' floors, represented drops of the Sun God's divine semen and the red berries of the other plant the sacred menstrual blood of his mother and consort *Muttererde* he would have never allowed the sprigs and garlands to be hung at Yuletide. The old woman did not tell him. She understood that the solstice was the seed-time of the year and that the blending of mistletoe and holly would spark the great change of the coming months. Nor did the priests of his faith for they knew that the people were slow and reluctant to change and that most did not understand the meanings of the old practices and customs but merely carried on traditions the significance of which they did not fully understand. The priests knew if they attempted to proscribe such practices that their decrees would be met with hostility and angry resistance. Instead of banning the old customs they found it easier, where they could, simply to co-opt them. They did not want to accept or tolerate the old rites but they had to squint and wink at them to achieve their goal. Christianity became paganized as the pagans became Christians.

The ceremonial holly-and-mistletoe garlanded Yule log, nearly an entire tree decorated with ribbons and pine cones and carved with wishes for the coming year brought inside both castles on Mothers' Night, carried there in joyous procession by the men and boys of the castle, to burn all twelve nights and days of the Yule celebration—each of which standing for one of the twelve coming months—blazed in the long pits of both places (though it was called the *Christklotz* at the Wartburg) after being doused with wine and dusted with fine, white flour before being lit with a leftover piece of the last year's log, specially kept for the occasion. The log brought prosperity and protection from evil. The remnant retained to light next year's log kept the protection across the year. No one dared squint at the burning Yule log and no barefoot woman would approach it. On Mothers' Night when the celebrants remained until dawn to honor the divine *Muttern* and the female ancestors who had long ago lived and died, the children would wassail the log and salute it with Musil or a concoction of mulled ale, apples, curds, and nuts. With their bowls of mead, the wassailers would then go outside and address their songs and loud shouts to the cherry and apple trees, charms to insure that the trees would remain whole and hale the next year so as to bring about a good fruit harvest. On the other eleven nights the revelers played riddle games, cast spells and made wishes on the still burning log and throughout the entire Yuletide and not only on one day of the tide, people exchanged handsels and competed for those presents in playful debate. Where her father always gave her some costly bauble at Christmas—usually a bright jewel—Oma and Oma's cohorts traded inexpensive and handmade presents. On several evenings the men and women adorned themselves with ribbons and bells and danced both indoors and out. One of the courtiers called for light and the servitors brought the tall candles. The trenchermen knights in their surcoats emblazoned with the Landgrave's coat of arms rapped the bottoms of their sword hilts on the oaken tables as the couples took to the floor to the noise of drum, the piping and warbling of flutes and hautboys and the fanfares of trumpets, on which many bright banners flapped and waved gaily. Hearts gladdened on hearing the musicians playing. The lords and ladies stamped, hopped and leaped in the air, but after a time the music stopped and the dancers disappeared, the men and women going in different directions. After a short time, all returned, each with his face blackened to scare off evil spirits or to mock the Wild Hunt then ongoing in the night sky. Handing round torches and lighting them from either the great hearth or from the flaming Yule log itself, they proceeded outside where the musicians again took up their instruments and the lords and ladies danced winding round after winding round to the musicians' curious strains while other somewhat shadowy individuals planted rods into the snow, beating the poles again and again into the ground until the rods stayed fast, their attempt to bring fertility to the land. On another night, mummers performed before all the company and enacted a tale where a hero returned home from a far land after which a villain dressed in black slew him. A learned doctor from distant parts then arrived and miraculously revived him. Oma told Beatrice to remember her dreams each night. Each night she would foresee in her sleep an event from one month of the coming year. Beatrice never remembered any of her visions until her eighth year when on the tenth of the twelve nights of Yuletide she awoke beaming. She would meet a little boy who could change into a fawn at will. Only she could see him and they would become the fastest of friends, the best Christmas present of all, of any gift ever given her in her young life. She told Oma the Christ child would come to her and that he had golden hair and the bluest of blue eyes. She called the child both Baldr and Christ.

On another night, Lucy Night, perhaps Beatrice's favorite of all twelve, the revelers and celebrants held a festival of lights and planted torches in the ground and laid a myriad of candles and oil lamps in concentric circles round each torch and left them burning there when they returned to the castle. On Lucy Night the stars from the sky came down to earth to melt all the accumulated snow and ice from the ground. Beatrice's favorite day of the twelve, however, was the one on which she accompanied all the others to the silver fir and pine groves and helped to decorate the boughs and limbs of the trees, weighed down as they already were with snow, with tinsel, symbols of the Sun, Moon, and Stars as well as effigies of departed loved ones like Beatrice's mother and her wrinkled pink baby brother in order to remember those dear ones but also to hang them on the green boughs like Jesus on his Easter tree as offerings to the various gods and goddesses of the forests and finally last of all they decorated the remaining limbs with fruits of the last harvest both to give thanks for the son god's bounty and to attract and feed the ancestral spirits, the land wights and the elves. Once they finished they returned to the castle, washed and mannerly went to their seats at the long tables all of which groaned and creaked with the weight of the great silver serving platters heaped with roast boar, duck, goose and goat as well as wooden bowls of dried fruit and red cabbage. Double dainties would be served to Beatrice at her table on the raised dais where she heard low chanting from a choir in a nearby chapel.

The same morning they went into the forest, farmers rode from great distances to Oma's castle where they repaired with the livestock and even horses to an oblong outbuilding without windows. Inside they downed tankards of ale and afterward got down to the grim business of the slaughter. Blood steamed and coursed into the runnels both from the livestock destined for the feast and from the sacrificial horses. The men gathered the steaming blood in sacrificial vessels. When the work was done, Oma who did not go with the others to the silver fir and pine groves made an appearance. She daubed the aspergill twigs in the blood and sprinkled the men's faces with the white goddess' blood. She said her blessings and took her leave. Afterward the farmers smeared blood and made handprints with blood on the walls within and without, then lit fires in the center of the room to begin roasting the meat for the evening feast. They bore a beaker of blood around the fire and each man took a long draught and made a toast to the reborn god. They then blessed the cooking meat and once more began downing foaming ale from the wooden casks.

In the mountains, Oma explained to her granddaughter that the burning Yule log stood for and was representative of the great Ash tree Yggdrasil, whose branches and roots extended through the universe. An eagle nested at its top and a great serpent coiled at its bottom while a squirrel ran chattering up and down the tree between them fomenting discord. On one root of the great cosmic tree dwelt the three Norns Wyrd, Verthandi, and Skuld spinning and weaving—none, not even Woden himself, could escape his destiny—about another lay the fountain of Mimir into whose waters all the wisdom of the universe flowed. At the doom of the gods the entire length of the great tree would ignite in one great all-consuming flame and the universe would end in fire but from the ashes a new cosmos would emerge and a new day would dawn. Oma called the burning ash log a herb of the sun. It brought the sun from the sky into the hearth during the long night—the longest night and shortest day of the year, the dark night of our souls when the new spark of hope at last ignites, when the Wild Hunt which began on *Winter Nächte*—the mid-autumn festival when the populace built great bonfires to fend off the dark spirits and the wandering dead which on that night which the Christians called All Hallows Eve roamed the world freely and without constraint, the mundane laws of time and space temporarily suspended and the thin veil between the nine worlds lifted—reached its peak, Woden astride his eight-legged horse Sleipnir, his spectral host of warrior horsemen as well as Thor, the assembled Valkyries, helmeted and carrying spears, who rode through the air on horseback during battles and brought the souls of slain heroes to the great fortress of Valhalla, the ancestral spirit the Yula *Alf* dressed all in red and green and standing erect in his war chariot drawn by the two steeds Donner and Blitzen and the loudly baying phantom hounds of the furious host of *Jólner,* "Yula figure," one of Woden's many other names, ran riot through the heavens throughout all of the longest night of the year. Hunters' horns could be heard reverberating from, depending on which was the case, the starry or the stormy firmament and the children put socks stuffed with hay outside their dwellings to feed Sleipnir. The hunt would reach its peak Solstice Night but would not end until May Eve just before the marriage feast of the God of light—the most beautiful and gracious of the gods, he who was destined to be struck down by a dart of mistletoe thrown by the blind God Hoder but aimed at its target by Loki, mistletoe the one thing in all nature his mother forgot to extract a promise from not to hurt her son—when the Thuringii performed magic rites to hasten spring and cause the land to bloom and the livestock to breed, young people again collected greenery and tree branches at twilight to adorn the houses of all the villages and the peasants once more lit bonfires or bonefires to drive away both the winter cold and to fend off the Black spirits, for *Hexen* and goat-legged *Teufels* rode to *Brocken* peak in the Harz Mountains to celebrate the annual night of the witches and to consort and dance together, the same night the Christians called *Walpurgisnacht* in honor of the English-born Saint *Die heilige Walpurga* who founded the convent of Heidenheim in Württemberg and who spoke out against sorcery and was canonized a saint on May 1, 779.

The little girl realized that while the twelve night celebrations in the forest and at the Wartburg had many similarities they also differed in marked ways from each other. Some activities occurred in only one or the other place. Sword dancing, for example, only took place in the courtyard of the Wartburg, where minstrels would also sing their competitive love songs or together pluck on their harps and in unison intone: "If Christmas on a Sunday be, a windy winter we shall see. Hours of sun on Christmas Day, so many frosts in the month of May." The dance began with a procession of men marching into the hall with uplifted long swords. The men then one by one would leap over two lowered swords their points touching in the middle or tuck into a roll and pass under them. The men would then proceed to engage in mock combat. A man would pretend that another dancer had stabbed him and would fall to the floor where he would feign pain and the death throes until as in the mummers' plays a magician or doctor would arrive at the last moment and heal him. Finally the sword dancers would lay all the swords on the floor in some elaborate geometric pattern at the dance's end. Also at the Wartburg the kindly priest would relate to a crowd of gathered listeners how on the first Holy Night the animals all knelt on bent knee and swarms of bees hummed and buzzed the 100th psalm. Finally at midnight on Christmas Eve the Landgraf Beatrice's father and Oma's son Arbogast ordered his courtiers to throw open all the many doors in the castle so that all imps, sprites, and evil spirits that had entered and snuck into his—the Landgraf's—home during the past year needs must depart.

As the great wheel rotated past Yuletide, Beatrice continued to gambol round and move in sync with it during its yearlong passage, celebrating alternately and together the Pagan holidays and their Christian counterparts. On February 14th, the high days of the two faiths again converged for Oma's Disting and her son the Landgraf's Love Feast of Saint Valentine, on which date the ancient Romans also celebrated Lupercalia in honor of the horned god Faunus, where two youths begirt in goatskins and impersonating rutting rams raced through the streets whipping passersby with strips of goatskin. The Pope had christianized Lupercalia in memory of the martyrdom of St. Valentine, who with the confluence of the two traditions became connected in the people's minds with the customs of the older Pagan festivals so that he was soon popularly regarded as the patron of lovers, especially of lovers in duress. Those who suffered from love wounds drear. To mark the middle or half way point of the dark half of the year, while the farmers held weeklong markets in all the villages—the Christians would later succeed in moving the fairs to February 1 or Candlemas, the feast of the Purification and of the Presentation of Christ in the temple—in the forest, two of the acolytes attending on Oma—the Fire Maidens—would cense the altar and the ecstatic celebrants making sacrifices to the female powers or *dísir* the Norns and Valkyries and finally light the sacred fires in the cause of peace and for all the maidens soon to become brides and mothers asking that the sacred fire burn also in their hearts. The keeper of the waters of Mimir offered a taste from the sacred vessel to all before offering the water to *Muttererde* to drink. The celebrants picked a tree to stand for the World Tree and dressed it, then Oma gathered the brides in a group, prayed to both the tree and the ancient mother in their behalf, asked that Yggdrasil the cosmic tree which connected all nine worlds and rose from the depths to tower in the heights also grow in each of the maidens' hearts and told them to open their eyes and see not only Yggdrasil manifest itself but also the Rainbow Bridge. She finally called on Heimdall the gatekeeper, he who would sound the ill-fated horn when one by one the giants ignited the limbs of the great tree, he who had the sharpest ears, ears which could hear both the green grass and the curly, crisp fleece of the sheep grow, to throw open the portals so the brides could glimpse the Shining Ones in all their glory. The wheel kept turning until night and day stood in perfect balance, with sunlight on the increase, the season in which the Christians celebrated the Feast of the Annunciation and Easter and those who clung to the old ways Ostara, the Vernal Equinox, the night and day sacred to the Saxon Lunar Goddess of fertility Eostre, whose emblems were the egg and the rabbit. Oma and her followers held ceremonies every full moon, for each of the thirteen during the year, to celebrate the gathering of the harvest and the change of the seasons—their power waxed with the moon and reached its height each month at full moon—but the *Samenmond* which occurred during Ostara marked the sacred as yet unconsummated marriage of the young God and the young Maiden Goddess, she who would again become the Great Mother. On seed moon, Oma and the other priestesses laid garlands of woodruff, violets, and gorse on her high altars. The Sun God's coronation would occur on May Day when the young people would hold hands and dance around the May Pole all day before spending the entire night a-Maying and at last the God and Goddess would lie together in their green bower amongst the blossoms and unite. That day and the nights before and after Beatrice's father would not let his daughter leave the precincts of the Wartburg. She went to chapel and heard the priests relate the life story of *Die heilige Walpurga* and her uncle Winfrid, who received permission from Pope Gregory II to evangelize the German lands and later when made a Bishop took the name of Boniface and in the town of Geismar felled an oak tree consecrated to Donner and was not struck down by lightning when the great tree toppled and fell. Next on the wheel came Midsummer and the Solstice, the longest day of the year when light and life abounded, which stood opposed on the great circuit to Yule, the shortest day and longest night, the time of year when the Sun God reached his greatest glory but from which date his light slowly began to wane and decline into the dark and everything began to dissolve into a single song of death-ecstasy, the day the lord of the forest embraced the green goddess, the Summer Queen, one last time in his deep, abiding, eternal love before embarking once more across the dark seas in search of the isle of light that is rebirth. The priests celebrated the feast of St. John the Baptist on Solstice Day, but from the door of their cathedral peered the face of the Sun King–Oma pointed him out to her granddaughter–his features partially hidden by a foliate mask. The next two heathen Sabbaths occurred on August Eve and on the Autumnal Equinox in September, the first of which marked the Sun King's decline into dotage and the beginning preparations for his funeral rites, the second the transformation of the green goddess into the Winter Crone. Winter Nights would follow on November Eve and Woden would once more embark on and lead the Great Hunt. It was on Winter Nights the year Beatrice turned eight that the miracle happened. Again she confused the two religious practices and mixed their tenets, dogmas and principles in her mind. At this time of year, the most beautiful season thought Beatrice with the bright, parti-colored hillsides the leaves orange-yellow-red-green-brown and the sweet breezes the air cooling with each day as the wheel spun round and the world once again went into transition, both Priest and Priestess spoke of the dead. The eve and night before All Saints Day which was also the *Festnacht* of the Pagan Lady and Lord of the Dead the Crone and her aged, doddering Consort a dark festival balanced at the opposite point of the wheel by the spring festival of *Baldrtag* or May Day, in the chapel at the Wartburg the tonsured priest with a long wide piece of white woolen cloth draped over his shoulders said mass for the Christians who had gone to God during the past year or else spoke to the gathered lords and ladies of the court of the first martyrs and said prayers with them for all those who died in the Faith. All next day they feasted in Arbogast's banqueting hall except when they went to chapel and sang praises for all the Lord's saints both known and unknown and the day following Hallowmas, November 2nd, they celebrated yet another feast of Mother Church, All Souls Day, during which they prayed for those suffering in

Purgatory. The night before, believing the dead returned to earth that night, the adherents of the one true faith would light tapers and long candles and leave them lit all night not snuffing them out until the cock crowed and the All Souls Day festivity began so the recent dead could wend their way one last time to their earthly homes, this even though the priests warned that spirits and *Hexen* perhaps even the Lord of Lies the Dark One himself accompanied and hid in the ranks of the homeward returning souls. During these same feast days Oma left word for her retainers in the *Rennsteig* to throw open all the windows and doors of the castle there so as to invite in all spirits and visiting souls. Like the Christians she and her fellow priestesses left candles burning in the windows of their homes to guide home not only the recent dead but also all the ancestral spirits, and they also set extra chairs round the table and in front of the hearth for the nightcomers. But to protect themselves from evil guests and ward off malevolent spirits they hollowed out turnips and carved fanged faces with slant eyes on their fronts and then put a lit candle inside to scare off the wicked and damned souls. The Sisters also buried apples at cross roads and beside their junctions with meandering forest paths for spirits who had wandered off course lost with no where to turn and to feed the wandering dead who had no descendants living to offer them food and drink. Oma herself stole to the cemeteries and the castle burial vaults where she knew the bones of the especially wicked lay and left the most notorious of the dead gifts of sweetmeats, cheese, and nuts to propitiate and mollify them so that they would not work mischief and bedevil the living. She told Beatrice to lock her yellow-eyed white-and-gray kitten Crème in the closet for the nights of the last day of October and the first day of November as malevolent elves would catch kittens those nights and ride on their backs as if the kittens were steeds and would hold mock jousts in which the kittens could be hurt or blinded. She also told Beatrice not to sit on the ground with her back to the trunk of a hawthorn as the kobolds and wood elves loved to dance on the grass there and would pinch and prick the skins of bad little boys and girls who had the audacity to profane with their buttocks the kobolds' dancing green. During the feast days the peasants the women wearing wimples to cover their hair the men with no headdress or at most a simple hood and the tradespeople of the town all bound by the Sumptuary Laws as to what they could wear as well as the indigents and the transients passing through the little kingdom dressed in their sleeveless tunics and shawls of fur with simple rolls of leather wrapped around their feet and tied with thongs for shoes took to the streets begging for coin or traipsing from house to house singing for raisin-filled soul cakes and the seasonal pastry known as Bones of the Holy which those in the towns doled out at their doors. Many of those parading through the streets either blackened their faces or wore hideous masks such as they donned during times of dearth and want or when the plague threatened in order to scare off malign spirits. Boys and girls wore disguises made of straw and dressed in the garbs of one of the opposite sex so as to confuse and bewilder any shadow that might strike out at them. The drunk and rowdy ran riot unhinging gates and posts, stealing ploughs, throwing cabbages at doors or blocking them shut from the outside. In the country, cattle and other livestock went to slaughter and meat was smoked for the long winter months ahead. The peasants built bonefires after the feasting in which they threw the white remains as offerings to the Nature Spirits to ensure healthy and plentiful cattle in the year to come. They also threw stones into the fire on which they made their own individual identifying marks. Depending on the condition of the stones after the fire burned out they could foretell the amount of prosperity coming their way. In Eisenach on All Saints Days the hooded executioner would behead criminals and people condemned to death for heresy and other sins by the church fathers. The headsman's axe fell on the necks of murderers and thieves after a tonsured priest read them a last sermon and heard their confessions. Oma and her followers dressed not in bright colors as at their other ceremonies throughout the year but all in white as if they themselves had gone through the great change and now roamed the world among the pale dead. They would tramp in long procession on the eve of All Souls Day to an ancient altar sitting in a forest meadow, a great blood-stained rock known as the stone of the Franks around which they would form a circle all of them holding hands. A bright white moon rose above the shivering, leaf-stripped trees and the stone altar. Oma brought Beatrice though she was of course too young. One of Oma's handmaidens carried a ball to roll to her in the grass and several wooden ducks for the child to play with. Oma however felt the girl at eight was old enough to receive some explanation of what she and the other grandmothers would undertake: how they would call down the spirits of the mothers, the *dísir*, the ancestors, the forest goddesses and ancient spirits, the unborn, the future progeny of the Thuringii, recently departed family members and pets as well as the elders of the faith and friends lost in the past year but now departing to the Summerlands for a blissful respite before once more embarking round the wheel in another life and again experiencing the endlessly repeating cycle of birth, growth, decline, and death. She explained that she and the other *Hexen* were white *Hexen* not the black *Hexen* who congregated and hovered over Brocken peak on *Walpurgisnacht.* They vowed harm to none and good to all, acknowledging love and light as their guides and when misfortune was enow each would wear a star of gold on her aged, wrinkled brow. They practiced by the elements, the Ancient Ones and nature and followed structured ceremonies passed down generation after generation by the foremothers, Priestesses, tree dressers and healers and female doctors wise in herb lore.

As Beatrice gamboled and pranked on the greensward near the sacred altar and she and Oma's young handmaiden rolled the golden ball in the grass between them, Oma and the other witches began the Circle Casting. In a singsong voice, Beatrice's grandmother old Oma chanted: "At this time and within our special place, I walk the circle and declare it now sacred space." A crone called each of the four corners and asked one by one the spirits of fire, water, air and earth to bless the circle with their presence. From the east came the sylphs and elemental beings of wind, breath, and mind to witness the rite and guard the circle. From the south slithered the red salamanders and gold-spangled newts, the elemental beings of flame, of passion, of soul and inspiration. From the west appeared the undines, the Shining Ones made of water, the cleansers and the healers, and finally from the north elves, gnomes, and kobolds arrived and manifested, the elemental beings of earth, of nature, sustenance and the body. Oma declared the circle open and in unison the old women began to call the spirits of the dead and unborn to dance in love and trust within the bounds of the circle. At that moment the ball shot past Beatrice in the grass and between two of the women right into the middle of the circle. Before anyone could stop her, Beatrice darted under the extended arms and held hands of the two women. She did not see any of the myriad descending spirits that the mothers had called forth, but she immediately espied a little boy with white hair standing at the circle's center on top of the Franks' Stone, his eyes closed.

He came from where dreams were born. The first words Baldr spoke to her, not yet raising his eyelids: "And I, Princess, consign myself to your ear and find that nest sufficient."

Beatrice and Baldr together

Eyes shut, he did not understand that he no longer stood on the shore of Spirit Lake, his toes buried in the hot sun-drenched silvery sand. Eyes still shut, he continued singing out his love songs to Beatrice each song or valentine an arrow he strung on his bow and shot out between the worlds blindly and at random hoping that one of his bi-lobes would wend its way to her then strike her—prick her—directly in the heart, resembling, if anyone who could detect his glassy see-through self standing there in the sun on the beach would understand the reference, a tiny amoretto or infant cupid except he had no wings. In another age and time he might have been a radio astronomer broadcasting signals out into deep space in an attempt to contact other sentient beings across the cosmos. In his mind's eye, standing there singing—his sweetest songs told of saddest thoughts, while his saddest told of sweetest—he saw a shadow behind him slowly extending on the grass waxing little by little until it stretched to the full length of a tall man's shadow cast at noon, then the silhouette till then dark as an inkblot began fading first imperceptibly then more rapidly until all at once in a flash a second it vanished utterly like a puff or wisp of smoke rising from the stone bowl of the Hocąk calumet, and Baldr at last opened his *blaue Augen* to stare directly into the smiling face and green-gray eyes of his heavenly beloved—the goddess now made girl. His eyes had to adjust. They sank deeper in the darkness, and the small dots of light in their pupils made them look like two long paths through tall shrubbery in the park of some mansion, over which summer and sunshine lie, broadly gleaming. Beatrice herself saw a little boy—a real freckle-faced blond boy who cast a shadow on the ground in the moonlight, his hair the color of the sun, and widened her eyes in disbelief. He had come! The Baldr Christ had come! She jumped up and down in her delight, clasped his hand and led him out of the circle. Oma and the other old women also wore joyous expressions on their faces. They saw and danced with the shades of their own passed loved ones and did not see the girl or her companion. In her arms Oma held her beloved daughter-in-law, returned from the Summerlands. For a fraction of a second she thought she saw her granddaughter holding hands and spinning round in dance with a dead child not her baby brother but did not worry. No spirit would cross with her out of the circle, and Beatrice clasped the ball to her chest and scurried right out, for Oma had not yet declared the circle open with love and trust. The dead who had entered were bound within its confines. She had not yet dismissed the Spirits of Earth and Water, Fire and Sky or even thanked them. Nor had the dead themselves stopped drawing nigh. She had many more old friends to meet and greet before she would command: "Return now to your normal place, while blessing all through time and space." And the dead departed while love and trust remained within the closed circle. Did not Oma remember that she had summoned not only those who had gone down into the ground but had also opened a wormhole through the thin veils of time and space through which souls not yet born could also cross back and forth between the many interconnected worlds? Different rules applied to souls and spirits. The living could not compel and bend to their will souls of the not yet living as they could the spirits of the dead, those who had once lived. From that time forward the two—who had immediately sensed their strong connection and instant bond to one another but did not understand their relation in its full complexity— they remained budding children and had only the understanding of children, only realizing that they loved each other to their hearts' full measure and capacity—would stand inseparable. Beatrice prattled to all and sundry about her new friend. Everyone saw her address the air, which did not answer back, but paid little heed to what they considered a passing whimsy on the child's part. Oma took deeper and sharper notice of course but Oma knew the child and the power of her young imagination—how she liked to make up stories and to pull the wool over the old ones' eyes. She also came to the conclusion that her granddaughter perpetrated an elaborate hoax to pull the legs of everyone and attract their bemused attention to herself. Not for months did she realize that an unborn soul had attached itself to her granddaughter, not until one day in the forest she saw Beatrice flying through the air riding on Baldr's invisible shoulders. Afterward Beatrice broke down under the old woman's questioning and related all. Once the girl finished, Oma admonished Beatrice to never speak about Baldr to anyone and especially to keep mum about the little spirit's name, it being the same as that of the old German god of light, the son of Woden and Frigg. Beatrice did not listen to her grandmother and prattled on the same as ever. When the two who had once mixed their irradiance in the land of eternal ideas again met in fallen form on earth, Beatrice in her joy did not immediately realize that she and she alone could glimpse the visage of her beloved. The truth dawned only gradually after repeated failures on her part to point him out to other children and to the handmaidens and retainers of the court. Baldr continued to tag along everywhere she went and Beatrice grew glad she had someone at her beck and call and all to herself. A joy all her own.

They walked together into the hills and explored the forest glades together, where they entered paths which began as circles of half-light which then extended into ever more narrowly enclosing darkness until the two children together saw a distant, glimmering point: the exit opposite into sunshine perhaps much brighter still. They laughed easily. The invisible boy let her mount his back so that she could ride him pick-a-back, and she raced him like a proud stallion and they fell down and laid on their backs amid the flowers. She taught Baldr Oma's herb-lore and he learned to identify heliotrope, mint and nutmeg as well as mugwort, allspice, catnip for Beatrice's kitten Crème, broom, sage, straw, sweet grass, deadly nightshade and the little screaming manikin or Mandrake root. And Baldr sang to her about Spirit Lake so that she could almost see its waters. He told her about his little den beneath the purple and red boulders, *kokopelli* and his flute, and the lone white water lily bobbing up and down atop the darkling water. In the hush Beatrice could almost hear the spirit voice in the lake murmuring over and over again the syllables *da-wa-kah-char-gra da-wa-kah-char-gra*.

It surprised the little girl that her friend did not realize who he was, the little Christ child come back and returned again to earth, but she recollected Oma saying that spirits coming from the Summerlands often lost all memory of their previous lives upon again descending from the Upper Circles. With a sudden gladdening of her soul, she perceived that it would be her especial joy and benefaction to teach the reborn child of hope and sunlight his own message of love and deliverance and immediately she began prattling her simple understanding of Christ's teaching and parables, the Sermon on the Mount and of course the Beatitudes. They attended mass together and went to see the kindly priest who each Christmas always related to a crowd of gathered listeners how the animals all knelt on bent knees the first Holy Night and swarms of bees hummed and buzzed the 100th psalm. All Beatrice's words were honey to Baldr's ear and as she returned to him what she thought was rightly his he paid attention to her words and grew proud to have borne such a loving message of redemption and hope to the people of the world, and with joy he accompanied her when she gave alms to the poor. In the forecourt of the chapel that morning, a dozen alms seekers of both sexes and representing all ages from youth to senescence, stood waiting for the conclusion of matins and the appearance of the Landgraf and his daughter who apparently were running late as the bells at the conclusion of the service had long since tolled. At last the church doors opened and the little girl appeared in the company of her august father the Imperial Elector, and the invisible little boy, who never strayed very far from her sight, as she alone of all people in the world could see him, stood as always right beside her. The little girl wore all black and although much too young, a mere child only, to have entered upon a novitiate much less taken any binding vows the girl of eight nonetheless looked in the beauty of her Baldr-induced radiance the perfect image of a young bride of Jesus, a future Saint beheld in her blessed childhood. She saw the holy spirit her Baldr Christ smile when her female retainer knelt before her and opened the ducal purse from which Beatrice drew the gold and silver coins she slipped into the postulants' hands.

The beggars fell on their faces and to their knees, sobbed, and tried to lay their gnarled and black-nailed fingers on the train of their benefactress' gown or kiss its hem with their trembling pale blue lips covered with sores. Beatrice gave out the last coin to the last in line and then she and her father turned around and again entered the church, little Baldr scurrying after them.

One morning, she took Baldr to the site of the future *Sängersaal* and explained to him that because of the lessons taught to her by her Oma she could see the shades of things yet to be and told him both of the gorgeous hall that would in the course of time be erected where they now stood and of the future contest of song there, and Baldr remembered that in the life they had chosen before plunging downward he was to have been one of the early strolling *Minnesingers,* those German lyric poets whose order was founded on the banks of the Danube by Der von Kürenberg, Dietmar von Aist, and Meinloh von Sevelingen and whose adherents the current minstrel exponents of courtly love at the time of Beatrice's birth were just coming under the influence of the Provençal troubadours and the *trouvères* from the north of France, from whom they adopted the seven-line strophe of the canzone. She took and gripped Baldr's hand and they both saw first the great hall itself with its pillars, steps and horseshoe arches its ceiling beams, frescoes, tapestries and mosaics then the great event which would take place there twenty-five years forward in time in the year 1207, the actual contest later celebrated in poem and song between the six Minnesingers famous knights all who had devoted their love and their lives to their own chaste, unreachable lady, vowing to obey her from afar and who had all foresworn and renounced physical contact and fleshly affection. One by one Wolfram von Eschenbach, Heinrich der Schreiber and Heinrich

von Ofterdingen, Walther von der Vogelweide, Biterolf and
Reinmar von Zweter filed into the hall for the Landgrave
Hermann's great singing competition. The translator of Ovid
Albrecht von Halberstadt also took part, as did many others.
Baldr watched each Minnesinger sing and as he saw and heard
them he came to know their life stories and beheld their courtly
loves as if from afar. But at the same time he heard the poem
being read, he envisioned an entirely different contest taking
place, one he drew in his own mind, and then farther hence
Bea and Bal entered and sat down together in the great theater
as the lights dimmed and the curtain raised upon a performance of Wagner's *Tannhäuser* (Wagner, with a poet's license had
placed the *Sängerkrieg* during the holy Elizabeth's residence at
the Wartburg or rather used the Hungarian Saint, whose life
Beatrice's so mysteriously prefigured and adumbrated, as a
model for his Elisabeth, *Nichte des Landgrafen*, the courtly love
ideal of his Wolfram so different from the actual *Minnesinger*
whom Baldr simultaneously saw, the penurious long-in-the-
tooth poet of the great oral epic *Parzival* who could not read
or write even his own name and who had a high-pitched tenor
voice very unlike that of the deep and pious baritone singing
from the stage. In the opera, to the accompaniment of the most
ravishing tones Baldr's ears ever experienced, Wolfram brings
Tannhäuser to the Singers' Hall where he tells his friend to
approach Elisabeth without fear where every glimmer of hope
vanishes for him from life as he hears her declare her love for
Tanny the Tenor, the girl Wolfie simply wanted to make happy
again and let her star shine once more! Now the noble lady's ear
will listen to the knights' competing songs. She agrees to judge
the contest. Wolf sings first and compares his Lady to the bright
most dazzling star in all the heavens the Evening Star which at

other times of the year was also Red Horn's Morning Star, the glowing orb Venus. Tanny breaks in and sings his own song, a hymn to physical love and to the Goddess Venus, who has entertained him periodically in her cave under the Venusberg:

> O Wolfram, der du also sangest,
> du hast die Liebe arg entstellt!
> Wenn du in solchem Schmachten bangest,
> versiegte wahrlich wohl die Welt!

And Wolf has to cool down the hothead knights who want to slice and dice him there and then but sings his own indictment of his friend and asks that sin be banished from the knights' noble and sublime circle before launching again into his own song of divine love where Lizzie's star shines forever. *O Himmel! Laß dich jetzt erflehen!* Defiantly Tannhäuser repeats his own verse and the knights rush at him with swords drawn. Lissa intercedes for him. Although Tanny dealt her death, she will plead for his life, and she dedicates her remaining years to offering prayers for Tannhäuser's salvation. Wolfram prays for her in her travail and asks God to grant her some relief though her wound may never heal. He knows that her path leads to heaven and sings to the Evening Star to salute her as she passes from the earth to become an Angel of the heavens. Wolfram's motives are born of the highest code of chivalry.

As the music died away and the two children again stood in the empty *Sängersaal*, a man with the bluest of eyes and the blackest of beards stepped into the room with them. The year is now 1867 and the second Ludwig not the count of Schauenberg who had clay from his lands brought to the summit which was not quite in his lands, so he might truthfully swear that the

Wartburg sat on his own ground but the other castle builder
the Swan King Ludwig of Bavaria who came to the Wartburg
expressly to see the Hall of Song on which he would model
the singing room in his own castle of *Neuschwanstein* which he
vowed would embody the true spirit of the medieval German
mountain fortress. When the vision faded, Baldr dropped to
his knees before Beatrice and launched into his own *Minnelied*:

> Dû bist min ich bin dîn
> des solt dû gewis sîn
> dû bist beslozzen
> in mînem herzen
> verlorn ist das sluzzelîn
> dû muost immêr darinne sîn!

Which in modern English could be rendered as follows:

> You are mine, I am yours
> Of that you may be sure
> Deep within my heart
> You're safely locked away
> But I have lost the key
> And there you'll ever stay.

One of the minstrel knights Friedrich von Husen, who at the
time of the war of the two faiths would join the entourage of
Friedrich Barbarossa and like his King die on crusade, heard
the little witch girl singing it in a cranny of the castle. He could
not get the words and melody out of his head and wrote them
down and put the manuscript of the little song in the codex
but did not ascribe it any authorship.

While Beatrice could show him the future, Baldr could show her the past. Baldr took her again to their favorite forest glade and held her hand in his and together they looked backward and in each other's company experienced the love of the garden. Not the Perfect Sky realm but the earthly garden where they experienced the tumultuous, primal force which drew the beasts of the fields one to the other and attracted Father Sky to Mother Earth, the power that transforms the uncertain misery-choked world of want, hunger and pain into a green paradise and gives ephemeral, fleeting life its beauty and splendor. In the garden, they remained good, kind, sweet children and stood side-by-side in a beautiful meadow in which innumerable kinds of flowers grew. Baldr merely had to look upward for the apples, every one of which was ripe, to fall down from the trees in a thick shower. Their comely bodies fitting but temporary vessels for their abiding, eternal souls, they gave names to all the creatures of the woods and forests and assisted thereby the All Highest in his continuous act of kaleidoscopic creation.

The weeks lengthened into months. A year passed. A bearded centaur galloped through the glade with little fawns dancing upon his back. Then in the spring, Oma and Beatrice, accompanied of course by Baldr, moved for a time to one of Arbogast's hunting lodges, a log cottage and hall tended by the good steward Ewald, his wife and their numerous children as well as a few other of the Landgraf's retainers, a journey of several weeks' duration deep into the green and rolling hills of the Thuringian countryside. Oma told her granddaughter that every year at this time *Muttererde* remembered anew her first beginnings, the dawn of the world and the commencement of time, when after the winter she once more felt the renewed stirrings of life in her womb.

Oma continued instructing her granddaughter: "In the summer, her face all radiant, our Mother announces her pregnant condition to the hills and mountains and even to Father Sky and the sun disc, the Day's Eye, whose golden rays in the springtime caused all the seeds within her to start sprouting and the vernal leaves to start shooting forth from all the branches of the dead trees. But as the wheel turns, for slow and sure turn she must, into the charged and weighty silences of autumn she learns to hold her tongue as you should also learn my daughter. For a wise tongue is in a still head, little girl. The Mother does not blare forth to the world the secret revealed by the season when death approaches in his guise of many colors, that the reawakening world does not confine itself to meadows, trees, and forest paths. Our souls too come back after resting for a time with the God and the Goddess in the Summerlands. Each year as we witness the annual rebirth and smell the sweet fragrance of the new all around us we must strive to take the sunlight inside our spirits and make it our own interior force and possession. We must remove it from the time-bound world, so we can experience the eternal, the timeless, in all its freshness and first youth in the here and now and in our hearts and in the presence of the Shining Ones, the immortal Gods and Goddesses. But, daughter, enjoy to your fullest your meagerly apportioned mortal youth and childhood and hold fast to whatever pleases you for happiness quickly flees us and life leaves us all each and every one with many regrets. If you want to be happy, daughter, be so today for tomorrow all may change. There is no certainty or promise of continued happiness or content-ment for any of us. For at all times the twilight of the gods approaches."

For at that moment Oma knew that her son the Landgrave Arbogast had departed with his train to the Harz Mountains to collect his new bride the Duchess Sigune, Beatrice's new stepmother and with her foresight she saw that the woman from the Brocken had a black heart and would be jealous and hateful toward the little child from Arbogast's first marriage, she who now remained all that still lived of the Elector's beloved wife Orgeluse. Light and dark both had to be tasted in life. Oma could only accept with resignation and calm the black fate which approached. At the time of first beginnings the die had been cast. Eons before on the great root of the World Tree, the weird sisters had spun the thread of her granddaughter's fate. How could she escape it when Woden himself could not evade or avoid the destiny which alone was his? Oma bowed her head and prayed to Mary's son the good Christ not the black one. Beatrice so wanted the others to see Baldr, to see that she was not making up stories. The reborn child of hope and sunlight had to show himself, and Baldr so wanted to oblige his Beatrice he tried to shout out the parables and teaching she had taught him—that she had told him he himself had first proclaimed to the world during the time of his First Coming in the Holy Land. But for all his hoopla and hosannaing, his lips remained as if sealed. No one could hear him but Beatrice. Then the miracle happened at last. Though none but Beatrice would hear his voice (for he would continue speaking to her just the same and in like manner after the metamorphosis) he found a way to make manifest his presence. As she whispered in his ear again how the first time he came to earth he changed the water into wine and then later the wine in a far greater miracle into his own blood, Baldr remembered how Red Horn had shown him how to transform back and forth from his *waika* self into his spirit

66

animal and suddenly Beatrice saw standing beside her a brown, speckled fawn. She called to the other children Ewald's sons and daughters, she called to Oma and the handmaidens and male attendants and the knight protectors who had accompanied them from the castle and they each in turn crowded into the small room. The brown, speckled fawn had meanwhile become albino. Two small spikes or rather felt-covered round nubs protruded from his head. Only the very first who came into Beatrice's room saw him brown and spotted.

Baldr felt such joy at being seen he bounded from out of Beatrice's chamber in the hunting lodge and out into the meadows and forests where he felt the eyes of all the woodland creatures turn upon him in wonder and love. But he could not bear to be out of Beatrice's presence for any great length of time. So he would race back to Ewald's long house of logs every day after making his jaunts into the forest. Beatrice would ride on his back in the meadow in front of Ewald's house of hollowed-out trees. Sometimes when she dismounted and they sat together on the green, Baldr would suddenly begin weeping uncontrollably and his limbs would start and shake and shiver. "Beatrice," he said, "How I fear someday that I will have to leave you." Beatrice patted him on the head three times I love you, one pat for each word, and said to him, "Be calm, dear fawn, I'll never leave you." Then she undid her golden garter and put it around the fawn's neck, and she pulled out some rushes and braided them into a soft cord and from thenceforward she would never unleash him in their walks through the forest. When they tired themselves walking, they at last turned about and headed back to Ewald's house of logs. Beatrice gathered leaves and moss to make a soft bed or nest for her fawn. Each morning before Baldr awoke, Beatrice went in search of food for them to share and in the forest she found abundant roots, berries and nuts as well as picked the long tender grass which Baldr ate out of her own hand and afterward he sported about her in mad, frolicsome dance before growing tired and lying down on the bed of moss and nettle. Beatrice would kneel and say her prayers beside her sleeping boy. Then she would make a pillow out of the fawn's back and go to sleep.

Everyday they wandered greater distances and one morning in a little glade beside a brook Baldr sat on the ground on his rear hips and straightened his back against a tree as if he were a sitting human child and reached upwards with his right front hoof which as he moved turned into a little human hand and removed first one nub and then the other off his head, then smiling he set a single horn at the center of his skull. "I can take them on or off," he explained to Beatrice, "and be one horn, two horns or without horns. Or all three all at once." He reached over and gave Beatrice one of the two little nubs. She held Baldr's little spike to her chest then handed it back and said that when she had touched the horn that it changed into her own rapidly beating heart and now she was giving her heart to him to guard and care for forever. He took her heart but just as fast handed it back to her with his other horn, which he said stood for his heart and that she should keep watch of both. Beatrice patted him on the head three times I love you, one pat for each word, and replaced both horns on Baldr's head. The summer passed and Beatrice welcomed the breezes and the cooler days of autumn. Horns blew, hounds barked, and hunters' shouts echoed through the aisles of the forest. Baldr heard the sounds and eagerly reared on his hind legs and danced he was so eager to participate in and lead the annual chase. "Sister," he pleaded, "Unleash me so I can run through the wildwood and show all and sundry the prancing Christ—the horned God—returned in all His glory! I can't resist any longer." Beatrice shook her head and her eyes moistened and her lip began to quiver. "Never, certainly not with all these wild hunters out and about looking to pierce your heart with their arrows. I will lock you inside our room in Ewald's cottage instead." "Beatrice, I am a spirit deer and can fly faster than any earthen missile, but if an arrow chances to strike me down, I will rise again in three days. But let us ask Oma what she thinks and let us abide by what she says. Her word shall rule us both."

Oma told the girl to unleash him, and Beatrice tearfully obeyed.

The first two days Baldr evaded the huntsmen and led them on a merry chase, returning each evening to Ewald's log house, where Beatrice waited for him anxiously at the door and when he returned again put on and fastened his golden collar.

As Beatrice made a pillow of his back, Baldr told her how he outwitted the sly hunters and was far too fast and nimble for them. The third morning the fawn awoke again to the sounds of the blaring horns and the men's voices hallooing. Once more he had to burst forth from Ewald's lodge and tear through the woods ahead of the baying hounds. He simply felt like jumping out of his shoes each and every time he heard the hunting horns. Once more Beatrice unleashed him and he bounded straight out the door and into the morning sunlight.

Baldr returned the third night limping, a shaft of mistletoe wedged in his hip. Beatrice was terribly frightened when she saw that her fawn was wounded. She and Oma removed the arrow, washed off the blood, applied herbs to the wound, and put the little fawn to bed. For an entire month, long after the hunters had departed from the woods he slept, and Oma thought he would sleep his way into the next world, but after four weeks, at the very time when Oma was making preparations for her and Beatrice's return journey to the castle—she had yet to tell Beatrice that her father had remarried since they had last seen the Wartburg—the fawn rallied and slipped out of bed to dance once more with Beatrice on the greensward. Oma petted their boy on the head three times. She then spoke seriously to both Baldr and Beatrice. Baldr would have to again return to being an invisible boy. He could not manifest himself as a fawn once they went home to the Wartburg. She then broke the news to her granddaughter that Arbogast had remarried. She warned Beatrice once again to keep her mouth shut and reveal not one word about Baldr.

Word about Beatrice and her foundling fawn, however, had already reached the Landgraf Arbogast from the pen of his retainer Ewald who had mentioned the girl's pet in a letter. Oma told her son that his daughter had released the young roe deer fawn back into the wild just before they started upon the journey home. When they came back, Beatrice discovered that her new stepmother the Landgrafin Sigune had moved her own two daughters into Beatrice's old room and Beatrice into a little closet at the other end of the castle, a room purportedly haunted by dark spirits. Sigune, too, had heard all about the little fawn. She had also listened to many tales about the young girl from the various servants and retainers, how she sensed things before they happened and how she had told all those that had the patience to listen to her preposterous stories that the Christ child appeared to her in visions. Sigune smiled. She saw that the little girl had a weakness and vulnerability she could exploit and make use of. Her husband Arbogast knelt down and worshipped the Black Christ of Intolerance and strictly adhered to the rigid, unwavering dogma of Mother Church. Blinded by the tenets of his doctrine, refusing to think for himself or to open his own eyes to the radiant, revealed truth disclosed each and every day and throughout the entire world about him, he would surely take extreme measures to save his daughter from hell fire and damnation. Confronting that which he did not understand, he only had to be made to think that Beatrice trafficked with incubi and he would surely immure the little girl in a convent. He would try to save her soul by caging her body—by burying her behind the convent's walls. Sigune had tricked him into thinking her black heart white. She would now undertake to blacken Beatrice's white soul in her father's frightened, prejudiced eyes. She cast the spell on the little pallet to make it a moving bed and she summoned the demon black cats, the dancing human leg bones or *Totenbeine,* the leering skulls or *Totenköpfe* and the red-eyed *Teufelhunde* or hell hounds to Beatrice's room each and every night.

Baldr, however, stood guard in the sleeping chamber and stilled the bed when it started to move on its own volition as if it were being pulled by phantom horses, and he made quick work of the nightly revenants and did not let the foul things disturb his Beatrice's sleep. Just as Beatrice had tended him after the shaft of mistletoe had pierced his pelvis, he cared for her now. He knew that in addition to Baldr and the Christ child he was *herok'aga* son of *he-šucka* and that he shared his father's prowess with the bow. Moreover like *he-šucka* he did not need arrows to kill. He merely had to breathe correctly in the correct *herok'a* manner and utter the word *ahahe* twice and let fly the empty bowstring and all his foes would fall over dead. When the black cats glared at him fiercely with their blazing yellow eyes, he let fly with his bow and dropped them one by one. "Oh, meow," he said "How cold we are now," and dragged the dead devils by the scruffs of the necks across the floor to the room's single window and heaved the dead bodies through it and let them drop down into the precipice yawning below. When the black dogs on their fiery chains emerged from every nook and cranny and made straight for his loved one's bed, he had to disobey Oma. He changed once more into a deer and leapt in front of them, turning them away from the bed as he led them in chase toward the open window through which Baldr would leap into the open air but instead of plummeting down and smashing himself on the rocks below Baldr hung suspended as the hell hounds fell and plunged downward. So much for the *schwarze Katzen* and the *schwarze Hunde*. Baldr also dealt with the *Totenbeine* and *Totenköpfe*. He made short work of them. He set up the human leg bones as pins and played bowls using the spherical leering skulls as balls. The leg bones all shattered when struck by the skulls which also chipped and splintered. In the end he brushed all the broken bone bits into a dustbin and emptied it out the selfsame window from which he also let drop each and every skull.

Beatrice slept soundly night after night. Even the din of the bowling did not awaken her. She opened her eyes refreshed each morning and told no tales of things going bump in the night. Sigune could work no mischief. Baldr thwarted and foiled her every attempt. Beatrice and Baldr's downfall, however, could not for long be averted, and Beatrice herself brought their defeat and ruin about, for she did not listen to her Oma and boasted and bragged about Baldr to her two stepsisters.

The wheel continued to rotate and Yule once again approached. For over a month Beatrice tried to befriend Sigune's two daughters, but the two girls steadfastly rebuffed her advances and feigned cold indifference to her. At last Beatrice grew angry and said she had her own secret friend and did not want to play with the girls any longer. Sigune's daughters' ears pricked. Their mother had told them to listen for any such confession on their stepsister's part and to report it immediately to her.

Beatrice so wanted the two to see Baldr, to see that she was not making up stories, so she insisted that the reborn child of hope and sunlight show himself both in his deer form and by allowing Beatrice to mount and ride his invisible shoulders. The sisters told her to bring her friend to the banqueting hall at midnight and that they would watch the two play from a hidden place behind an old arras. But it was not the girls that stood behind the arras at midnight. It was Arbogast and Sigune. Arbogast gasped and cried out when he saw the little fawn materialize from nowhere and he ran from the room when he saw his daughter fly through the air while riding on Baldr's invisible shoulders. The next day he summoned the nuns and monk to haul the child away. The twilight of the gods was at hand. Before the sisters and the monk arrived at the Wartburg the following week, Arbogast confided in his mother, and it was then that old Oma determined on her subsequent action. She had to separate the two children, the one living, and the other as yet unborn. Oma decided to erase all memory of Baldr from Beatrice's mind and to send him packing to his own world. She composed a knotting spell of nine lines, one line for each of the nine months of gestation, to return the unborn soul of Baldr to the future:

At knot of one I've my spell begun
At knot of two my word ringeth true
At knot three the fairy child can our world no more
   glimpse or see.

At knot of four his vision ceases to blur
At knot of five in another sphere the fawn remains
   yet alive
At knot of six our lot stands fixed.

At knot of seven a star disappears from heaven
At knot of eight, I meld with fate
But at knot of nine the child wraith's mine.

She committed the spell to memory and bided her time. She hated what she had to do, but Beatrice's life could be in danger. The Christians had already begun the practice of burning witches. The night before the nuns were due to arrive to collect Beatrice, Oma prepared a draught of forgetfulness for Beatrice to drink and poured the wine into a magic cup and served it to the little girl who obediently drank it down. The potion would not take effect until after Beatrice fell asleep the first night after Baldr had departed for his own world.

The next day the nuns arrived in their gray habits, as did the monk in his cowl and scapula. The nuns forced Beatrice kicking and screaming to accompany them across the drawbridge and out of the castle. Oma came with them and would also make the long journey to the faraway convent. Beatrice smiled when she saw Baldr following on the heels of the monk and the two nuns. Oma saw her smile and silently spoke the words of the knotting spell. Baldr felt himself beginning to fade. He knew immediately what Oma had done. How could Granny inflict such mortification on them, he wondered. Baldr ran to Beatrice and slipped the little spike that represented his heart into Beatrice's outstretched hand while he clutched the other horn that stood for her heart tightly in his own and then disappeared. The tears streamed from Beatrice's eyes and continued streaming the rest of the day until the monk, the nuns, she and Oma reached the inn and Oma put her to bed. The next morning she awoke and told Oma that she had a wonderful dream in which she had seen a beautiful unicorn dashing through the forest. The unicorn had allowed her to mount its back and away she rode into the night. Tears came to the old woman's eyes.

Turmoil at Spirit Lake

or

Baldr and Beatrice worlds apart

Baldr returned to Spirit Lake a human boy in all respects except for one: he cast no shadow. He could, however, be seen by all if he carelessly allowed himself to stray into someone's eyeshot or if he strode out brazenly and deliberately into the open from behind the natural cover of the whispering pines. The first time Red Horn noticed him and called out to and confronted him, after Baldr related all that had happened in Thuringia, the father of all raconteurs told the child that Beatrice's love had almost but not completely transformed him from a *waika* into a *worak*. Red Horn said it was proved by the fact that Baldr did not appear as a glassy play of lines but as real flesh and bones, albeit his flesh looked as white as a bleached bone, certainly not as brown or red as a normal-nosed domesticated brother and native son of the Hocąk tribe. Indeed with his piercing blue eyes, Baldr was the strangest looking long-nosed wild Twin war captive Red Horn would ever assimilate, but Wears Faces on His Ears remembered that Baldr had first appeared to him as a fawn, a fawn whose skin was sometimes brown and speckled and sometimes entirely white. He accepted Baldr as one of the People of the Big Voice, for, when the morning star shone resplendently in the eastern sky and its reflection blazed in the lake, Baldr had heard the words *da-wa-kah-char-gra da-wa-kah-char-gra* as Morning Star-Red Horn uttered them. Shortly after the boy's return, something else miraculously happened. Baldr started to grow and age. He did so rapidly and in a period of a week shot up in stature to nearly twice his former size. Later he would tell Red Horn that he had simply resolved to grow. From Red Horn's considerably longer point of view, Baldr's transformation from boy to man seemed to happen overnight, and he handed him two sets of the copper god maskettes. The blond youth of nineteen or twenty wore *hejąkiga* and *herok'aga* pinned onto both his earlobes and his nipples as he ran skyclad along the quartzite rock cliffs beside the lake or went bouldering over the extended stretches of red and purple rock or scaled the gorgeous buttresses and secluded crags.

The teller of this tale—the present raconteur—previously stated—perhaps too hastily and too categorically—that six hundred and more rotations of the Wheel of The Year with its eight spokes indicating the solstices and equinoxes, the four greater and the four lesser Sabbats, separated the time period of Beatrice from that of her beloved, but the abysses and gulfs between the unborn spirit and the mortal girl actually varied and shifted, for when Baldr first arrived at Spirit Lake and when he appeared again as a seeming human boy, albeit a boy who cast no shadow, whom every Ho-Chunk could behold and not just the great shamans and medicine men, none of the Hocągara had yet seen a white man. Baldr was the first. He kept apart from the Hocąk (for he knew he was not of their world), but they occasionally glimpsed the garbless white child wearing a thong with a single deer spike around his neck in the woods and at the lake shore nonetheless, but in a blink of an eye he was gone, for Baldr could move more swiftly than any creature in the forest and he ran faster than any arrow shot by bow. The Hocqk gave the spirit boy the name *wanagi* or ghost. To avoid observation *wanagi* would hide for many of the sunlit hours inside the empty hollow of a tree stump. One morning several Hocqk children saw *wanagi* emerging from his place of concealment and began calling him Stump after his hiding place, so Baldr became known by two names among the people of the nation. Semi-divine "transitional" beings, Baldr and Red Horn had a different sense of time than mere mortals. From the day Baldr had descended from the sky and had first landed at Spirit Lake to the time he opened his eyes and found himself within the confines of the witches' circle *vis-à-vis* with his Beatrice, generations of ten-toes had lived and died, and, during the "week" he "rapidly" aged from a small boy into a youth of nineteen or twenty, mothers gave birth to sons who in turn grew into men who fathered children of their own. Only when Baldr himself reached adulthood did six hundred some rotations of the Wheel of The Year divide the boy-man from his dearly beloved. By then others with white skin had made their appearance in Red Banks. Generations before the current one, everyone in the Hocqk nation had already heard tell of *wanagi*. The entire tribe, even the children, knew of Ghost's existence and that over many mortal lifetimes he had grown from a boy into a youthful brave. In the same manner as their forefathers, the Hocqk of 1825 reverenced him. They viewed the other pink skins with anything but reverence, however, and a generally tense though still peaceful state of affairs existed between the Hocqgara and the hoards of palefaces then coming into the Michigan Territory—present-day Wisconsin—from the south and from the east. A short time earlier, a new wave of

settlers had started overrunning Hocąk land to the north of
Galena, Illinois. The lead boom had attracted miners from both
Illinois and Missouri who in their search for new deposits had
traveled up the *Rivière aux Fèves* into Hocąk lands. Throughout
the years, Fever River (as the English would corrupt the French
river name) would bear other titles. Just like the French, the
English originally themselves called it Bean River due to all
the wild legumes growing along its banks and later it would
bear the names of both Galena and Wisconsin, but the armed
conflict in the southwest region of what is today the state of
Wisconsin between the Ho-Chunk tribe, local militia and the
U.S. Army which broke out in the summer of 1827–the Le
Fèvre Indian War–the first important Indian disturbance in
the United States and its territories since the war of 1812 and
the immediate and determinant precedent to the much bloodier
1832 conflict the Black Hawk War–took its name from the
original French designation for the river up which pushed
many of the approximately six to seven thousand disgruntled
wage-slave lead miners from Illinois and Missouri, who had
come to the Galena country starting in 1824 to work the (for
the owners) hugely profitable mines there, in their hunt for ever
new deposits of the lustrous silver-blue element which darkens
when exposed to the moist air.

Prior to the outbreak of hostilities in 1827 between the
Hocąk people and the government of the United States of
America, the Indians of the region, despite the best efforts of
the American government to compel the tribes to live in peace
with one another–for bitter experience had taught the westward-
bound American settler that war could not exist between the
Indians without its becoming inconvenient and dangerous
also for him–fought constantly among themselves, engaging

in internecine feuds in which small bands of marauders committed retaliatory murder after retaliatory murder. For over a century the native peoples—all the nations from the headwaters of the Mississippi, both the Siouan and Algonquian peoples, including the Siouan Hocqgara—warred amongst each other. Sauk, Fox, Menominee, Ojibwa-Chippewa, Potawatomi, Hocqk and Kickapoo battled amongst themselves, and often agents of the United States government acted as mediators and peace-brokers between the warring factions hoping to restore the general peace. When Red Horn handed Baldr the two sets of copper god maskettes in 1824, the Hocqk had carried an on-and-off war with their rivals the Ojibwa-Chippewa for nearly a decade. All the tribes, however, considered Spirit Lake a holy place, and Baldr, who never strayed too far from the blue lake's sandy white shore, never witnessed bloodshed among the *worak*.

Then the United States imposed common boundaries in contested areas and regions between both the separate territories of the tribes themselves so that the lands of each tribe were clearly defined and between Indian territory generally and lands formerly recognized as belonging to the Hocqk (whom the United States referred to as the Winnebago, a name given them by the neighboring Algonquians: the Fox, Sauk, and the Ojibwa-Chippewa) and/or other tribes but now occupied and given over to white settlements. All the tribes Siouan and Algonquian agreed to the lines drawn on the map and their representatives signed a general peace treaty at Prairie du Chien on August 19, 1825. But again and again the various nations would send out marauding parties and new warfare would commence.

Ironically, at the same time the native peoples battled and disputed, the lead miners coming into the region also fought and feuded. Claim jumping led to countless deaths among the whites. Those who came from Illinois waylaid those who came from Missouri and vice versa. Both sides spoke derisively of one another. The Missourians gave the Illinoisans at the Galena mines the name "suckers"—this for two reasons: one, because in the springtime many Illinoisans from the south traveled up the Mississippi River by steamboat and worked in the lead mines during the warm months then embarked down river to their homes come fall, thus establishing a similitude between their migratory habits and those of the fishy tribe of the same name, and, two, because poor people from slave states—those unable to purchase their fellow human beings for profit and gain and those whom the wealthy southerners considered a burthen to genteel society—had originally fled the south to escape the distain and imperious domination of their wealthy planter neighbors and had settled in the southern part of Illinois and thus resembled the sprouts or "suckers" from the roots and stems of the tobacco plant which the Negro slaves stripped from the weed and threw away with the tobacco worm itself, as, when they removed to Illinois, they too had been plucked in a sense from their parent stem and gone away to perish like the not-missed "sucker" of the tobacco plant. As insults always breed insults among the sarcastic, the southern Illinoisans by way of retaliation called the Missourians "pukes." Missouri had taken a great puke, all the Illinoisans claimed, and vomited forth hordes of uncouth ruffians and riffraff—all her worst population—from its lower, already worked and depleted, lead mines to the pristine and as-yet untouched, lead-rich Galena country. Illinoisans and Missourians would be trading insults and calling each other suckers and pukes forever, but an Illinoisan would rob a fellow Illinoisan just as quickly as he would a Missourian in the lawless Indian country north of Galena.

While all these hostilities were erupting, Baldr experienced a fever inside himself. His guts churned ever so badly. Lovesick, he felt the stoneache, but the experience was an entirely novel one. He did not know from what he suffered. He missed Beatrice so fervently! Moreover the world had become so strange as of late! In a race no *worak* Hocąk could keep pace with him, for he ran it seemed as fast as the wind itself. Yet recently he encountered a brave with a ruddy complexion called *warora* who looked the very image of Red Horn himself. Their eyes locked across the distance of an open glade. Baldr instantly turned on his heel and sprinted in the opposite direction, but rubicund *warora* immediately started running after him and soon came up right behind him and followed on his heels as they sped round and round Spirit Lake hour after hour day and night in seemingly endless competition until at the end of a week *warora* collapsed from exhaustion, his magical more-than-human stamina at the last falling away and giving out. Thereafter Baldr avoided the miraculously endowed *worak* youth wherever he could, for as an adopted son of the People of the Big Voice, Baldr knew that the youth, garrulous as little Beatrice, would boast to all who would listen that he had almost tied *wanagi* in a footrace and that he would now scour the forest for Ghost to seek a rematch.

At this time, Baldr suddenly experienced difficulty sleeping. In the past his eyes would simply slant shut with the sunset, their tired, irritated pupils suddenly drained of their former blue hue to become gray and virtually colorless just before Baldr's eyelids drooped shut. Now he lay still as could be but could not sleep though he feigned perfect sleep. He would toss, turn, and wake throughout the night. But the mornings became the golden hours of his day, the time he "spent" and shared with Beatrice, when he luxuriated in that interrealm between sleep and waking, the hour when the morning bells rang in Thuringia, a time he dubbed "Beatrice matins."

Blessed interrealm, which seems so real, realer than the waking world! As he lay sprawled in the sand in front of the purple and red boulders, the deerskins he used as covers kicked off him and overturned on the beach, and the light from the opening Day's Eye came streaming down on his pallid deathly white face, half-awake and half-asleep, Baldr-*wanagi* visualized—in his mind's eye—his immortal beloved, for long before he had discovered that a sort of assignation with his other half could occur in the shadow world, the interrealm peopled and populated by the unchained sleeping mind where the imagination ruled supreme and the semi-conscious, semi-dreaming puppet master that was oneself could travel from here to the moon in a wink of the eye but could also control and shape the dream, could chain the unchained and move the dream wherever he wanted it to go and make happen only what he wanted to make happen. If he fell off a cliff he need not plummet. He could sprout wings and turn into a *kaǧi* or a Thunderer. In the interrealm all that Baldr-*wanagi* desperately longed for came true. He could make the little girl materialize beside him, and once more he became his fawn self and she used his back for a pillow after making them a soft bed of moss and gathered leaves and kneeling down and saying her nightly prayers. In the manufactured dream, each morning before Baldr awoke, Beatrice went in search of food for them to share and in the forest she found abundant roots, berries and nuts as well as picked the long tender grass which Baldr would eat out of her own hand and afterward he would sport about her in mad, frolicsome dance. He would spring out of Ewald's log lodge and dash through pastures and forest paths, where he would lead the hunters and their hounds on a merry chase, outwitting them one and all. Old Oma would also appear before his eyes, scratch him under the chin and pet him on top of his head one-two-three I love you. If in mid-dream, Baldr chanced to wake, he would will himself back under to recommence the dream at the point where it had broken off. He could fool himself into thinking that he held his Bea in his arms. Nothing in the world about him carried Baldr so far away that he could not find his way back home. Throughout the day but especially in the mornings he could enter the interrealm at will. He needed no quiet, no pillow, no darkness, to forget the world. He simply sat on one of the hard pink boulders, shut his eyes, and, leaving all behind, entered his waking dream.

There was no pleasure that would make Baldr forego his morning dozes. He wished that he could lie in the arms of Morpheus eternally. We have it from the highest authority that, "Surely that man is the greatest who keeps faith with and yearns for the night, the while he performs the mightiest tasks of the day." Yes, that very great raconteur rightly hymned "sleep, sweet sleep." Yes, we can all "hold to be the benignest, the most moving of all the great facts of life that daily the night falls; that over stresses and torments, cares and sorrows the blessing of sleep unfolds, stilling and quenching them; that ever anew this draught of refreshment and lethe is offered to our parching lips, ever after the battle this mildness laves our shaking limbs; that from it, purified from sweat and dust and blood, strengthened, renewed, rejuvenated, almost innocent once more, almost with pristine courage and zeal we may go forth again." Baldr, however, preferred the half-sleep of morning to the deeper, perhaps more refreshing total sleep of the night, where one relinquished all control and one's dreams went rampant and spun wildly out on their own. Baldr feared the unleashed subconscious. No pilot stood at the helm at night. In the morning, half-awake Baldr attached a golden garter, a soft yet resilient cord of braided rushes, around the neck of the subconscious and from thenceforward would never give a free rein to him in their walks through the shadowy interrealm. Growing from a boy into a man, Baldr discovered that he could no longer exert complete control over his body, which, though he did not cast a shadow, was at least partially *worak*. Moreover, he feared the night and deep sleep because then when his subconscious had free reign his body could do unspeakably vile things without his having any say in the matter.

The week-long race with *warora* in which the two ran round and round the circumference of Spirit Lake and which ended on the last day of April 1826 with red *warora* collapsing and falling to his knees on the hot white sand also left pale Baldr exhausted and on May Eve he fell into a deep sleep but not a particularly sound or restful one—at least not for the first watches of the night. His body took control. He relinquished all mastery of it. Anyone watching would have seen his limbs and extremities twitch and dance as he lay unconscious on the sand. His eyes flickered and fluttered behind their lids. Deep within stirred a particle of consciousness. He felt as ashamed as if he had lost domination over his bladder and bowels as foul, strange things occurred about his intimate person and secret places and he felt himself leaking, trickling, oozing and making puddles outside of himself as the white sand clumped. Total blackness supervened. An almost narcotic sleep clutched Baldr-*wanagi* in its talons and held him down, a dark dreamless overpowering blackness that seemed to blot him out as it tried to negate and extinguish him—to snuff out his spirit, as if its light had never existed at all in the Summerlands, the realm of eternal ideas of which everything here below presents but a transient image, a pale copy or reflection. Baldr-*wanagi* felt as if he was being sucked and pulled into a swirling dark vortex, like a drowning man caught in a powerful undertow. He fought for the light of consciousness and in his desperate life-and-death struggle he heard chiming from afar silvery, bell-like tones. Achieving the light at last he opened his cobalt-blue eyes but still felt benumbed and deadened. He blinked and heard the laughter of young women in first bud intermixed with dulcet flute tones. Across the water does of the familiar four-legged kind emerged from the forest and plunged into the water and swam in *kokopelli's* direction. The skyclad olive skins also fearlessly plunged into the lake and swam out toward the fluteplayer standing in the shallows in profile in his breechclout of deerskin. Thousands and thousands of waterbeads little transparent globes or eggs glistened on his great humpback and atop his head he wore an otterskin turban fringed with turkey beards, the otter's snout brought round in a circle so it could clasp its tail in its teeth. Standing in the shallows, *kokopelli* slipped the thong bound to his flute back round his neck and then plunged both his hands under the front flap of his breechclout and caught the great wriggling eel from where it writhed, squirmed and made a prominent bulge and unleashed it that first morning of May into the water where the two- and four-legged does all swam and bathed. Then the interrealm came out into the world or the outside world was drawn into the interrealm. For upon awakening and observing *kokopelli*, Baldr went into a dream, or real and dream somehow became blended and one, and a great time later in his fallen existence when he returned to Thuringia

Beatrice herself told him that years and years before she too had dreamt the same dream so Baldr could not after all feel at all sanguine about dismissing what had happened as a mere vision or reverie, a fata morgana, and he remembered old Oma saying that on Beltane when the lads and lasses went a-Maying the God and Goddess would use young couples as avatars so that the Great Mother in the guise of the young Maiden Goddess could at last touch with human fingers her reborn son and the two could lie together in their green bower amongst the blossoms and unite. Beatrice said she suddenly became aware that she was running in a dark forest. Through the fringes of the trees she saw both the beach and the gleaming water glistening for more than a quarter mile across. Baldr's eyes followed the sun as it slanted across the blue ripples between gigantic trunks of ancient titans of the forest. He first saw her emerging from between two pines and stepping out on the white sand. She had come. Come to Spirit Lake. Come to Paradise Lake surrounded and ringed by conifer and deciduous hardwood forest, a cobalt-blue pupil in the southern range of metamorphosed sandstone, a gorge plugged on both sides by terminal moraine and mantled by gleaming pink-maroon and darkish purplish talus. Beatrice too had grown. A woman and not a girl stood before him skyclad like he was and wearing a necklace round her throat from which depended a spike or horn, the partner or twin of the spike he himself wore. He ran his hands through her frizzy hair as his blue eyes locked on her green-gray ones and she smiled her toothiest smile. She detached the heart-horn he gave her, his heart, from the necklace and held it out to him in her cupped hands where he saw the red muscle pump and beat. Time, distance, separation seemed cancelled and annulled, and soon Baldr was kissing, touching and tasting his beloved and for a brief moment he experienced the sweetest of surrenders pure, skyblue, overpowering and above all sunny, sparkling and scintillant as Beatrice grasped each of his ears in her hands and Baldr sipped and probed and sucked and at last took the communion wafer in his mouth. His skyclad body remained clean and radiant and pure. As did hers. What had happened between them was not foul or untoward but a holy sacrament, a knitting of two lives into one. He held mastery over his own body. He found himself again in the light exceedingly in the light but the darkness soon enshrouded him. For a time the two states interchanged, and Baldr felt alternately eclipsed and transfigured as he passed from shade to sunlight and back again. He saw himself as puny and insignificant then brilliantly miraculous as if some capricious god, now bored and now enchanted by his creature, had turned upon him at one moment an eye of withering indifference and at the next, with his love, had bestowed upon Baldr some of his own divinity, and when Baldr next opened his eyes what seemed whole eternities later he lay sprawled, spent and alone on the beach.

Later Baldr told Red Horn of the incident and Red Horn promised to help him reunite with Beatrice. *He-šucka* said he came from afar to furnish all his particular powers to address and set right the imbalance in his son *herok'aga's* life, that he would bring harmony to his spirit and aid *herok'aga* in the divination of the proper path for his journey through life, that he would instill inspiration, wisdom, and power in his boy and bring him happiness, contentment and abiding love on his path of life. He would use all his magic and the fires and sparks of the primal creation to make sure that all he promised might actually be. He would take his sick son's soul in his arms and hold as at the same time he took his body into the sweat lodge for healing and purification, for the fever and imbalance in *herok'aga* had infected the entire world. *The imbalance of the one had brought about the imbalance of the other.* That which was broken needed to be set right and quickly. That very spring right at the time Beatrice had come to Baldr, the Method family of Prairie du Chien had been massacred near the Yellow River in what one day would be Iowa where they had been tapping the Maple trees which were gorged with sap and sunshine their limbs bulging with new green, and six Winnebago men had been arrested for their murders. The white settlers soon released four of the Indians but bound over two of the braves for trial whom they placed in confinement at Prairie du Chien's Fort Crawford.

The wheel of the year made one full rotation while Red Horn tended Baldr in the Medicine Lodge. Spirit time differed from *worak* time and seemed to pass more slowly. Baldr continued to lie in his blood and far from getting well his condition further deteriorated and he could not for days at a time get up from his pallet. In his delirium, Baldr told Red Horn that he was the reborn son, the Christ child. When Baldr's fever went down and he again became lucid and himself, Red Horn asked him about his past life and Baldr repeated to his father all that he had learned about Mary's son from Beatrice and tears began welling in Wears Faces On His Ear's old eyes, for he knew the strength it took to lead a war party but had never considered the strength it would take to turn one's cheek or to lay down one's life for others. Not members of the tribe but total strangers. The Christ he realized was a new and a most powerful kind of god, but the Sky Father who allowed the Romans to hang his dear innocent boy on a tree and refused to come to the boy's aid as Red Horn now came to Baldr-*wanagi's*, Red Horn found terrible, his action heartless and ghastly. Such a being could not come from Overworld but belonged in Beneath World, the dark realm of chaos where the Underwater Panther threateningly and stealthily swam and where also dwelt the multi-headed green-and-red horned serpents, the especial antagonists and foemen of the Thunderers, the Birdmen and Falcon Beings of the Overworld, with whom they forever stand in fierce, mutual opposition, as well as the ancient Corn Mother or Woman Who Never Dies. During the course of the first year of Baldr's fever, the garrison at Fort Crawford relocated to Fort Snelling in what would be the future Minnesota, leaving Prairie du Chien undefended by federal troops. The soldiers took their Hocąk prisoners with them, but the Indians received word that the two accused Hocąk had been put to death.

Periodically Red Horn left the side of his ailing patient and made sorties throughout all of Red Banks to see how events would unfurl in "this time of troubles." He always looked dejected, nervous and preoccupied when he returned to the lodge and the news he brought back to Baldr was always bleak. During the summer months of 1827, a Hocąk war party surprised a band of twenty-four Ojibwa-Chippewa traveling across Hocąk land in Red Banks and slew eight of their number. As by treaty the Chippewa had right of passage, the army commander at Saint Peter's turned four of the accused Hocąk who had meanwhile come into his custody over to the Chippewa who summarily executed them with their long rifles. The executions further exacerbated tensions between the Hocąk and the whites. At the urging of the prophet *wabokieshiek* (White Cloud) who would later give his wholehearted support and approval to the Sauk chief Black Hawk during the bloody rebellion of 1832, the noble-looking Hocąk leader and war chieftain Red Bird determined on avenging the shooting of the four Winnebago warriors and led a war party against the Chippewa but returned disgraced, his band of brothers soundly defeated by their hereditary enemy. Again at the behest of *wabokieshiek* and to prove his worth after the recent fiasco, Red Bird resolved to attack the whites who had abetted his enemies and who continued to invade his country in such large numbers in order to seek revenge for the four who stood in front of the Chippewa firing squad but also for the purported executions of the two warriors held by the U.S. Army for the alleged murders of the Method family in the spring of 1826. Red Bird and his warriors journeyed to the undefended Prairie du Chien, arriving there June 27. Red Bird, *wabokieshiek,* and the rest of the war party burst into the home of James Lockwood, but, finding the house empty, they continued a few miles southwest of the settlement to the home of one Registe Gagnier, who had in the past welcomed Red Bird to his house as a friend and who on that day invited all the Hocąk men inside for a hot meal. As they sat down to table to eat, the Indians shot and scalped their host and then proceeded to attack his hired man Solomon Lipcap, who tended the garden outside. As they scalped and killed Lipcap, Gagnier's wife fled from out the house with her three-year-old son, and the two ran in the direction of the home of a neighbor. She fled but left behind in her crib the couple's year-old daughter. After butchering the gardener, the Hocąk reentered the house, discovered the baby girl and partially scalped her—miraculously the infant would survive and recover—before fleeing the vicinity, for Mrs. Gagnier's neighbors would raise an alarm and a crowd of men from Prairie du Chien would rush to the scene of the murder, by which time Red Bird and the other warriors had long since disappeared and slipped back into the forest. The white settlers around Prairie du Chien immediately formed a volunteer militia to defend their families. Red Bird and his confederates headed northward to attack elsewhere and in July struck two keelboats which came up the Mississippi laden with supplies for Fort Snelling. Seven Hocąk fell and two crewmembers from the keelboats died from their wounds while four others lived. The frontier settlements were now all up in arms, but Red Bird and his Potawatomi and Sauk allies including the notorious Black Hawk, who now joined in Red Bird's operations, carried out guerilla actions to the south, slaying some settlers along the *Rivière aux Fèves* and striking the Galena lead mines themselves. All hell broke loose. The miners raised their own considerable mounted force after fortifying Galena itself against any possible attack. Colonel Henry Dodge took command of these auxiliaries. The Governor of the Michigan Territory Lewis Cass happened to be visiting the Illinois town. He ordered his subordinates Abner Field and Lt. Thomas Martin to form a militia in Illinois to reinforce the volunteers at Prairie du Chien and then wrote to the Secretary of War to apprise him of the uprising. Troops from Fort Snelling were soon dispatched to reoccupy Fort Crawford, and Illinois Governor Ninian Edwards wrote General James Harrison to detach a fourth of the regiments of his brigade located on the east side of the Illinois River. Thomas M. Neale of the 20th recruited six hundred volunteers from Sangamon County and arrived in Galena with them. Troops from Jefferson Barracks in St. Louis, Missouri, under the command of Brigadier General Henry Atkinson also headed to the Michigan Territory, and in short order a massive body of regulars and volunteers began marching its way up Fever River directly into the Hocąk country.

Occupied and concerned as he was about his patient, Red Horn called on Morning Star and together they spoke the words *da-wa-kah-char-gra da-wa-kah-char-gra* so that the big voice combined of their two voices again rang out and all those who had their ears open could hear Red Horn's now anything but jocular and laughing voice warning his tribe that they could not possibly resist or overcome the forces arraying against them. Red Horn spoke to Red Bird, *wabokieshiek*, and the other war chieftains individually according to each one's ability to perceive and comprehend. He implanted in their hearts the complete futility and terrible cost of any further struggle. The good tidings he had heard, the teachings of the reborn son, also influenced his advice. The white settlers professed to worship the Christ. If the Hocąk now turned the other cheek, if they lay down their weapons, beat their swords into plowshares and acted like sheep perhaps the white generals would also show mercy and forgive their red brothers. Red Bird, *wabokieshiek*, and five other warriors all voluntarily surrendered to save their nation from the miseries of war and sure defeat from such a superiorly matched foe. The main culprits were kept in jail a long time awaiting their trials—some of the small fry who had taken part were acquitted and a few local leaders convicted and executed, but *wabokieshiek* and a number of the bigger chiefs and warriors, including Black Hawk would eventually receive Presidential pardons after the Hocąk by a new treaty ceded northern Illinois to the United States for $540,000 to be paid to the tribe in annual installments of $18,000 over thirty years and an additional $30,000 worth of goods to be dispensed immediately. It was the noble-looking Red Bird's fate alone to pine and gradually waste away in prison, where he at last died in confinement, the victim of regret and sorrow for the loss of the liberty he had known and grown accustomed to in the fresh green woods. Red Horn would weep bitter tears for his caged son.

His adopted war captive Baldr, however, began to rally in the Medicine Lodge once the tensions and war fever began to abate, and Red Horn brought him from the lodge back to the shores of Spirit Lake. There he throve with the other Hocąk, and like them waited impatiently the next appearance of the morning star, for he knew that due to the turbulence of the times Morning Star-Red Horn would have important things to say to each and every member of the tribe including the adopted war captives like himself. On the appointed day, before dawn, a goodly portion of if not the entire nation from the reverend elders in their ceremonial garbs with special designs and feathers woven in the cloth, their faces, arms and chests painted, and copper long-nosed and short-nosed god maskettes suspended from their pierced ears to the old and young women in their long full deerskin dresses, their necklaces of fawns' hooves, and their three styles of headdress to the countless children all naked and some splashing into the water had gathered on the beach to watch and listen. The harbinger of the sun began ascending in the east and as always the spirit voice began to speak the word *da-wa-kah-char-gra*, but then a great shadow like the silhouette of an enormous swan—a great old devil of a black swan—rose up in the air from below the treeline, stretching out its neck and spreading its dark wings which beat in the air a few times before extending to their full length. Outspread at last, they blocked the light radiating down from the morning star so the silver beams no longer reflected in the waters of Spirit Lake and the word *da-wa-kah-char-gra* was broken off in the middle after the syllable "kah." Baldr flinched at the rifle shots as to the left and right of him Hocąk men and women pitched forward or fell back as lead balls ripped through entrails or broke and snapped bone. The women and children not hit began to scream

and wail and Baldr heard the report of more rifles and bodies
began to pile on top of other bodies. The growing silhouette
of the swan could be seen by all who faced the portion of the
sky where the morning star had just disappeared, but none
but Baldr, Red Horn, his spectral form as glassy and transparent as Baldr's had been before his return to Spirit Lake from
Thuringia, and a few of the more gifted of the medicine men
and shamans—indeed one of their number pointed first to the
evil spirit and screamed *herecgunina*, the Hocąk name denoting
the dark entity who eternally opposes Earthmaker—could see
the figure casting the shadow: a great horned and winged beast
walking on the water with its cloven feet. Its head resembled
that of a goat, with a black candle set between the horns. The
claw on one human arm pointed upward, the pincer on the other
extended to almost touch the water. The demon had a scaly
green belly like a fish, above which fell two blue and sagging
female breasts, largely nippled. The sexual organs consisted of
a penis and a vulva, as in a hermaphrodite. A tail like that of
an elephant, an orange eye on either side, curled upward over
the fanged and tusked anus. The spiral eyes on the head circled
round and twisted and coiled out from two bright red dots.
Succubae danced on the laughing *herecgunina's* fingertips.

Red Horn came running down the beach and with one great
spring launched himself in the air and out across the water, but
just as his fingers were about to close round *herecgunina's* neck,
a great black-bearded giant of quite different stock and line-
age from that of the local red-haired long-nosed man-eating
wage-rucge stepped out from his place of concealment behind
herecgunina's back, a flaming sword uplifted over his head, its
hilt grasped by both his hands. He brought the blade down in
one great stroke—a triple-strand necklace of wampum beads

hung from Red Horn's throat; the sword cut through it, and the individual shells and whelks scattered—and severed at the outstretched neck Red Horn's huge head from his great, strong and powerful body. Red Horn's blood burst furiously forth and both head and body proceeded to fall into the water below where they floated on the waves, the open-eyed face at first up but then rolling round, so that the hair wound and coiled in an occipital bun with a long red braid dropping below the severed neck could be seen. A smiling and winking face depended and bobbed from the exposed earlobe. *Herecgunina* shrieked delightedly. "You were always a wraith and lifeless counterfeit, *he-šucka*, but now you are truly lifeless," the enemy of *mą'ųna* exulting and proceeding to viciously kick the facedown seat of the imagination and intellect across the water to the opposite shore with his furry, matted goat's foot as if it were an outsize soccer ball. *Herecgunina's* fiery red eyes locked on Baldr's cobalt-blue ones. His pincher extending like an eel from its hiding place inside a cleft of ocean rock caught Baldr in its vice around his abdomen. *Herecgunina* lifted the nineteen year old high in the air and placed him atop one of the great chimneys looking down across the lake where he could view the sandy stretch of beach from which he had been just plucked and where numerous Hocąk corpses now lay. From his perch atop the high chimney, Baldr watched horrified as the ragtag militia of volunteer lead miners—paleskins or *wanagi* like himself—emerged from their hiding places behind the trees and continued raising their long tubes which spat fire. Each time the tubes spat, more Hocąk men, women and children fell and their blood stained the sand. One of the whites a somewhat spindled figure bore no rifle but ran in the forefront and egged the others on and seemed to be the group's leader. He wore a badger cap tugged at one ear, and on the other side reddish hair extended from the temple upward. Reddish lashes rounded likewise reddened eyes. The face looked pale as a cheese, with the tip of the nose bent slightly askew. He wore a stocking-knit shirt striped crosswise, untowardly tight trousers and worn, yellow shoes. He constantly waved his fat-fingered hands and shouted out in a steady, slow voice, a schooled voice as it were, with pleasant resonance in the nose: "Kill the murdering heathen and devil worshippers. These savage, bloodthirsty Wuinebagoes call this Spirit Lake. Hereafter and henceforward it will be known as Devil's Lake, for these savages that hew, hack, and scalp worship the Black man of the forest!"

Both *herecgunina* and the fire giant suddenly grew. They increased in size dramatically until both their faces loomed down at Baldr. *Herecgunina* addressed his hireling: "Surtr, I imported you from Norse, Germanic legend—in such a case this is no special bother. It is permitted us to transmit spirits from different climes, cultures and millennia. Behold woven upon the loincloth which doesn't hide my goat's pecker all the swastikas, crosses in circles and tri-lobes—the last indicating my ability to travel to and from all the interconnected times and spirit worlds and underworlds. Like a certain German colleague of mine, who lamented in his expeditions and flights with his bondmaster the learned mage and scholar that among the non-native sprites he seemed to flounder whereas with his familiars the northern witches his control was stronger, I hit a lot of foreign spots and do a lot of favors, services for which I expect just remuneration. Some of the locals find my company so congenial they follow me through the wormholes between the worlds. I simply have to snap my fingers thusly for me to have a surrounding prodigy! See, the wanton company of roguish flirts as they skip and skim before me."

Skeletons, souls, imps, ants, griffins, sphinxes, sirens, Lamiae, will-o'-the-wisps, warlocks, fireflies and whole and half-witches, a sea of hexendom glowing, sputtering, burning and stinking began to swirl in an array of bright colors around the monstrous form of *hereçgunina*. Again the evil spirit thanked the *jötunn* Surtr. "You may return to that place of dreadful light and heat, that region of fire said to be located in the far south Muspelheim. I wish you luck when you do battle with Freyr. The pitch I gave you will insure that the flames you bring forth after you slay Woden's champion will engulf the earth and that you will destroy the Gods with fire at Ragnarök. But do me a final favor before you go. Retrieve Red Horn's head from where it bobs in the water near the opposite shore and climb the bluff on that side to the fantastical outcroppings at the top and ask the red-haired long-nosed *waǧe-ruǧe* who reside there to hang it from their lodge scalp pole so little *herok'aga* here can see it from across the lake." The *jötunn* Surtr dashed off, and Baldr saw the fire giant as he clambered up the cliff across the lake with *he-šucka's* head and reaching the top hand it over to the chief of the *waǧe-ruǧe*. Later that night something occurred that *hereçgunina* had not foreseen. In the eternity—the eons and eons of time—that followed when day after day Baldr was forced to witness the events of that day and night interminably repeat themselves, he looked forward to the last occurrence of the evening just before he lost consciousness—the only thing to give him a tiny smidgeon of hope. The *waǧe-ruǧe* kindled a great fire around the lodge pole from which the head of Baldr's father, whose hair had by now turned quite white, hung. The giants standing guard had painted their bodies half red and half black and as the moon rose they began a celebratory dance round their bonefire. Across the lake, Baldr heard the word *da-wa-kah-char-gra* ring out from across the water. His father Red Horn-Barbarossa's head was calling out to the spirits with a death song, the kind sung by prisoners about to be executed, and the red-and-black giants standing guard upon hearing the big voice of *he-šucka* immediately jumped into the flames of the fire and their flesh and even their bones were reduced to ash.

Herecgunina again turned his goat's head with its red dots for eyes in Baldr's direction.

Baldr spoke up: *A long time ago I fell from on high but my journey's end was not this world. You, Black spirit intercepted me and with that great claw of yours knocked me off course, so now I am divided from my heart, from my sweet Bea. I crossed over to her once as a child and later she a young woman seven years older than myself visited me on the shores of this lake but once again we have been pulled apart and separated which has been nearly the death of me. Now you come here and profane this holy lake and slay my adopted father and his people. Why do you persecute me?*

Herecgunina stared and stared at Baldr with his red eyes. The youth quaked and trembled and felt the blood flowing through his veins turn to ice. The evil spirit spoke. His voice sounded just like that of the red-haired ringleader of the miners' militia on the beach below. A steady, slow voice, a schooled voice with pleasant resonance in the nose: *We should doff our hats and be properly introduced, friend Baldr. I am the spirit that negates. I steal shadows. I snatched those of all the Hocąk lying dead on the beach—a good harvest—just before the little spinning spheres of lead hit them and made them all grave men. He jests at scars that never felt a wound. Their hurts cannot be much. Little wounds I grant you one and all. Not so deep as a well, nor so wide as a church-door. But 'tis enough, 'twill serve. You worak durst not lose your shadows. They're an immaterial yet integral part of you all.* Baldr winced as he heard the report of more gunshots. *I have been collecting shadows for a long time now. The Egyptians called one a* khaibit

and considered it an individual's most vulnerable part. I know that it was a
very wicked thing to do, but back in Thebes I enjoyed walking on a person's
shadow and holding it down on the ground with my foot as he or she blithely
strode on not realizing until later and then with horror and despair what I
had stolen from them, their precious khaibit. All the time they performed
special rites to prevent its theft. For the khaibit accompanied a person after
death and became the khaibit of the sahu, the soul which was a replica of
the human body which, provided the right ceremonies had been performed, set
out through the underworld to the Hall of Judgment. Without one's khaibit
one remained trapped a ghost and wandering spirit on this side of the great
divide forever, as you are trapped at Spirit—or rather—Devil's Lake, wanagi.
Volleys of new shots followed upon one another. What a harvest
I am having today! See how great my shadow grows. The silhouette of
the swan continued to wax and wax and suddenly became
immense. Fire came from its nostrils and its two vast wings
extended in the gloom as if the bird had become a great dragon.
Heregunina continued: I have been called many names. The followers of
Zoroaster or as some call him Zarathustra, those who worshipped Mithra,
the ancient Indo-Iranic god of light, called me Ahriman, the dark destroyer.
The ancient Slavic people knew me as Chernobog or "dark god," the mortal
enemy of Dazhbog, another deity of light. Oma called me Black Christ, and
her son Arbogast remained his entire life my devoted servant, and, see, I can
walk on water and not sink beneath the waves just like the fabled White Jesus.
Indeed I'm the son of that privileged Pharisee who enjoyed Roman citizenship
and suffered from epilepsy. During one of his fits he had a vision of me and
the to-then-fanatical devotee of Jehovah grew enraptured, intoxicated with all
the possibilities of mischief which I offered. With threats of hellfire and eternal
damnation, we exacted obedience from the adherents of the new faith and through
fear forced them to renounce and forego all of life's pleasures, and together we
made a great odyssey through Asia Minor and the Aegean so as to swell and
proliferate the ranks of the intolerant and bigoted and to convert the gentiles to

our brand of Christianity which emphasized the wrath and vengeance of the stern, unforgiving Father and thereby stifled and choked the original message of White Jesus, the gentle lamb. What a legacy we two would produce. We fooled untold scores of good people into leading miserable lives of dirt and squalor in the hopes of a better life to come. We encouraged our converts' masochistic and sadistic tendencies. They would flagellate themselves and burn and otherwise torture and slowly put to death all those who did not tow the line and strictly adhere to every line, jot and tittle of our hateful dogma which we ruthlessly promulgated from Palestine and Syria to Greece, Crete, Sicily and Rome. Our creed would bring about the age-long persecution of Paul's own race and upon it was founded the Holy Inquisition, which persecuted and made suffer thousands upon thousands.

Yes, Baldr I am the spirit which negates. I wish creation to return to primal darkness, for all to fade back to black. I want quiet, pure quiet, and not all this tumultuous hubbub and uproar, this constant, deafening ruckus and fuss. The All Highest needs to give over his silly procreative fun. The cost of his selfish masturbatory enterprise must be brought home to him. You and your love, Baldr, are among the apples of his eye, and therefore I'm your sworn enemy. Yes, out of spite and malignity, I diverted you off course when you first made the journey down and I vow that you will never lead the life you and Beatrice envisioned in the realm of eternal Forms and Ideas. O it would hurt and wound our friend the demiurge if you two his confederates, co-creationists, and willing helpmeets would switch sides and help me douse the light. The Hindus reverence Siva as much if not more than they do Brahma. Destroying has its compensations, my son. It can exhilarate one's soul every bit as much as creating. No, Baldr, if you bow down and worship me and if you promise to make Beatrice worship me too—well, that is probably too much to ask—why demand the impossible? —I tell you what Baldr, I'll turn Beatrice into a most obedient wife; I'll use one of my pincers as if it were a narrow rotating blade in a cannula to make an incision into the frontal lobe of Bea's brain severing the nerve fibers. I see you wince. I assure you it won't *hurt at all. All my assurances won't help of course. I see I will have to take another tack. Well, I can be a kinder, gentler devil if I put my mind to it.* Hereupon Black Christ cracked a smile. *Well, I know the very trick. You'll recognize the article I have in mind, little* wanagi. *I will make you a little golden garter to put around Bea's neck. I'll weave some rushes and braid them into a soft cord. Once you drape the noose—um, necklace—round her throat from thenceforward she will never oppose you and do anything you say.*

Baldr's answer came as quick as day: *A Hocqk from the green wood, I know how it feels to stand leashed when you feel like bounding through the forest, and Beatrice God bless her loved me enough to let me go. She saw that a deer must remain a deer. I will not cage her. Not even in a golden cage. I will not leash her. Not even with a golden garter. I want my love. A* worak *not a* wanagi *Beatrice.*

Black Christ looked highly amused. *Are you so sure, Baldr? Many a good man desires a taming of the shrew. Xanthippe put Sophroniscus' son through his paces and there was never a nobler more high-minded man than he. All virtues, contrary to his teachings, do not converge into one. This unseemly creation would be a little more palatable if only you goody-two-shoes and artist types walked the earth. Though I would still find all your noise unbearable. For few who make the great fall downward remain as true and steadfast as you and Beatrice, dear Baldr. This world might not be such a bad place if everyone was a little Mozart, if you* worak *could all be swans of Avon and join hands with the creators in producing the sublime. For the small minority which succeeds, countless others fail. The All Highest's miracles come at great cost. All those that depart the Upper Circles have the best intentions of course. God is very wasteful. For every Mozart, Goethe, or Leonardo he succeeds in cultivating, numerous others go to seed. Something becomes perverted in you when you arrive here, and I'm not the agent of the perversion. You kill and maim each other and otherwise treat one another abominably. The All Highest's few successes do not justify the many abortions. For such a seemingly beautiful place, this middle world is foul, foul beyond all belief. Yet the All*

Highest won't give over his little experiment, and the body count goes on and on. I hold my nose. I will not serve and abet such a selfish wasteful master. I may be Black Christ but I am still Christ. I see all the horror and heartache. I hear the noise and din from constant conflict. The Prince of Peace only wants peace. Baldr no longer looked at a goat. Suddenly he beheld an obsidian Jesus beautiful, pure and kind. *Help me then, Baldr. Let us together put an end to all suffering. Choose another life now that you have come here.* But as the God spoke Baldr remembered his Beatrice and shook his head no for all time and with complete finality. *Take pity on the little lost ones, the grieving and the hurt, on all the suffering ill,* the dark god urged sweetly. *Pity the deluded monkeys, lemurs and fools that think they are their bodies. End transience and mutability. Give the peace that passes all understanding. Suffer the children to come into the eternal night and taste the oblivion of sleep, sweet sleep.*

No, shouted Baldr. *I will never help you.*

Then suffer the consequences, screamed Black Christ. Instead of the wolf in sheep's clothing—the beautiful obsidian face—Baldr again saw the goat with the red dots for eyes. *You will assume all their collective guilt and the All Highest's too. But hold. I will give you time to reconsider. All the time in the world, for Devil's Lake shall become your Purgatory. A nice Catholic invention to fleece the flock. Pay up and Father will say a mass and light a candle for a lost soul purging his sins in fire on our high holiday, All Souls Day.*

Baldr stood rooted to the spot, where he was made to watch the massacre over and over again. With tears in his eyes, he continued singing his love songs to Beatrice. Everything seemed weighed down and between tick and tock time slowed to a snail's pace then all but stopped as Baldr's molecules hardened and solidified into ice. Each day every day he saw his brother and sister Hocqk slaughtered. Universes and galaxies came into being out of swirling clouds of hydrogen gas rotating in starless space. As the clouds spun, eddies formed in them in which gravity began to lump particles of matter together into larger bodies. Internal temperatures rose within these compressed masses and the first stars ignited and lit up. More spinning clusters appeared elsewhere. As they became thicker they grew hotter. Some clusters came in pairs and triplets. Others remained single. New stars flickered. Old and dying suns expanded, turned red and then died in great fiery explosions. One enormous glowing disc of dust in which lumps formed as in a pudding became the solar system. One fiery lump orbiting the Day's Eye would eventually turn blue. Hot dense clouds darkened the cooling earth and eventually began dropping rain which boiled off the molten rock below as steam—the water in Devil's Lake at the same time seethed and bubbled and the elongate basin of quartzite bluffs surrounding the lake became the rim of a great witches' cauldron—but with time the rocks cooled and the water furiously fell down from the sky and filled the vast hollows of earth's surface forming the oceans. *Mą'ųna* thrust up great peaks and ranges which over the millennia the rains would slowly wear away after first digging valleys, gullies, and huge canyons. At tears and rips in the earth's crust lava spit up and flowed. The seas gave rise to life and a long pageant ensued. From shadowy beginnings arose an infinite variety of things. Sunlight touched the face of the waters and single-celled organisms—little transient transparent life forms that only half existed danced in the light. Trilobites grew to a foot long. Tiny-shelled animals, starfish, snails and two-horn corals like strange potted plants appeared. Thick seaweeds wound on the ocean floor. The first land plants such as Nematophyton and Psilophyton moved ashore. Life forms ever gave rise to newer life forms and eventually great crested lizard-birds with sharp teeth and claws walked the planet. Still each and every day, Baldr awoke to see the same dreary spectacle. He saw each and every death infinite times over as different days he focused his eyes on different sections of the killing fields. Lead balls again and again passed through the same bodies. His lips clenched as his stood on the chimney and mentally kept singing to Beatrice despite the utter and proven futility of his countless, previous attempts, each song or valentine an invisible immaterial arrow he strung on his mental bow and shot out telepathically between the worlds blindly and at random hoping that one of his bi-lobes would wend its way to her and that she could somehow bring him aid and deliverance. Silver beam after silver beam of bi-lobed arrow flights streaked upward into the sky but all the myriad arrows bounced off the ever expanding breast of the great devil swan and fell back either to the earth or hissed as they hit the blue waters of Devil's Lake. A great meteor crashed into the Yucatan peninsula and the lizard-birds that tramped the earth and glided through the air for millions and millions of years all died in an eye blink. The age of the thunder-footed scaly giants had come to an abrupt and sudden end. Tiny mammals emerged from their holes, dens as small as little glassy, transparent Baldr's had been underneath the red and purple boulder field on the lake's marge. As always, life forms ever gave rise to newer and newer life forms. Bothriodon, Protapirus, hungry Hoplophoneus and the graceful grass-eating Proëbrotherium roamed the savannahs. Sky beings from far across the heavens touched and caressed with their long magic fingers the pea-sized brains of a tiny tree-climbing species of lemur and caused them to expand and grow at a greatly accelerated pace…. Then came the coming of the cold. Ice ground across the plains, rounding valleys and creating new lakes and rivers. Vistas of time-coulisses opened out infinitely, yet each and every day, Baldr awoke to see the same dreary spectacle of murder and death. From the days before Set, civilizations arose. Atlantis and Lemuria, itself but a remnant of the old Gondwana continent, sank beneath the waves and a great knowledge and light went out forever. Someone built a couchant lion in what was not yet a desert and the Chaldeans raised their high tower, but still Baldr needs must watch the same bloody events. Each night as he closed his eyes he prayed never again to awake in the world. He had descended from on high and fallen down it seemed to the lowermost pit in hell but at last a comforter came to him. A little girl with blonde braids flowing down from a white linen cap fringed all round with tiny bells and pink and blue lappets she said had been her grandmother's visited him in his sleep and claimed that she was his and Beatrice's daughter not in the current world but on a parallel plane. She explained that in the night in her sleep Beatrice had somehow heard Baldr's song even though during the day where she prayed constantly to Mary the mother of God for intercession and guidance her ears remained closed and stoppered to him. She remembered Oma's kettle—though she wouldn't recollect one snatch of what she dreamt when she woke in the morning—and peered into it until she found the particular reality in which little Orgeluse lived and breathed, for as old Oma taught all that can be is— everything that can possibly happen does happen simultane- ously and all at once—and indeed on one plane of reality all that Baldr and Beatrice envisioned in the realm of eternal forms and ideas before taking their plunge downward occurred and unfolded exactly as they foresaw and they had their children together. Orgeluse would never be in this time strand, even if Baldr managed to escape from *herecgunina* and return to

Thuringia, but nonetheless Baldr could meet the darling little girl that would never exist in his particular version of life in the interrealm, where his Beatrice had dispatched her, and she could not only give him succor and comfort, she could aid him with her love in his most desperate hour. Father, she said, stay awake a fraction of a second more and observe what happens across the water on the far bluff. Red Horn dies only temporarily. Have faith in your father, and something wonderful will at last finally happen. The wheel of the year kept circling and circling and Baldr each night kept his blue eyes open for an infinitesimal bit longer and at long last the year 1174 rolled round again and he saw Beatrice's light for a second time fall from the sky and later that night as his eyes were about to slant shut he saw rubicund *warora* creeping between the fantastical outcroppings of rock on top of the far bluff holding in his hands Red Horn's magical bow. Two *waçe-ruçge* guards stood by the scalp pole from which the now white head of Baldr's father hung. They had painted themselves red and black and plugged their ears with clay so they could not hear the spirit of *he-šucka* sing his death song. Baldr watched *warora* who looked the very image of Red Horn himself string a charmed arrow whose shaft was feathered with red and black quills. The arrow pierced the throats of both guards, and the Ho-Chunk warrior who had almost beaten *wanagi*-Stump in their great race grabbed Red Horn's head from off the scalp pole and ran with it. The entire *waçe-ruçge* tribe pursued him, and as he ran and the giants gave chase *warora* shot arrow after arrow behind him, each shaft killing many hundreds of man-eaters. When he had used all his arrows up, *warora* stopped running and stood his ground. He used *he-šucka's* great bow now as a club and slew the remainder of the giants except for a little girl carrying a baby on her back as he did not want the race of giants to become extinct. The strength of his father came into him. *Warora* caught hold of the two *wąge-rucge* children and slung them half way round the world so that they could no longer pose a threat to the Hocąk nation and then ran down the bluff to the waters of the lake where Red Horn's headless trunk still floated near the sandy shore. Baldr realized that he would have to divert *herecgunina* for the evil spirit had heard the great din and racket across the lake and was pivoting round to see what was happening. Ghost would come to the aid of his twin Flesh. Baldr shouted that he would capitulate, that he was ready to make terms with *herecgunina* and the red dots turned quickly back to him. Baldr vowed that he would make Beatrice bow down and worship the evil spirit if *herecgunina* would ease his torment. He would do all that the devil would have him do and more. He would win him more converts than Paul-Saul. He would aid him in extinguishing all the lights if only *herecgunina* would uncage and unleash him. Meanwhile *warora* ran like the wind with Red Horn's head tucked under his arm. He flew down the bluff trail to the lake shore then dove with the head into the water and swam out to the headless, floating trunk. Both his legs kicking and the fingers of both his hands clutching the tangled white hair, *warora* pushed the head in front of him and at last the halves of the severed neck would join when he fitted head with trunk. He slowed his speed just before head and body touched. He did not want to remain in a flurry when he blessed the cuts and called upon Red Horn's name. The split blood had to have time to run back and be sucked in again. He made sure one last time the head was face down and that the starlight fell upon the back and buttocks of the headless trunk; that the body still floated on its belly. He did not want to put the head wrong way round so that Red Horn would have to run with his face on backwards. The severed neck halves finally touched and *warora* said twice the word *da-wa-kah-char-gra*.

In a fury Red Horn rose up from out of the water. He clutched his ancient club with many knobs, the same stout stick he beat his wicked brothers with after the race but whereas he turned them all into foxes and coyotes he changed *herecgunina* into a skunk after knocking the evil spirit off his legs where he stood on the water and belaboring him with his stick. As Black Christ fell and tumbled, his shadow the devil swan also veered and pitched and morning star's light again hit the lake. The sun rose and all the dead Hocąk stood alive at the lake to greet and wave at him. In a trice, Red Horn joined Baldr on the chimney. "You must cross to the other world, my son. Your fever from being separated from Beatrice has thrown this world all out of balance. You must leave Spirit Lake and assume your original life as a Minnesinger. Grab hold of my hand, little *wanagi*." Baldr took hold of the proffered hand and shut his cobalt-blue eyes. He opened them and saw that he now stood on the beach where departure gifts had been laid out for him by all the gathered Ho-Chunk. A Spanish sword and a conquistador's helmet and cuirass lay on the sand. He stood and put out his arms and his brothers attended him and put on his armor, but first the olive-skinned girls gave him underclothes of woven nettle fiber. They also had knitted him a gambeson, a quilted coat stuffed with linen and grass which would serve him as underpadding for the cuirass and also a surcoat, with belt around the waist, to be placed over the armor which bore the figure of a spatulate hand lifted high in the air, a human eye gazing out from the palm. The crowd parted as *warora* led forward a beautiful chestnut mare he had liberated from the

U.S. regulars, Flesh's parting gift to his brother Ghost From The Hollow Place Inside The Stump.

Baldr looked up to see the glassy spectral form of his father *he-šucka* who handed him a seashell from inside which a particle of star brightly shone. "I bring you my son *herok'aga* a bit of Morning Star himself—a light for dark places—so you can cross over from world to world." Baldr mounted his horse, and Red Horn whacked the mare's rump. "Make for the center of the lake *herok'aga*, my son. The horse's hooves will gallop right on top of the water. The two of you will not sink for you are *wanagi* the White Christ! Ride to the center of the lake where you see morning star reflected. Unite the tiny star particle back to the great parent and a portal will open and in a trice you will be with your Beatrice."

As he approached the wavering, watery star, he heard the spirit in the lake's voice. It asked him: "Wilt thou wed this fate and give up all behind thee?"

Baldr firmly pronounced: "I will." *I love her that much.* "Beatrice, pray to God and ask Him to speed me over to you." He spurred his horse and saw the shores he had relinquished shrink to an infinite remoteness.

Baldr entered the light and returned to Thuringia.

Worlds in transition

He entered the wormhole a beautiful golden-haired youth of twenty but emerged as a balding, paunchy man in his mid-to-late thirties. Perhaps the eternity he spent in Purgatory had something to do with his aging and his exiting the wormhole at a later date in time from the one he intended. His eyes had to adjust when he rode out. They sank deeper in the darkness, and the small dots of light in their pupils made them look like two long paths through tall shrubbery in the park of some mansion, over which summer and sunshine lie, broadly gleaming. The journey between the worlds itself reminded him of his and Beatrice's explorations of the forest glades together as children, where they entered paths which began as circles of half-light which then extended into ever more narrowly enclosing darkness until the two children together saw a distant, glimmering point: the exit opposite into sunshine perhaps much brighter still. Snow lay on the ground on the far side, for there the wheel had spun round to that time of year the sun approached closest to the earth. The wheel had again reached Mothers' Night, Solstice Night or Yula— the longest night and shortest day of the year, north of the equator—the dark night of our souls when the new spark of hope at last ignites, each day after which the sun climbs a little higher in the sky as the dark half of the year declines and gives way to the growing light. On the first try this year, the *Christklotz* took fire. He had come! The

Baldr Christ had again come! Beatrice felt him approach and rushed to wake her adolescent sons Gawan and Gramoflanz. She heard her Minnesinger sweetly singing to her even before he entered the portal. His voice, which only she could hear, emanated from the tiny deer spike she wore round her throat. In her mind's eye, she saw the son god and his horse crossing the water of Spirit Lake to where the reflection of the morning star gleamed blue-white, and her childhood memories repressed for so long returned to her full force. She had known him and would him again in many other worlds. Baldr kept singing his love songs as he made for the exit opposite into the sunlight. He too experienced foreglimpses and dreams of their other lives together as he rode his horse through the dark tube and emerged onto the *Rennsteig* into the falling snow. He would forget them a short time after crossing over.

The powers of light and the god of the waxing year–the newborn Oak King–his topmost branches crowned by the solstice sun–would overcome the god of the waning year, the Holly King with his shadowy mantle, but the two would contest again in June, on the shortest night and longest day, with differing results. The two long separated lovers immediately sensed each other and Baldr spurred his horse and made his way to Oma's old castle, for in his heart he immediately knew his now matronly yet still chiseled and well preserved Beatrice's location. Her scheming and conniving brother-in-law had sent the *Witwe* back to her relatives in Thuringia an exile or *Verbännte* from her deceased husband Frimutel's ducal kingdom on the Neckar when he assumed the throne, her sons small friendless boys and no threat to him. Her half brother the Landgraf looked the other way and ceded her the castle in the mountains. Baldr did not stop singing, not until he had the old ruin in sight. His heart remained in his joyous throat throughout all the long night of his journey.

My sunshine, my dearest friend, my love: how I want to romp and frolic with you, our arms entwined. I want to give you my all. All that is best within me and share with you all the beauty that I have ever come across in life, wherever I might have acquired it: every jewel and gem in words and music, every majestic panorama and vista from the blue and starry skies to the snow-peaked mountains and the mist-enshrouded dark forests of the Landgraviate to my home territory of Spirit Lake with its brilliant foliage and irruption of scintillating color, its maroon and purple boulders, its bluffs with fantastical stone outcroppings, and its cobalt-blue waters. For can one enjoy alone? Yes, to a certain degree, but it's so much more wondrous, beautiful and uplifting to share and experience together. I love the mischievous green eyes of my Beatrice as she holds enfolded and enclosed something secret in her hands. Is it alive? I wonder. She holds out her surprise to me and asks me to guess: she is the best friend I've always imagined but didn't believe could really exist outside of my imagination: but I in no wise want to idealize: she is sweetly human, more so than most of us: she is simply the woman I adore most in life, the sweet other of my heart: how I long to breathe the air she does, to live beside her: to eat of the same food and idly chit-chat about our days: how we would play and romp and have good times: we would have no major differences of opinion: all might not be perfect harmony, but there would be no real dissension: how I have wanted to stand by her side in mutual life-adventure: being with Beatrice would be the fulfillment of my life: I love many things, but I love my Bea more than anything: she is all the delight and richness in my life: I'll swoon when I see her, I will find her so beautiful! I'm dazzled and dazed, shot through with red-horned Cupid's arrow. I will ask no more of life than that Bea be in my life. That she finds her true place at my side and we share everything together, for Bea is my heart. I love nothing more fervently than I love her but I'll accomplish anything asked of me, complete the hardest task, giving it my very all, so mote it all be with my be-all and end-all my Beatrice and me. For too, too long I have been divided from my heart. I ask nothing more of life than to finally show her how devoted and in love—fervently in love—I am. I'm her captive, slave, and subject: I pine and pine for her: want to hold her in my arms: how wonderful I feel when I kiss the arches of her feet in adoration and veneration, I so love her: and I know when she looks me in the eyes she can see my love welling there. How I love to ramble down the street with my baby, her hand in my hip pocket, my arm round her shoulder like we were kids all over again sauntering down Beaver Avenue on our way to the arcade to play Pac Man and Centipede. But what is it again and again that she holds playfully and mischievously enclosed in her hands as if it were a toad or frog: she asks what it is, to guess: I shake my head and say I don't know: it is her greatest jewel, her treasure, her pearl without price: I so long to hear her say those words and I know the truth of those words: how I want to see her smile and hear her say: it's beating and living within my hands: you know what it is: for you, Baldr, gave me this treasure. You gave it before Oma sent you packing to Red Banks and Spirit Lake: it is the gift of your living, beating heart: it is the gift of your love and my greatest treasure. My heart's with yours always. Both are enclosed in my hands, and the two Beatrice's and Baldr's beat as one.

As he sang and followed the ancient path over the summits of the main ridges of the ancient somewhat-difficult mountains and slate hills and through the aisles of fir and pine, the tree limbs covered and weighed down with snow, that looked to Baldr like an army of green-and-white snow and frost giants on the march, the snow storm abated and broke off. A giant orange-silver moon appeared at intervals from behind the scudding clouds. Baldr could see his horse's shadow ballooning across the white snow. No rider sat upon the horse. Baldr still cast no shadow. In his hazy, dreamy state, Baldr wondered as he glanced at the shadow of the riderless horse cast on the opposite snowbank, if he could hire some great painter to paint a false shadow on the snow, so he could see the shade of a centaur instead. He imagined the painter asking him how on earth could he have lost his silhouette and inky outline and he replying that the previous winter while he traveled in Russia, it froze so bitterly one day that his shadow became fixed to the ground, and he found it impossible to remove it from where it lay frozen. The painter refused the commission, saying that Baldr would lose any false shadow he could possibly paint. It would fall from him when he made the slightest movement. Only if he stood forever in one spot could a false shadow be painted. Oh, Baldr lamented, if only someone could fetch or manufacture him a well-fitted, moving shadow. He had some prevision that his not having one would somehow prove deleterious to Beatrice, that he a shadowless transitional being and not a real flesh-and-blood *worak* had practiced a wicked deception and as a child and youth stolen away the pure and angelic heart of the innocent girl. She returned love for love with all the full and youthful fervor of an innocent heart. Her love was a true woman's love. She was no half wraith.

Beatrice stood in the white yard in front of the castle's entrance, a son's hand clasped in each of hers. She wondered if they would see him arrive, for at the time of his last coming, except when he manifested as a fawn, only she could see him. Not even old Oma herself had been able to make out his lineaments. Perhaps her boys would inherit her ability to see Baldr. She gave each of her sons' hands a simultaneous squeeze. Perhaps her touch would convey the gift to them and their eyes would magically see. Both had been but small boys when their father went on crusade. They knew the image of a face reinforced by the graven likeness on a locket. They remembered kindly eyes. A mischievous smile. To wed Frimutel she had at long last left the convent. From her first day with the sisters she accepted that someday she would join their number and become a bride of Christ but then she had a dream of a blue paradisiacal lake ringed by conifer and deciduous hardwood forest and a beautiful blond youth standing skyclad in the sand and she knew that it stood her fate to bear children—sunbeams emanating from him, the sun's son, would pierce her dark womb and make her bear forth children of light—and to Arbogast's great chagrin and annoyance she steadfastly refused ordination and would not cut her hair. Sigune had meanwhile born him a whole stable of sons, so at last he found his daughter from a former marriage a suitable husband and sent her packing from the kingdom. A goodly gentle husband to his wife, Frimutel nonetheless valued service to God and King more than love, for despite Beatrice's remonstrances—all her pleading and begging for him to stay home—Frimutel went on crusade and was killed. Sir Hero needs must leave his bower and go off to the wars in which he first revels and finds his life's true meaning—he had dreamt from boyhood of slaying the infidel and of proving his virility and manhood by test of arms and he received ample confirmation of his gift and talent for war—and then finds, all unlooked for, sudden and early death. A life cut off abruptly and neatly. His younger brother fell on his knees and gave thanks, his way to the throne now clear. "Baldr-Christ is Heavenly Father's son," Beatrice explained to the half awake, surly, and grouchy Gawan and Gramoflanz, "But he'll be your spirit father now." The eyes of both boys widened for at the far end of the forest path they saw a strangely goldhelmeted knight, his tired and overworked horse foaming at the bit, come pricking forth, singing mightily the words of an old child's sweet and tender song, something almost but not quite forgotten. Tears came to their mother's eyes and she too began singing:

Dû bist min ich bin dîn
des solt dû gewis sîn
dû bist beslozzen
in mînem herzen
verlorn ist das sluzzelîn
dû muost immêr darinne sîn!

Baldr dismounted and fell on his knees before Beatrice in the snow. "The love of a poet is not lasting," he said, and lifted the conquistador's morion from his head. "His brush is for the rose in its season, at its height and bloom and full glory." Although if she focused on his piercing cobalt-blue eyes, she would lose herself in their depths and start deliciously dreaming of the young boy at the lake, Beatrice saw the ravages that time had wrought on her fawn. "Nonetheless, I have always worn the little fawn's horn round my neck, and I see that you also wear yours, my Bea."

"My love for you," he continued, "is now more like that of an old dog, who knows but one form to worship in its poor stupid fashion and would perish for her. If I lose you again after having refound you after long years, I will howl and howl then crawl under some front or back porch, retreat from the light entirely and await my sad, sordid, shabby end. And if I see anyone try to hurt you, fear not, like an old dog, I will not be able to smother my low growls but will bare my teeth and wolf-like spring to the attack. Truly like an old dog, I'll devote all the days of my remaining life to you, my mistress and love. If only you knew the insuperable difficulties I have encountered and met crossing over to you, but from this day forth, we never more shall be parted here below and for a time and season and even though quite belatedly we can still together experience the opposite of the timeless and eternal and as we envisioned we would before we fell from the realm of eternal forms and ideas we can still assist and partake directly in the All Highest's continuous act of creation, and perform as agents of that creation—sharing and taking part in His ceaseless, never-ending toil if only in a time-bound way and for a span of three score and ten. We were to have children but you are now past the age. No matter. You already have two strong boys. I shall simply adopt the two war captives and make them mine, for as well as Baldr I am *herok'aga* and, having kept *herecgunina* diverted and occupied so that my brother *warora-hejąkiga* could reattach our father Red Horn's head, I have become my father and am Red Horn as well." He addressed Beatrice's boys directly. "Little speckled fawns without nubs. Let me adopt you. *Herok'aga* and I are one and the same. When I wear my *herok'aga* guise I am still *he-šucka*. Thus it is I the great horned one who is the true protector of all the little fawns. Yes, boys, you shall undergo assimilation into the Hocąk tribe. Your adoption into the nation becomes complete with the calumet ceremony after I give your beaks several symbolic trimmings. At each stage of the process, I'll turn over to you a new set of copper long-nosed and short-nosed god maskettes to pin to your nipples. On each maskette *herok'aga's* nose is trimmed shorter and shorter until at last it is the same size as *hejąkiga's*."

In the months that followed Baldr-*he-šucka* taught the two young war captives the Hocąk way. He fashioned Gawan and Gramoflanz bows and wove them headdresses of gold and red feathers. He taught them how to spot and follow tracks in the woods, saying to them that it was equally if not more important to learn to follow the tracks of men's thoughts—the written word—made up of many individual squiggly little words—across the snowy face of the vellum page. When Gawan brought down his first red roebuck with forked antlers, he smeared the cheeks of the boy's face with the bright blood of the kill and taught him a prayer of thanksgiving to offer to the animal's released spirit. "Oh, Grandfather, I thank you for your life. Your body and blood will nourish mine and your life in the change and circle of existence shall become my life. Some time in a future being and incarnation, our roles may be reversed and after a strenuous and noble chase—for I will not simply lay down for you—I will let myself fall a sacrifice to your need and hunger and to the need and hunger of those you love. I will return life for life, for you great horned one have become my spirit animal and Grandfather."

Beatrice had only a very small contingent of retainers but every one at the castle could see the middle-aged balding Baldr— the pale guest who visited Dame Beatrice for six months every year. See him that is during the period of his fixed stay. "The Noble from afar," as Beatrice referred to him before all the serv- ants—one wag in their number said, after the Lady had retired, "Noble from afar? Why not say wight from the Moon?"—annu- ally arrived at Yule and departed into the night at the Summer Solstice. During the longest day in the kindled majesty of the sun, all would see him waving goodbye. None saw him after sun fall although spies watched for him everywhere, for here today he was gone tomorrow. He disappeared in a seeming eye blink. Those at the castle who if they did not practice the old ways of Oma and her followers, the other white crones, knew and had not forgotten the old legends and stories identified the stranger as Baldr the Sun and Oak King who struck down and banished his nemesis the King of Holly and Mistletoe at the height of his season and power on Mothers' Night, from which time the days each day began to wax longer, but in turn would be overthrown after the year's longest day by the Dark One when the waning half of the year commenced and the days began to shorten—at first ever so slightly.

Baldr never slept until the short night of the Summer Solstice. The first year what happened came as a total surprise and shock. He stood in the banquet hall alone with Beatrice. He had thought that they would never more be parted. As he approached the wavering, watery star, he had heard the spirit in the lake's voice. It had asked him: "Wilt thou wed this fate and give up all behind thee?" and Baldr had firmly pronounced: "I will." He never thought that he would see Spirit Lake again. But as he stood talking to Beatrice, a great exhaustion overtook him. Beatrice watched as his eyes suddenly drained of their former blue hue to become gray and virtually colorless slanted slowly shut. In a moment the man of flesh became but a glassy outline, a nearly transparent thing, which then faded and disappeared completely. Ghost opened his eyes to see the blue waters of his home lake. His fear and sadness—his anxiety, uncertainty and grief—knew no bounds. Would he ever see his Beatrice again? He called out for Red Horn. He called out for great *kokopelli*. And he even called out questioningly, "*herecgunina*, did you bring me here?" No loud, resonating voice replied to his summons. He listened to the waters of the lake but did not hear the spirit murmuring and intoning the words *da-wa-kah-char-gra da-wa-kah-char-gra*. He did recognize the Ho-Chunk gathered on the beaches. The faces were the same ones he knew from the time of the Le Fèvre Indian War but now just a little older. He saw the prophet *wabokieshiek* or White Cloud as he and the other medicine men and shamans conferred. After the peace the lake had devolved into a mere *worak* lake. All of Earthmaker's five sons *wakdjąkaga* (Trickster), *wadexuga* (Bladder), *kecągega* (Turtle), *he-šucka* (Red Horn), and *wacdjįgega* (Hare) had departed to hunting grounds in the far west. White Cloud said they could not abide the people's dishonor or the increasing depredations of the white fathers against the people and the land. Even Red Horn, who had initially advised the tribe to put down the hatchet and turn the other cheek to the *wanagi*. When the morning star appeared before the rising sun, its image could still be seen reflected in the lake's waters but none of the Hocąk any longer heard the rumblings of the Big Voice. All the lesser deities who together formed Red Horn's war party to attack the evil spirits who lorded it over humanity including the great thunderbird *mą'e-manįga* Storms-as-he-walks and his brothers Sleets-as-he-walks and Snows-and-Hails-and-Lightnings-as-he-walks; the fabulous Birdmen of the Overworld Falcon Dancer, Red Bird, and Raptor and Great Black Hawk; the two nephews of the *wakcexi šišik* who had befriended Red Horn while their relatives the bad water spirits held the winner of the race in captivity and planned to eat him, Otter and Loon; and one of the Twins red *warora* had also pulled up stakes and uprooted themselves. Only *wanagi*-Stump could still be sometimes spotted at the lake.

The wheel turned and summer became fall and the Canadian geese made a great V in the sky as they honked together in the air and headed south. Baldr desired the lethe of sweet sleep. He did not know if he would ever see his Beatrice again and in his dejected state he did not sing a single love song. He deemed all such efforts futile and pointless. All the spirits had abandoned the lake and magic and hope had gone with them from the place. Baldr no longer had faith that one of his bi-lobes could wend its way to Beatrice after crossing between the worlds or that even if miraculously it somehow did she could bring him aid and deliverance. He desired oblivion and forgetfulness and remembered how he slept for century upon century as an unborn sprite. He determined to hibernate once again through the cold, cruel winter and retired to his old hiding place in the hollow stump where he curled up in a ball just as the snow began to fall and accumulate, burying the world under a deep and heavy mantle of white for the long months the earth lay freezing cold, dormant and inactive. But he awoke to find himself again hurtling through time and space on Mothers' Night, and he heard Beatrice's voice calling out to him through the little horn he still wore round his neck: "Return to my castle my love. Return to Beatrice and your two young sons."

The journey between the worlds itself reminded him of their explorations of the forest glades together as children, where they entered paths which began as circles of half-light which then extended into ever more narrowly enclosing darkness until the two children together saw a distant, glimmering point: the exit opposite into sunshine perhaps much brighter still. When he emerged on the far side, he found himself standing before Oma's old castle, his feet ankle deep in the white snow. His eyes had to adjust and refocus. They sank deeper in the darkness, and the small dots of light in their pupils made them look like two long paths through tall shrubbery in the park of some mansion, over which summer and sunshine lie, broadly gleaming.

The picture that finally came into view made him fall to his knees and give thanks to the Heavenly Father. As had been the case twelve months before, Beatrice stood in the white yard in front of the castle's entrance, a son's hand clasped in each of her own.

After that first time he knew that his years thereafter would be divided in two halves one light the other dark and he would spend the waking part in Thuringia and hibernate in Red Banks but the months in each place would alternate from sunny and warm to dreary, wintry and cold. Baldr always came to Red Banks in mid-summer and he'd stay awake through the gorgeous fall with all the colored leaves except that in the early mornings he would sometimes consciously dream in the interrealm and return home to Thuringia or draw the Landgraviate, Beatrice, and her two children into the interrealm from across space and time. He only slept deeply after all the green-and-red horned serpents and the lance-head vipers went underground and the constant month-long snow falls bringing down their huge, towering accumulations began. In addition on full-moon nights during the months he spent mostly awake in the Michigan Territory he could sing to Beatrice and she could hear him through the horn-heart, and she could sing to him and he could hear her. Ancient ones—spirits of the air—drew nigh and blessing them with their presence in both worlds turned their voices into signals that passed through and from those on one side to their opposite numbers on the other at which time the signals became voices again after passing through the hollow horns. Baldr smiled when he first heard Beatrice's voice coming from nowhere. He sat on a pink boulder at the shore of the Lake of the Big Voice and she excitedly said that from where she was she could also hear his long absent voice and that from henceforth she would confine hers to his ear and find that nest sufficient and he first realized that not all the spirits had departed from Spirit Lake. Baldr enjoyed his stays in both worlds, and, year after year, during the sixth months he spent at Red Banks all remained serene and placid there, and the Hocqk and the *wanagi* kept and lived by the terms of their truce, and the Indians, if anyone, fought only amongst themselves.

Of course, at the time of their strange guest's very first visits, a few of the servants saw, some of their number noting it almost immediately, that Baldr cast no shadow. Others forgot everything else but a bewitching pair of blue eyes. Bedazzled they slunk away and tittered. Beatrice ordered the castle rooms brilliantly lit up so that one did not readily discern shadows. None cast them or at most ones of respectable size though of only the faintest hue. The precise relation of the Lady Beatrice and the Noble from afar was a subject of constant conversation amongst the lower orders. They would repair together to her room, the blue chamber, only on rare occasions. But what happened when the doors shut and the two stood alone none knew. The guest when he, the *Witwe*, and her two sons sat to their meals offered prayers of thanksgiving to Earthmaker. Baldr also accompanied Beatrice and the two boys to chapel three times during the week and the older pair, the man and the woman, narrated nightly to the younger, Beatrice's two sons, episodes from Jesus' first life. For instance how he healed the soldier's ear at Gethsemane and taught to those whose ears were opened to listen that those who lived by the sword would also die by the sword. Shortly after his arrival on Mothers' Night for which miracle Beatrice unobtrusively, secretly, and in private gave thanks to the *dísir*—prior to his annual appearance, she ordered the servants to throw open all the doors and windows in Oma's old castle, so she could invite in all ghosts and holy spirits—on Christmas day he accompanied Beatrice and her sons to the evergreen-bestrewed banquet hall where the Yule log burned and the stranger, the Lady and her two sons before sitting to the feast table all stood before a kindly faced priest who related to the assembled four the story of the first Holy Night, when the animals all knelt on bent knee and swarms of bees hummed and buzzed the 100th psalm.

Word eventually reached the ear of Beatrice's half brother that a strange Lord from afar visited his elder sister and stayed for a full half year each and every year. That he arrived annually at Yuletide and departed precisely at midsummer. Eventually the Landgraf sent an emissary to convey his cordial regards to his beloved sister and to entreat a word or two in private with her friend from foreign parts. Was Beatrice staging some sort of elaborate mummers' play? Her half brother the Landgraf wondered. Baldr chose to receive the emissary dispatched from the Wartburg in the evening under the cover of the trees of Beatrice's garden, but, as the sky had clouded over and the moon could not be seen, he accompanied the courtier on a long walk down the *Rennsteig*. Baldr anticipated all the formal interrogatories and gave ready answers. A friend of Frimutel, he had promised to look after the needs of his friend's wife and sons at Frimutel's dying side, a paynim blade broken off in his belly. No he did not seek the Lady's hand. He had his own wife in the Palatinate. He simply fulfilled his pledge and made his bond his word. He vowed to spend a full half-year each and every year with Frimutel's lady, and he would keep her company in such a wise from now until the day one of the two of them died. He spoke earnestly to the emissary and saw that the Landgraf's servant found his answers all seemly and acceptable. So intent were the two on their conversation they did not notice the orange moon as it emerged from behind the clouds at their back. Had the emissary looked down on the ground he would have perceived only his own shadow before the two. Baldr did at last notice the single shadow. Beads of sweat started dropping from his brow. He imagined the emissary looking down at the ground then turning to gaze at him with terror showing in his eyes, then looking down once more in search of Baldr's shadow. What a tale he would have carried back to the Wartburg! The moon slipped back behind the cloudbank without the knight catching sight of what so clearly and patently but only momentarily it revealed. After they finished speaking, Baldr shot with the rapidity of an arrow out of the man's eyesight and into the trees. Baldr vowed to avoid all such follies and to be more careful in the future.

Oh the dreams he had when he next returned to Red Banks and again found himself in the interrealm after sitting for a while in the genial warmth of the sun on a fragment of pink rock beside the sandy white beach. On the sunlit sand before him flit a shadow without a master the size his shadow would and should have been. "Are you in need of a master?" he called to the inky outline. "Then in me you shall find one." He sprang forward to seize it, fancying that if he could succeed in treading so exactly in the traces as to step in its footmarks, it would attach itself to him, and in time become accustomed to him and follow all his movements. The shadow however fled over the purple and red boulders and into the piney wood, among whose shades Baldr necessarily lost it.

Afterward he could not tell if he had awakened or if he slept and while dreaming had drawn the *worak* lake and the surrounding countryside with him into the interrealm but all there had changed and war had come again to Red Banks, and Black Hawk, the great war chief of the Sauk, Fox and Kickapoo led his "British Band" against both militias from Illinois and the Michigan Territory as well as the United States Army.

Black Hawk had crossed swords with the United States twice before. He fought against the American nation in the War of 1812 and then again in the Le Fèvre Indian War of 1827.

In 1804 certain Sauk and Fox leaders had signed a treaty with the then Governor of the Indiana Territory, William Henry Harrison, in which they ceded all lands east of the Mississippi River to the U. S. government in exchange for an annual remittance of $1,000.00. The tribes could remain in their traditional homelands until agents of the U. S. government surveyed and sold the land. A task which would take many years. It had been a long-standing policy of the United States dating from as far back as the Jefferson administration to gradually but slowly and surely relocate all Native American tribes living east of the Mississippi west of the river. Harrison's treaty, signed by the native representatives in St. Louis, would move this policy forward and start ever so slowly to accelerate it. Those negotiating and signing for the tribes had not, however, received permission from the full tribal councils to relinquish and yield territory.

The land given away included that on which lay Black Hawk's home village, the main village of the Sauk, Saukenuk. Saukenuk was established in the mid-1700s after Sauk and Fox refugees from the Fox Wars of 1728-1733 fled from the Great Lakes region further west into lands stretching from the *Rivière aux Fèves* in the north to the Illinois River in the south. Born in Saukenuk in 1767, Black Hawk spent much of his early life there and he considered his country sacred and inviolable. It was only natural that he would side with the enemy of his enemy, the British. His main rival at the Sauk council Keokuk chose to cooperate and make terms with the Americans. In May 1816, Black Hawk signed the general peace treaty, ignorant of a provision that reaffirmed the Harrison treaty of 1804. After the second war with Great Britain, settlers came pouring into Illinois. Again and again individual Sauk and Fox leaders signed other pieces of paper promising to eventually vacate their settlements east of the river but pressure for them to do so did not begin in earnest until 1830 when President Andrew Jackson signed the Indian Removal Act into law. Meanwhile Keokuk made yet another reaffirmation of the old treaty at Fort Crawford in Prairie du Chien, in which 26,500,000 acres of Sauk land east of the river—including the village of Saukenuk—were for all time deemed finally ceded and sold. Black Hawk and his followers determined to remain on the disputed land despite the opposition of Keokuk and returned to their old village after winter hunting in the spring of 1831. Illinois governor, John Reynolds, declared the reoccupation of the village an unprovoked and hostile Indian invasion. Federal troops mustered and forced Black Hawk and his men again west of the Mississippi and Black Hawk made his mark on yet another surrender agreement, but on April 5, 1832, unable to bear the jeers and condescension of Keokuk, Black Hawk and his five hundred warriors and a thousand followers—mostly old men, women and children—from the Sauk, Fox, and Kickapoo nations returned to Illinois yet again. Crossing the Mississippi near the mouth of the Iowa River, they followed the Rock River northeast, skirting the ruins of Saukenuk and making for the village of Black Hawk's old ally the Hocąk prophet *wabokieshiek*. White Cloud committed the whole Ho-Chunk nation, but only his own followers in the end would lend their support to Black Hawk. Other Hocąk sided with the United States Government or remained neutral. During the course of the war, the Menominee and Potawatomi also remained on more-or-less friendly terms with the Americans.

Another of Black Hawk's allies Neapope said he could secure secret British aid from Canada. Because of the chief's participation in the War of 1812, he and his warriors received the name "the British Band," but no aid from England would be forthcoming as Black Hawk would soon find out to his chagrin. He would also shortly become aware that White Cloud had painted too sunny a picture and that apart from the prophet's own following of warriors most Ho-Chunk and Potawatomi would refuse him all aid and that some would even take action against him. Sauk and Fox tribal councils immediately sent orders for him to turn tail and recross the Mississippi westwards.

Meanwhile Brevet Brigadier General Henry Atkinson who had previously led troops north of the Galena country in the Le Fèvre War would prosecute the new war for the Federals.

An Illinois militia commanded by one Major Isaiah Stillman entered the disputed territory in pursuit of the British Band and razed White Cloud's village. Always a pragmatist, Black Hawk had decided to retreat into Iowa, but Stillman's men crossed paths with the Band at a point north of the Kishwaukee River, a valley destined to bear Stillman's surname. Black Hawk requested a parley with the militiamen and sent three Sauk who spoke English to Stillman's camp. The Illinoisans killed one of the three and subjected his body to mutilation. Infuriated at the outrage, Black Hawk led forty mounted warriors and attacked Stillman's encampment at dusk, throwing the militiamen who outnumbered the Indians at least six to one into fluster and disarray. All cohesion on the side of the militia collapsed and Black Hawk's band of Sauk and Fox scored an unlikely victory. The newspapers created a great hue and cry and stoked the flames of the subsequent panic. They reported Indian depredations across all of northern Illinois.

The next four months would see more massacres, skirmishes, and raids and then several decisive battles that would restore the badly shaken public confidence. Black Hawk and his allies perpetrated enough bloody offenses on their own, but the newspapers magnified each and every lurid detail. The policy makers in Washington connived with the publishers for they saw a general solution to the Indian problem east of the Mississippi at hand at long last. The long-desired removal westward of the tribes—even those who had cooperated in good faith with the U.S.—could be effected if tensions, latent hostilities and fears could be brought to a fever pitch. Abraham Lincoln, Zachary Taylor, and Jefferson Davis would all later make political hay out of their participation in the war, as would a number of future state governors. Small skirmishes not directly related to the war or Black Hawk's warriors were nonetheless connected and tied together with the greater rebellion so that it seemed that a vast organized Indian uprising was underway, as when a handful of Ho-Chunk warriors unaffiliated with Black Hawk and without sanction from their own tribe killed and mutilated United States Indian Agent Felix St. Vrain and three confederates in Kellogg's Grove, Illinois, on May 24, 1832. Area residents blamed the Ho-Chunk when they discovered the scalped and mutilated body of a civilian miner in June near Fort Blue Mounds in present-day Dane County, Wisconsin. The belief spread that the Hocqk nation had decided to align itself after all with Black Hawk's British Band.

At first the militias and Federals did not seem as if they had the wherewithal to squelch the rebellion. Atkinson's troops appeared ineffectual and disorganized. Washington dispatched "Old Fuss and Feathers" General Winfield Scott and one thousand federal troops westward to Illinois from Buffalo. A cholera epidemic at that time ravaged many of the eastern states. The troops embarked on barges, which made for Chicago. Many of the men came down with cholera while aboard ship. The vessels landed in numerous towns to drop off the dead and dying. Soldiers deserted and ran from the ship and the disease soon also began to spread through the civilian population of the state. When the remainder of the troops at last reached Chicago, Scott had to cancel his march into the war zone.

More Indian attacks occurred including the Spafford Farm massacre. Near present-day South Wayne, Wisconsin, a band of Kickapoo marauders descended upon the farm of Omri Spafford where they slew five men including Spafford. Two of Spafford's party of seven escaped however and made their way separately and unbeknownst to each other to Fort Hamilton, one of whom mistaking friendly Menominee inside the fort's walls for belligerents thought the fort overtaken and fled back into the forest.

Colonel Henry Dodge—the same *wanagi* soldier and hero who took command of the lead miners' auxiliaries in the Galena country during the Le Fèvre War—at the head of a mounted force of twenty-nine volunteers—pursued the Kickapoo to the Horseshoe Bend of the Pecatonica River and shot most of the marauders down, an event later termed a major turning point in the conflict. Kickapoo and Sauk also clashed twice with volunteer troops near Kellogg's Grove in Illinois. The first encounter, a small skirmish between militiamen and eighty or so Kickapoo occurred the same day of the Battle of Horseshoe Bend, resulting in three militia members killed and six Kickapoo warriors dead. A somewhat larger clash, a vicious fight at close quarters with bayonets and long knives between a party of renegade Sauk and another local militia commanded by James W. Stephens, wounded in the fray by a musketball to the chest, took place in nearby Waddams Grove two days later.

Black Hawk himself attacked the hastily constructed Apple River Fort, the militia there under the command of Captain Clack Stone, near what today is the Illinois town of Elizabeth. A force of two hundred Sauk and Fox warriors rode with him. Only twenty-five defenders stood behind the pales and stakes, most of the fort's detachment then out on patrol. The Indians stormed the defenses for a full forty-five minutes. Both sides exchanged heavy gunfire, but Black Hawk deeming the fort more strongly guarded than it in fact was signaled for his band to retreat. On June 25 a third, much larger confrontation occurred at Kellogg's Grove, when native forces joined together under the command of Black Hawk furiously and unrelentingly attacked a unit commanded by Major James Dement in which twenty-five horses, five militiamen and nine Sauk, Fox, and Kickapoo fell. Then on July 21, Illinois and Michigan Territory militiamen under the command of Henry Dodge and James B. Henry surprised the British Band near today's Sauk City, Wisconsin, and the Battle of Wisconsin Heights began. The encounter proved a devastating defeat for Black Hawk who lost upwards of seventy men, many of whom drowned helping women, children, and aged grandfathers flee to safety across the *Rivière aux Fèves.* Their reprieve did not last long. Near today's Victory, Wisconsin, Army regulars and militia caught up with the fleeing Indians and the very one-sided, two-day final battle of the Black Hawk War followed. The Federals had the use of an armed steamboat in the fray. Black Hawk and his native commanders separated from the main body by about two miles escaped but, by the end of the second day of fighting, the casualties to the British Band exceeded two hundred and fifty.

The militias lost only fourteen men. The victory would lead to further white settlement in the Michigan Territory. Both sides had committed countless bloody atrocities. Black Hawk, his son Whirling Thunder, Neapope, *wabokieshiek,* and other native leaders surrendered and were taken under armed escort to Jefferson Barracks in Saint Louis where Brevet Brigadier General Henry Atkinson extended the leader and chief culprit every courtesy during his confinement. The war did not turn out well for Atkinson who lost all the prestige and reputation that had come to him for his victory in the Le Fèvre War. Fated to remain out of favor for the final decade of his life—President Jackson held him responsible for the early poor prosecution of the war—Atkinson realized that his name thereafter would forever be linked with that of his famous prisoner. Black Hawk later dedicated his autobiography to the General, and when the two first met, he warned him: "The path to glory is rough, and many gloomy hours obscure it. May the Great Spirit shed light on yours—and that you may never experience the humility that the power of the American government has reduced me to."

After eight months of imprisonment, the men traveled east at the orders of President Andrew Jackson. Conveyed by steamboat, carriage, and railroad, the celebrities drew crowds at every stage of their trip until they at last arrived in Washington where Jackson himself held an audience with the Sauk leader, before he was again incarcerated at Fortress Monroe in Virginia. This time the stay behind bars lasted only a few weeks. At Fortress Monroe the war chiefs posed for a series of portraits by various artists. Subsequently they were paraded before large crowds in New York, Baltimore, and Philadelphia. While crowds burnt and hanged effigies of these same Indian leaders in the west, they became the center of a spectacle in the east, where a circus-like atmosphere ensued everywhere the British Band toured. Chief Keokuk and General Winfield Scott signed the treaty ending the Black Hawk War in 1832.

All the Native Americans of the region—even those who allied themselves with the U. S. government during the conflict—paid the price for Black Hawk's resistance and rebellion. Few of any of the tribes managed to stay east of the Mississippi River. Keokuk's people had to sell prime lands in eastern Iowa at the price of eleven cents an acre in the Black Hawk Purchase as an indemnity for the war. The United States forced similar terms of peace on the Hocqk, most of whom had to exchange their lands in Red Banks for ground in western Iowa. Within the next decade the federal government would buy up all that land too. The last tribes would have again all moved further westward by 1845.

In 1836, Henry Dodge received appointment as the governor of the newly created Wisconsin Territory, a section of land apportioned from out of the formerly much larger Michigan Territory.

Baldr could hardly tell if he sat within or without the interrealm. He realized that he was dreaming when he found himself away from the Hocqk lake at one of the war's many skirmish sites or battlefields or in one of the *wanagi* ghost towns by the wharves where the paleskins had stacked on top of each other like logs in a cord of wood the bodies of the cholera victims with the eruptions of rose-red spots on their chests and abdomens. Yet during the late summer of 1832, Baldr spent many hours by himself by the lake sitting on one of the prominent purple or red stones in the boulder field. Few Hocqk visited the lake. A single white-haired shaman passed through after the attacks at Blue Mounds and Spafford Farm and Baldr learned of the new war from listening to the old medicine man's prayers to *mą'ųna*. Often Baldr thought himself lucid and quite awake when he began to see Indians falling wounded and bleeding at the lakeshore. He saw the suddenly materialized men, women, and children collapsing before he heard the first rifle shot and he feared that he had somehow slipped back into Purgatory. But, no, he realized he merely dreamed what he saw and that he had in his hands the means and power to move the dream in whatever direction he wanted. He knew that, even though it still looked exactly like the *worak* lake, he had entered and stood inside the interrealm and that his momentarily unchained sleeping mind had peopled and populated the place and set off all the bloody and horrible phantom yet very real-looking events. In the interrealm, however, he became the semi-conscious, semi-dreaming puppet master. His imagination ruled supreme. He could travel from here to the moon in a wink of the eye. If he fell off a cliff he need not plummet. He could sprout wings and turn into a *kaği* or a Thunderer, for he could control and shape the dream. He could again chain what had become unchained. Baldr simply had to attach a golden garter, a soft yet resilient cord of braided rushes around his own neck, for he after all was the dreamer and the small part of him which remained alert and awake could turn the dream in the direction he wished it to go. In the interrealm all that Baldr-*wanagi* desperately longed for came true. As Black Christ fell and tumbled, his shadow the devil swan also veered and pitched and morning star's light again hit the lake. The sun rose and all the dead Hocąk stood alive at the lakeshore to greet and wave at him.

The wheel turned and summer became fall and the Canadian geese made a great V in the sky as they honked together in the air and headed south. A few families of Hocąk spent several weeks at the lake, and Baldr learned of Black Hawk's defeat. A great exhaustion overtook him. His eyes, drained of their former blue hue, suddenly became gray and virtually colorless. As always at that time of year, he desired oblivion and forgetfulness and he remembered how he slept for century upon century as an unborn sprite. He determined to hibernate once again through the cold, cruel winter and retired to his old hiding place in the hollow stump where he curled up in a ball just as the snow began to fall and accumulate, burying the world under a deep and heavy mantle of white for the long months the earth lay freezing cold, dormant and inactive. Usually after entering a dark and deep sleep—if he dreamed he had no memory whatsoever of the dream afterward—he awoke to find himself again hurtling through time and space on Mothers' Night and again hearing Beatrice's voice calling out to him through the little horn he still wore round his neck: "Return to my castle my love. Return to Beatrice and your two young sons."

This year, however, he found himself caught and caged in a nightmare, a nightmare from which he could not wake but lay in, forever prostrate. *Herecgunina's* goat face hovered over him. Even though Baldr's eyelids were shut, he could see from underneath them *herecgunina's* devil's eyes. Spirals wreathed and coiled out from two central, bright red dots. *You've been dreaming, Baldr. You have never stopped dreaming but simply crossed from one dream into another. Your little lemur-ape brain has conjured this entire dreadfulness up. I judge creators by their creations. You wanted to help ole Earthmaker and tell stories of the Good Lord, did you? Beautiful parables and such. Well, you won't even look straight on at what you make. You look through rose-colored spectacles that prettify and spiff up. I'll unblinker you so you can see the true horror show! The war between the redskins and the* wanagi *out there—it is you that are the cause of it. You're at war with your brother* warora. *You want to rip your twin's face off. Papa always loved his blood son the chosen one* hejȧkiga *more than any adopted war twin non-relative. Flesh is a true, living breathing man. You are only* wanagi-ghost. *A half wraith without his* khaibit. *See your great creation. How in truth it actually appears. Man the paragon. How bestial are his desires and lust. How green-eyed and hateful his jealousies. See what's always at work at the back of your minds though you do your best to hide it from yourselves and act always as if it remains unbeknownst to you. Rise from the depths into the light great serpent with two horns. On many worlds I have beheld dragons but none so foul as this worm. Not even the vipers from the Marble Cliffs. There the lance-heads shoot like lightning flashes from the crevices and red clefts and then glide through the garden beds like pale whipcords, until raising to a man's height, they sway their heads like slow-beating pendulums, their fangs, bared for the attack, gleaming like lancets of curved glass.*

Deep devouring jaws wide-gaped, the serpent heaved itself out of the water, its long brass-scaly metallic back like a great hill. His red body patterned with gleaming triangular scales monstrous, horrible and vast, the color changing at the head to a jewel-like green. A great frill of horn rose up from behind the swaying triangular head, the frill decked with sharp spikes along its edge, the outside of the dragon's head decorated with extra bumps and points of bone. Above the eyes the two small horns—one green, one red—glinted in the sunlight. A cloud of smothering smoke and sulphur steamed out of the creature's stinking gorge and the air about the white sand of the beach where Baldr stood in defiance singing his love songs to Beatrice filled with smoke and stench. "When he swims to the surface he first exhales all his stale, old, poisonous, vomit-inducing air," *herecgunina* professorially explained, "then he will take deep breaths for hours as he fills full his hollow skull with clean, fresh, new air before descending at last back down to the bottom. Watch the two horns, Baldr, as my pet swells his neck and swings his head to and fro. See first the red one. Watch it as it swirls and rotates."

Baldr steadfastly continued singing his *Minnelieder* as the red horn of the serpent spun and spun and one by one a hundred fantastic obscene forms emerged from it, each metamorphosing into a beautiful full-breasted, large-nippled Hocąk Flower Maiden. Baldr heard the laughter of young women in first bud: bright, bubbly and babbling as any brook or rill, and, turning his head again toward the lakeshore, he saw them, their hair wound in long single braids which descended half way down their backs, as they stood at the water's margin and slipped off their bead necklaces and medicine bags from around their necks and kicked off their soft squaretoed footgear whose upper front reminded Baldr of the split upper lip and dark nose of a doe and then began divesting themselves of all their garments, first their waist sashes, then their long tanned deerskin shirts with their bead and quill designs, and finally their underclothes of woven nettle fiber and the fingerwoven garters which held in place their leggings, and stood skyclad before the youth, for Baldr once more had become but a nineteen year old. He rutted with them all over and over for a seeming eternity as if he were again in Purgatory but the lewd coverings brought him no pleasure or relief, only pain. He cried at the loathsome foul animal he had become as again and again he betrayed his Beatrice as his body did unspeakably vile things on its own without his having any say in the matter. It simply took control. He relinquished all mastery of it as his limbs and extremities twitched and danced and his eyes flickered and fluttered behind their lids. Deep within stirred a particle of consciousness. He felt as ashamed as if he had lost dominion over his bladder and bowels as he felt himself leaking, trickling, spurting and oozing from his most intimate, secret place. Total blackness supervened, but then he saw his face reflected in the creature's green horn. Suddenly he stared into the mirror of Beatrice's green eyes but it was not his own face reflected back to him but his brother Flesh's. *Warora* embraced Beatrice in his stead. He roared like a mad bull, his anger grew so great and horrible. Suddenly it was he, Ghost, and not the red-haired miner wearing a badger cap tugged at one ear, who egged the other *wanagi* on and seemed to be the group's leader. He screamed for the others to shoot. He constantly waved his fat-fingered hands and shouted out in a steady, slow voice with a pleasant resonance in the nose: "Kill the murdering heathen and devil worshippers. These savage, bloodthirsty Wuinebagoes call this Spirit Lake. Hereafter and henceforward it will be known as Devil's Lake, for these savages that hew, hack, and scalp worship the Black man of the forest. Their hussies the women with four, five, and six vaginas part their legs for one and all."

Baldr seeing his other self leading the charge screeched no! Whipping his head back and forth in agony, he had reached his own dark night of the soul, where it seemed as if no spark of hope would ever again ignite. Then unexpected and unlooked for assistance began pouring down from Above World....

A new birth

The great thunderbirds Storms-as-he-walks and his brothers Sleets-as-he-walks and Snows-and-Hails-and-Lightnings-as-he-walks as well as all the Birdmen of the Overworld—Falcon Dancer, Red Bird, Raptor and Great Black Hawk—came swooping from the white clouds, their talons extended to cut and slash their enemy the red-and-green horned great serpent. A great black cloud composed of hundreds of individual ravens or *kaǧi* spirit birds, however, preceded them from out of the west and reached the lake first—the spirits of all the Hocąk warriors who had died in both the Le Fèvre and Black Hawk wars. The birds had rainbow plumage and their wings shone brightly with color unlike ordinary ravens. All the individual dots comprising the vast cloud descended one, two, and three at a time to alight on the serpent's scaly back, pecking with their beaks wherever they landed. But then all the wicked spirits from the Beneath World, the cold dank realm which one could find an entrance to at the very bottom of Devil's Lake began rising to the surface in even greater and greater numbers. Twelve more green-and-red horned serpents—many multi-headed—came lashing up out of the water to—deep devouring jaws wide-gaped—spring out and snatch hold of their especial antagonists and foemen, the Thunderers, the Birdmen and the Falcon Beings of the Overworld with whom they stood in fierce, mutual opposition. Plunging downward like souls from the Upper Circles to the Beneath Realm of stubborn, refractory, formless matter, the three Thunderers each caught a horned serpent in its talons and then lofted upward again into the blue to return to their eyries high in the cliffs and fantastic outcroppings overhanging the cobalt-blue lake, where they would feed their offspring torn-up red-and-green snake dollop by bloody dollop. As they flew off a greater and much more powerful opponent that hybrid cougar-rattlesnake-deer-and-hawk, the Underwater Panther itself ascended from the depths and broke the surface just as Red Horn led a select war party of Turtle, Wolf, Bladder, Trickster, Otter, Loon and the Twin Flesh–Baldr-*wanagi's* brother *warora*–out from behind the aisles of fir and pine. *Warora* tossed a bow to Baldr where he sat transfixed on the pink rock; it struck and bounced off *wanagi*, waking him from out of his trance. Baldr snatched the weapon off the rock and breathing in the correct and proper manner aimed at his foe the original serpent which, its red body patterned with gleaming triangular scales badly pecked by *kaǧi* spirit birds, nonetheless still writhed and slithered at the lake's shore. Baldr uttered the word *ahahe* twice and let fly the empty bowstring; the beast gaped its jaws even wider and shrieked demonically as it toppled over to its side and quivered in its death throes. All of the war party began attacking the other evil spirits still emerging from the seething waters, the great chief, as he reached the water's edge, cutting off the single, very red horn from off his forehead and tossing the braid into the water whereupon its surface burst into flame, immolating all the evil beings which called the water home.

He-šucka cried, "Henceforth no man shall call me *he-šucka*. I have burnt my braid to save humanity. Hereafter all shall call me *herok'aga* or Without Horns because I have caused myself to be without any. Father and son have now in truth become one.

Little *wanagi*, you are at last becoming a *worak*, but when you dream you can still enter the *waika* world. You simply crossed over from the *worak* lake below to the *waika* lake above. One of the infinite *worak* Devil's Lakes below. At Spirit Lake, my select war party always defeats the evil water spirits. There is only ever one ending to our battle up here. Down there, there are as many outcomes as there are lakes. The Indians usually lose, but not in all the worlds. At a couple of lakes, the whites, never having crossed the great salt waters, do not even appear on the scene. In a few others the Hocąk snatch victory from seeming sure defeat. Your fate no longer is here with us, *wanagi*. I don't see what will happen very far into the future in your or any particular world. Only for a short distance can I make out and glimpse what will be. You will wake on Mothers' Night in Beatrice's castle and from now on you will sojourn in Thuringia the entire year." Then the star-deity of the Overworld, a *waika*, an immortal, grand and imposing and commanding allegiance, became his familiar funny old human self. Red Horn flashed his son *herok'aga* a great stupid grin. The two little faces on his ears also made funny faces and stuck their tongues out. "And once you are there, you will begin growing a shadow.... You will no longer be able to return to me, but I can and will visit you, my dear son. "

When Baldr-*wanagi* opened his eyes, he lay on the regal bedstead in his suite of rooms at Beatrice's castle. Through the window he saw a gray day dawning and the snow already beginning to thickly fall. A great fire roared behind the grate. A drowsy Baldr smiled. He remembered Red Horn's words of parting. He felt warm and safe and pulled the covers from off the bed and crawled under them. He could stay in bed and drowse this cold winter morning.

Unbeknownst to him, however, something from his long—and according to Red Horn—last winter dream in Red Banks had come back across with him. For at the beginning of the new year, a red-haired friar began preaching in the streets of Eisenach. He warned its good citizens that persons of high birth in the Landgraviate had taken up the Blacks Arts, that the world itself would soon end in fire, and that the Black Devil himself brazenly pranked in their midst. He spoke of Hell's tortures without end and the green-and-red worms that would gnaw through the eyeballs of the damned in the lake of smoking brimstone and lava for time eternal.

Almost four centuries later, a man with his exact appearance, hair, and facial features became the Prior of the Convent of Cologne. Along with his colleague Heinrich Krämer of Innsbruck, this said Jacobus Sprenger would author and in 1486 publish the *Malleus Maleficarum*—"The Hammer of the Witches," a quarter-million word dissertation on witchcraft and demonology, its preface Pope Innocent VIII's bull of three years before, *Summis desiderantes affectibus*, the same bull, initially aimed at Germany where the Pope considered Satanism especially rife, which created the Holy Office or Inquisition. The Pope had declared war on all those who kissed the Devil beneath his tail. The bull authorized inquisitors duly appointed by the Holy See to sit in on all trials for heresy, to overrule local powers, and to prosecute anyone of whatever rank and ultimately to burn, or otherwise put to death, anyone they judged guilty. "The Hammer of the Witches" became the inquisitors' Bible. Edition after edition would go to the presses and it would be translated into most major European languages. Ultimately forty thousand souls accused of practicing witchcraft would perish at the hand of Mother Church in the fanatical inquisition's indiscriminate reign of terror.

Cologne would not be the last place where someone of this same general appearance would be seen in Germany. *Herecgunina* would again return to his former stomping grounds just outside of Eisenach. Yes, in 1521, a red-eyed, red-haired monk, invisible to all eyes except one pair only, would forever torment and constantly distract the high strung and erratic, disguised Martin Luther, freshly excommunicated by Pope Leo X and under an edict of seizure from the Diet of Worms, as, hidden away deep in the bowels of the Wartburg, he labored on his magnificent and inspired god invention, the great heroic feat of translation of the Bible—at the Wartburg he worked exclusively on the Greek Testament—into beautiful and sonorous High German. The fiend so exasperated the special guest of the Duke of Saxony Frederick the Wise, known to his hosts simply as Junker Jörg—the Knight George—that he heaved a bottle of ink at the red-eyed, red-haired fiend and fairly blinded him.

Eisenach, the point of initial infection, lay some distance from Beatrice's castle on the *Rennsteig*. Four years would pass without Baldr and Beatrice ever hearing of the mysterious friar's crusade against the witches.

In the meantime, as Red Horn predicted, Baldr began casting a shadow. It grew bigger and darker and fuller each year as the Summer Solstice drew nearer and nearer and then shrank and faded away almost to nothing, only the palest bluest outline, as the wheel turned round and Yule once again approached. The *Witwe*, her two sons, and their guest Frimutel's friend, the Knight Baldr, lived a quiet, retired life. A very ordinary matter-of-fact life but one in which Baldr experienced more magic in the everyday and the routine than in any fantastic spirit world.

Daily, he experienced the re-enchantment of everyday living. Joy suffused his entire being as he sang to Beatrice and she wove her colorful tapestries. Together they made a home, something they had not done since childhood and their stay in the good steward Ewald's house of hollowed-out tree logs, where she used his fawn-back for a pillow after making them a soft bed of moss and gathered leaves and kneeling down and saying her nightly prayers. The *genius loci* of their new home together revealed itself slowly. The first of the wall hangings and tapestries Beatrice worked so assiduously on all depicted one landscape, but seen from different angles, heights, and perspectives. She even made a great hearthrug for the banquet hall on which one peered down on the very same place but as if from far above—as if one plummeted downwards from highest heaven. Two ranges of metamorphosed sandstone rose upward, together forming an oval ring of hills. In the southern, wider range, the hills all adjoined or set adjacent, whereas the rises and mounts curving northward stood farther and farther apart from each other until one saw in the distance only isolated, small, flatcapped buttes. In the southern range, a cobalt-blue pupil surrounded and ringed by conifer and deciduous hardwood forest gleamed brightly from an elongate gorge, a basin plugged on both sides by great rocks and glacially moved earth. The gorge's glistening sides varied in color from pink to maroon to darkish purple.

One wall tapestry featured a great field of red and purple, cascading boulders coming down to the waters of the lake, four or five cat o' nine tails whipping in the wind and a stone's throw from the shore a lone white water lily bobbing on the darkling bosom of the blue water.

Another showed the lake in autumn with its brilliant foliage and irruption of scintillating color. Others portrayed animal and bird tracks in the silt loam soil and the effigies of lynxes and other animals traced on small mounds, chiseled there by unknown hands. One showcased the spectacular East Bluff and the tallest and most precipitate of the rock formations that rose highest into the blue heaven. Riven, jagged crags where the nimblest hands and feet would be rendered useless and only wings would avail the power and means to reach the topmost summits. In yet another the elongate basin of quartzite bluffs surrounding the lake became the rim of a great cauldron, down into which the outsize face of a young girl peered.

Beatrice strove to illustrate all Baldr's songs. She wove portraits of Red Horn, *wabokieshiek* and Red Bird, Otto, Loon, *hejąkiga, kokopelli* playing his flute and the two- and four-legged does bathing. She even depicted the great final battle at the exact moment Baldr slew the red-and-green dragon with his magic bow.

Afterwards she also composed pictures of her and Baldr as children, an albino fawn, a burning and beribboned Yule log, and a blond and blue-eyed Christ on the cross. At the height of her creative powers and at breakneck speed, Beatrice produced a string of amazing wall hangings. She wove images of the Fire Maidens censing the altar and the ecstatic celebrants making sacrifices to the female powers or *dísir*, the Norns and Valkyries. She depicted the three sisters Wyrd, Verthandi, and Skuld and Erda's daughters, the assembled warrior maidens, helmeted and carrying spears, who rode through the air on horseback during battles and brought the souls of slain heroes to the great fortress of Valhalla. She portrayed the Great Mother herself, who to Baldr's eyes looked exactly like Oma, her granny who used to pat him on the head one-two-three. Beatrice figured forth and dressed the World Tree Yggdrasil which rose from the lowest depths to the uppermost heights as well as stitched the Rainbow Bridge, as Heimdall the gatekeeper—he who would sound the ill-fated horn when one by one the giants ignited the limbs of the great tree, he who had the sharpest ears, ears which could hear both the green grass and the curly, crisp fleece of the sheep grow—threw open the portals to disclose the Shining Ones in all their glory. On Winter Nights one year, she unveiled her masterpiece. It covered the entire wall of the castle's greatest hall—where Baldr sang for her as if he stood in the great *Sängersaal* of the Wartburg itself—and which naturally represented the great hunt: Woden astride his eight-legged horse Sleipnir, his spectral host of warrior horsemen, the Valkyries, the ancestral spirit the Yula *Alf* dressed all in red and green and standing erect in his war chariot drawn by the two steeds Donner and Blitzen and the loudly baying phantom hounds of all the furious host.

As much as Baldr enjoyed remaining within the stone walls of the castle during the cold winter months, where he could gaze lovingly at Beatrice's tapestries depicting the Hocąk lake whose real shores he had renounced and never more would see though he missed them bitterly at times, in the spring, summer, and fall, he would bound out from the cage of the castle, and he, the *Witwe*, and her sons would live outdoors, Baldr having instructed the boys how to make tents from deer hides. He and Beatrice would spend many hours tending to her herb and vegetable gardens, and he would make repairs to the castle, the mews, and other outbuildings if need be, but he and the boys would also constantly track and hunt game, as Baldr took pride in his skill with bow and arrows and that he could live off the land. In the spring, he and Beatrice would tend to her numerous fruit trees. With offerings of bowls of mead, the two would address their songs to the cherry and apple trees and recite charms to insure that the trees would remain whole and hale all year so as to bring about a good fruit harvest in the fall.

Each full moon, Beatrice and her love would perform a full-moon ritual, for Beatrice had found a closet full of scrolls which constituted old Oma's Book of Shadows, or collection of spells. The two would enter their circle, each carrying a white torch, and, asking for their guidance and protection, they would call down the great Spirits of the East, South, West, and North—the Four Quarters—the Wise Ones of Air, Fire, Water, and Earth. Then they asked Great Mother to nourish and feed them as they continued down the path of life and round about the eternal circle. They vowed to remain true to their hearts and asked that the above reflect the below and vice versa. They begged that their actions and wishes would bring harm to none.

On clear nights, Baldr looked up and reveled and gamboled underneath the great Pearl. He would see his black shadow trailing on the ground and smile. If clouds obscured the moon, he closed his eyes and breathed deeply. Beatrice told him to picture himself striding along a mountain path at dusk and descending into a meadow freshly mown. She told him to enjoy the sensation of the grass between his toes and that he would see a knoll in the middle of the field. She told him to make for the knoll and, when he reached the summit of the little hill, that the sun would have already set. Baldr listened to the birds cheeping and twittering in the tree limbs. He reached the hilltop and looked around at the shadows—including his own—darkening in the twilight. "Look," Beatrice said, "to the east, and you will spot, just cresting the horizon, the Pearl ascending to her zenith. As she rises her colors start changing from a deep orange to a sandy brown, then, as she grows smaller, to a light gray. As she reaches her zenith, she becomes a brilliant silvery orb. As you stand transfixed, raise your left arm, my beloved, and receive the energy, she so willingly gives to the true of heart. As you stand with your left hand up, you see her silvery beams descending toward you. You can feel her energy flowing down your arm, through your chest, up and around your head and down through the rest of your body. As this happens, your own aura becomes bright and brilliant and changes colors as you absorb her energy. Point your left hand out slightly and cup it as if holding an egg. See a small ball of white light appear in your hand, as if it grew from inside you. Let the ball roll around in your hand and allow your third and only open eye to examine it closely as it turns and rolls. Observe it melt into a golden pool in the cup of your fingers. Your hand feels as if you are holding it above a lit candle. Enjoy the warmth. Play with it. Shift it from hand to hand and rub it on your forearms. Notice when you stop playing with the fluid moonshine and you return your hand to the cupped position, the pool slowly reforms there. Concentrate on that warmth and will it back to the ball of light—the great Pearl—in the sky, then return it to your hand. Do this several times. Again focus on the pool and you'll notice a gentle warming sensation spread-ing up your arm. When it reaches your shoulder, it spreads to your head and the rest of your body until it fills every part of you. Bask in the warmth and then remember the ball of light as it first appeared in your hand. You now see the silver orb again hovering above your palm. Cover it with your other hand, and repeat with me, 'Lord and Lady, let it be known, you have granted me refreshment from within my own. I realize my quest for knowledge, not nearly complete, is but yet freshly begun.' Now extend both your arms to the sky and see the Ancients standing by and give thanks for their attendance. Lower your right hand to your side with the palm turned out and give back to *Muttererde* the pearly warmth you do not need."

Baldr opened his eyes and looked upward. Two eyeholes appeared in the clouds and a yellowish light peeped through. The Lady looked down. Baldr and Beatrice took each other's hands and said in unison: "We are a circle within a circle with no beginning and no end. Our power flows and all our hurts mend. With your guidance, Shining Ones, from above, we will practice perfect love and perfect trust. Blessed be." This dismissed the gathered spirits back to the Four Corners. "If you must go," Baldr and Beatrice called, "go in peace and power." As the circle opened and they again gave thanks to the Great Mother, Baldr once more looked up into the sky. The curtain of cloud had parted in the center. A halo of mist swirling in a circle around it, the Pearl shone in all her glory. A dazzling silver ball.

After the first Summer Solstice, after his shadow reached its greatest length and started to slowly shrink and decline—and yet he remained in Thuringia still—Baldr gave to his beloved his most precious possession aside from her heart which thenceforth she wore around her neck with Baldr's spike or little bit of antler: the seashell with a particle of Morning Star which Red Horn had given him on his departure from Red Banks. "Dearest," he said, " I know we usually exchange gifts at the other solstice during the coldest months, but in thanksgiving for my remaining here with you, my Evening Star, I hand you a light that will never dim, a bright, burning speckle or fleck of Morning Star, Evening Star's other self—just as you are my other face, my love." Beatrice smiled and said, "We are made of many parts, Baldr, but you are what my soul is made of." And Baldr softly sang:

Dû bist min ich bin dîn
des solt dû gewis sîn
dû bist beslozzen
in mînem herzen
verlorn ist das sluzzelîn
dû muost immêr darinne sîn!

After several rotations of the great wheel, one autumn when the falling red leaves drifting down in death from the grieving parent tree recalled to him the loss of his own beloved boy, Red Horn bethought himself of the promise he made to his son *herok'aga*, just prior to the boy's departure from Spirit Lake, to someday pay him a visit, and he set out to travel between the earths. A star-deity of the Overworld, a *waika* who had tri-lobes indicating his ability to journey to and from all Earthmaker's worlds woven on his clothes, he simply had to will himself to his destination and he would arrive there, so Wears Faces On His Ears—after tying a false red beard made from a fox's pelt onto his chin (for he remembered that Baldr had first called him Barbarossa after a great king of his people—a king with a red beard, such as Red Horn would subsequently see some of the male *wanagi* wear—and Red Horn thought it best to travel incognito)—simply shut his eyes, thought, "my son Baldr's true home," and opened them to ... find himself standing in Asgard amongst the luxurious palaces and halls of the Aesir, the chief and most beautiful of which was the "Shelf of the

Slain," Woden's Valhalla—and thus became the first and only being ever to enter the home of the Shining Ones who had not gained access thereto by crossing the rainbow bridge Bifrost, guarded by the watchman of the gods Heimdall. The present raconteur can only think of two, perhaps three, reasons why this happened. First, just as Red Horn was also Morning Star, the fallen-semi-divine-part-*worak* being called Baldr was also on another plane the son of Woden and Frigg whose name he bore and thus Asgard was indeed his true home, or, second, Red Horn, a *waika*, simply crossed from Above World to Above World—to his proper sphere, so to speak, and, only after bridging that great gulf, could he descend to the Middle World of the two-legged walkers on the other side, namely Midgard. Then again, as nine worlds existed in the cosmogony of Germanic religion—Alfheim, the world of the elves; Asgard, the world of the Aesir, or higher gods; Jötunheim, the world of the frost-giants; Midgard, home of mankind; Muspelheim, the home of the fire-giants; Nidavellir, the home of the dwarves; Niflheim, the ice world of the dead; Svartalfheim, the world of the black elves; and Vanaheim, the home of the Vanir, or the lesser, vanquished gods—perhaps, in his confusion, Red Horn simply did not know where to alight. At any rate he found himself in a crowd of slain warriors from many various tribes and races preparing to take part in the great annual winter or wild hunt. To the untutored and far from sober eyes of his fellows—much mead was drained that day in Valhalla—he did not appear too strange and out of place. As Baldr, on hearing it spoken, understood Red Horn's language without effort, so too did his adopted father comprehend everything said in the welter of different tongues about him and thus learned that each and every night for the next six months, the furious host of spectral horsemen would ride through the stormy sky with all their ghostly hounds across all the many regions of Europe. The mortals below would hear the horns of the dead warriors reverberating above the woods and meadows and looking up into the sky they could behold between the lightning flashes the spectral band as the slain warriors of Valhalla accompanied by the Valkyries and other immortals and led by Woden, *Langbardt* Eyepatch himself, streaked together across the starry heavens.

Red Horn-Morning Star bethought himself that if he could make himself conspicuous in the night sky—if somehow he could come to the forefront of this raging host of warriors—nay, even lead the pack itself—Baldr might see him from below or he might espy his son from far above—and the two could at last be reunited. An idea slowly began forming in the crafty brain of the father of all raconteurs. He listened to the fallen heroes as they sang the praises of their great chief. They hailed Woden as the god of wisdom, war, battle, fury, and death but also excitation, mind, poetry, prophecy, and victory, and Red Horn realized that he would momentarily be closing with a being much like himself. He listened and learned of the god's great feats—how he plucked out and traded an eye for a sip from Mimir's well which lay deep under the roots of Yggdrasil and which made him all wise and all knowing and how (like the Christ, Red Horn, thought) he made a sacrifice of himself for himself and hung for nine days of fasting and agony, pierced by his own spear, on the World Tree, where he learned nine powerful songs and from which on the ninth night he fell screaming having had revealed to him in a flash of insight the secret of runes and writing, how certain arrangements of rune letters could be put to use as wards or charms, particularly on swords and spears, but also could cure and heal and bring love and also safety for ships on the Whale Road. Nonetheless no rune magic would help him advert his fate or prevent the final destruction of the world, the dreaded Twilight of the Gods or Ragnarök. Woden would still in the end feel Fenrir's teeth sink in his throat before the great silver wolf swallowed the sun.

At that moment in the hall of the slain heroes, Woden rose to his feet from his throne Hlidskjalf, from where he observed all that happened in the nine worlds and where during the six months he did not ride in the sky he waited the coming of Ragnarök. He did not realize that his kingdom had been breached. His one eye blazing like the sun, in flowing capes and robes and full battle dress, he lifted in both hands and placed on his crown his great peaked helmet with a white swan's wing on either side, his ring Draupnir, which every ninth night somehow dropped out of itself eight new gold rings to fall to the ground or floor and spin and roll until the greedy scooped them up, gleaming from the fourth finger of his right hand, a second eye on that side of his body to make up for the patched, covered, and hidden sacrifice to wisdom to the above left of his highly symmetrical, great curving nose. Lifting it from the corner where it leaned braced at the meeting place of two walls, he brandished and held aloft Gungnir, the spear that never misses, and strode out into the setting sunlight and crowd of dead outside his great hall, his wolves Freki and Geri following at his heels. All his gathered men hailed and saluted him. Red Horn knew the chief for who he was instantly, for two great ravens—or as Red Horn knew them *kaǧi*—descended out of the sky to alight on his opposite shoulders. Indeed, as he realized, *he-šucka* faced his opposite number in this other dream world, for the *kaǧi* was also the spirit animal of the Hocąk tribe. All the Hocąk came initially to Red Banks as migrant *kaǧi*. At

Spirit Lake the very same birds obeyed him as supreme spirit master and occasionally one would swoop down from the sky to perch on his extended wrist. In the German states below the *worak kaği* swore allegiance to the Holy Roman Emperor and were known as Barbarossa's birds. Woden made for the Great Stable, and the dead resumed their carousing. Freki and Geri nosed about and played with and snarled and bared teeth at and bit the black hell hounds of the warrior dead and let their master sweep past them out of their sight. Red Horn crept softly and stealthily nine steps behind his quarry. Before entering the horse stalls, Woden dismissed and sent out his two ravens Huginn and Munnin—thought and memory—to fly above and around Midgard in order to gather and bring back to him intelligence of all that was happening in the world below. As they departed downwards like shafts of lightning, Red Horn placed in their minds the image of an irresistibly lovely cobalt-blue lake bound by red and purple boulders. Forgetting all else they changed their course and embarked on their new quest to find this paradise lake, where all the other *kaği* had rainbow plumage and their wings shone brightly with color unlike ordinary ravens. Woden thus stood alone before the stall of his eight-legged, gray steed Sleipnir—that cross-species monstrosity sired by a *jötunn* stallion on the trickster god Loki, who had disguised himself as an alluring mare to lure the giants' magical stallion away from the task of carrying great stone blocks to its masters then busy constructing the fortress walls of Valhalla to win the hand of Freia who tended the apples of Idun which kept the Aesir forever young—without any of his animal protectors or defenders. Eons ago he had stripped his greatest minder and guardian his daughter Brünnhilde of her immortality and banished her to *worak* existence in one of the numerous parallel below worlds after first kissing her on her eyelids and putting her to sleep and then causing a magic ring of fire to spring up all around her so only the greatest of heroes—one without fear—would awaken her, after first having the courage to pass through the wall of flame.

Red Horn clutched his ancient club with many knobs, the same stout stick he beat his wicked brothers with after the great race. He came up on Woden's blind side and knocked the Lord of the Aesir off his legs from where he stood before the wooden stall. Woden from where he lay bleeding interposed Gungnir, but *he-šucka* again brought down his knobby club and struck the spear from *Langbardt* Eyepatch's hands, and, though the spear did not snap in two, from his post at the gates Heimdall of the acute ears, ears which could hear both the green grass and the curly, crisp fleece of the sheep grow, caught the sound of an almost inaudible crack. Red Horn belabored the fallen god again and again with his stout stick until at last Woden lay unconscious. But as soon as he stared into the great stall, Red Horn knew that he would never mount the monstrous snorting wild-eyed beast within. His brother *kunu* had extra limbs—namely four arms—and had always proved a fast friend, but the multi-legged creature rearing before him looked anything but friendly. The great mountain of a horse suddenly calmed down. Red Horn looked the beast directly in the eye and the eye sure enough seemed to laugh back at him. The sly and cunning beast—in every sense his trickster-father-mother's son—gave the impression of saying, "Mount me if you dare, foolish one. I'll allow you to climb on and remain as placid as still waters, but just as you gain back all your confidence, I will throw you off and trample you to death with all eight of my unshod hooves." So Red Horn quickly passed down the row of stalls—all empty save for the last in which, his back to the Hocąk chief, stood the Yula *Alf*—that always jolly, rotund, red-cheeked, hazel-eyed ancestral spirit with a full white beard and dressed all in red and green—hitching his two stallions Donner and Blitzen to the front of his war chariot. Although he was loath to do so—the spirit seemed so kind and beneficent; sensing someone behind him, the elf turned around smiling, his eyes twinkling brightly—Red Horn brought his club down on the old man's pate and laid him low and unconscious with the mere faintest of taps—a love tap really— and then after clapping the ancestral spirit's tapering red cap, a white snow ball at its tip, onto his own head, Red Horn leapt into the great chariot and took up the reins, but Donner and Blitzen would not budge and remained stock still as if turned into stone statues. What a fix! *He-šucka* sighed in despair, but then a solution came to him. Wears Faces On His Ears knew where he could find replacements for the two recalcitrant horses. Quickly he removed the two earbobs he had won in the great race, the live little faces on his earlobes which so resembled and eerily prefigured those of his own two sons *hejąkiga* and *herok'aga*. "Boys," he said as he dropped the two earrings to the ground, "I need you to become your spirit animals." Right where the bobs fell, they transformed into two red deer—one with a single spike on its head and the other without any. Now he had his own Donner and Blitzen. Quickly he unhitched the two steeds, and, with his brawny red arms, he pushed the chariot from out behind them—for the two horses still stood stock still and motionless—and then proceeded to hitch the two deer to the front of the chariot in their place. This year the great hunt would truly become a great hunt, and surely Baldr would notice Red Horn and the two bucks pulling the sleigh-chariot through the sky from below as the slain heroes and their barking, excited hell hounds gave them chase. Red Horn cried *ahahe* twice as if he let fly an arrow from his bowstring and then snapped the reins hard, and his sons *hejąkiga* and *herok'aga* leapt off the ground and into the air where they hung suspended until Red Horn again called—this time piercing loud so all the dead below would turn their heads in his direction—*ahahe* twice and with a great flourish once more whipped the reins whereat the two stags bolted across the night sky pulling Red Horn and their misbegotten booty behind them, and as Red Horn beforehand saw would be the case the *schwarze Hunde* and the fell wolves ran after them and gave chase also jumping up and leaping into the night air, the legions of the grateful dead and the Valkyries upon their phantom horses following and riding behind in frenzied, joyful pursuit. The most ferocious of the baying and yelping black dogs leading at the front of the pack broke their fiery chains which rattled and clattered and shook behind them in the night breeze.

Back and forth, up and down and all across the night skies of Europe for the next two months, did Red Horn and his two sons lead their pursuers on a merry chase. Red Horn had not had such a splendid time since, when a young *worak* boy, red from head to toe, and just then learning who and what he really was instead of merely a two-legged walker, he turned himself into a winged arrow and shot himself ahead of all the other competitors to win the race—for which great victory he received the two names *įco-horúšika* and *he-šucka*, the former for the two little human faces on the lobes of his ears which came alive when he attached the earbobs he had won in the race to his ear bottoms. From November Eve, the very first night of the great chase and night hunt, those from town and country who had stepped out into the night after leaving candles burning in the windows of their homes to guide home not only the recent dead but also all the ancestral spirits and setting extra chairs round the table and in front of the hearth for the expected nightcomers, looked up, gasped and pointed to the eerie prodigy, the starlight shining through and illuminating the spectral, glassy, warlike figures flying, dashing, running, and furiously riding their see-through phantom horses through the clear night sky, intermittently lit up by lightning flashes. Far in front of devil dogs foaming and slavering at the mouth raced a war chariot pulled by two deer and piloted by an elf with a bright red beard. Those below had taken to the streets to beg for coin or to sing for raisin-filled soul cakes and the seasonal pastry known as Bones of the Holy which those in the towns doled out at their doors. Many had blackened their faces or wore hideous masks such as they also donned during times of dearth and want or when the plague threatened. Boys and girls wore disguises made of straw and dressed in the garbs of the opposite sex so as to confuse and bewilder any shadow that might strike out at them. To protect themselves and ward off all malevolent spirits they hollowed out turnips and carved fanged faces with slant eyes on their fronts and put a lit candle inside each turnip. A few wise women buried apples at cross roads and beside their junctions with meandering forest paths for spirits who had wandered off course lost with no where to turn and to feed the wandering dead who had no descendants living to offer them food and drink. The wisest and oldest of their sisterhood stole to the cemeteries, the crypts and burial vaults where the bones of the notoriously wicked lay and left gifts of sweetmeats, cheese, and nuts to propitiate and mollify the evilest dead so that they would not work mischief and bedevil the living. Through the towns, the drunk and rowdy ran riot unhinging gates and posts and throwing cabbages at the mayors' doors. In the country, cattle and other livestock went to slaughter and meat was smoked for the long winter months ahead. From above Red Horn saw the bonefires dotting the hillsides below in which the dancing revelers threw the white remains of the horned bulls and cows as offerings to the Nature Spirits and to ensure healthy and plentiful herds of cattle in the year to come, and he thought of the *waŋe-rucge* guards who stood in front of the huge bonfire before which rose the scalp pole from which his severed white head hung and how the giants standing guard had painted their bodies half red and half black and as the moon rose how they too began a celebratory dance round the fire. Red Horn-Barbarossa sweetly sang the word *da-wa-kah-char-gra* and began a sad, mysterious death song, the kind sung by prisoners about to be executed, and the red-and-black giants standing guard upon hearing *he-šucka's* big voice immediately jumped into the flames of the fire and their flesh and even their bones were reduced to ash. A bonefire truly. In the German states, rumor, that many-tongued, blatant beast, held that Frederick Barbarossa had awoken from his sleep in the misty caverns underneath his magic mountain to rise forth at the time of his nation's greatest need and that the denizens of Hell itself pursued him flying through the night sky trying to reclaim the escaped soul for the Black One, or that Woden had relinquished the leadership of the Wild Hunt to him as in the past he had done to other legendary rulers such as King Arthur, Charlemagne and Herla.

As many times as Red Horn and his sons crisscrossed the sky as they sped ahead of and evaded the furious host and all the trailing, yapping, ghost hounds, they did not pass over Eisenach until near Yule. Red Horn had looked downwards from the Yula *Alf's* sleigh and scoured the moonlit rolling hills and countryside and the streets of all the cities and towns and all the great thoroughfares, highways and byways of the great continent in search of any sign of his beloved boy Baldr-*wanagi*. He knew that the particle of Morning Star he had given Baldr inside a whelk or seashell would blaze forth brightly like a beacon when he—Red Horn—drew close to it and he would thereby discover and quickly home in on his mark. He looked everywhere but did not see the silvery beam shooting upward from that little bit of star. Baldr, who no longer wore the whelk around his own neck, however, saw and immediately knew his father and rejoiced as he saw him streaking like a great arrow across the night sky. He and Beatrice's two sons Gawan and Gramoflanz had journeyed far into the mountains and slate hills on their own *worak* version of the Winter Hunt. In this instance, the above did in fact reflect the below. The two-legged walkers could not call attention to themselves though they shouted and waved. Red Horn simply flew too high above them for him to spot them on the ground, much less hear their shouts and cries. Baldr, however, knew where the whelk was and that Red Horn would eventually be attracted and drawn to Beatrice, so he ordered the boys to break camp. They would no longer pursue the winter game but would beat feet back to the castle, where his two adopted sons would meet his own adopted father.

Just prior to detecting coming from the direction of the *Rennsteig* and Oma's old castle the silver beam of starlight—the bilobed arrow shooting up toward his sleigh from the seashell which Beatrice now wore around her neck in addition to Baldr's felt-covered nubbin or first horn or point, Red Horn flew over Eisenach and felt *herecgunina's* presence, the smile on his falsely red-bearded face disappearing instantly. He heard Black Christ speaking from the pulpit of the cathedral but also at the same time heard him addressing Beatrice's half brother the young Hermann, Landgraf von Thüringen, at a private audience at the Wartburg, at which his aged dam the *Witwe* Sigune also sat in attendance. He spoke with a steady, slow voice, a schooled voice as it were, with pleasant resonance in the nose. In large numbers children and aged people in the Landgraviate had come down with the stomach fever and not only suffered from diarrhea and dehydration but also developed abscesses and obstructions in their bowels. The townspeople of Eisenach stacked on top of each other, like logs in a cord of wood, the bodies of the Plague victims. All the dead from the very young to the very old had eruptions of rose-red spots on their chests and abdomens. Jacobus the friar inveighed on behalf of the dead little lambs whose lives God's Death Angel took to punish the Thuringian people for their acquiescence, quiet submission and passive consent to all the deviltry and witchcraft brazenly taking place in their midst. Before the young, the infirm and the old began falling ill, Jacobus began his weekly diatribes at the cathedral by railing at the fact that a Pagan devil Baldr, the old German god of light, the most beautiful and gracious of the Aesir, his face and features partially hidden by a foliate mask, peered from the very doors of God's House, a graven image carved by some idolatrous stonemason no doubt. That no one had felt indignation enough to knock it off or otherwise deface the figure spoke volumes about the citizenry of Thuringia. Their own apathy and slackness would call down just retribution on their heads. The good Lord would smite them as he had struck the Egyptians and the wicked inhabitants of the cities on the plain. Jacobus always began his address or proclamation quietly and composedly. Almost inevitably he mounted the pulpit late—sometimes up to an hour after the originally appointed time. He drew his listeners slowly yet securely and tightly into his meshes and great web and made of them his secret partners, assuring them they stood on the side of right-eousness. Then midway into a sentence, he began to shout. His auditors felt the raw nakedness of his emotion and trembled. They experienced his anguish and anger. As he spoke he dis-played a genius for stagecraft and oratory and invective. He held his auditors spellbound. Then the children began to die and his dark prophecies and predictions seemed to the good citizens to all be coming true. The sun-face with the foliate mask was soon chiseled off the door and smashed. The head lost its countenance. Jacobus preached that the world would end in hell fire and that the Black Devil himself brazenly pranked in the people's midst. Thuringia had in times past been a Pagan kingdom. The old practices and folkways carried and continued on, often so craftily disguised that those who still performed them did not realize how they risked and imperiled their immortal souls. And, of course, he enumerated all of Hell's tortures including the green-and-red worms that would gnaw through the eyeballs of the damned in the lake of smoking brimstone and fiery lava for time eternal. During his discourses, he hinted that persons of high birth in the Landgraviate had taken up the Blacks Arts. He did not mention Dame Beatrice by name. Yet somehow the old stories about the little witch girl—Arbogast's daughter to his first wife, she of the blonde braids and the pink-and-white cap, Dame Orgeluse—all resurfaced and once again got bruited about. Beatrice's name was on everyone's lips. The people remembered that her father Arbogast had immured her in a convent after she told one and all that she had visitations from a young spirit boy, who first attached itself to her on All Hallows Eve. She claimed that the spirit was the reborn Christ child and that his coming had been announced to her in a dream the previous Christmas. But hadn't she also called him Baldr, the very same devil Brother Jacobus recently denounced? The entity could manifest itself as a fawn. At the hunting lodge of the good steward Ewald, many saw the demon animal. True, the nuns supervised the girl for many years and after she grew into womanhood. But she refused to take orders or to shear her ringlets, and, at long last, Arbogast took her off the nuns' hands and found her a husband—the good Frimutel, who died for God and country in the Holy Land. Banished from the kingdom by her brother-in-law after her husband's early and untimely death, she had returned to the Landgraviate and retired to her grandmother's old castle on the *Rennsteig* where from all reports she led an exemplary if an unobtrusive, largely hidden, life, that is until she began receiving yearly visits from a strange knight who arrived each year at Yule and departed at the Summer Solstice and whom many swore did not cast a shadow or had not cast a shadow until recent years. Now he kept company with the lady for the entire year. Some maintained that beginning the day after the wheel's longest day, the newly minted shadow he had begun to cast began to shrink and fade away, a little each day until the week before Yule it had faded altogether. Did not visitors to the castle say that this knight also went by the very same name of Baldr? Could the witch's demon consort have returned? Did it not initially manifest itself as deer? Could not two deer be seen now every night dashing through the evening sky? Jacobus received his expected summons to the Wartburg. When he arrived and a knight ushered him into the presence of the Landgraf Hermann and his mother the aged Sigune, the red-haired monk smiled as he sensed the latter's black heart, and Sigune realized at once that her Master stood before her and that he knew each and every one of her many crimes including the fact that she had hastened her husband—Hermann's beloved father—on to his heavenly reward by seasoning his food with certain of her select but secretly tainted herbs and spices. Immediately she fell on her knees before her son and related how years before his two stepsisters had come to her with the tale that Beatrice had so wanted the two to see Baldr—the reborn child of hope and sunlight—and to see that she was not making up stories, she told them that she would bring her spirit friend to the banqueting hall at midnight and there he would show himself in his deer form and allow Beatrice to mount and ride his invisible shoulders and that they could watch the two play from a hidden place behind an old arras. Arbogast and Sigune went in their stead and stood behind the arras at midnight. She and Arbogast saw the girl cast her magic spell. They gasped and cried out when they saw the little fawn materialize from nowhere and then saw little Beatrice fly through the air while riding on the incubus' invisible shoulders. The next day, as was his duty as a good, Christian father, Arbogast had summoned the nuns to haul the child away, hoping thereby to save the little girl's soul. The old woman lowered her head and the tears streamed from her eyes. The rumors and accusations, which her beloved and noble Hermann—her dear, dear son—had called evil and base, indeed had their basis in God's truth. She had advised her son to squelch all such talk—how dare the peasants abuse anyone belonging to the royal family—but she had just now agonizingly experienced the piercing agenbite of inwit. What if the demon had indeed returned and had caused the deaths of all the innocent children? "There is no doubt, madam," Jacobus interjected, "that the imp of Satan has come back, though he now wears the form of the middle-aged knight who used to stay with her but half a year but now remains at her side for all twelve months, although when our Saviour's birth approaches by the Lord's dispensation his evil is exposed for all to behold and see, for he ceases to cast a shadow like a creature of flesh and blood and walks shadowless. No doubt he has known Beatrice carnally, has become her demon lover. When he first returned to the kingdom, he had no shadow at all and returned to the fires of hell each year on the blessed feast day of St. John the Baptist. She has drawn and kept him here. It is her energy that gives him his strength and power. We must lay the death of the children all to her. I see your tears, my son, and I know that you love your half sister. What your beloved father tried to do, you can still accomplish if you have the resolve and strength, but it will take very great strength and willpower, Herr Hermann. Beatrice may yet spend all eternity with the Blessed Ones. You can indeed save her soul as your father Arbogast so valiantly and nobly tried to do. But to escape hell fire, she must burn here. When your men reduce her body to ash—and she must die by flame; she must scream and suffer as her flesh melts; you must give strict orders that none of your men draw the misericord and administer the mercy stroke—the Plague will come to an end. No further innocents will die." "You must sign the orders, my son," Sigune said, gripping his forearms with each of her liver-spotted hands, "So we all can meet again in Paradise." Hermann affixed his signature to the proffered document.

Red Horn saw or sensed all that happened below him in Eisenach and at the Wartburg but then immediately saw coming from the direction of the *Rennsteig* and Oma's old castle the silver beam of starlight—the bilobed arrow shooting up toward his sleigh from the whelk or seashell—and, thinking that he would shortly greet his son Baldr, he descended as a silver arrow—the two deer first vanishing in an eye blink and the two little faces at the same time reappearing once again in their wonted places on his earlobes—and struck the snowbank in front of the portcullis, the wooden grating let down in the snow at the gateway of the fortified ruin, whereupon *he-šucka* once more assumed his human, *worak*, two-legged walker form. Wearing around her neck in addition to Baldr's horn the seashell with the particle of Morning Star, Red Horn's beautiful daughter-in-law rushed to the gates and ordered the portcullis raised. After first taking her into his arms and embracing her like the loving parent he was, Red Horn grew serious and asked Baldr's whereabouts, and Beatrice informed the Hocąk chieftain that several weeks ago he had gone winter hunting with her two sons Gawan and Gramoflanz.

Red Horn warned her of Black Christ's presence and the plans afoot to offer her up as a sacrifice and wergeld. Red Horn, however, would protect his new daughter from the evil one. Beatrice replied that although he was many things—she knew, for she had met him in his several and always diverse guises throughout all her life, and he had been almost all things to her—her saviour and redeemer, her advocate and high priest, her life, lord, love and hope as well as her hurt and suffering, her babe in swaddling clothes, her kind, affectionate husband, and her wise all-knowing father—all things but nothing evil or cruel. Here, she tried to proselytize. Red Horn had heard it all before and had even for a short time been a sort of convert. He ho-hummed when she started in about God sacrificing His only son on the flowering dogwood tree.

In his delirium, *wanagi* had told Red Horn that he was the reborn son, the Christ child. When *wanagi's* fever went down and he again became lucid and himself, Red Horn asked him about his past life and Baldr repeated to his father all that he had learned from Beatrice and tears began welling in Wears Faces On His Ear's old eyes, for he knew the strength it took to lead a war party but had never considered the strength it would take to turn one's cheek or to lay down one's life for others—not members of the tribe but total strangers. The Christ he realized was a new and a most powerful kind of god, but the Sky Father who allowed the Romans to hang his dear innocent boy on a tree and refused to come to the boy's aid as Red Horn had come to Baldr-*wanagi's*, Red Horn found terrible, his action heartless and ghastly. Such a being could not come from Overworld but belonged in Beneath World, the dark realm of chaos where the Underwater Panther swam. The good tidings he had heard, the teachings of the reborn son, had also influenced his advice to his people during the Fever River war. The white settlers professed to worship the Christ. If the Hocąk now turned the other cheek, if they lay down their weapons, beat their swords into plowshares and acted like sheep perhaps the white generals would also show mercy and forgive their red brothers. Red Bird, *wabokieshiek*, and five other warriors all voluntarily surrendered to save their nation from the miseries of war and sure defeat from their superiorly matched foe. The white men, however, did not practice what they preached. Far from it.

All of Earthmaker's five sons *wakdjąkaga*, *wadexuga*, *kecągega*, *wacdjįgega*, and of course he—*he-šucka*—as well, had departed the *worak* Spirit Lake—to hunting grounds in the far west, as they couldn't abide their people's dishonor or the increasing depredations of the white aggressors against the Hocąk nation.

Red Horn inwardly smarted and felt scarlet shame because he initially advised the tribe to put down the hatchet and turn the other cheek to the *wanagi*. When the morning star appeared before the rising sun its image could still be seen reflected in the gray and cobalt-blue waters of the lake but none of the Hocąk any longer heard the mellifluous rumblings of the Big Voice.

Beatrice told her father-in-law that Black Christ was not the true Christ and that even Below World Baldr Christ was not Above World Sun Christ, and that here below we see but through a glass darkly. All goes wrong somehow almost always in the world below the stars and Shining Ones. The twilight of the gods is ever at hand. But Christ's Kingdom is not of this world. Eventually the glorious day would come when He shall gather all those who received and accepted His redeeming love and with them He will enjoy the fullness of that which He purchased with His blood. Red Horn was yet a babe in Christ, but with the help of His grace, he would grow into the fullness of the spiritual man through consecration, study, and prayer. Black Christ could have her life—she would gladly lay it down—for she knew she would again meet her Baldr—her true Christ—in the eternal Summerlands. She had glimpsed them often with her third eye. Here she took Red Horn by the hand and led him to view her tapestries of Baldr-White Christ's Lake. Seeing his own sacred space, Red Horn understood. She said essentially the same thing as he had when he told his son the last time he came to his rescue that he—*herok'aga*—had simply crossed over from the *worak* lake below to the *waika* lake above. One of the infinite *worak* Devil's Lakes below. At Spirit Lake, *he-šucka's* select war party always defeated the evil water spirits. There was only ever one ending to the battle up there. Below, there were as many outcomes as there were lakes, but in almost all of them the good people suffered a sad and undeserved fate, but not in all the worlds. At a couple of lakes, the whites, never having crossed the great salt waters, did not even appear on the scene. In a few others the Hocąk snatched victory from seeming sure defeat. Perhaps the stern Sky Father was just another of his own opposite numbers, like Woden. Maybe they all had to make a sacrifice of themselves for themselves? Maybe in all the Above Worlds, the Highest had to at some point become flesh precisely for the sake of his offspring, to redeem his children from error and point the way back home? He too shared in the sin. He too in his own person experienced the fall—the descent into hell—because he loved his offspring even in their perishable, pupal state. He understood that He lived in them and they in Him and what seemed sin truly wasn't, for his children the name givers were his co-creators. Only through these agent-witnesses of his puissant creation did He attain his Godhead.

In very short order—a matter of a few days—Baldr and Beatrice's two boys arrived at the castle, and Baldr learned of the approaching danger. Red Horn, Baldr and Beatrice conferred together, as to their plan of action. At first *he-šucka* wanted all four *worak* to flee and he alone would surprise the enemy when the monk and the Landgraf Hermann's men started their siege of the castle. Oh what a surprise would lay in wait for the evil one. But then the father of all raconteurs bethought himself. Beatrice had become *heregunina*'s chief target. With flaring nostrils, he scented her like some great demonic bloodhound. If she left the old ruins of Oma, he might, subtle fiend that he was, somehow detect it and follow her instead of falling into Red Horn's set trap. In the end, the three decided that Beatrice would remain at the castle under Red Horn's protection. *He-šucka* had after all defeated *hereçgunina* numerous times. Baldr had witnessed his father vanquish the black one again and again, and Wears Faces On His Ears promised that he would once more transform old goathead into a skunk before he would let him singe one of Beatrice's curly locks. *He-šucka* wanted his son, however, as far away as possible from the scene of his and *hereçgunina*'s impending confrontation. Although everyday, due to Beatrice's influence, he was becoming more and more a *worak,* he still had, and always would have, something of a *waika* nature, which would make him vulnerable to *hereçgunia*'s attacks in ways Beatrice never could be. For while *he-šucka* always triumphed over *hereçgunina,* *hereçgunina* held the upper hand over Baldr. To separate the two lovers remained the goat's chief aim and delight. With a wave of his hand he might again contemptuously banish Baldr back to Purgatory or cause him to fall into a new dream, a dream per chance that Baldr might never awaken from. So it was agreed that after they all took a festive last supper together—an early Christmas feast and banquet—that Baldr would spirit away Beatrice's two sons to safety. They agreed that he would make for the hunting lodge where the pair had bedded down together as children, where the aged Ewald still remained master. Beatrice herself scribbled instructions to her father's old retainer. Ewald's son also named Ewald would in turn journey with the two boys southward and smuggle them across the mountainous Swiss border.

Leaving Beatrice in Red Horn's care and protection, Baldr and the two boys set off. He would return for Beatrice after Red Horn had soundly defeated and trounced *hereçgunina,* and the two would follow her sons southward.

Within a week, Jacobus and the Landgraf's men arrived to burn Beatrice. Red Horn met them at the castle gates. With a sweeping motion of his arm, Red Horn knocked the knights riding in the vanguard from off their horses. Those coming up behind them turned their animals around, spurred the beasts' flanks and in great fear and consternation, rode off. Jacobus hurled abuse at them. Red Horn shouted, "Turn, hell-hound, turn! I have no words. My voice is my sword, thou bloodier villain than terms can give out." Then Red Horn and Jacobus faced off, and Red Horn to his horror and complete surprise discovered that his powers were not nearly so efficacious in this world as at Spirit Lake. The monk did not instantly transform into a black-and-white skunk. Jacobus took the iron cross from around his throat and flung it like a throwing star so that one side of the horizontal piece near the top wedged in Red Horn's throat from which the bright, red blood began to pour. *He-šucka* became light-headed as he reeled and staggered back through the gateway, and Beatrice lowered the portcullis. "You were always a wraith and lifeless counterfeit, *he-šucka,* but here you are truly lifeless and without power," the enemy of *mą'ųna* exulted. You can't help the Christians like you did the Hocąk. They do not fall on their knees and worship you. They trust no god but their own, and make no mistake deep down Beatrice is a Christian. You have no power here! You are nothing but a *wanagi* or a ghost. A great paper tiger."

Beatrice ran to support Red Horn and half carried him into her hall of tapestries where he collapsed on the stone flags. Beatrice took down the wall hanging of the white fawn—the closest thing she had to white deerskin—and used it to bind Red Horn's bleeding neck. Beatrice blessed the wound and offered prayers to both Mary the mother of God and the great Earth Mother for Red Horn's recovery. "I can't protect you, my child," the father of all raconteurs gasped. "My daughter, I can never see what will happen very far into the future in any of the *worak* worlds. Only for a short distance can I make out and glimpse what will be." The old man broke off in mid-sentence. Beatrice saw his face formerly beet-red drain of all color as tears began streaming down his grieving face. For he saw Beatrice chained to a stake, defiant and serene as the flames rose up all about her. She cried out: "I forgive you. I forgive you. See the radiant rainbow. The great bridge. It appears. It appears. Heaven unfolds its golden portals and I can see the Shining Ones. Amid the angel choirs, my Oma stands radiant. She clasps the White Christ, my beloved fawn, to her breast. They stretch forth their arms to me in love. I mount. I fly. Back rolls the dwindling earth. Brief is the sorrow, endless the joy."

Red Horn bethought himself. There yet might remain a way. If not in this life and particular world, in another. My daughter do you remember what your Oma revealed to you as a little girl after you looked into her great kettle and beheld visions of other worlds as well as other eras and epochs of your same below world?" Beatrice unhesitatingly replied, "Out of the air her voice, at the same time the voice of the ancient and all-powerful World-Mother herself, told me, 'All that can be is. Everything that can possibly happen does happen. Simultaneously and all at once.'" "Yes, my daughter. And often you beheld multiple reflections of yourself and sometimes the other Beatrices weren't merely parallels. They did not share the same face with you. Their lips might be less thin or more full, and the color of their hair and eyes would differ as would the girls' often bewilderingly odd apparel. Nonetheless you felt yourself alive in each of the girls." "Yes, dear Opa, I remember. My Oma said they were the many cups, the many daughters, I would pour myself into, that my essential self would manifest again and again. I would have many different embodiments, and, for the briefest of instances, I could see out their eyes and glimpse into all their far-flung worlds so at variance from my own, and I not only knew that I was still myself but I also understood all the strange things of those many multifold worlds." "Alas, daughter, with my death vision, I see that *heregunina* will again succeed in separating you and Baldr. You have made my son almost all *worak*, but as Baldr never took birth—as he is not of woman born—he can never become completely human. He was to have entered life in the flesh seven years after you as a son to educated commoners or tradespeople. Despite such humble beginnings, he was to have risen to the rank of Minnesinger and because of his prowess at song writing to have become a knight and vassal of a great German lord. However, a spiteful shadow-being and thief of others' shadows to darken his own—a horrid angel of the gloom and murk—this same *heregunina* or Black Christ that threatens us now without—waylaid Baldr as his soul descended to take birth. Arms stretched aloft, talons at the ready to catch the fluttering flibbet as it flew by him, the Black Prince snatched in his loathsome claws Baldr's mote of light and diverted it far from its intended destination. But I know where Baldr's intended blood will at long last enter and mix with my own. A descendant of the two who should have been Baldr's parents will in the state of Pennsylvania in the great country known as America one day marry a daughter of one Christian Poole, a raconteur-storyteller who will live to the great age of one hundred and twelve and stand six-feet two-inches tall. Far in the future, he will be buried at Spring Mount, near the little town of Warriors Mark, Pennsylvania. He'll marry a woman to whom he will give the Christian name Catherine, a full-blooded Sioux who'll meet Christian in Washington County, Maryland where he'll find himself pursuing some fantastic claim against the government—a land grant to his father, a teamster in the Revolution, signed by General George Washington—when her people are driving a herd of bison to the Federal City at the request of the Great White Father, President Andrew Jackson. Will any future Beatrice find her way to those far parts or that general vicinity? For as Baldr can never become a full man here anyway, I will simply change him back again to his spirit animal and he will cross over from the spirit realm to another, future, life like the ravens from the spirit world came to Red Banks during the time of the Great Migration. No black claw will knock him off course this time and a *worak* Baldr will encounter you in one of your other lives, instead of an unborn spirit."

Beatrice rushed to the secret closet which contained all Oma's old scrolls. She knew what stood on its three legs at the far corner in the very back.

Beatrice spent the next several hours staring in Oma's kettle for a suitable Beatrice for Baldr to find in the future as a "reborn" human and eventually found a Pennsylvania girl—a descendant of Gramoflanz—who reminded her very much of herself. Red Horn nodded and said he would choose the right recipient for Baldr's soul, a descendant of Baldr's intended parents and of Christian Poole and Catherine, his Sioux bride, and that he would make sure that this *worak* Baldr would enter the world a full seven years after the birth of Gramoflanz's distant daughter. Beatrice smiled to the old man and told him that for poor Baldr's sake she would make a sacrifice out of herself for herself. "My daughter," Red Horn replied, "I don't see what will happen very far into the future in your or any particular world. Only for a short distance can I make out and glimpse what will be. But I will tell you this ... your love will again return to you at Yule." He turned his head to one side where he lay slumped on the floor and lost consciousness. To Beatrice, he appeared as if he lay dead.

When Red Horn again rose, on the morning of the shortest day of the year, Beatrice had already gone to her fate. Wears Faces On His Ears recognized a horrible odor, one he recalled smelling from the time he sweetly sang the word *da-wa-kah-char-gra* to begin a sad, mysterious death song—the kind sung by prisoners about to be executed—and the red-and-black painted giants standing guard at the scalp pole upon hearing *he-šucka's* big voice immediately jumped into the flames of the fire and their flesh and even their bones turned to ash—the pungent sweet scent of a bonfire. Red Horn bounded out of the castle, veiling his eyes so as not to behold the grisly scene in the castle yard. He thought now only of his beloved son. He would be approaching fast and must at all costs be prevented from seeing this horrible scene. As fast as one of his arrows, as if again he competed in the great race, Red Horn shot whizzing down the *Rennsteig* until he reached his son as he came rushing back homewards. The two almost collided. Restored and made whole at the time he had awakened, the chief of the *herok'a he-šucka* with a wave of the hand such as he used to change the face of the evil spirit who stole the appearance of the Forked Man's grandfather back to that of an owl—its true features—attempted to turn Baldr into his spirit animal the roebuck. He said the magic word twice—*da-wa-kah-char-gra da-wa-kah-char-gra*—but Baldr merely blinked and smiled at him before asking, "Father, what news? Why do you weep so?" "I cry for joy, little *wanagi*. Beatrice's love works miracles. She has at long last succeeded in transforming you from a spirit into a man." The white-haired chief told the truth. For indeed a Christmas miracle had happened. On the shortest day of the year, during the last few sunlit hours preceding Mothers' Night, the longest night of the year and the dark night of our souls when the new spark of hope at last ignites, Baldr cast a full-length shadow. It extended behind him on the snow as dark as any inkblot. Red Horn could not now merely snap his fingers and change him into his spirit animal. Now the fawn could only emerge in one way. In his haste to return to the castle, Baldr had already taken a few steps past his father. "Beatrice has crossed to Red Banks, my son," Red Horn hurriedly called forth. "*Herecgunina* reigns supreme in this world. We shall leave it to him. We too shall return home, and henceforth he shall be forever banned and barred from Spirit Lake. I anticipate your fears, my son. Listen to me now and I will strive to quell them. First, I have already sent Storms-as-he-walks southward to fetch Gawan and Gramoflanz. He will cross over with them and on the far side we all shall be reunited in one great family." Under his breath, very softly and almost inaudibly, Red Horn began muttering again and again the magic words *da-wa-kah-char-gra da-wa-kah-char-gra da-wa-kah-char-gra da-wa-kah-char-gra*. He knew the terrible thing he had to do. He had to make a sacrifice of Baldr for Baldr. Had the miracle not happened, had Baldr not suddenly emerged from his cocoon a complete *worak* with an intact shadow, or had Red Horn merely to slay an Evil Spirit, he would have but had to breathe correctly, utter the word *ahahe* twice and let fly his empty bowstring. He would not have needed any *worak* arrow. He had a shaft of mistletoe in his quiver, but Baldr stood too close to him. He did not have the arm room to use his bow. Nonetheless, to make himself stronger and steel himself to his task, Red Horn thought of Baldr as a great buck of Red Banks. A terrible sacrifice was called for on the chieftain's part too. He would have to kill what he most loved. He remembered the prayer a Hocąk brave offered when he struck down his first red buck with forked antlers and the other warriors smeared his cheeks with the bright blood of the kill, a prayer of thanksgiving to the animal's released spirit: "Oh, Grandfather, I thank you for your life. Your body and blood will nourish mine and your life in the change and circle of existence shall become my life. Some time in a future being and incarnation, our roles may be reversed and after a strenuous and noble chase—for I will not simply lay down for you—I will let myself fall a sacrifice to your need and hunger and to the need and hunger of those you love. I will return life for life, for you great horned one have become my spirit animal and Grandfather." Red Horn again silently uttered those words. He could not bear to see Baldr's bright blue eyes—so like the color of Spirit Lake itself—staring into his. "Look yonder, my son, and you shall see our lake and Beatrice standing on the hot white sand." Red Horn again silently muttered the magic word *da-wa-kah-char-gra.* Baldr turned his head and indeed saw. A little evening breeze blew over the clearing and the leaves rustled and the wind waves flowed up the green pool. Red Horn raised his war club above his head. His hand shook violently, but his face set and the hand steadied. On his red-ochre face above the spatulate nose two red dots suddenly gleamed in the eyeslits, and for a brief moment, *he-šucka* felt great anger and hate for his adopted son *wanagi,* the orphan he welcomed to Red Banks, the first of the ghosts, the evil invaders who would eventually dispossess the Hocąk of all their native ground, to have arrived there. He brought his club savagely down, but then tears began rolling down his face as he looked down at his son's body and his red-stained golden hair. Red Horn dropped to his knees and laid his weeping face in the snow and began to bitterly wail. He now knew the pain of the Heavenly Father upon seeing his only son Jesus on the cross, of having to Himself make the same sacrifice He had first asked of His servant Abraham. After weeping and crying for a very long time, the old Indian at last looked up. Baldr's soul—an albino fawn—hovered over his prostrate body. Red Horn quickly made a medicine bag in which he slipped a few pieces of quartzite from Spirit Lake which he fumbled out of one of his pockets. He tied the hastily made quantra around *wanagi*-fawn's neck. Then with a wave of his hand, Red Horn changed Baldr's soul into an arrow, which he quickly fitted to his bowstring. With his brawny arm and his beautiful well-shaped hand, the father and greatest of all raconteurs drew the arrow back to his ear, from which a small earring depended, and aimed the shaft upwards into the darkening sky. Never before had *he-šucka* pulled the bowstring so hard or so far back. It would take all his great strength to launch his son Baldr across all the centuries and into his future life.

Red Horn stood in the snow many hours. At long last, he cried *ahahe* twice and let the arrow fly.

No black claw would knock his son off course now.

worak

Richard and Natalia

Richard opened the screen door and again stepped outside into the sunlight. The date of his departure December 19th had at last arrived.

[From way up high, the present raconteur—Marceric Frederickson—elsewhere called M. Prime and perhaps known to the reader already if she has chanced to read or browse through another of this raconteur's books, a big, hefty tome entitled *Symphonie Fantastique* after the well known "program" symphony of Hector Berlioz—the present raconteur had intended to write, "Michael opened the screen door" but in the final few seconds before he commenced typing, Marceric or rather M. Prime decided that, after turning away from them for so many years to investigate other subjects, when at long last again writing about his two favorite and most beloved characters, he would have to rename and indeed recreate them. That in this new little book, the second part of which he was just now starting to write, they could no longer remain Michael and Elissa. So instead of Michael he typed Richard. Actually the pair had appeared in another novel before M. Prime's own and in the very lofty guises of John Milton and Kalliope, the muse of epic poetry, a book by the present raconteur's distinguished teacher and master, the inimitable PW. He knew and encouraged the young Marceric and read the early drafts of Marceric's book, his tale of virginity lost and his fall into language subsequent to his near death on the operating table at the age of nineteen and of his heartbreak at, and the physical and psychological scars occasioned by, his love "Elissa's" departure from his young life. W had heard all the tales—Marceric and "E's" fabled verbal fencing, their wicked and cutting exchanges with one another, came up as a regular subject of gossip between Bob and Tom during their morning shoptalk and bs session around the mail room coffeepot and even Jack and Phil squawked about and gave odds on which of the two would next outshine and outfox which—all the tales of the student-couple's storied rivalry and their witty give and take while co-editors of the student literary magazine *Kalliope*, though Marceric's love never sat in on or audited one of the great P's classes. He knew only the Elissa of Marceric's book. PW's novel ends with two images of Milton. First we see him as an aged man, a virtual skeleton in a rocking chair looking with affection at his own death, still yearning to be of tender service to his long-gone Amaryllis-Kalliope: to massage her feet, to kiss her eyelids closed, to smooth out with a flat hand the black velvet of her stomach. He wonders where she went and what she had become. Then we see the young Milton, immediately after his Muse's departure, capering up and down a narrow beach howling, seizing handfuls of wet sand and plastering his face, getting it in his eyes the worse to see. No moon shone, no light beckoned. Marceric's own novel ended almost as bleakly (both Milton and Michael, struck by a lightning bolt, enjoyed the great/paltry consolation of language—dejected as they were, it stood at their command), but he added an addendum when he finally published the book, as part of another book, twenty years later in which the actual M. Prime and E. Prime and not the fictional Michael and

Elissa of his novel come to meet again in later life and how she
unseals his lips and helps heal the wound that plunged him
into despair and silence, the wound occasioned by the death
of his grandfather. Feeling the wellsprings of his art renewed,
M. Prime realizes that he will have to tell both the story of his
time in the slough of despond but also that of his miraculous
resurrection. He feels impregnated. A new novel begins taking
shape in him. Intimidated and scared, he decides, at least for the
present, to use the familiar and comfortable names from the old
book Michael Bolanger and Elissa Hexfore when writing about
himself and his dear friend. Michael had a forefather named
Christian Poole. But as M. Prime or Marceric actually had a
forefather with such a name who had reputedly lived to the great
age of one hundred and twelve—who indeed maintained himself
that he was that old and had long articles written up about his
longevity in various newspapers and periodicals of the time in
which the writers referred to him as the durable Dutchman
of Centre County, Pennsylvania—Marceric saw no reason why
his new word-self Richard Mercer could not descend from
him also. Thomas Wolfe—perhaps E. Prime's all-time favorite
raconteur—provided the analog for splitting oneself into two
nearly identical but differently named fictional selves, for when
Wolfe switched publishing houses between *Of Time and the River*
and *The Web and the Rock,* for contractual and copyright reasons,
Eugene Gant became George Webber. As the earlier book ends,
sailing from Cherbourg home to America, Gant encounters
Esther, a woman twenty years older than he, who will become
his destiny (after he is renamed Webber; she is still called
Esther but also given a surname, Jack), a character modeled no
doubt on Wolfe's own much older love and eventual wife Aline
Bernstein. In the *worak* section of *Baldr and Beatrice* we will come

up on our familiar but magically subtly-and-cunningly altered, newly named, characters at about the same time in their lives as when they last appeared in their familiar old disguises of Michael and Elissa in M. Prime's hurried (far from final) new first chapter draft, which brings to a conclusion his addendum to *The Mozart Machine*, the comic, clockwork third movement of *Symphonie Fantastique*.]

After combing his still curly brown hair one more time over his bald spot and looking deep into the mirror only to see his own gray-green eyes staring right back at him, Richard Mercer put the comb in his pocket, stepped out of the living room into the foyer, opened the screen door and again stepped outside into the sunlight and the cold, crisp morning air to see if his friend Ned had yet pulled up out front, Ned who would drive him shortly to the train station in Altoona. Richard felt uneasy and nervous at the prospect of traveling. Having lived so long with a shut-in, he had become something like a shut-in himself. He had remained pretty much in the little Pennsylvania town of Mercersdale for the last eighteen years, his trip farthest away a drive to a university town in upstate New York twelve years before, chauffeuring a former professor of his from Penn State, whose epilepsy precluded him from sitting behind the wheel, to a conference to give a paper as a personal favor. Both Owen, his maternal grandfather, and Ida, his sweet but always pugnaciously argumentative paternal grandmother, had been still alive at that time.

Richard had hardly slept at all. He bounded out of bed at first light. He was at present experiencing both great excite-ment—he was finally going off to see Lynn—and what amounted to almost fear at the prospect of the journey which he would

soon be undertaking. His remaining for so many years in one
place had much to do with his current trepidation—staying put
in utter obscurity, hidden from all view, in the heart of the heart
of Pennsylvania or rather what amounted to the new millen-
nium's version of Tobacco Road, little Mercersdale, a whole
world in itself for always the microcosm reflects the macro-
cosm, the town founded by and named after his joint paternal
and maternal ancestor Heinrich Mercer, a Revolutionary War
soldier who hailed from Germany and, before entering the
service, had knelt before royalty as shoemaker to King Louis
of France. The Mercers and the Merciers, it turned out, were
after all related, as his grandfather Owen always half suspected.
George Mercier Sr. had not, when he and his family pulled up
stakes in Filthydumpia shortly after the Civil War, picked the
destination of the little, obscure, hamlet of Mercersdale arbitrarily. He had come with a reason and a purpose—as Rich and
his grandfather discovered while researching at the Philadelphia
genealogy museum just after Richard turned eleven. Richard
himself made the conclusive find in a registry of Lutheran mar-
riages and baptisms of the 1700s. Henry Mercer had a wife
previous to Mathilde Streckmann and a son William to this
first wife, Elizabeth Dreißer, who died giving him birth during
the Yellow Fever epidemic. The Dreißers raised the boy who for
some reason added the extra letter to his surname. Owen had
his grandfather George senior's Family Bible. It listed George's
father's name as William. A little more research would confirm
that the two Williams were the same person.

At the time of his parents' marriage those events lay over
a century in the past, and the couple did not believe that they
both descended from a common root. It fell out they were
sixth cousins twice removed. Only after Richard and Owen

discovered proof of the connection, which Owen always had thought possible, did Richard's father Hugo Mercer—the famous critic, distinguished professor of literature and radio commentator for the San Francisco Opera—concede the point, for he had always pooh-poohed his father-in-law's "crackbrained ideas and notions." Owen had steadfastly maintained since the time of his daughter's engagement that the fact that both Mercers and Merciers had settled in the exact same place, albeit at different times, made the story that they were supposedly unrelated suspect. The surnames stood simply too close to preclude that possibility.

Had Richard not stayed in one place for so long, his disinclination to make trips and excursions, his positive fear now of traveling, would seem strange, especially considering how much of it he had done in Europe and America with his family in his youth. As a small boy he always so looked forward to Christmas, Easter, and to the trip which always took place sometime in the summer (during which his grandfather would always go driving in the state forest with Richard and his sister to see if they could spot deer, turkey, or other wildlife)—for him the three most magical occasions of the year—he could hardly contain himself when the time for each trip again came round—to riding in the taxi from the suburbs to the awesome, huge international airport, boarding the plane outbound from San Fran and flying across the continent with his parents and sister back to the grimy, smoky city of Pittsburgh and then taking the United commuter flight to the little regional airport located in the middle of nowhere—all around it state forest and game land—at the top of Cold Mushroom Mountain, sawn off and steamrollered in World War Two to make a runway, where Owen wearing a red tie and one of his porkpie hats would be waiting in the parking lot inside his ancient, green Rambler. Richard always looked forward to spending his Christmases and other vacations with all four of his grandparents, the Mercers and the Merciers both. All four spoiled, fawned on, and showed constant delight in their two grandchildren. They simply showered them with affection. From very early on, Richard developed an especially close and tight bond with Owen, whom he for some reason called fawfaw and whom he always requested to tell stories. Owen told wonderful stories—thrilling and funny both—usually just after bed time when Richard lay snuggled between his fawfaw and his Nanny Ina (whom her son-in-law Hugo always thought looked like the Irish actress Una O' Connor of *Bride of Frankenstein* fame, who, early on in the great camp classic, throws up her arms and flees in terror from the monster who, it turns out, had not perished, as everyone thought, in the burning windmill, screaming "It's alive! It's alive!" as she runs), both sitting up in bed, their backs to the headboard, in their pajamas, a cone-shaped orange lamp burning brightly on the nearby dresser. He told him how faw-faw and Rich fled from Long John, Pegleg Pete and the other pirates (Pirates also being the name of the baseball team he watched on the TV with the anchors all different from the ones at home) into the cave entrance, the left eye socket of Skull Island, where the buccaneers had previously buried all their ill-gotten gains and now made their way toward to add their latest haul to the already vast treasure. A friendly spider spun a great web for the best friends to hide behind. They came out only after all the pirates had left, and then the two made off with all of the gold piastres. Or how Grandma Ina had been so careless one day as to knock over a box of macaroni and spill some elbows into the kitchen sink, which was filled with dishes, water and dishwashing liquid. To make matters worse she turned on the wall fan. Soap bubbles formed and rose up and floated into the air and out the open window. Eventually the bubbles would pop high up in the blue sky and the macaroni elbows caught and imprisoned inside them would drop like bombs to pelt people on the head. Owen would also pin his arms back and put him in a bear trap or bear hug from which he would encourage Richard to struggle or wiggle his way out, playfully nipping and biting his ear—making an ear sandwich, he called it—the while. Richard and his younger sister Angharad would eventually make trips to Pennsylvania on their own to visit their grandparents during the summers but the trips they took there as children with their parents would stay with them all their lives. During the Christmas season the lampposts of the main streets of all the run-down little towns near Mercersdale wore bright lights in the shapes of twinkling stars, snowmen, red and white candy canes, angels, or silver and golden bells, and multicolored bulbs blinked from the outside trees, the windows, eaves and doors of all the houses. Everyone tried to outdo his neighbor and the electric bills people ran up during the winter had to be enormous. This annual display continued year after year, from the time of Richard's childhood right up into his middle and late thirties and the time of Ida's and Owen's deaths, until today when Richard had reached the age of forty-six. During the 1990s, he would bundle up both his two ailing remaining grandparents and walk them slowly and carefully to the car, get them settled inside with a blanket spread over their knees, then drive them around the town and its adjacent residential areas to see all the rainbow-colored lights. A sinful waste of money, his father had always said. The people here could find better, more practical and beneficial, ways of spending their hard-earned dollars. Always hard up for cash throughout the rest of the year, everyone put on the dog at Christmas. The squat, flabby, no-nonsense people, laconic to the point of taciturnity most of the year, made merry and acted in boisterous fashion at Christmas. The churches also put on opulent pageants—Richard and Angharad particularly enjoyed the "annual hanging of the greens" service at their grandparents' little house of worship, where it seemed like all the congregation participated in the beautifying, decorating, and adorning and even the youngest children strewed evergreen boughs and helped hang the fruit-and-nut twined wreathes. Again his father decried the waste "when people were starving overseas and there was such great need and want in our own inner cities." The townspeople never had to lock their doors in Mercersdale. The whole town behaved like one great extended family. Most of the young people who went on to college, however, did not return but found jobs elsewhere in the country, in some cases many states away as was the case with Richard's parents. Owen said that those good looking enough or smart thinking enough always moved on elsewhere, leaving only the rubes behind to mate among themselves. Despite these last remarks, Owen stood the town's biggest booster, forever singing its and the state of Pennsylvania's praises. "You like coming here, don't you?" he asked his grandson. "Always remember that Mercersdale is your real hometown." Richard loved and remembered those childhood trips when all four of his grandparents were alive.

Ina died first when Richard was only twelve. Aware of her heart ailment for years—poor Ina, she had angina—she had told Richard that if something ever happened to her whenever he felt the wind buffeting his cheek, she would be giving him a kiss.

Even though only a mere boy, he perceived that his grand-father's grief was of such a staggering order of magnitude that he would shortly follow her, unless he—little Richard—could somehow distract him and hold him back.

For sometime, Richard's father Hugo had been planning a nine-country European tour for his sabbatical year—the family so used to flying back and forth across the American continent would shortly fly across the pond—and Richard proposed taking Owen along. Owen accepted. Inviting him and persuading him to come, Richard indeed saved his grandfather's life and staved off death and the grim reaper. So deeply interested in all aspects and ever detail of his family's history, Owen suddenly had something to look forward to and anticipate, for Hugo planned to visit one of their ancestral villages. During the course of that memorable trip during the summer of 1974, all five of Heinrich Mercer's descendants visited the little town of Wallheim, the town from which Heinrich's father Johann Georg Mercer hailed and from which he departed forever as a young man when he embarked on his journeyman years as a shoemaker which took him across Germany to the duchy of Saxe-Coburg, where he settled and married the local shoe-maker's daughter and where his son Heinrich would be born in 1751. Richard had many vivid, sparkling memories of that wonderful vacation to England, France, Switzerland, Italy, Greece, Yugoslavia, Austria, Holland, and especially Germany, but his father's and his grandfather's enthusiasm for family history having infected young Richard, his imagination had kindled and caught fire when they traveled through Württemberg, the place of their family roots, and, of all his many memories, he most treasured those of his family's time in the two little adjoining towns of Wallheim and Besigheim.

An electric power plant was under construction in Wallheim at the time of their visit, and workers from elsewhere had taken all the rooms in all the hotels. The little American family could not find a place to stay, but a concierge telephoned and found them lodgings a littler further down the line in neighboring Besigheim. Happily the two towns stood as close together as Owen's Mercersdale and its tiny neighbor to the west, Nestor Hill. As the family walked the short distance and crossed from one town to the other at about eight pm, Richard's grandfather pointed out to Angharad a man from inside pulling fast the second-story window shutters of his house. They observed that the shutters of the neighboring homes were also all closed. As they walked, ahead of them, they saw an elderly man with a cane. Richard's father Hugo who had planned and orchestrated the family's trip, who spoke three languages other than English, and who had studied the third of those, Russian, for military purposes while stationed in Germany with U.S. Intelligence in the 1950s, hurried to this gentleman and spoke to him in German, telling him that he and his family were of German extraction and bore the name Mercer and that they would like to meet persons of that name. The gentleman guided them to a corner building that housed a tavern restaurant. They entered and were greeted by the owner who acted as hostess. Very impressive was this gray-haired lady attired in a beautiful black dress with white lace. Hugo conversed with her in his best German. The hostess took them to a table and she went and brought her daughter, who unfolded the family's story to the other patrons in the dining room. This group was having an enjoyable evening like the Germans love to do—friendly fellowship, playing of a popular card game and, of course, eating and drinking. Everyone listened intently. Here, a family group had come from abroad, claiming to be descendants of wine gardeners of the old German towns of Wallheim and Besigheim. Next came the introduction of Mercer to Mercer. Eugene Mercer, who sat at table playing cards with friends, was a retired shoemaker from Wallheim. This when related brought a smile to both Hugo and Owen. Hugo then told how their ancestor Heinrich Mercer's occupation in Philadelphia had been that of a shoe and boot maker and that he possessed some of his tools. When the storytelling and greetings at last came to an end, the gracious and friendly hostess honored the American family by serving them some of the famous local white wine. Even Richard and Angharad took a sip. Later Owen would tell Richard that he felt the spirit of Heinrich's grandfather old Conrad Mercer (whose wine cask on the barge rolled over, when the Neckar grew wild, and knocked him over into the water causing his death) looking down at him saying, "Grandson, you will never taste anything so sweet as Neckar River wine." Later the four Mercers and the one Mercier would visit the eleventh century winery on the Besigheim side, still in operation, and they would photograph the hillsides of Wallheim covered with grape vines bursting with grapes. Even though centuries had passed since Hans Conrad's time, cultivating the grape remained a productive and profitable farming enterprise for the area. The group in the inn was there for the evening—a way of German life. The American family did not observe the entry of any persons since they had arrived, but everyone at the little inn seemed to be having a grand time. Owen wished he understood the German language. At last Hugo told their hostess they must leave. She said that they might not find their way home. Someone volunteered to drive them to their hotel. They soon arrived safely, and, with an expression of good will, they shook hands with the driver as they parted company at the hotel. Next day, they walked through and toured the very ancient small city of Besigheim. A pamphlet on the city Hugo translated for them wished Besigheim's visitors many happy and wholesome hours in "our old city." It told the visitor to take in the beautiful scenery, to enjoy the medieval character of the town and to be sure to enjoy a glass of Besigheim wine. It also gave a little of the town's long history. Archaeologists had uncovered an altar rock used by a Mithra cult there in the year 90 AD. Hugo explained that Mithra was a Persian god of light, defender of truth, and enemy of the powers of darkness. The pamphlet explained that in 1886 excavators unearthed the remains of six buildings used by the cult. They also recovered Roman coins and earthenware. The pamphlet further stated that in 260 AD, the town received its name. The Basinge clan or tribe lived there. People called the town the home of the Basinge—or Basingheim, from which the town's current designation Besigheim ultimately derived. The four Mercers and the one Mercier walked from their hotel a short distance to the river Neckar. The wide, brown waterway flowed right through the center of the town and under an ornate bridge with flower box after flower box full of well-cared-for flowers running down its side. Additional flower boxes sat below all the windows of the town. The school grounds also had beautiful flower areas. This evidenced the pride of the townspeople, Owen said. It made you think, "I too should have pride in my ancestral area of abode." A sizeable fountain stood in the town square. On its ornate pedestal stood a stone knight. Nearby sat the town hall, a beautiful stucco building, flower boxes at each of its windows. A balcony towered over the building's entrance, its front all flowers. Richard's family strolled through the cobbled streets, where the drivers raced and speeded just as crazily as the local yokels did back home in Mercersdale on Saturday nights; Hugo clutched his son's hand so in his eagerness he would not dash out into the street and in front of a car—until at last they came to an area that had a stone wall running round it. The air was so fragrant that Owen became curious. Finding an entrance he passed through the metal gate and once inside beheld a most beautiful cemetery with family plots one after another, all covered with flowers and green growth and large markers. As Owen and the family walked slowly about, they came to a large monument that read: "Resting Place of the Mercer Family." Hugo met a woman in the cemetery. Conversing with her, he discovered that she knew local Mercers. She took him to a recent grave of a Mercer lady, a friend of hers who lived to be eighty-four years old.

Returning home from Europe at the end of the summer, Richard and the rest of the family learned of the declining health of Richard's paternal grandfather Cornelius, who had suffered a severe stroke while they all were on vacation. Nanny Ida and Hugo's sister, Richard and Angharad's Aunt Audrey, had decided not to interrupt the family trip. Cornelius would die that autumn on the fourth of October, the same day as the poetess Anne Sexton committed suicide. A sad precedent established itself in Richard's life. For the first time, something terrible happened shortly after something splendiferous and wonderful, a pattern that would repeat and repeat itself through-out his life. Because Richard had saved one grandfather, death in retaliation took the other. Richard had deeply and equally loved this other grandfather, the more low-keyed and often shy, taciturn Cornelius, who each year planted wonderful vegetable and flower gardens and who especially enjoyed cultivating blue irises and who each summer took Angharad and him to the woods to pick blackberries or huckleberries for his wife to make homemade cobblers. They would disappear down the railroad tracks, Richard slinging a great empty pail and Cornelius carrying Angharad on his shoulders. During the last several years of his life, Cornelius began having problems with his memory and was afraid that he would forget the names of his children and grandchildren. Every day he would write them down four or more times. Cornelius had walked to the Mercersdale bus terminal to see the travelers off as they embarked on the bus to New York City, where they would catch their KLM flight to Amsterdam, the first stop on their European trip. When they all arrived back in Mercersdale, Richard was the first to walk to Cornelius and Ida's. Ida opened the door, and, when Cornelius heard Richard's voice below, he grew so happy and excited, he struggled and succeeded in getting up from bed, fell to the floor, then crawled to the top of the staircase and slid on his backside down the steps in order to greet his grandson, come back in time to see him still alive. He smiled and his eyes beamed, but he could not say hello, only grunt and go "mmm" like the Frankenstein monster. During the next several weeks his condition worsened and doctors diagnosed a brain tumor. He had to have surgery and after the operation was admitted to a nursing home for the last few weeks.

Richard would again fly to Europe in October 1977 when he and his grandfather Owen returned to Germany on a Bavarian tour in company with a group of Masons and Shriners. Both a thirty-third degree Mason and a member of the Shrine, Owen had learned about the trip at one of his lodge meetings and determined to make it. He would foot the bill for his grandson, a boy of fifteen, to go along. Richard's parents gave their consent and obtained a permission of absence from school for Richard. Unlike the family's earlier trip where Richard's father had planned everything out and the family traveled on their own, the Masonic tour would be hosted and chaperoned by professionals, and Richard would finally get to see *Neuschwanstein* castle, a place Hugo had wanted to take him on the previous trip but had been unable to at the last minute because Owen lost all the family's travelers' checks and it took a whole weekend to replace them, during which the family remained sidelined at the hotel in Munich. When Hugo received the new checks from the American Express on Monday morning, the family had to keep to their schedule and leave for France. Hugo had also contemplated visiting Saxe-Coburg during the 1974 trip, which Owen badly wanted to do, but had decided on a jaunt to Salzburg to attend a performance or two at the summer opera festival instead. *Neuschwanstein* was on the itinerary of the guided tour. Saxe-Coburg was not. Richard, however, had not been frightened of traveling then. He suggested to his grandfather that they skip the scheduled bus trip to Dachau with Owen's Masonic brothers and on their own take the train from Munich to Coburg instead. Owen had his misgivings about the venture but let his grandson persuade him. Richard had studied German in high school and had just enough knowledge of the language for the pair to manage to get by. Everything went smoothly; the two in their matching caps, scarves, and sweaters switched trains in Nuremberg, and traveled on to the city of Heinrich Mercer's nativity situated at the southern extremity of the Thuringian forest near the East German border—their train after they disembarked went on across the border—where they visited both its ducal palace on a hill above the city, where Martin Luther found refuge in 1530, and the Saint Moritz cathedral, where

Heinrich Mercer was baptized and presented to the lord two hundred and one years later, Owen snapping photograph after photograph on his Kodak camera, going through reels and reels of film. No, Richard had not been frightened of traveling then.

Richard chose Penn State as his university, at least in part, because of its close proximity to Mercersdale, so he could again be near his beloved grandparents Ida and Owen. Keenly aware of their advancing age, he wanted to spend time with these greatly beloved persons, dear to him since childhood—who would always in a way represent childhood to him—while he still had time, so he sought them out when he went to school nearby. The university, of course, opened up a whole brave new world of discovery and experience for him and he did not spend nearly as much time with his grandparents as he originally had intended. At a student writers' group he met Lynn—who in those days, dreaming of herself as the tragic heroine in a story or play by Chekhov, a novel in verse by Pushkin, in immaculate Russian prose by Turgenev, or even in immaculate English by the more recent Vladimir Vladimirovich—still went by her first name Natalia (she would switch to her more prosaic middle name Lynn after beginning her teaching career at DePaul), a graduate student in English and a poet all of twenty-five, bright, energetic and pretty, who had taken off a few years after earning her Bachelor's, living on the family farm near Ephrata with her Mennonite grandmother, knitting and embroidering and leading a very quiet, retired life, her boyfriend at the time, friendly Fred, a sailor in the merchant marines. She of course knew of his father—the famous Hugo Mercer—and she had even got advance word of Richard through reading *Style and Precision,* Hugo's primer on writing, literary investigation, and critical analysis and cogent argumentation for young persons, in which the elder Mercer related how his young son, a precocious reader in his early teens, had come to him with what he thought to be a great literary revelation and flash of insight: namely that Charles Dickens had modeled the appearance of the Ghost of Christmas Present in his celebrated, forever beloved "A Christmas Carol" on that of the seemingly equally mystical, weird and unnatural Green Knight of the Old English early Arthurian poem "Sir Gawain and the Green Knight," which Richard had read in modern English translation, for which bit of chutzpah Richard received some early notoriety, even though his father mercilessly deflated and punched holes in his young son's contention and claim. Indeed the two specters did outwardly slightly resemble each other. Both wore green robes bordered with fur, had bushy or white beards. The two were also giants, the "fay-man knight" who green all over glowed the largest man on middle-earth in measure of height, the Ghost of Christmas Present "a jolly Giant, glorious to see" who bore a glowing torch, in shape not unlike Plenty's horn. The knight holds in one hand—in the other he clasps his axe—a holly bundle that is greatest in greenery when groves are leafless. Scrooge's second-of-three spirits wears on his massive head a holly wreath set here and there with shining icicles. Hugo's son saw this resemblance and assumed that Dickens must have known the medieval poem. A major error and leap of faith on young Richard's part. The diligent scholar would first check all available sources to see if Dickens had ever read or was even familiar with or heard of "Sir Gawain and the Green Knight," before venturing to make such a bold and unsubstantiated assertion. Perhaps at this date the fact could not be established if Dickens knew the earlier work or not. Perhaps the medieval poet and Dickens had merely drawn on the same ancient traditions and

sources of the Yula *Alf*? Hugo warned the young and eager not
to be too precipitate in jumping to conclusions in their youthful
enthusiasm and enjoined upon them the necessity of patient
and thorough scholarship. Lynn liked the fact that Richard
chose Penn State so that he could be near his grandparents.
She too had a very strong bond with her grandmother and
when Fred went to sea and they eventually broke off and ended
their relationship, she found solace living off the land on the
family farm. She had a very earthy, simple, and practical side
to her character and fell in love with salt-of-the-earth type men
who could fix toasters and do, not only the minor, but most of
the major repairs on their automobiles. She took Richard's
virginity and indeed did love him, but right from the very
beginning she sized him up as a beautiful fool—he had worn
only a green corduroy jacket to the writers' group on a very
cold winterish autumn night. While she wrote journals more
voluminous than Anaïs Nin's, an occasional brilliant, well
constructed poem and the most gorgeously descriptive travel
letters, she set her goals on a teaching career and secondarily
on the publication of literary criticism in scholarly journals.
Richard wanted to surpass his father and make him not only
proud but also green with envy. He wanted to write novels in
his own signature style, make his scratch on the face of ano-
nymity. She felt that despite his enormous precocious intelligence he was too young and too emotionally immature for
her and broke things off quickly, but he really, really, loved her
and became almost suicidal when she started seeing the man
she would eventually marry, a fellow graduate student who
studied philosophy but handcrafted furniture and could fix a
toaster. She and Shane continued on to another university, for
a time split up, during which period Natalia still kept in contact

with Richard, and in the summer of 1984, four or five months before her marriage, she paid him a final visit at Cold Mushroom State Park. He had been out of school for about a year living with his grandfather. He regretted that he had treated her rather shabbily in several of his student short stories where he portrayed her as selfish and promiscuous. Nonetheless he remained jealous of her boyfriends, past and present. He himself had been rather promiscuous his final year as an undergrad after she had received her Master's and had gone on to Chapel Hill to pursue her Ph.D. In 1985, Richard was accepted into the Brown MFA program and for nearly a decade after graduating he tried to become a writer but stopped seeing anyone, he still felt so in love with the blonde, blue-eyed Lynn. He did not date for seven years. After receiving his MFA, he rushed back to Pennsylvania just as he had rushed to Owen's arms when he and Lynn first broke up. Hurt he headed straight for his childhood pal and fawfaw with whom in the always happily ending bedtime stories he always made off with all the pirate treasure. He realized that even though he had studied under and won praise from Coover and Hawkes and that he was the son of the well-known Hugo Mercer his MFA was worthless unless he published. Owen thought he could get him a job as a stringer with the Mercersdale *Courier* but never quite managed it. He worked for a year as Assistant Activities Director at the local Lutheran nursing home, the same one his grandfather Cornelius had been admitted to years before, but saw in what a ghastly manner the aged and demented were cared for and could not stomach the work. He vowed that he would never see either of his grandparents end up in such a death factory. His grandfather and parents completely supported him and his father continued to list him as a dependent on his federal income tax seemingly forever. He lived with Owen in the old Mercier row house on Second Street on the second and third floors. Owen let the downstairs apartment to a series of elderly ladies. Richard would rent out both apartments after Owen's death and again and again run into difficulties with his tenants who either damaged and ransacked the place or failed to pay their rent or both. Year after year Richard churned out his literary or "experimental" fiction. For six years he lost all contact with Lynn. She wrote to him in 1995 after telephoning his mother for his address and whereabouts to discover that he again lived with his grandfather as he had been doing when she had last seen him in 1984. He had spent many more years with Owen than she had with Anna. He had remained in Mercersdale for over half a decade without ever finding a job, but he had turned out unpublished novel after unpublished novel, all of which he sent her in one great bundle to her work address at DePaul and all of which she would read and admire. She and Shane had two sons—Sean and Micah. They did not live in Chi but across the border in Wisconsin, where, approaching Kenosha, outside a rural town, they owned a small farm, a white farmhouse and barn, where Shane made handcrafted cabinets, cedar chests and other furniture. He had not pursued a Ph.D. but helped to support Natalia when she went for hers.

Four years prior to Owen Mercier's last illness, the death of Ida Mercer *nee* Sayers, Richard's pugnacious paternal grand-mother, into whose brick two-storied house he would finally move after Owen also passed, came as a sharp blow to Richard and a bit of a surprise even though she was eighty-eight for she had kept her deteriorating health a secret from him as well as virtually everyone else but Owen, whose eagle eye of omniscience detected what others failed to see. Do the old just know? Richard wondered. Do they have some secret sense, a "deathdar" that allows them to perceive and intuit the reaper as he approaches other seniors—their friends and peers—long before younger persons ever see or realize what's being dealt in the cards? Several weeks before Ida's heart failed her, Owen said to Richard, "Something isn't right. Your grandmother isn't at all well." Richard remembered pooh-poohing him, saying, "Ida seems fine to me." For years now he referred to and addressed both his grandparents and parents by their first names. After a month or so of grieving, he resumed his normal life and writing. After composing his grandfather's obituary, Richard would not sit down at a keyboard for nearly seven years, or rather he would spend hours in front of his computer screen, but nothing would come or he was never satisfied with what little did, and he knew the agonies and frustrations of writer's block first-hand.

Although both his grandparents resided in the same small town, Richard's life had not been nearly so interconnected and entwined with Ida's as it was with Owen's. He saw Owen each and every day and spent many hours in his company. In contrast, he visited Ida once or twice a week for a couple of hours. He performed for her on her piano but could not attempt to learn new pieces but only practice and polish up old ones, as her nerves were not up now to hearing him curse or pound the keys in anger and mounting annoyance as he failed to master a difficult passage, shared a weekly meal with her usually bought at the little Corner Store a block from her house, rubbed and massaged her feet as she said her husband Cornelius once had, argued about politics (she was as staunchly conservative as he was liberal) and took her to the movies. She objected to most contemporary films but delighted in seeing old stars such as

Lillian Gish and Bette Davis taking their final turns before the camera. Swan songs such as *The Whales of August* were must-sees for her. Sentimental, old-fashioned pics like *Driving Miss Daisy*, she likewise awarded a thumbs-up, though Richard did not fail to note that almost invariably his grandma, his nana, would nod off sometime during the course of the film and therefore always miss a pivotal fifteen minutes or so of the story. He had a hard time inducing her to go at first to a show at the Garland Theater, one of only two movie houses that she had ever regularly patronized, the other the Majestic, the Garland's competitor, having shut its doors some thirty years before. The two theaters maintained a fierce rivalry during the thirties, forties and fifties. Mercersdale had two competing movie houses just as it had two competing fire companies, Mercy and Spirit, which had engaged in fact in merciless, spirited contest since their organization in the 1880s. The Garland had always been the town's "A" theater. The huge, baroque movie palace had been built in 1916 and both pairs of Richard's grandparents had patronized it from their youths on. The Garland fell on hard times in the early seventies. New owners screened x-rated films there on weekends. Richard remembered seeing the placard for one titled *Milk Jugs* when driving past the theater the day of his grandmother Ina Mercier's death. His parents, his sister, and he had flown into Pittsburgh, where his father had rented the car at the airport. His parents did not tell him his Ina had a heart attack until they had arrived in Mercersdale and pulled over at a gas station. In the restroom his father explained why they had made the unexpected trip. They had not arrived in time for his mother to see and speak with hers. He went to the movies with his grandmother Ida far more often than to the doctor's. During all the years he later lived in Mercersdale, he had accompanied her to medical appointments on only one or two occasions, those few times his granduncle Jim was out of town or otherwise occupied. His grandmother and granduncle were respectively the oldest and youngest siblings in a family of fifteen children and a special bond existed between them. Many years James' senior, Ida had already married Cornelius and begun her own family years before his birth. Both Richard's father Hugo and his aunt Audrey were a full decade older than Jim. Ida's third child, Richard's long-dead Uncle Todd, however, was his uncle's junior by little more than a month. Ida discovered that she was pregnant for the third time a few weeks after learning that her mother was once again with child. Ma's really the most unfortunate woman in the world, Ida remembered saying, as she shook her head upon hearing the news. Although Todd Mercer entered this world within weeks of his uncle Jim, he left it far sooner, dying at the age of twelve as a result of a fall from a tree, a backyard hemlock he had scaled countless times, but, attempting to break the record and better his speed reaching the top, the little monkey had lost his footing. He died from blunt force trauma to the head. His older sister Audrey had been timing him with a stopwatch from below. The attending physician said that had he lived he would have been blind.

Ida had always been closer with her older brothers and sisters, the ones nearest to her in age. Over the years her parents Pop and Mom Sayers kept on having children. It seemed they had three families instead of one. The older, middle, and youngest children formed separate subsets and the children of each group were generally most attached to the brothers and sisters they themselves had grown up with. The fondness and special devotion, which gradually grew between Ida and Jim, developed only after their parents had died, Jim had reached adulthood, and Ida's son and daughter had moved away. It did not date, as Richard initially speculated, from the time of Todd's accident. Indeed visiting her mother and seeing her tending the child of her old age when death had snatched away her own son had deeply disturbed Ida at the time, but with the passage of years Jim would indeed come to look at his eldest sister as a kind of mother figure and she would view him as a sort of surrogate son. She never wanted to bother the faraway Hugo and Audrey with her medical concerns. Nor did she disturb her nearby grandson with them. His grandmother remained practical and realistic. Jim already had a house and Richard would one day need one. She willed him hers. Six months after her death, a year after Lynn had again come into his life, Richard's friend also lost her grandmother Anna, who had just reached the great age of 103. Richard remembered the letter Lynn had written to him then. She had learned of the incredibly long-lived and beloved lady's death while attending a PMLA conference during semester break just before Christmas and on the flight home to Chicago she looked down at the night lights blinking below—the windy city lit up like one big Christmas tree—and thought of her grandmother taking wing to heaven and also looking down at all the Christmas lights. Richard had never gotten the opportunity to meet the august Anna but felt like he knew her from all of Lynn's accounts and descriptions. His grandmother had died on Memorial Day, hers early the following December. Years later, in a poem, he would write about the two on high together looking down and watching over their beloved grandchildren in their time of greatest need and suffering.

But not even his grandmother's Memorial Day passing had hurt him and plunged him into such despair, as would his grandfather Owen's death four years later. The only time he experienced comparable pain and desperation—when he had separated from Lynn in his early twenties. Rejection in love had nearly done him in then. His survival in large part was due to his grandfather Owen. Each had saved the other once, struck down and beaten at the loss of his beloved. He wrote to Lynn back in those days that he was rereading Walt Whitman at a time in his life when the poems from all the many versions of *Leaves of Grass* touched him deeply. He found certain of them especially relevant and meaningful. The song coming out of the mockingbird's throat in "Out of the Cradle Endlessly Rocking" was also his song, for he, too, was separated from his beloved and starved for her love. Alone in his icy isolation, he pined for her and withered, shrank and became diminished in her absence. He found himself alone, profoundly alone. Sick and sorrowful, with his just-sustained note, he announced himself to her. His gentle call was for his missing love. The dusky spot he saw in the distance, how he wished it were she, his missing mate, flying to him. Out there somewhere, did she hear faintly and from afar his sad sweet song?

Richard started drinking in college and never stopped. In the mid-nineties he finally mustered enough courage to begin picking up women in bars, provided that they had a place to go for he certainly couldn't take them home to Second Street. Nothing too serious ever developed, but he had once more started dating—to use the polite word—when Natalia Lynn Lefebvre—she still used her maiden name professionally—again entered his life. Still awfully fond of her, he no longer felt under her spell and power. They could be just friends now. He hoped she was happy in her marriage. She seemed to be and experienced enormous joy on becoming a mother. Whenever she passed through Pennsylvania—once or twice a year visiting her parents or in-laws—she contrived to stop in Mercersdale to see him. She, he, and Owen occasionally shared a meal together. She wrote him letter after letter and post card after post card, eventually confessing that her husband had no patience with or interest in the inner world that constituted such an important part of her and that therefore she would forever reach out to Richard as a friend, as he supplied a magic and fulfilled a large, great lack in her life. He vowed that he would love her in whatever limited manner he could and stand satisfied. An infrequent correspondent, he telephoned her in the office during or just after office hours, and they both grew enamored hearing once again an old, for years unheard, beloved voice. They continued living their separate lives states apart and Richard continued his drunken hunt for two-legged does at the bars and clubs—the game remained elusive; Richard only occasionally scored—took care of his grandparents (or perhaps they took care of him) and continued tilting at windmills or, assuming the overpowering importance of his soul, writing as if the world were well lost for art. Shortly after Ida's death he sold his first story to one of the quarterlies. Not until four years later in 2000 did his agent—the assiduous Rhonda, whose nationally famous radio commentator grandfather from the big city had, coincidence of all coincidences, famously called Mercersdale "little Chicago" in the 1930s after a black barber was shot there by his lover, an older white woman, who would later be acquitted when in her defense she claimed that the barber had never told her he was Negro though the man was coal-seam colored, in an infamous love-triangle murder which received national attention—at last placed his first book *The Dragoon*, a fictional account of the life and times of his Revolutionary progenitor, whom in the novel he named Conrad Semler, having come across the surname in *The Sorrows of Young Werther*, where a pivotal scene occurs in a town called Wahlheim, where a young farm hand murders his rival for the affections of a widow. Werther thoroughly identifies himself with and feels compassion for the criminal, whose predicament so mirrors his own. Werther is, of course, such a sensitive soul! It disturbs him that so few people have any sense or feeling for the precious things of the world and, in the passage where Richard found the name, he mourns and laments the loss of several noble walnut trees in a parsonage yard. The wife of the new pastor demanded that the trees be cut down because they deprived her of sunlight, their falling leaves made her yard damp and dirty, and, when the nuts grew ripe, local ruffians pelted them with stones to knock them down and this disturbed her profound meditations weighing the differing arguments of "Kennicot, Semler and Michaelis." In true *Sturm und Drang* style, Richard's novel opens in Saxe-Coburg with the young Semler enmeshed in a Werther-Lotte-Albert type of situation, the complications of which necessitate his hurried departure from the city of his birth.

The years between Ida's and Owen's deaths were productive and pleasant ones for Richard. Lynn continued to pay him yearly visits. 1997, Mercersdale's bicentennial year, proved particularly memorable. Known far and wide as Mercersdale's foremost, most knowledgeable, historian and biggest town booster, Owen had been chairman of the committee that planned the town's sesquicentennial celebration in 1947. Fifty years later the town named him grand marshal for Mercersdale's bicentennial parade. The organizers said he was everyone's hands-down choice. No one had better credentials or greater love for his little hometown deep in the heart of the Alleghenies than this particular native son. Eyes twinkling, he boasted to the reporter from the Mercersdale *Courier*: "My maternal grandfather was born here in 1820. My dad was born here in 1871. I was born here in 1907. Why, I'm doggone half as old as this town and I'm a descendant of the town founder to boot. This darn place is in my bones." During the week-long celebration the ninety-year-old Owen, who now wore a hearing aid and limped a bit but still remained spry enough to stand and chat for hours, could be seen everywhere telling and retelling all his many stories of days past and the town's old glories, but on the afternoon of the big three-hour parade he took center stage in a horse-drawn carriage with the beautiful Angharad, with her model's good looks now a television personality in L.A. She flew in especially for the event to sit beside and wave to the crowd with her grandfather with his warm smile, pink cheeks and deep-set blue eyes. The two appeared together on the local Action News along with highlights from the magnificent firework display from later that night. Richard would also have his moment of glory but not until the following afternoon when Civil War reenactors staged a third and final skirmish in a farmer's field just out of town, where both a local group, the 48th Pennsylvania volunteers, and their guests, an outfit from Virginia, set up Union and Confederate encampments on opposite sides of the wide mown meadow. No Civil War battle, of course, had ever taken place outside of Mercersdale. Richard had enjoyed watching the two earlier skirmishes. He liked the fact that reenactors made history come alive for the onlookers, but the organizers of the bicentennial made no mention in any of their literature of an important if tragic part of Mercersdale's history, the sad tale of the indigenous Seneca Indians whom the white settlers called the Cornplanters, after the great Seneca chief, the son of an Indian woman and a white father, who led war parties with another Indian called Red Jacket for his allegiance to the British against colonial forces during the American Revolution. Cornplanter, however, signed the Treaty of Fort Stanwix in 1784 and thereafter advocated peace and friendship with the United States for which the government issued him a land grant on the Allegheny River, where he lived to a very great age. For a time the Mercersdale settlers and the Indians managed to live in near proximity to one another and to carry on a thriving trade. The Europeans—including, no doubt, the town's founder, Richard's ancestor good old Henry Mercer—fleeced the poor Seneca blind. The Cornplanters traded moccasins, raccoon, fox, deer and other skins for blankets, shawls, handkerchiefs, beads and other gaudy, worthless trinkets as well as for whiskey, brandy, sherry and cognac. At the time of the 1812 war, the Seneca in the region were again looked upon with suspicion. The government forced most of the tribe, both the converted Christians and the followers of the peaceful prophet Handsome Lake, who influenced by the Quakers nonetheless preached his own moral and religious teaching advocating giving up the traditional Indian ways and taking up agriculture, to depart from their encampments in the Alleghenies to take up residence on guarded reservation land in the state of New York. In 1947, when Owen was planning the week-long sesquicentennial festivities, he wrote to New York and as a good will gesture invited the tribe to participate in the celebration, and over three hundred men and women came and marched in the parade in traditional costume. In 1997, as no one made any mention or acknowledgement of the Native Americans living in the area at the time of the white settlers' arrival, Richard hatched a plot with his fellow barflies to draw everyone's attention to the Seneca tribe's place in Mercersdale history. He and eight other conspirators decided to mount a Cornplanter attack on the Union troops the day of their final skirmish with the Virginia Confederates. From out of the nearby woods they would charge the rear of the Union lines. Each of the tribe claimed Indian descent. None of the participants came from Seneca stock. The one or two drops of Indian blood in Richard were Sioux. On one of her collateral lines, Owen's mother could claim descent from Christian Poole, the famous "durable Dutchman," whose bride had been the Sioux princess White Feather, who took the Christian name Catharine when she wed the man destined to live longer than any other resident of Centre County, Pennsylvania. Due to the fact that he was the grandson of the grand marshal of the bicentennial parade, Richard felt sure that he could get away with the stunt without any serious repercussions. But to insure this, he enlisted the help of his distant relative Dean, a World War Two Navy veteran and a beloved country music disc jockey on Mercersdale's single radio station WMER and also, like Richard, a descendant of Christian Poole. He made Dean Chief and borrowed an old Exalted Order of Red Men deerskin costume and headdress—the Red Men were a fraternal lodge in Mercersdale at the turn of the century—from the town museum for Dean to don during the mock attack. The other tribe members male and female wore no such fancy trappings or fine beaded regalia, but a turkey did make the ultimate sacrifice so that everyone in the tribe could wear tail feathers in their hair, and all the men—even the bushy bearded—bearded to the navel—Dude Merrill shaved. A half an hour before the start of the skirmish, the tribe met at the local Amvets and applied their war paint before proceeding to the woods alongside the farmer's field. A number of Richard's other friends chickened out. The tribe was supposed to have been twenty or thirty strong and had not been limited to only those who had Indian ancestors but the eight brave souls who did follow and go through with Richard's plan all did. The bluebellies had heard rumors all week of an incipient Indian attack but bets went two-to-one against Richard. Either they didn't think he had the stones or that he couldn't possibly pull it off. Nonetheless when the disgruntled Cornplanters angry at being snubbed and not being invited to the big two hundredth anniversary birthday bash came howling out of the trees, all the boys swiveled round and trained their vintage Harper's Ferry muskets not on Chief Cornplanter Dean but on the whitest-skinned redskin—pale, ghostly white—that ever was, Richard himself. As they fired he leaped high in the air and into a somersault, then came crashing down on his backside. The crowd cheered wildly. Verisimilitude would demand that he stay dead, but not so Dude Merrill. He only played dead but after awhile got up and charged—the children on the side-lines screaming "That Indian's not dead"—and blocktackled the mustachioed blond Union corporal, the local State Representative. A Union sergeant scooped up one of the girls kicking and screaming and carried her off for a bride. The bluebellies one by one kept picking off the Cornplanters, but Chief Dean and a mother-daughter pair, the girl an up-and-coming star of the high school track team, managed to dash across the whole length of the meadow past the Confederate entrenchments and into the crowd, where stood their plant, bald, jovial, red-cheeked Rudy, today wearing an Afro-style wig over a bare pate smeared with ketchup. The track star took the scalp as the crowd started spontaneously clapping and screaming, and two Confederate pickets put paid to the three remaining Indians. All the tribe then got up and took a bow and Richard then dashed over to his grandfather, father, mother and sister where they sat in their lawn chairs. The bicentennial would prove the final time that the European travelers, the four Mercers and the one Mercier, all came together in a single group. Richard did not pay for a single beer that night at the Amvets. All the Confederate reenactors sat at the bar. They had been prepared to dutifully lose for the third boring time. Never in their wildest imagination did they expect to see Indians coming out of the damn woods. No, they would never forget Mercersdale. The one picket kept saying, "I'm sure sorry I killed that girlie."

As per plan, Richard completed *The Dragoon* in time for Mercersdale's bicentennial celebration and his grandfather read the manuscript six or seven times, the seventh time just as eagerly and fascinatedly as the first. Richard had written the book for him and now had the thrill and reward of seeing Owen read and enjoy it. The novel made the old man tremendously proud and happy. He positively beamed and constantly conveyed his joy and approbation to Richard. Over the years, while he never took a real job, Richard did a lot of gratis community service, fundraising and public relations work, for his home-town. Shortly after returning there after receiving his MFA, he became affiliated with the Mercersdale Historical Foundation. He applied for numerous government and private grants on behalf of the town's little museum, and a number of his grant applications were successful and received funding. With the assistance of his friend the State Representative, the same fellow Dude Merrell so brutally tackled in the Cornplanter Indian attack, he obtained a state grant from the Pennsylvania

Museum Commission for fifty thousand dollars to catalog and preserve all the artifacts in the Mercersdale collection. Of all the grants he had written thus far, this one brought in the most money and, as Owen said, put the spotlight squarely on him. The same year, he also secured funding so that the Foundation could place metal identification markers on all the graves in Mercersdale's Founder's Churchyard, as many of the old headstones were broken or their inscriptions worn to the point where the names, epitaphs and dates could no longer be read. Yet another grant of his procured the museum a microfilm reader/copier.

The year after the bicentennial, Richard undertook and put into effect his most ambitious scheme yet when he assumed the chairmanship of the Heinrich Mercer House restoration project. At the bicentennial, the Mercersdale Historical Foundation decided to take upon itself the task of preserving for posterity Mercersdale's oldest extant home, a two-story hewn log structure built in 1807, the second of two homes in the town which Mercer raised and resided in and to which, in about 1820, he built a large frame addition. As chairman, Richard participated in numerous brainstorming activities and engaged in strategic planning with restoration architects, historical preservation experts, project donors and volunteers. He prepared numerous press releases for the project, which locally received a great deal of media attention. He also served as the chief grant writer and was responsible for all the project's direct mail solicitation, raising over $130,000.00, mostly from private donors. Finally, he spent many volunteer hours engaged in the very dirty business of "undressing" the one hundred and ninety-one year old structure. During the bicentennial year, a distant cousin of Richard and Henry Mercer descendant

Hildred Russell and her husband Robert purchased the house which over the years saw use as a shoe shop, tavern, night school, and Erie Turnpike stagecoach stop and then after Henry Mercer sold the place for a time served Mercersdale as the town orphanage and poorhouse, and then as the nineteenth century turned into the twentieth and moved onto the twenty-first, housed a bakery and later, for several decades, became the headquarters for the local Salvation Army before finally ending up a three-unit rental property. The house looked shabby and run down when the Russells purchased it in '97 and donated it to the borough, which would continue to own the historic site but which the Mercersdale Historical Foundation would restore and administer. With the exception of the foundation members, few people in town realized the building's significance or, if they did, did not consider it worth saving. Most thought it an eyesore. There were those in town who wanted to tear the whole thing down and make the property into a parking lot, including a couple of geezers on the borough council, who had the last names of Evans and Novak—just like the famous television commentators—but who both shared the first name of Dave. Under Richard's leadership, slowly but surely, the gem beneath the crumbling, gray siding began to emerge. A crew of volunteers removed the siding to expose the weathered clapboards, which someone somewhere down the line—no one knew exactly when— placed over and covered the hand-hewn fifteen-inch-in-diameter squared logs which rested on a foundation of dovetailed, beautifully crafted and fitted river stones hauled to the site from the Cold Mushroom Creek. Richard felt that only professionals who truly knew what they were doing had better tear off the clapboards, so he and the Adventure Tuesdays crew who spent every Tuesday for months upon months working on the house moved inside. While traffic rolled down the street and people strolled the sidewalks outside oblivious to the noise and commotion within, the crew, their noses and mouths covered by safety masks, removed layers of drywall, plaster, and wood. With wrecking bars and claw hammers, they raked the ceilings and unleashed a downpour of laths, horsehair plaster, square-cut nails and furring strips until finally they exposed, amidst clouds of settling dust, the original ceiling beams. They removed six or seven layers of flooring to uncover the original wide but all but worn away floorboards and bashing away at the plaster walls and ripping off all the laths they at last revealed the logs themselves. The fingerprints of those who had last chinked the structure could be clearly seen. Richard's crew photographed and documented each and every stage of the discovery process. They uncovered a near pristine section of hand-cut, side-lapped wooden shakes or shingles where the rear addition met and overlaid what had been the log structure's original roof. One of the experts from Old Bedford Village restoration and preservation group who would later complete and finish the restoration would tell them that shakes that old and intact were rarer than hen's teeth. They also discovered two pairs of shoes—shoes undoubtedly hammered together by Richard's forefather the Versailles shoemaker himself—in what was left of the crumbling chinking between two logs. The same expert from Bedford Village explained that it was a German custom, when completing a new house, to so inter and cover over the newest shoes of the oldest person moving in for the future good luck of his family and descendants.

At last the Adventure Tuesdays volunteers completed all that they themselves felt comfortable doing. Richard would always remember that first wonderful open house at the restoration site-in-progress. People talked, laughed, and shared stories as they drank cider and munched gingerbread in the old tavern room of the log home, where storyboards and picture albums chronicled the just completed discovery phase of the restoration from start to finish. For a final time, Owen shined in all his glory, as he regaled visitors with tales of Mercer family history and how one day a Cornplanter Indian came to the place to have his moccasins hemmed and stitched and how Henry's grandson Eberhard—Hugo Mercer's great-great-great grand-father—high-tailed it upstairs and hid under the bed for fear of being scalped. Owen would not see the project completed. Because of his grandfather's suddenly diagnosed cancer, Richard would step down as chairman after hiring the Bedford Village group. It took a number of months to interview all the prospec-tive candidates for the final bit of work. As Richard's cousin Luanne told him on innumerable occasions, "They only had one shot at doing this thing right." It took time for Richard to find the right people—individuals whom he could fully trust to complete the project on time and without cutting corners. He wanted an accurate and historically correct restoration. Nonetheless the two Daves on council groused and complained that the project was taking forever. The property needed to be brought up to code now. The borough owned the place. The borough, through its code enforcement officers, fined other property owners for not complying to code—how bad it would look if the borough itself did not maintain its own property to set standards. Nails protruded from the exposed logs. Someone might be scratched. The people from the Historical Foundation did not keep their word. You couldn't trust the Mercersdale Historical Foundation. Might it not be better to pull the eyesore down? The town could always use another parking lot. The comments deeply disturbed Richard's dying grandfather. They would rankle and smolder for years in the back of Richard's head. The cancer ate way at Owen, yet he carried on bravely and for a long time he still seemed his old self. Richard, as had been his custom for years, continued taking him for car rides through the nearby state forest and game lands. Once, turning a wide corner, they came up on a doe and two fawns crossing the road, and Owen's face immediately lit up and he smiled a broad smile and to Richard he looked every bit as eager and excited as a very young child. He would later take comfort in this memory, one of the few bright ones of that period. Owen grew progressively weaker and weaker, and Richard's mother Rebecca flew in from the coast. She had always regretted not arriving in Pennsylvania in time to see her mother before her death, so Richard made damn sure she got there now. Angharad also would periodically visit, and all three would tend the failing ninety-three year old. Owen enjoyed playing with Angharad's two frisky Pekingese pugs, with their long silky hair, their diminutive snub noses and short legs. A few days before Owen's death, Richard's friend Dude Merrell, again bushy bearded, caught a huge bass and gave it to Richard to prepare for his grandfather's breakfast—Owen had been asking for fresh fish. That breakfast would constitute for Richard a last golden memory of his time with his grandfather, for Richard's fawfaw had often taken him fishing as a boy and had many times fried him fish for breakfast. Their roles stood reversed now. Owen said that the bass would be much too much for him and that he would certainly have to share it with Richard and Angharad. Of late he had been eating very little. When Richard served the fish to him, however, he found it so tasty and delicious he ate the whole thing—every last bite. His eyes sparkled and he seemed happy and jolly. Once more the two friends shared together a sunny hour. The following week Owen would eat hardly anything at all and would lie convulsing in pain. He did not want to go to the hospital, so Richard and his mother had him attended by hospice nurses. He received shot after shot of morphine the final several days but the injections did seem to ease his distress and the nurses began to administer larger and larger doses. Richard would never forget the expression on the one nurse's face as she looked up at him before giving the last shot. It was a questioning look. Richard nodded not once but twice before she performed the injection. In the weeks and months to follow he came to understand first-hand the grief and guilt of Paul Morel in *Sons and Lovers*.

His mother stayed with him in Mercersdale well after the funeral and helped him with the move to Ida's house. Only after she left did he really begin to grieve for his loss. He could not read much less write and began drinking heavily. He found the holidays especially hard. A little more than a year after his grandfather's death, he drove to State College the morning of September 11th in order to purchase the Bob Dylan album *Love and Theft*, which was officially released and on the store shelves that day. He saw the second plane hit the second tower just as he walked into the National Record Mart. The clerk had on the television over the register. Richard knew that he would never fly again. He had not flown anywhere for years and years. Owen had long been too feeble to travel out of state. Richard saw his parents and sister when they came to Pennsylvania and visited him in Mercersdale.

Aside from them, his only visitor was Lynn. She continued her annual pilgrimages to Richard when she passed through PA. During that dark, unproductive period of Richard's life when he could only write very little or not at all and when he drank and smoked far too much, those said visits were for him oases of sunlight and delight. Indeed she was forever pulling open all the curtains of his deceased grandmother's little brick house to let in the light. When she drove off, the darkness surrounding Richard seemed redoubled.

In 2003, she told him that she and Shane had separated and that she had filed for a divorce. It turned into a protracted, bitter affair. Richard tried to support Lynn as best he could throughout the nearly three-year struggle. She fired off letter after letter to him. He could only ever be bothered to write once in a great while, but he telephoned her at home every Monday and Thursday night, which would become a regular practice for the next seven years. He vividly recalled one of their calls from that time. She told him how pleasant, almost divine, it was to be speaking with him. She seemed to drift into some nebulous place. She was uncertain where she was. If he were here or she were there. Her medicated mind gave her nights of peace and helped her through the confrontations with Shane and all her own mental wrangling. With his every word, but also just as clearly expressed in his silences, her husband showed that he did not intend to be fair to her.

Lynn spent her fiftieth birthday with Richard in the spring of 2005. He presented her with a copy of John Woods' just published translation of Thomas Mann's *Joseph and His Brothers*, one of his all-time favorite books which he had read for the first time—in Helen Lowe-Porter's earlier translation—as an undergraduate at Penn State. During that trip, they spent the morning at their old alma mater and the afternoon at Whipple's Dam State Park, an old haunt of theirs. A tremendous storm had overturned a great number of trees and they found hiking hard going. Somewhere down the muddy trail, Richard at last kissed his love. They would continue to kiss and embrace on all her subsequent trips and visits. Throughout the year, on each and every holiday, she would send bright cards and packages upon packages of brightly wrapped and beribboned gifts. She always remembered him at Christmas and Easter, two of the hardest and most lonely times of the year for Richard Mercer.

In June 2007, at last he met Sean and Micah: at the Mercersdale McDonald's. Lynn had left them there eating that Saturday to pick up Richard at the now completely restored Henry Mercer House, which the historical society kept open every Saturday from Memorial Day to Labor Day from twelve to two, and where that day Richard had been giving tours. A few weeks before this visit, in a Monday or Thursday night telephone conversation, he finally worked up the nerve to ask her if something more than friendship might develop between them. She said perhaps but that he would have to come visit her in Wisconsin. She invited him at Christmas, when her two sons would be out of state with her ex, though they would rejoin her at New Year's.

Ned arrived punctually.

Richard had been looking for him the last two hours. He stepped out on the porch to see Ned pull up to the berm, then slipped back through the screen door, bundled up in his new performance outerwear from Athletech with its outer shell and inner zip-out liner with interior zipper pocket for MP3 player or cell phone and snow skirt with draw cords at the hem for additional wind protection, buttoning it over his green sweater before pulling on his black tossle cap and slipping his hands into his gore-tex gloves. He lifted his luggage out onto the front porch, pulled fast his door and locked it. The bright sun and glaring snow made him wish that he had worn sunglasses. Sunny yet freezing, bitter cold. Cold enough that one saw one's own and everybody else's exhalations.

Yet not so cold as in Wisconsin. Lynn had urged him to purchase and bring snow pants. He had not worn snow pants since he was a white-haired little boy, yet he bought a pair along with all his other new "trip" clothes—he wanted to look his best—at the local Wal-Mart. Lynn had written to him on the second of the month, on what she described as another blustery, cold December night. The previous Friday and Saturday, they had three inches of snow, and then a half-inch of freezing rain. She and Sean still went out to saw down and drag in the Christmas tree on Saturday, but her dog Rusty would not come. The sleet stung Lynn's face the whole time. As she wrote, the tree still lay on the porch. She would bring it in the next day after she finished work, but she had already finished decorating the house for Christmas, watching the snow blow and listening to Christmas music as she did, glad to be in with her new furnace running, a new furnace which she would have to start paying for next month with money tight from the alimony and child support she had to pay as the primary breadwinner. She enjoyed her weekends when she could sleep her fill. She lingered in bed Sunday morning, the day prior to her writing the card. As no one would plough her rural road on the weekends, she would not attend Quaker Meeting in Kenosha. She went nowhere on Saturday either, but hunkered down with her boys in a cold, white world, her wooden farmhouse, except for its green metal roof, also all white, the brown weeds in front poking up out of the snow. Yes, a stark world outside her windows, the dog curled on the south porch. She covered him with blankets and doled out scraps of Thanksgiving food she had saved for him throughout the day. She never glimpsed the sun once when she stepped outside to tend to her copper-colored hound. On Monday, however, she and her boys ventured out even though the roads were still bad. They drove to Kenosha and went to the IMAX to see the matinee showing of *Beowulf* together, a great 3-D film and a provocative feminist reinterpretation of the medieval poem. Afterward they went to an electronic store to shop for Micah's birthday presents—all his goodies came at one time of year—then drove back to their rural refuge. All week, she wrote him, the highs were to be in the twenties. Light snow was also forecast. She promised to work on some new poems. She also, however, had to deal with the furnace man, who had a little more work to do, and to take care of some financial stuff she had been putting off for months. Living on the farm, she always had plenty of home projects to keep her busy, not to mention her work duties at DePaul. She tried to take pleasure in all her tasks—none greater, none smaller—all a part of her liquid life. How she looked forward to his visit in less than three weeks!

Perhaps Wisconsin could serve as a stand in for Labrador, Richard thought. He had finally started working on a new novel—his most ambitious yet—though he had great trouble progressing with it, a multi-generational tale about a Pennsylvania Moravian family, the patriarch Polycarp Schober a musician and missionary from the 1700s, his descendant Wencel Hilderbrandt, a twentieth-century American composer who studied with Pfitzner and Strauss in Germany in the 1920s, but who suddenly lost his capacity to read and compose music after a brain injury in an automobile accident. Hilderbrandt's inability to compose would mirror Richard's own incapacity to write following his grandfather Owen's death. Returning home to the states from Germany, Hilderbrandt would enter a Moravian seminary and for a time become a Moravian minister. In Richard's outline, he would experience a crisis of faith in the 1950s, at which time he would abandon his wife and young daughter and for decades impersonate an old-style Amish farmer, but as the book ended, he would begin composing anew after reencountering his daughter, a troubled child of the turbulent seventies who had dropped out of college to live for a time on a commune, during the early days of the Reagan administration. Part of the novel would be set in Labrador, where Polycarp Schober would seek converts among the Eskimos—or, as he called it, "Strive to gather in for the Lord first fruits." Ned got out of the car to help Richard with the luggage. Within minutes, Richard's suitcase and laptop were in the boot and they were off. They did not proceed directly, however, to the Amtrak station. The train would not depart until late in the afternoon and Richard did not have to report until half an hour before departure. Richard wanted to sleep for as much of the thirteen-hour trip as possible. He also wanted to quiet his nerves. Now. He started downing beers, first at a couple of Mercersdale bars—Ned had soda—and then at the home of a mutual friend of his and Ned's, where Richard wanted to stop to tender his holiday greetings. He continued to feel uneasy and nervous about the trip ahead of him, as he and Ned knocked on Mitch's door and Mitch shortly afterward opened it and ushered them inside. Mitch's brother Barry was back home from school visiting. He and a group of his college friends sat and stood around the kitchen table partying. Richard and Ned joined the circle. A spliff and a bottle got passed. Richard knew none of the younger people. But the college sophomore beside him had not only heard of Richard but also, having seen his book *The Dragoon*, recognized his face from the dust jacket. Or so he said. The young man stood medium height. Scraggly, beardless, and strikingly snub-nosed, he had red-orange hair and milky, freckled skin. Blear-eyed, sneezing and coughing—reddish lashes fringed his reddened, bloodshot eyes—he had a large sore on his upper lip.

At 3:00 pm, Richard nudged Ned and said that they best be going. In forty-five minutes, Ned pulled up in front of the Eleventh Avenue Amtrak station. As Richard still had twenty-five minutes before he had to report, the two took a short but brisk walk, as Richard would soon be seated and seated for a very long while. They reached the old movie palace—the historic Mishler Theater—no more sumptuous and opulent, however, than Mercersdale's own Garland—then turned back and retraced their way to the car, where Ned retrieved Richard's baggage from the boot and helped him carry it into the station. He watched all the stuff while Richard strode up to the ticket office. Richard had booked his seat on the Internet and so had to pick up his tickets at the window. He had to provide the clerk a confirmation number and show him his AAA card—as he received a discount on the ticket price as a Triple-A member—as well as two other forms of ID, one with a recent photograph.

Traveling in the United States was altogether different after 9/11.

Ned said goodbye and that Richard needn't worry. He would pick him up here at 10:30 am on the morning of January 4th. A clerk broadcast over the p.a. that the train would arrive on time. Some twenty minutes later when the same person announced that the *Pennsylvanian* would be boarding in ten minutes, Richard took the stairs to the outdoor platform instead of riding up in the elevator. The liner coach waited on the tracks. Gripping his laptop in one hand and rolling his wheeled suitcase by the extension handle behind him with the other, he walked past several cars until he found one without a long line. A redcap helped him aboard and toting his tagged carry-on luggage, the suitcase now hoisted in the air and held by its regular handle, he mounted the six or seven metal steps into the car and made his way down the aisle until, finding an empty window seat, he stored his bag in the luggage rack above and sat down. After depositing the laptop by his feet, he put his seat with its white paper napkin for the head all the way back and stared out across the four sets of rails—a Conrail freight train, the sides of its maroon cars all covered with graffiti, flew past down the farthest, most distant track—at the brown and white warehouses, the blue sky and the gigantic white moon. The first hours of his trip would be in daylight at least. He would enjoy looking out at the Pennsylvania winter wonderland. His current train Amtrak's *Pennsylvanian Limited* would reach its western terminus—Pittsburgh—at 8:05, where he would have an almost four-hour layover. The train to Chi would not depart until 11:55. For the time being leaving on his tossle cap, he pulled off his gore-tex gloves and took off his coat, which he draped over his knees, then turned his head and looked across the aisle and to his front at his fellow passengers: people of all ages, grandparents and grandchildren, young couples and college students going home on break, military personnel in uniform—home on leave, Richard thought but then heard one GI say to the person sitting beside him that his unit was deploying to Iraq and how his leaving just before Christmas was especially tough on his wife and kids. A large contingent of Amish. Richard noted the features of one elderly yet still burly man with a silver-lined black beard, straw hat and snow-white hair. A possible model for Wencel Hilderbrandt. At last the train lurched and began to roll out. A ticket collector did not appear for about fifteen minutes. Richard was off: crossing to Bethlehem, to see Lynn on her home-turf four states away.

The conductor's voice boomed over the intercom. The train would shortly be rounding the famous Horseshoe Curve. Richard looked out of the window at the snow-covered, glistening Allegheny Mountains with their bare stone outcrops standing on the far side of a large frozen-over water reservoir. The conductor said that the curve bent in a tight arc of approximately 220 degrees and that the workers of the Pennsylvania Railroad or PPR had accomplished an incredible engineering feat when they succeeded laying tracks through this rough terrain in order to avoid blasting through the summit of the Alleghenies, that the curve had been in continuous operation since it was built, and that while it originally had a two-track configuration, the triple-track mainline now saw daily traffic of at least fifty trains including twice each day, one in each direction, Amtrak's *Pennsylvanian*. Because of the curve's immense importance to railroad traffic, Union troops guarded it throughout the Civil War and it was a target of German saboteurs in World War Two. Germany's spymasters named their plan Operation Pastorius. As Richard continued looking out his window, a freight train approached the great curve from the opposite direction and passed round it simultaneously with his. As it worked round the grade and flew past, Richard noted, instead of the traditional caboose, a helper engine at its rear. He enjoyed his front-row seat at this railroader's wonder and thought of how Owen had taken him to see steam shovels and trains as a child and how the two in their matching outfits had traveled by rail in Europe thirty years before—heavens, it did not seem that long—in 1977. Richard continued to enjoy the sun-drenched Pennsylvania winterscapes as the coach chugged westward until at last the sun set. Then he enjoyed looking at the Christmas lights and street decorations of all the little towns through which the *Pennsylvanian* passed. From the interior zipper pocket of the zip-out liner of his new Athletech coat, he fished out his new toy, his recently purchased Tracfone, and proceeded to call first his mother in San Fran to tell her that he had made his train and was underway, then Lynn to relay the same message—he left a message on her answering machine—and finally several of his friends in Mercersdale whom he had not seen before departing in order to tend holiday greetings and best wishes. Before arriving at Penn Station in Pittsburgh, the coach stopped for passengers to detrain and for other passengers to board at Johnstown, Latrobe, and Greensburg. It arrived in the Steel City a little late and Richard who passed through the station as a graduate student on his trips back and forth to Brown once more saw the familiar grayish brown terra-cotta structure with office tower behind, at Grant Street and Liberty Avenue. Flying in from Providence to Pittsburgh, he would have had to have waited almost a whole day to catch the next commuter flight to State College (in the early 1980s United had moved these flights to the new airport there from the older facility at Cold Mushroom Mountain). So instead he hopped a shuttle to the Port Authority bus terminal a block away from Penn Station and carried his bags up the hill to catch the eastbound, *Broadway Limited,* an Amtrak passenger service since discontinued. Since 2005, for the first time in its railway history, only two daily passenger trains, the *Pennsylvanian* and the *Capitol Limited,* served the city. The first thing Richard noticed after taking the elevator down to the

Amtrak waiting area below was that coin-operated lockers no longer lined the station walls. Passengers now had to sit with their luggage during layovers or else check it at the service window. No one would be planting any bombs and skipping out of the building. He remembered how similar precautions stood in effect in Europe in the 1970s. He recalled seeing wanted posters in the Munich *Bahnhof* for the leaders of the notorious Baader-Meinhof gang and Red Brigade. As he did not wish to check his luggage, he dug into his bag for a book. He had planned to rent a locker and take a stroll downtown and have a couple drinks at one of the many nearby bars. He thought about carrying his luggage across to the Port Authority Terminal and using a locker there but decided against it. He did not want to take a chance on being mugged and someone making off with his laptop, which held all his precious book files. The concourse of Penn Station was also no longer open to the public but transformed for commercial spaces on the ground floor, all the paint now removed from the great central skylight. Throughout the nearly four hours of his layover, he looked up from his book to look at the clock on the wall or at one of the television screens hanging from the ceiling. All were tuned to the same channel with the volume turned down so low that it was only barely audible. He got up several times to feed dollar bills into the vending machines or to take a drink at the water fountain. He watched the bags of the lady sitting beside him so she could use the restroom. Later she would do the same for him. He took note of the many faces of the people sitting and waiting. He recognized the Amish contingent from his car on the earlier train. While the only blacks he had seen on the *Pennsylvanian* had been the redcaps and the ticket punchers, half of the people who now waited in the station were Negroes. At 11:15, the man at the counter announced that the *Capitol Limited*, which Richard would take on to Chicago, shortly would be arriving from Washington. After the train came in, he saw people both coming down the stairs and out from the elevators. Some proceeded out the glass street doors to a row of yellow taxis. Others greeted friends or relatives in the lobby and, after exchanging kisses and hugs, also headed outside to the parking lot. A good third of the people sitting in the waiting room got up to mount the stairs or to ride up to the platform in the elevators before the announcer made the boarding call. Richard overheard a redcap say that the train would not depart at its scheduled time because a hydraulic brake had frozen and maintenance personnel would have to de-ice it with water hoses before the liner could proceed. When the call to board came, Richard followed behind the group of Amish men and women whom he had traveled with on the earlier train up the flight of stairs and into the chilly night air. The *Pennsylvanian* remained on the adjacent track. Porters for the *Capitol* directed the passengers to different cars, depending on their destinations and if they had booked sleepers or were riding reserved coach. Everyone had to flash their tickets and a picture I.D. before boarding. A much longer and larger train than the *Pennsylvanian* with upper and lower levels to each of its cars, the *Capitol Limited* had also seen many more years of use and service. The passengers traveling to Chicago had to walk the furthest. Richard passed both the closed dining and lounge cars and the glass-topped dome car before at last boarding one of the rearmost coaches. Although he could stow his suitcase below in a special luggage area at the foot of the steps, he chose to take his carry-on bag and not just his laptop up the long staircase with him. Most of the seats were occupied and some of those already on board had their laptops plugged into the electric outlets underneath the wide rectilinear windows. He again slid in by a window, at the rear of the car. An elderly woman sat down in the aisle seat next to him. Had he been traveling at another time of year, the seat beside him would probably have been unoccupied and he could have sprawled across it as well as his own during the night so as to better sleep, but not at Christmas. The woman turned on one of the two pushbutton lights above their seats. Once all the travelers had boarded, but before the repair crew finished with the brake, a conductor moved the empty *Pennsylvanian* out of the terminal. Looking out his window, it seemed to Richard as if his own train was moving as the other liner rolled past. Ten minutes later the empty train backed into the terminal again but on another track three or four tracks down. Shortly thereafter the *Capitol* lurched forward, preparatory to moving out, and in a few more minutes they were underway. Richard looked out at the skyscrapers and the barges cruising down the river and at the belching smokestacks of the factories. Again, as had been the case on the *Pennsylvanian*, some time passed before the ticket puncher came through the door and slowly made his way down through the car. A woman employee followed on his heels and passed out a blanket and a pillow to each of the new arrivals. Unlike the stuffy and quite warm compartment on the *Pennsylvanian*, the older *Capitol Limited* passenger car seemed drafty and cold. The couple and two young children sitting in the four seats directly in front of him spoke French. Had the lounge car been still open, Richard would have probably slammed a few more drinks in order to put himself out for the long trip ahead. He would sleep hardly at all during the night as his train crossed through Ohio, Indiana, and Illinois and made numerous stops at the different cities and towns on the way to Chi.

The draft running through the car seemed to drive a nail through Richard's temple. Shut up in the moving metal shell, Richard closed his eyes only to jolt awake again after a short interval, pins and needles in his legs. He looked out the window at the snowy world outside and watched the trees, hills, and towns pass in soft yet perfectly defined focus. The car wobbled continually from side to side. When the train passed through Cleveland, Elyria, Sandusky and Toledo, Richard looked out at the floodlit buildings. He saw a great deal of urban sprawl, endless malls and fast food restaurants. Such a big country. So many people. Passengers detrained and boarded at all the stops. As he watched them, Richard dreamed of Lynn. Soon he would cross over into her world. He saw her smiling face before him and felt as if he clutched her hand within his own. He slept until the train arrived at the Elkhart, Indiana station. He recalled that the Public Library in Elkhart was one of the four hundred and fifty libraries across the country to purchase *The Dragoon*. He learned this from www.worldcatlibraries.org. Dawn finally broke. The sun would shine on the final leg of his trip just as it had on the first. Richard didn't go to the dining car for breakfast. As the train rolled through the flat, snow-covered Illinois countryside, Richard saw gigantic red silos, grain mills and elevators dotting the terrain for mile after mile after mile. At last they arrived in South Bend, the final stop before the *Capitol's* terminus.

It seemed to take forever for the train to reach Union Station in Chicago. On Chicago's outskirts he saw line after line of freight cars parked on adjacent tracks, switches and spurs, their sides all covered with gangland insignias, Arabic and Persian characters, hearts, flowers and other graffiti, and, in the distance and then up close, he glimpsed Lake Michigan. The train sped past stockyards and steel-fabrication plants. An endless stream of cars zoomed by on the multi-laned expressways and boulevards. Chi appeared to extend out infinitely, a gigantic hive of brick row houses and brownstones, warehouses and meatpacking plants, parked automobiles and chain fences, grocery stores, churches and mosques, basketball courts, food and clothing outlets and fast food restaurants. Everywhere he saw numerous billboards and hoardings. 747 after 747 descended over the metropolitan area, as Richard's train rushed toward the city's heart. The underground approach and storage tracks to Chicago's Union Station ran for about ten city blocks. It was a long walk from the trainshed to the concourse, a double stub end with tracks coming into platform from both the north and south. Richard proceeded down the middle of the station past the numerous vendors, information desks, and newsstands. He took the escalator up to the Canal Street exit. Magnificent skyscrapers, canyons of great white buildings and brown and tan, antennaed and thousand-windowed towers—gleamed in the sunlight. CTA buses pulled up in front of the Beaux Arts structure, the great train station in front of which he stood. Cabs also waited near the exit. Richard took one, told the driver his destination and rode to the three-level Student Center at the Lincoln Park Campus of DePaul, where the College of Liberal Arts & Sciences was located, a ten-dollar fare away, a quick zip up the Lincoln expressway. As Acting Head of the English Department, Lynn was attending administrative meetings at the Cultural Center. She also had an appointment with the committee determining on whom to next bestow the semi-annual Oeuvre Prize, which the department awarded usually well-known writers, recognizing significant contribu-tions to belles-lettres. She would meet him at the Arby's next to student services at noon. After locating the restaurant, as he still had several hours to kill, he entered the cyber café to check his e-mail on his laptop and to otherwise waste time surfing on the Internet. Tired and sneezing, he logged off his computer after about an hour. He wandered up and down the Student Center and eventually found his way into the Saint Louise de Marillac Chapel. He had always heard the Catholic Universities only hired Catholics. Lynn said that such was simply not the case. She, after all, was DePaul's Quaker poster child. Richard snickered. Rather its quota Quaker. He made his way back to the Arby's at fifteen minutes before the hour. Lynn ran a little late. She bent down and kissed him on the mouth where he sat eating, a display of affection that slightly startled him.

Soon they were speeding homeward toward Wisconsin in her red Ford Windstar SUV. Richard immediately caught sight of the **Bring Our Troops Home** bumper sticker as he stored his luggage in the back. He dozed in the front passenger seat. She woke him when they pulled into her driveway before the snowbound white farmhouse. He noticed the numerous wind chimes on the gallery striking and jangling as a blustery current of air continuously roared and saw in front of every window a bird feeder on a tall pole. Fat, bushy-tailed gray squirrels as well as their sleeker, tabescent, more ratlike red cousins climbed the wooden and metal posts to steal the seed. Lynn shouted out at and shooed away two squirrels at the feeder nearest the front door. She commented that on such a chilly white winter day, her copper-colored hound probably still lay buried in his blankets on his bed on the south porch. Richard would dis-cover that his Lynn had no mercy—any stirring of compassion whatsoever—for these arboreal rodents or "the rats with tails," as she called them. Even in the fall when her lawn lay covered with fallen black walnuts they preferred to rob from the birds and chase them from their feeders. Rusty would put paid to them, however, if they did not watch it. Her dear dog tangled with all sorts of wildlife on her twenty acres. As she, Rus, and the neighbor's dog Cassie ran a three-part course on her property on the mown paths that twisted and turned through the sunny fields and the Black Forest-like plantations of pine and hemlock, her rufous hound would forever be flying off to tree a coon, chase a skunk, or scuffle with a porcupine or badger. She did feel pity once for a poor baby possum they came up on eating an apple. Before it could dissemble and feign death, Rusty fell upon and made short work of it, scooping the squealing creature up in his jaws and snapping its neck with a swish of his head. Lynn had seen numerous such bloody kills on her runs. Once Rusty and Cassie had quite literally pulled apart a young raccoon right down the middle, Rusty clenching its skull in his mouth, Cassie its hind legs in hers, and each tugging hard in opposite directions in an attempt to wrest the prey away from the other. During the course of his visit, Richard would see Rusty chomp down a gray squirrel in three great gulps. On a day on which Lynn commuted to Chi and he remained—writing and reading—at her beautiful white country home with its gleaming hardwood floors, through the large curtainless window, through which the sun streamed and he periodically looked to see cardinals, jays, and gold and purple finches alighting at the feeder, he espied a squirrel staging an attack on the birdseed, so, imitating Lynn, he tapped on the pane loudly and repeatedly with his bare knuckles. Hearing him do so from his station on the porch, Rusty leaped into the snow and came bounding round the house. The squirrel likewise dove off its perch on the feeder and shot up a high oak and out onto the very end of a limb bent down by heavy snow. At the foot of the tree, Rusty bayed so persistently and piteously up at the quivering squirrel, it lost its footing in the wet and dropped to the ground, then made a mad dash for the nearby treeline, its speed no match for that of the fleet copper-colored dog who instantly pounced upon it and crunched and gobbled it down.

Dead tired, Richard stomped the snow from his boots and followed Lynn into the entryway. As they approached the porch and the bright red door with its great beribboned green wreath, Lynn said to him that he should think of the farmhouse as his own, her home his. They both kicked off their footwear, and Richard dug in his bag for a pair of slippers. Lynn had tennis shoes waiting for her on the throw rug beside the closet. On the broad shelf or ledge-like sill of the great picture window looking out at a bit of white, ice-hardened front lawn and the detached garage into which Lynn had backed the Windstar, sat numerous plants and gourds as well as seashells, Southwestern Native American pottery and sculpture, starfish, candles and an assortment of Christmas decorations and sprig upon sprig of red-berried holly. Christmas cutouts had also been taped to the glass itself. Richard would soon discover that red-nosed reindeer, jolly Santas, elf helpers clad in green, Frosty-snowmen, crèche figurines of wise men and shepherds and green-potted scarlet poinsettias sat upon every table, desk, and light stand, and Christmas cards lined the many bookshelves and the fireplace mantelpiece on which hung four stockings. The entryway led directly into the copious kitchen. Beside a bulletin board hung a framed lithograph of the stone Heinz Hulbert House in Ephrata. Built by one of Lynn's forebears, it antedated the Heinrich Mercer House in Mercersdale by more than one hundred years. Mistletoe dangled from the ceiling and on one of the countertops sat three Charles' Chips potato chip tins with their dark brown lids. Lynn had brought these antique metal containers with her from Pennsylvania. Richard had seen tins just like them at the homes of both his grandparents in the early 1970s. Lynn led him through the living room and past the huge as yet only sparsely decorated Christmas tree. Plants peeped out from every corner and hung in all the curtainless sun-flooded windows with views of decks and bird feeders outside. Along with framed art prints and pinned puppets, several of her own canvasses—paintings Richard recognized as hanging on her apartment walls in their long-ago college days—graced the bright walls, with their Gauguin-like colors with interpenetrations of light and dark, calculated geometric designs, and purposely flattened two-dimensional forms. She led him to the guest bedroom through a small study or den. Two PCs with large flat-screen monitors—her sons'—sat side by side on a common desk. Framed photographs of Sean and Micah at different ages adorned the walls of all the rooms she had led him through. Christmas cards, like little tents, and yuletide figurines stood atop all the bureaus and dressers in his bedroom. The walls were decorated with bits of embroidery and needlework Lynn had stitched her name to in junior high school. One featured fourteen or fifteen species of bird.

She told Richard she would see him when he awoke and that he needed to make up for not sleeping a wink on his long train trip. After she kissed him on the cheek and pulled shut the door, he opened his suitcase on his bed, found his pajamas, changed into them, crawled under the warm, snug woolen covers and the newly laundered sheets, and in no time at all lost consciousness and snored loudly. He slept for fourteen hours and arose with a phlegmy cold. The entire first week of his trip, he rummaged in Lynn's medicine cabinets for decongestants and pain relievers. He used up her supply and had to replenish it for her. She kept her home well stocked and provisioned for the cold, unfriendly winter months. One of his first nights when his cold still prostrated him and the weather outside turned frigid dropping to fifteen below and nine inches of new snow fell, he slept only fitfully, awaking repeatedly to the weird sometimes frenzied tinkling of the chimes as the wind again and again whipped up. Once he heard Rusty howl mournfully twice. He huddled under the covers warm, safe, but sick. He needed a few hours of complete rest. No doubt his sickness caused his dreams. Earlier that day he had purchased a Scandinavian troll in a little souvenir shop in a nearby town as a joke gift for Ned. When he last awoke he saw two bright red dots—its eyes—across the room on the dresser. Outside the chimes jingled and pinged. Richard was sweating under his blankets. Coupled with everything else, he was experiencing a slight disorder of the stomach, no doubt brought on by his sampling variety after variety of rich mustard at a shop in the same town he purchased the little carved troll with its fringe of black hair. Though it seemed he would never fall back to sleep, eventually blackness supervened. An almost narcotic sleep clutched Richard in its talons and held him down. He saw the face of the night visitant and Christmas ghost, an ancient crone and ghastly witch with fanglike teeth and slanted slits for eyes. Her frost-stiffened hair and cerements were both snow white. She wanted him gone from her bed, which he profaned with his hated presence. Richard screamed and did not know where he was when he awoke in the strange room. As he sat up sneezing and hyperventilating and again heard the spectral bell-like chimes, his memory came flooding back. He recalled that Lynn said that she had only recently purchased the bed in his room at a Wisconsin antique store. The next morning he matter-of-factly informed her she had a ghost, and she replied that it did not surprise her, as the white farmhouse dated back to the 1850s. In the 1950s a photograph of it had appeared on a Christmas calendar. He said that he felt the crone had come in with the bed. Fortunately she did not reappear to haunt him. She manifested only the one time.

The close-to-two weeks Richard would spend with Lynn would prove if not the happiest time in his whole life at least his most blissful and exultant in years. He had not had such a memorable Christmas since early childhood when he, his parents and sister flew to Pennsylvania from their home in California to see Owen, Ina, Ida and Cornelius in the friendly, prosperous Mercersdale of long ago.

With the persistent three-decade downturn of the local economy, the little town had declined into little more than a retirement community and ghost town. Business after business had folded. Office space on Front Street lay vacant and for rent. The hospital had gone into bankruptcy and shut its doors several years after Owen's death and patients now had to drive to Tyrone, Altoona, or State College, each at least twenty-five miles distant. Only one of three grocery stores remained open and in business. Folk most assuredly locked their doors at night. Young people strung out on pills, without jobs and roaming the streets late, overdosed all the time. Opiates were all the rage in the rural areas as well as the cities. Older residents of the region, who had trouble paying for food and their prescriptions both, fought against the opening of Methadone clinics and halfway houses in their cluster of communities. The police logs reported robberies and break-ins all the time. Every year people lost homes, as they were unable to pay their taxes. All the little towns had to disband their local police forces, as they could not afford the high costs, and had to ban swimming in the local reservoirs and dams because of the liability risks. The lakes of the State Parks no longer had lifeguards. One swam at one's own risk.

During their vacation together, Richard and Lynn talked shop and debated the merits of novelists and poets, and Richard read to her every night—Tennyson and *A Child's Christmas in Wales* and Truman Capote's short story *A Christmas Memory*. Richard had purchased the lavish format stand-alone edition of the Capote work as a Christmas present one of their years together at Penn State and she claimed that she had reread it every year since, as she pulled the treasured little volume from her bookcase and with a great gleaming smile handed him his ancient gift, asking him to read the story to her again. Richard remembered buying the book and dramatically interpreting and intoning it to her many years before, but had long forgotten the tale, yet, as he read and the story again unfolded, it seemed all vaguely familiar. Seven-year-old Buddy and his best friend, an unnamed elderly but childlike female cousin who exhibits the first signs of dementia perhaps but who also had never been quite right or normal her entire life, live with their guardian relatives and their dog Queenie in rural Alabama. The two together pinch their pennies for Christmas when they collect pecans and all the other ingredients including whiskey, for which they take a trip to see bootlegger Haha Jones, in order to mass produce fruitcake after fruitcake for four consecutive days. They send the cakes to people with whom they have only had the briefest acquaintance and to public figures such as FDR whom they'll never meet. After all the baking, the two polish off the bottle and become tipsy to the chagrin of their prim, churchgoing guardians. The following day the old woman and man-child trudge for the Christmas tree at the eccentric cousin's favorite select spot a far piece from home and manage to drag it back. For the several days leading up to Christmas, they make homemade presents for each other, the dog, and their easily mortified, faultfinding relatives. Like they do every year, the cousins make each other kites, though they keep their presents to each other a big secret. On Christmas morn, Queenie receives a bone, Buddy old cast-offs and hand-me-downs and a subscription to a religious magazine. The eccentric cousin shares her Satsuma oranges with Buddy and receives some pretty hand-knit scarves. But the two then exchange their kites and go off to their heavenly hidden grove to fly them and joy in each other's company the while. This will be their last Christmas together, for the next year Buddy will attend military school and his ailing cousin will forget who he is as her dementia worsens in the months prior to her death. Far away, Buddy senses her passing. When it happens, he knows it: "A message saying so merely confirms a piece of news some secret vein had already received, severing me from an irreplaceable part of myself, letting it loose like a kite string. That is why, walking across a school campus on this particular December morning, I keep searching the sky. As if I expected to see, rather like hearts, a lost pair of kites hurrying toward heaven."

On the long cold, dark nights as the snow fell continuously and the wind blustered and howled and the chimes outside rang eerily and hauntingly they also watched a number of foreign films on DVD, which Richard had brought with him from Pennsylvania. They both loved cinematic adaptations of the great books and had attended scores of such films at the Kern Graduate Building at Penn State in the early 1980s. Together they put together an elaborate three-dimensional Moravian star to hang from the ceiling of the computer room and decorated the great tree with tinsel, electric lights, metal beads, strings of fresh popcorn and with Anna's precious antique glass curios. But they made several dozen of their own wooden ornaments as well. They painted the little snowmen white and penned in black eyes and triangular orange carrot-like noses and cut them red and green felt coats and hats which they glued to their heads and trunks. They tied scarves and little bells round their throats and made them teensy-weensy hands out of tiny bits of pinecone. Richard learned each room of the house upstairs—including Lynn's bedroom with its lace curtains and two hundred-year-old family baby cradle sitting on rockers at the foot of her mahogany four poster—downstairs, and in the basement, where on an end table in the rec room he found—purposely laid out for him to see no doubt—several copies of the first issue of *Kalliope* as well as a large silver-framed black-and-white of Natalia as a little girl astride a stick pony, wearing a cowboy hat, a silver cap gun in each of her hands.

In this same room, Lynn would work out on a mini-tramp to Bruce Springsteen's "Born in the USA", "The Lovers' Waltz" for solo violin and piano, Ottmar Liebert's "Poets & Angels", Andrew Botticelli and Sarah Brightman histrionically and in grand operatic fashion belting out their duet "Time to say goodbye", Bix Beiderbecke and his orchestra changing up the pace with Rogers and Hart's "Thou Swell", and finally Billie Holiday soulfully and exuberantly confessing how stars fell on

Alabama. Richard sat, stared, and slavered as Lynn exercised to the music. But after a time he got up from his seat and explored the nearby fruit and wine cellars. A small chalkboard hung by the new furnace on which he saw drawn seventeen cartoon mice heads with Xs for eyes and tongues dangling out. Multiple mousetraps lay on the concrete floors of the wine and fruit cellars.

Lynn made him the most sumptuous and exotic of meals—he particularly loved her nutmeg flavored squash soup—and had baked and exchanged with her friends countless cookies. Her freezer and fridge were stacked with tin after tin of goodies, which she told Richard he could raid as much as he wanted. Richard would not let her be his maid but helped out in the kitchen and thought how he and his grandfather had always shared such duties. One washed while the other dried. Lynn wanted him to go cross-country skiing with her and had borrowed boots, skis and poles for him from a male friend. She had forgotten about his bad foot eversion, which had caused him to always fall behind her when they jogged together at the edge of the Penn State golf course years before. Choosing not to tempt fate, Richard declined the loan of the skis. Nonetheless he followed her out in the snow in his regular boots, wearing double socks on his feet and his baggy snow pants over jeans and long underwear. As the sky turned an unbelievable pink streaked with red but gave no heat, he and her hound, coppery as the sky, followed her as she swished down the paths between the evergreens in her red beret and long black coat, leaving their prints—the dog's four paws and his Charlie Chaplin feet—alongside her two parallel ski tracks, the hound baying and hallooing joyously. He selected the right book for her, wrapped and hidden amongst the sweaters still in his suitcase: Virginia

Woolf's *Flush*. Rusty probably would have eaten Elizabeth's cocker spaniel even though their coats so resembled each other in their color. Unlike Flush who at least initially felt nothing but intense dislike for Mr. Browning, Rusty did not set his teeth on edge when Richard approached him. Rather he lifted his head up to the outstretched hand.

On several occasions, the couple drove into the fourth-largest city in Wisconsin, the nearby Kenosha, bound to its east by Lake Michigan. The first trip Lynn slipped into professor mode. She informed Richard that Paleo Indians had made their homes in the greater Kenosha area for over 13,500 years. Pre-Clovis culture settlements dating from the time of the Wisconsin glaciation were discovered, she believed, in the 1970s. The Potawatomi named the area *gnozhé* or "the place of the pike." The Ojibwa Indians, on the other hand, called the region "where the trout all come at the same time." Spawning fish entered all the many rivers from Lake Michigan. Between 1902 and 1988 when the AMC Lakefront plant shut down all its operations, Kenosha turned out AMC trucks and automobiles by the hundreds of thousands. Richard reflected that Owen's beloved green Rambler had probably been manufactured in the city. Lynn drove him to Harborpark on the lakefront. In the summers, she participated as a crewperson on a sailboat racing team. Afterwards they stopped at a favorite bar of Lynn's, The Scarlet Tanager, and checked their coats. A salsa band played and couples danced together in provocative fashion. Lynn had a glass of red wine and Richard a ginger brandy for his cold. At their table, Lynn proposed a writing exercise. She took two pens and two small notepads from her purse. They would each describe the scene before them. Lynn wrote with ease and accurately and minutely described a number of the dancing couples. Her output surpassed Richard's by a wide margin, though he managed to churn out a few perfunctory sentences concerning the crimson strobe light which cast round little rubies and cherries on the walls and dance floor so Richard felt like a starship captain piloting his vessel through a galaxy of only red giants, a galaxy of Betelgeuses. On the two Sundays he spent visiting, they drove into Kenosha to attend Quaker Meeting and eat out. As they sat through the period of silent reflection and meditation, Richard felt so thankful in his heart for the wonderful happenings in his recent life and for his reunion with Lynn, he prayed in earnest for the first time in many years and asked that good things befall his enemies in Mercersdale, the two Daves and the tenants who abused his trust as landlord and not only cheated him of money but who purposely trashed and maliciously damaged his two units on Second Street. One weekday, they visited the Dinosaur Discovery Museum, the Civil War Museum, and the Kenosha History Center and took a walk in one of the city's recreational parks. Lynn also drove him through the campuses of The University of Wisconsin-Parkside, Carthage College, and Gateway Technical College. She told him, rather pointedly he thought: "You know Richard, if you decide to come out here, you must come for yourself. You can't expect me to support you while you just write." That night, the two held each other man to woman, woman to man for the first time in twenty-five years. Unbelievably their love had reached the quarter of a century mark. Richard felt renewed and undiminished.

During Richard's stay, the couple took two longer road trips in the red SUV, the first to Galena, Illinois, a popular weekend destination for Illinoisans, Iowans, and Wisconsinites. On the way, they stopped at several antique stores while still in Wisconsin, including one in Cuba City where Richard purchased Lynn an antique pin of a peacock with an Argus-eyed spread tail. The clerk wrapped it hurriedly for him and on the sly while Lynn browsed elsewhere in the shop.

Lynn loved Galena's Main Street with its quaint brick buildings and mom-and-pop stores. She wanted to do some after-Christmas shopping but knew that Richard would enjoy the city's many historical associations. Galena got its name from the mineral, the natural form of lead sulfide. Native Americans dug the ore first and used it to make body paint. French trappers were the first Europeans to reach the place. They too began excavating lead. The big boom came in 1816 after retired colonel George Davenport succeeded in shipping the first boatload of ore down the Fever River to the Mississippi. Galena quickly became the most important port north of St. Louis. During the course of its incredible history a great number of famous people had walked Galena's streets including Dolly Madison, Martin Van Buren, the Mormon prophet Joseph Smith, General Tom Thumb, Jefferson Davies, the "Swedish Nightingale" Jenny Lind and William Jennings Bryan. Lynn told Richard that he would not be the first important literary figure to pay a visit. In the 1840s, Herman Melville often called on his uncle, a prominent Galenian who helped found the town's Chamber of Commerce. Mark Twain had also passed through and stayed at the famous DeSota House, a Galena landmark and Illinois' oldest operating hotel which served as presidential campaign headquarters in 1868 for Ulysses S. Grant, who had lived in the town and worked in his father and brother's leather shop in 1860 and 1861. He returned a conquering hero in 1865 and the town presented him a furnished house in which he resided until he assumed the presidency. Grant's home appeared much the same today as it did in the 1860s. Aside from Grant, eight other Civil War generals called Galena home. Lynn planned on their visiting both the DeSota and the red brick Georgian residence of the vanquisher of Lee. First, however, they window-shopped. They spent the early afternoon frittering away time at the many specialty stores. At last they entered the historic DeSoto a little before three and picked up the brochure for the self-guided walking tour. In the lobby they admired the graceful, curved staircase, the high tin ceilings and patterned carpets. They stopped at all the display exhibits to see the artifacts and stood in front of the framed woodcuts and photographs that hung in the hallway above the central courtyard. The hotel had in its time hosted many prominent guests. As a candidate for presidential elector, Abraham Lincoln had addressed a crowd from the balcony overlooking Main Street in 1856. Steven Douglas had taken rooms in the DeSoto two years later to prepare for his famous debate with honest Abe in Freeport. The hotel had a separate ladies' entrance. A special staircase led to the ladies' parlors on the second floor. At one of the hallway displays, Richard learned that in the 1880s the once five-story hotel had downsized. Workers raised the hotel roof on jacks, removed the two upper brick stories and then lowered the roof over the third floor. He and Lynn proceeded into the Quiet Room, a lounge with comfortable plush seats and sofas where videos detailing the DeSoto's rich past played continuously on several televisions. Richard did not pay attention to the tapes but instead stared at Lynn. She smiled, and they sat contemplating each other, green-gray eye looking into blue, for at least a quarter of an hour. Then they had an early supper at Vinny Vanucchi's, a favorite Galena restaurant of Lynn's, perched halfway up a cobblestone street. As they waited for their meals, Lynn asked him to do some more automatic writing. She gave him pen and paper and told him to describe the dining room. Richard groaned but complied. He would later tuck the paragraph into his suitcase to store with all his other hesitant, fumbled beginnings. He had a whole collection of such false starts:

> As I sit in an Italian ristorante in the nineteenth-century town of Galena, my eyes are drawn to the old elaborately framed portraits (photographs) on the wall of those long dead. I reflect on the short duration of all our stays on this plane of existence. This is not a new subject of meditation for me. In fact, earlier in the day in Cuba City, the subject was very much on my mind as I leafed through old photographs and daguerreotypes from the 1850s. I remarked to the elderly clerk how sad it was that no one had written the names of the persons on the backs, that the identities of the individuals had been lost, that the countenances have become anonymous. In Mercersdale, we have a whole cabinet of such faces. Many years ago, Owen put up a sign, "Do you know any of these people?" On the backs of all his personal photographs and of many of the pictures on display in the museum, he would write down the name of each family member or face he recognized. He had a mission. He didn't want people to be lost to time. He did not like the fact that we all fade and blur and become forgotten. It is a challenge to look into the anonymous faces staring down at Lynn and me from the walls of this restaurant. I try to imagine the lives of these dear people so like us, who lived, loved, etc. Of course, I'll get the details all wrong, but perhaps knowing ourselves, we also in some wise know them. If we can see ourselves in them, can imagine our face superimposed over theirs, a double exposure, a palimpsest....

Richard broke off in mid-sentence, signed his name and wrote down the date: 12/26/2007. After eating, the two returned to the parked car and drove to the Grant House. As they arrived, the elderly female volunteer dressed in period garb was concluding the final tour of the day. She told them to come back tomorrow.

Richard wanted to see the Mississippi, so Lynn decided to take him to McGregor, Iowa. She had written him from the Riverview Restaurant there after one of the great Midwestern floods of the 1990s on a day she played hooky from work as her own basement had flooded and she had had a horrible mess on her hands. Did he remember? She had always found river towns intriguing places. At the time she was recalling, a dike had broken just south of McGregor and the town had flooded as a result. When she arrived, clean-up crews were scraping the river mud from the streets. The coffee she drank tasted suspect. It had the oddest muddy flavor. Looking out the great window, she looked at the sandbagged buildings and the tree-covered islands; the flowing muddy water had risen as high as the trees' lowermost branches. The town of Prairie du Chien sat opposite McGregor on the Wisconsin side of the river. A ferry went back and forth from town to town during the spring, summer, and fall. Nearby attractions included a riverboat casino and Effigy Mounds National Monument.

As they trekked westward across the snowbound countryside of southern Wisconsin, Lynn only had one hand on the wheel. She clutched Richard's hand with the other as they listened to Mozart on the CD-player. He delightedly stared at her profile. She wore sunglasses as it was a brilliantly sunlit winter day but so bitter cold one believed oneself inside an icebox. One's skin could freeze; one was easily frostbitten. They pulled into the village of New Glarus for lunch. Lynn had a lot of favorite hideaways in the state but none could have appealed more to Richard than this little town of Swiss-style chalets, all with red flower boxes at the windows. Lynn told him that in the spring and summer red geraniums bloomed in all of them. Richard thought for a moment he was in Europe as they drove by the little restaurants, meat and cheese markets, bakeries, art stores, fashion boutiques and Swiss-style souvenir shops. Lynn related that the original settlers who together arrived at the land office in Mineral Point in 1845 all came from the canton of Glarus in Switzerland where continuous crop failures had caused food shortages and plunged much of the population into penury. Before they built homes here, only Indians had roamed through these two miles of fertile basin along the Little Sugar River bounded by rolling hills and pine forests that reminded the new homesteaders of their native Switzerland. They ate at a little German *Stube* where Lynn had only a Rueben sandwich but Richard dined on *Wienerschnitzel, Spätzle* or "small sparrows," kernel-sized fried dumplings made with eggs, flour, and salt, and *Röschti*, a great pancake of grated potatoes, onions, Swiss cheese and fresh herbs. Everything tasted wonderfully authentic and the white-haired man at the next table saw the delight in Richard's eyes and said, "You must be in heaven sitting here eating this good food alongside your pretty wife." Lynn did not correct the stranger, and later in the day commented several times about the friendly old man who took her for Mrs. Mercer. Of course, Richard sampled one of the local brews. He chose the wheat Spotted Cow. It too tasted like a true German *hefeweizen*. Lynn told him that in 1993 Deborah Carey founded the New Glarus Brewing Company, which she had pointed to as they drove past it, as she also did to the great outsize statue of a brindled cow. Deborah was the first woman in the United States to operate a working brewery. After visiting several gift shops with their imported cuckoo clocks, cowbells, beer steins, and handpainted Russian and Polish stoneware and purchasing a freshly baked loaf of pumpernickel and a hunk of leek-and-dill cheddar at a little *Konditorei*, they drove on through Dodgeville to Mineral Point in Iowa County, Wisconsin. Originally a lead-and-zinc mining center—in 1827 large amounts of galena were discovered near the settlement in shallow deposits; by the 1840s these easily accessible veins had run dry and an influx of Cornish miners came to Mineral Point, long experienced in digging deeper into the earth, who all erected houses and cottages of the same identical local stone—the town was now home to a number of galleries, artists' studios and specialty shops. The two visited several as they walked down High Street. The Five and Ten reminded Richard of many similar stores he had seen in rural Pennsylvania. Richard read the historical marker at the intersection of High and Vine: "In 1836, Col. Henry Dodge, here in Mineral Point, took the oath of office to become the first Governor of the newly created Territory of Wisconsin." They passed the Pendarvis Historic Site where the stone dwellings—stone like the Heinz Hulbert House and not log like the Mercer Tavern—of some of the early Cornish immigrants had been restored to their original appearance. These were all closed for the winter. Traveling north on Commerce Street, they saw to their left another historic marker. Despite the bitter cold—Richard's cheeks had turned red and he had tears in his eyes from the cold; frigid Wisconsin could certainly stand in for frigid Labrador—Richard stopped to read it: "In June 1832, an alarm spread throughout the mining region that Black Hawk and his band were on the march north from

Illinois. Hastily built stockades were erected throughout the lead region. Fort Jackson was built on this site using vertically placed logs arranged in a square that enclosed cabins housing the garrison and their families. Two-story blockhouses fitted with gun ports were installed on the southeast and northwest corners." Grateful to return at last to the heated SUV, Richard only half listened as Lynn spoke about how she used to drive here during her divorce. He had a bad habit of finishing other people's sentences for them, which he had inherited from his father. Once he realized what someone's next word would be, he would blurt it out first. Even though he wasn't paying close attention to what she said, he now cut Lynn off and finished one of her sentences. She roundly scolded him for fifteen minutes. It reminded her of their *Kalliope* days and just how domineering and impolite he could sometimes be. At last they glimpsed McGregor across the frozen river, tucked beneath a bluff. The temperature in Iowa was a bit warmer than it had been in Mineral Point. Richard and Lynn explored the downtown district with its antique shops in antique Victorian buildings. A clerk in a used bookstore had seen a copy of *The Dragoon* pass through his shop. Richard was reminded of a storefront set in an old western. They saw the white steamboat casino at its permanent landing as they crossed back into Wisconsin. They stopped at a little park in a wooded area alongside the river, on which they observed ten or eleven ice fishermen. They took a little stroll through the snowy trees and Lynn picked some orange-yellow bittersweet berries split open to reveal their one-or-two seeds from a climbing vine on one of the treelimbs. Richard would take a few sprigs home with him to Pennsylvania. On their return trip, they again stopped in New Glarus where they dined and danced at the New Glarus Hotel, where the music was very different from that of the Scarlet Tanager in Kenosha. They waltzed and polkaed—Lynn leading, as Richard was only a novice dancer. In traditional Swiss garb, the members of the band also yodeled. The friends did not arrive back at the farmhouse until the wee hours of the next morning.

Lynn's two sons Sean and Micah arrived a day earlier than expected. Lynn had to attend a campus meeting that morning in Chicago, so Richard welcomed the boys back on his own. The eldest, a junior in high school, had driven them from their father's new place in Kenosha. Richard watched the two raid their stockings and the cookie and goodies tins in the fridge. They then played video games all afternoon on their computers. They particularly liked one called Worlds of Warcraft, which had a fantasy realm setting and featured dragons, wizards and elves. The games he and Lynn had competed at at the arcade on Beaver Avenue in State College during their college days had very primitive graphics in comparison even though they were state of the art at the time. Both boys were polite and friendly. During the final days of his visit, Richard would develop a particularly good relationship with the younger of the two, a strategic thinker who loved board as well as video games. The ninth grader thrashed Richard at both chess and Stratego. It disturbed Richard to hear Lynn say that Micah although bright was not a big reader and that she simply could not motivate him to read more. When they next went into Kenosha, Richard had Lynn stop at a Borders. As he had not brought either boy a Christmas present, he now purchased each a book as a New Year's gift. He selected J.R.R. Tolkien's modern English translation of *Sir Gawain and the Green Knight*—a poem he had himself read as a teen and had a famous literary revelation concerning, which was celebrated in his father's celebrated book *Style and Precision*—for Sean, as he heard his mother say that, having first seen the movie adaptation with Micah and her, he had just read and enjoyed a modern English *Beowulf,* and for Micah, the nonreader, he selected *The Hobbit,* hoping that the boy's love of fantasy would spark his interest and spur him on to read it. He also had brought several DVDs he thought the boys might like, including *Apocalypse Now Redux.* Lynn didn't appreciate the previously deleted nude scenes. She cooked a terrific traditional New Year's dinner of pork and sauerkraut. Richard made sure to take a double dose of Prilosec, as he always had gastric problems whenever he ate the dish, a favorite of his before his intestinal surgeries in the early 1980s. With the boys now home, Lynn asked Richard to say a blessing before every meal. He asked everyone to take hands and channeled his grandfather Owen, who had always said a wonderful grace.

Richard wrote many letters to Lynn the first few weeks after his return home to Mercersdale. Some of them, she later told him, made her blush scarlet. As he put down his words with his ballpoint pen, he clutched in his other hand his favorite of all her Christmas gifts to him, the one he had to specially ask for after ardently brushing her hair one evening while the two listened to Chopin's *Regentropfen-Prelude* and *Revolutions-Etüde* on CD, a single blonde lock, a ray of sunshine from his sunshine. At his desk sat her Christmas card, a Metropolitan Museum of Art reprint of Suzi Singer-Schinnerl's *A Doll For Christmas,* a color lithograph first published by the *Wiener Werkstätte* in Vienna in 1912. Inside she had written: "Happy Holidays My Dear One! I am so glad that we can have this time together at last. Love, Lynn."

Dearest Lynn, I dream about you and again it is that sweet June night in 1981 and again I am being initiated in the Eleusinian mysteries and find myself in Elysium tasting the sacred, secret fruit. Such closeness belongs only to you. Love comes back. It returns as a weeping wetness and I spill seed into my sheets before arising to coffee and Chopin. For your letter arrived yesterday and you tell me that you love me, and, emerging from succulent, torrid dreams, the nexus of the interrealm, I sit down to my piano for the first time since returning from Wisconsin and celebrate with Chopin for one full hour dreaming of the bluffs of the Mississippi and the town of McGregor and my beloved driving in her sunglasses, ice fishermen on the frozen river, and the two of us plucking bittersweet. Surfeited by music and dreams I draw the "Plucking Flowers" card from the Waterhouse box and commence writing to you, swiftly and wildly. I love the mothers. I clutch my lock of your hair in my hand as I write this. I don't know if you ever noticed, but on a little display rack fastened to the bright yellow wall of my kitchen sit two crocheted knickknacks: a butterfly and a chicken. The display rack is heart-shaped. Each of my grandmothers made one, Ina the chicken, which I believe she gave as a gift to Ida (I think its purpose is to get a better grip on mason jar lids when opening them, though I don't use it for that, it's far too sacred), and Ida the butterfly. My mother purchased me the wooden heart. Both grandmothers are gone of course, but I still feel their love for me, and in your love for me I also feel theirs. I was only eleven when Ina died, but I know that she deeply loved me. She lost her own son Chester when he was only nine from appendicitis. Her first grandchild was a boy and how she delighted in her little Richard, her angel returned to her, and called him her little chickadee. She always had the loveliest Easter baskets for me when I was a child, and she would die at Easter. That year, in '73, she had a basket all prepared for me and also a wrapped coloring book of movie monsters with my name on it. I remember watching on television the old Frankenstein, Wolfman, and Dracula movies as a boy with her and Owen and she holding my hand tightly and how as a little child I would crawl into bed between the two, and they would have a little lamp with an orange shade on it and Owen would tell me pirate stories. I still have that lamp in my attic. Your caring tenderness sending me Christmas gifts and especially Easter candy brought back her love for me, profoundly echoed it. Love is a powerful, potent force in the universe. It reverberates and comes round again in a circle. We feel it as it throbs back to us from new sources. I feel my Nanny Ina's love for me renewed and intermixed with yours. And my Nanny Ida's too, bless her. My foot rubbing ritual with her you have inherited. Oh, blending and strengthening of old and new loves! How we need love, both to give and receive it. This letter is swelling and growing out of control, but I still have more to say, and if I'm in love and therefore gushing, gush on I say. Gush on. Where before there was a trickle, now there is a cataract, a veritable Niagara, and having disposed of the Nannies—though not really, there is still much to say about them, especially Ida's and my combating over politics ... she was a true-blue, dyed-in-the-wool Republican who cried when Wendell Willkie lost to FDR and a ferocious and tenacious arguer ... I recall <u>our</u> own fencing and swimming competitions and our tiffs on the editorial board of "Kalliope" when I think of her—I must move onto my mother Rebecca. I wish to thank you for writing the thank you card to her. She seemed touched when she spoke to me about it on the phone yesterday. Didn't I tell you in Wisconsin that I thought mommy love was the deepest, most profound love of all, and that men look for their mother's reflection in their beloved? That, to a child, mother and God are synonymous? Didn't I tell you my mother was a brunette as I brushed your hair though hers was as straight as an Indian's, not sprung yellow curls like yours? Proust knew how deep and profound mother-love is. Like Marcel we wait in our beds with such great longing for our mother to leave the party and tuck us in. How I envy Rusty with his plush green rug. I blink and see myself under a lime-green sleeping bag back at my basement apartment in the 1980s between my two operations, still ill and not knowing it and you coming to see me and bringing me roses. And I think of the green blanket you made me and sent me in Mercersdale, an echo of the blanket I spoke to you about, the one Ina made Owen and told him that, when she was gone, he could wrap himself in her blanket and still feel the warmth of her love. How I envy Rusty and, yes, even though I don't know them all that well yet, I feel love in my heart for Sean and Micah because they are extensions of you. I see you in them in the soccer and lacrosse photographs you sent me. Love transcends time, space, and generations. I loved the framed photograph of the little girl with the stick pony, the six shooters and the big smile that I saw in your rec room. Somehow I recognize my beloved in her. Yes, mommy love is strong, and how I long to be reborn in you, the next avatar or incarnation of myself, however sexed male or female, to be growing and alive and kicking in your womb. I want you for my mommy! I would even settle for the sweet existence of your dog. Oh, to be Rusty and to be tucked in by you every night. As I'm not a dog, I won't fetch a deer leg or kill marauding squirrels stealing seeds from your bird feeders, but I will retrieve something beautiful out of my word-hoard and lay it lovingly at your feet–the poem "Chopin" by Gottfried Benn.

Richard

For a change this week, I thought we would switch off from Waterhouse to Vincent van Gogh. Almost every object in my house has a specific memory or memories attached to it. Things are just things until they become invested and imbued with memories. The chain of associations attached to an object are often more precious than the object itself. The object comes to stand for the memories that are associated with it: a vessel into which one can pour a lot of feeling. The miracle of metaphor! The thing is transformed. The tawdry, little possession becomes transcendent and animate. Windows open and beautiful memories are triggered. Your little stuffed horse Sheddy—the unicorn who lost or "shed" his horn—is for you such a treasure, imbued with more than ordinary significance. At this moment I'm staring at a ceramic white cat with blue eyes and a pink ribbon around her throat, the one you sent me several Christmases ago. I'm recalling two different moments in my life. During my final year at Penn State, my blue-eyed Siamese cat Snowflake died— the cat who brought the baby rabbit and laid it down in front of the empty guinea pig cage the day after my sister's pet guinea pig caught its neck between two bars and strangled trying to break free. Snowflake had been the love of my childhood. She slept on my chest every night and licked my face with her sandpaper-rough tongue. My father told me if I would have died from my intestinal surgery, he would have put her asleep and buried her with me in the casket. Well, my sister was distraught and my father who was visiting me at Penn State—this was the year after you graduated—suggested that he take my Crème home to California. I wavered and hesitated. You know how much I loved that little kitty I saved from the dumpster, whose voice box was so badly crushed she could never meow. But in the end I relented and allowed him to take my sweet kitty to my inconsolable teenage sister. I remembered Snowflake earlier bringing her the baby bunny. Six months would pass—and I would graduate from Penn State—before I would see Crème again. I had fallen asleep on the living room floor. My father saw what happened when Crème saw me for the first time. As I say I lay sleeping. She came into the room, slowly crossed it, walked straight up to me, extended her face forward and touched my cheek with her little pink nose, my father says "kissed" her rescuer, who she hadn't seen for what must have seemed like ages. I'm also remembering the moment you arrived at the Arby's in the DePaul Student Union. You greeted me with a kiss, a buss on the lips. I had journeyed a long way to see my Dutch girl, but the kiss surprised me—at the time I didn't see it coming and the memory of it is one of the very sweetest that I carried home to Mercersdale. True, there would be other caresses long sustained and more fervent, other "act-poems," as Walt Whitman calls them, of eyes and hands, embraces at the time I wanted to go on forever and of which I was so unwilling to leave and see end, but that initial little kiss, so freely and spontaneously given it made me shy and start, how I treasure the memory of it, a precursor of all that was to come, our union of souls, bodies, and hearts. Oh how I love you Lynn and long for your embraces in the morning and in the night. How I wish I could touch your cheek with a moist pink nose like Pinky Crème's to acknowledge my great love for you.

Your Kitty Me-Now

As hard as he tried to win at board games with Micah, he soon found himself engaged and locked in contest with the dark opponent which had shadowed him all his life, the spirit who immediately seized on and took his Mercer grandfather in angry retaliation for Richard snatching his Mercier grandfather away from the slash of his scythe, and who when he finally did claim Owen took him at the moment of Richard's triumph, the publication of *The Dragoon*. Not satisfied yet in its vengeance, the nemesis caused his agent Rhonda's daughter to be in a car accident one week after they buried Owen, and Rhonda, who had worked valiantly for years to see Richard triumph and had invested so much time in establishing him as an up-and-comer, had to leave the business to tend to her now paraplegic child. The fiend sought to cut him down in one stroke, but the sunshine prevailed and grew even stronger in the wake of the attack. Lynn loved him that much, and he drew from her strength. The contest between light and dark became a war of attrition. For two years he sent out teaching applications. No one called for interviews. He tried for all sorts of editing and writing work, even sending résumés for jobs in Chi itself, though he could never see himself commuting like Lynn. Driving in a city petrified him. Eight years had gone by since he had published his first novel. He had not followed it up with a second book. He still could not write anything new, yet he began reworking his earlier novels, entering one in a contest. To his surprise it won. The one who never believed in contests benefited from one. A second work of his reached print—issued by a university press. Lynn visited him on a yearly basis, and he again took a vacation to Wisconsin two year later in October 2009, two months after the appearance of his collection of related novellas.

Six months from that time he would lay prostrate, love sick and trounced.

Poleaxed, he remembered how she had not blamed him for what happened after Christmas. How he unwittingly made her sick. The tears streamed from his eyes when he recalled her clutching that bottle of pills. He had come down with a bad cold on his train trip just before putting into Chicago. Love sick and prostrate, he thought of her conduct so loving and understanding toward him then—she did not react with anger or make hurtful recriminations—and he now saw that he was not nearly so good a person as she. Devils do persecute us and do their diabolical best to destroy our happiness. When she fell ill, he despaired of everything. His life seemed as if written by Thomas Mann. Again the dark spirit struck, the demon of deceitfulness in human affairs. Fate or god deceived him with the promise of happiness. He stood betrayed. That the one thing he kept for her—that he saved only for her—from that night twenty-six years before when she had initiated him into the mysteries of love—his greatest joy and sweetest surrender and which he dreamed about repeating with her—only her—behind closed doors and in private—would come to have such hurtful, sad consequences for her was almost more than he could bear. He had prayed and prayed in thanksgiving at Quaker Meeting, and Jesus would let this happen to him! Jesus loved him, sure. If Jesus didn't, Lynn still did. The darkness burned away, dispersed in her light. They still held each other when they met one another once a year. And Richard continued checking the Internet for employment in her state and region, as he started doing during the long Presidential campaign and continued to do after Obama replaced Bush in the White House, and everyone felt a change coming on.

When, after that second trip, the darkness again fell between them, Richard felt as if under a cruel, hateful spell. Never had he such strength. Never had the adrenalin surged through him day after day like this. He slept only two to four hours a night and drank a case daily. When as emotionally wrought up as he now was, he felt and feared that his mind could bring matter to heel and make it obey its every behest. He had always felt he willed his appendicitis and intussusception in college. After Owen died he developed the precancerous polyps in his sinus and had to have the operation, which, if botched, could leave him blind. So he tried to direct the excess energy outwards, and strange things happened. His grandmother's clock, which

he dreamed of punching, the following day flew off the wall
of its own accord. Miracle of miracles, the seventeen pills did
not work. He got up four hours later, his body full of surging
energy. He could put it to use. Albeit if only in heart's blood, he
knew he could still write. Richard had reached the dark night
of the soul when the new spark of hope ignites. He felt like
Moses graving the commandments into the tablets. A pair of
horns shooting out light emanated from beneath his forelocks.

He booted his computer and clicked open the first of his
three work-in-progress files. He did not know for sure what piece
of writing would appear first. He had not opened WIP1, WIP2,
or WIP3 for months and couldn't remember now which fragment he labeled WIP1. The ancient newspaper clipping which
he retyped came up first—what was to goad him into a Lynn-like
writing exercise. The woman for whom his mother was named
had cut the item out from a newspaper years and years before.
Shortly after Owen's death, she gave Richard the clipping. He
wished that he had discovered it before writing *The Dragoon*.
In 1796, Heinrich Mercer's neighbor in Filthydumpia was no
less a personage than Louis Philippe, Duc de Orléans, son of
Philippe Egalité, the Bourbon who considered an unlimited
monarchy antiquated and oppressive. The son also sided with
the revolutionaries but fled when the Terror began and his father
was beheaded. For a time he lived beside the *ci-devant* Versailles
shoemaker Mercer on Prune Street, and in Richard's novel he
resided by Conrad Semler, Mercer's fictional stand-in. The
clipping Rebecca had given him indicated that the future King
of France actually came to and inspected the laid-out town—
axe marks on the trees indicated the future lots—which would
become Mercersdale a few months prior to Henry Mercer and
the eleven other settlers arriving there to erect the first primitive

lean-tos and cabins. Rebecca had thought that the article was written by Henry W. Shoemaker, America's first State Folklorist and a pioneer of national conservation, who promoted and/or manufactured numerous Pennsylvania legends, such as that of the Indian princess Nita-nee, for whom central Pennsylvania's Nittany Mountain is named and who played a pivotal role in helping to create Pennsylvania's State Parks and forests and establishing the Historical and Museum Commission. Rebecca, however, was not certain. She had only been interested in the part of the article concerning the future King's visit to the site of the projected frontier town. She had only saved the opening paragraphs, not the whole of the romance. The supposed historical visit also interested Richard more than the missing folktale, as it was the only reference he had ever come across for Louis Philippe's inspection of the site. He tried to find the rest of the article searching through the indices of Shoemaker's published books but to no avail. He thought he himself, for kicks' sake, might compose his own version of the missing tale. Other than retyping the part of the article Rebecca had cut out and preserved, he never proceeded with the project:

Rattlesnake Tavern
Scene Of Romance
Of Many Years Ago

There is an old deserted tavern formerly known as the Rattlesnake Tavern on the road from Unionville to Mercersdale, now known as the Bald Eagle Highway. Today it is almost hidden from the road by a dense growth of sumacs, but in the late 18th century, French royalty visited the tavern. It was also the scene of a famous romance at that time.

Emanuel Gunsalis, of Spanish descent, whose grandson became the famous wolf and panther hunter of Snow Shoe, was the landlord of the tavern.

The tavern was in a small clearing in a dense pine forest. One snowy night in the Christmas season of the year 1796, four mounted travelers rode up to the tavern. Three of them were French princes in exile, the older of whom would later be known as Louis Philippe, King of France. Then they were simply known as the Messrs. Orleans. The fourth man was Philip Palmatier, of Huguenot origin, a land prospector and explorer, whom the young men had met while guests at the home of the Honorable Baron de Beelen Berthoff.

The princes had become interested in Palmatier's tale of his adventures in the wilds of Pennsylvania and they invited him to act as guide to take them through the northern and central parts of the state to the newly laid-out town of Mercersdale, where there might be business opportunities.

Peter Hauntz, a ventriloquist, had a marionette show, which performed at the tavern each night. Hauntz's wife was a beautiful....

Richard clicked open the second of the three files. For a time, he had considered writing a sequel to *The Dragoon*, which would take place in Mercersdale one hundred years after the events of the first novel and deal with Henry Mercer's descendants, Mercers and Merciers both, at a time when the town first hit the skids after the coal mining and lumbering booms had reached their height. He recalled Owen once speaking about his grandparents and had tried to recreate his grandfather's voice on the page. In this his first draft, he had not yet changed the family surname from Mercier to Semler:

George Sr. was a fine man and loved and respected in Mercersdale, but his sons degenerated into common slobs. Harry, William, and George Jr. became the terrors of the town. They loved to fight and they loved to get drunk and clean out the saloons. My father told me that one Saturday night at the Passmore Hotel, William Mercier rammed a drummer head first through a cigar case. These men looked all alike—tall and spare—and they all possessed exceptional strength. William was the strongest. A semi-professional boxer, he could bench press a tremendous weight. George Sr. and his shunned-Quaker wife Amanda also had two daughters, Sally and Sue. In her youth, Sally married a good for nothing named Davis. They had one son who died at six or seven, then Davis disappeared and good riddance. Then she married an insidious little bandy-legged son of a bitch named Albert Jackson, who drank himself drunk each and every day. He had a walrus mustache and a hooked nose. When drunk, he sometimes wet himself like a little child. As a youth, he inherited money. He lit his cigars with ten-dollar bills. He latched onto Sally for a living. Sally wasn't crazy, merely forty cents short. She had hair of a dull gray hue and when let down, it laid on the floor. She would laugh like a booming cannon, pound the table, and declare, "Al said, haw haw haw, Al said," and Al merely sneered at her. He never did anything else. All of us loved Aunt Sally and hated Al. Harry, Bill, and George Jr. all called him, "our insignificant little brother-in-law." He was, however, a fine machinist, one of the best. Later in life he did work and eventually he died horribly from cancer. Al could see the bad points of the Merciers. He liked to imitate Harry taking a miscreant to jail by the scruff of his neck. This act was a riot and always goaded Aunt Sally into one of her stentorian laughs or guffaws.

The Merciers always held their heads high. They never sub-scribed to any namby-pamby fawning and if they had something in their craw they said it. They were outspoken men who looked everyone squarely in the eye. A giant at that time if not today, Harry stood six-feet three-inches tall and weighed two hundred fifty pounds. A handsome man, imperious but not domineering, like all the Merciers, he had great strength. In Philadelphia, before the family removed to Mercersdale, he married Francis Tern of Baltimore. Full breasted and better than medium tall, she had a serene countenance. Tall and queenly, she stood erect with a fine figure and wore her clothes well. She had the hauteur of a fine lady, which she was. She died in Mercersdale at the age of fifty-four of cancer of the liver. She suffered greatly before she died. She gave birth to twelve children—no stillbirths. I know I would have loved her. She was my grandmother. The family lived on Ninth Street in Mercersdale. All of them lived on Ninth Street, and if one did not get along with the Merciers one should avoid and not even walk on Ninth Street, for the Merciers ruled there, where they resided ever since George Sr. first came to town. He could not have picked a worse place. At that time the country, especially the west was coming to life. Pennsylvania, anyplace in Pennsylvania, was old hat. The wealthy land barons and the insidious coal and iron police had the commonwealth strangled. The timber was gone. Slash took its place. Even the magnificent deer herd had disappeared by the 1890s. The state had to import deer from Michigan and Virginia. The legislature had to enact strict laws so that the new herd would survive. Harry and Francis settled down to a life wherein the wife had a baby on the floor, one at her breast, and a new one coming in her womb. Harry became the Pennsylvania railroad agent in Mercersdale, then the town constable. The people would elect George Jr., like his father before him, mayor, and the two brothers would control the town between them. Harry organized the National Guard Company in Mercersdale and rose to the rank of Captain and from that time on everyone called him Captain. As a lawman he was a holy terror and single-handedly maintained law and order in the entire surrounding community, and he saw every downtrodden victim of the coal and iron capitalists as a potential thief. Not that these people were actually that bad. The people of that time were poor and I mean poor. They worked like dogs for the robbers of the toil of men and received damn poor pay. Harry was also the big politico of the area. The ignoramuses always consulted the Captain, and he told them how to vote. The intimate of Senators and Governors, he never secured one state appointment worth a damn. He did their dirty work for nothing. He spent most of his time taking criminals to Bellefonte or Pittsburgh and attending court there. His family was like Topsy. It just grew. Every time some screwball ran amuck in the entire surrounding area, the people cried, "Send to Mercersdale for the Captain." His appearance settled riots, and, when miscreants learned that he followed on their trail, they simply grew small and gave up. He was a deadly manhunter. That was true. One time he traced a man and woman to Harrisburg, who had taken a large sum of money from a curmudgeon who never did anything but count it and were bent on running through and spending it. According to the Mercersdale *Courier*, the Captain interrupted them having a most splendid time. The paper crowed: "I tell you no one can capture criminals like our Harry. He does it with neatness and dispatch." One time a misguided Negro from Baltimore came up here and stole a mine payroll. The crime was committed on a country road at gunpoint. Of course a hue and cry went out for the Captain. At that time a roundhouse where mechanics did repairs on locomotives stood in Mercersdale. Someone saw the man getting on a coal train for Tyrone, so they stoked a boiler, placed a caboose on it, and the Captain followed the coal train over the mountain. It turned out that the man had two confederates with whom he had earlier robbed a drummer and other men on the highway to Mercersdale.

The Captain caught up with all three in the freight yards of Tyrone. He called on them to surrender and they all fired on him. He then shot one, one surrendered, and one fled. Harry went to fetch the latter when the authorities later apprehended him in Baltimore. The Bellefonte court convicted all three, and the man Harry shot later died in the state prison at Pittsburgh. And the town bugle trumpeted: "Tell you what boys, no one can match our Harry. He remained as cool and calm shooting the malefactor as sitting at his table at home and eating one of his wife's palatial meals."

By process of elimination, Richard knew what he had written of the Moravian novel—a single long section where the voices of the two protagonists, the eighteenth-century missionary and the twentieth-century composer alternated like verses of a psalm or hymn chanted or sung in response to one another—would come next, the last of his three works-in-progress. He did not know whether the unfinished passage would come at the book's beginning, middle or end, only that it would appear somewhere in its course. It was the only part of the proposed work that he had actually written:

Antiphonal

At last my life begins, the meaningful essential part. For finally the occasion long sought for, but always denied, comes now that I have reached, and indeed am well into, middle age and fast approaching either borrowed time or the Death Angel. Daily I meditate on the atoning wound made by the centurion's spear. Daily I contemplate passing through that deep cut, that portal to Paradise. Oh how I long to part the curtain to the Holy of Holies, to crawl into, and rewomb myself, in Jesus' side wound and thereby enter into the closer presence of the Saviour. For it is through that side hole that we are reborn. Daily I contemplate my complete union with Christ, expect to receive that fondly anticipated, long-awaited, final kiss, the Saviour's summons home. We must be prepared for that consummation—to pass through the wounds of Jesus into the mother city—at any time. For he plucks flowers from all his choirs. During the course of my life, I have progressed from the Infants' to the Younger and Older Boys' choirs and from thence to the Single Brothers' and the Married choirs and for twelve years I have taken my seat with the Widowers'. I wed late in life, years after the General Economy, much to the chagrin of Brother Joseph, had been dissolved in Bethlehem—years after that blessed time when we Moravians worked for a common stock and ate at a common table yet men and women, even married pairs, lived apart, when choirs did not intermix but attended separate *Singstunden*, kept together throughout the day as much as feasible—though like bees in a hive, each of us had individualized, specialized functions—and slept in the common dormitory throughout the night. No, in these bleak days and fallow time for the church in Bethlehem, husbands no longer live with the Married Brothers or wives with the Married Sisters in the common choir house, a husband joining his wife in the blue cabinet only on rare occasion, but reside, the two together, in many separate homes and dwellings. Although Anna and I both remained virginal in our hearts, now a much more difficult thing to do, and nonetheless maintained the purity of our marriage, sadly my much younger wife died but two years after the Lot brought us together after giving birth to our twin sons Christian Jacob and Johannes Frederick. We laid her to rest with the other sisters in the *Gottesacker* for, although couples were now permitted to live together, the bodies of men and women were still buried in the old way, in separate sections of the cemetery. After her passing, my interim, proxy marriage over, my thoughts naturally turned more and more to the slaughtered Lamb. After the funeral procession *mit Musik lieblich und munter*, even as we lowered her into the ground, along with all the Brothers and Sisters, I prayed: "Keep us in eternal fellowship with the entire perfected congregation, especially with our sister Anna Schober, and let us rest in the same manner with them in your wounds." But to tell the truth, all my life I have had the vision of that gaping purple hurt before me and have stood ready to be drawn deeper into that dear Side. Before I lay naked and bare on her lap, when she lived with the other pregnant sisters whom the Lamb deigned to carry side-hole creatures for Him under their hearts, my mother sang to me of the Lord's sacrifice when I was but a member of the embryo choir, and all my life that holy mark, that gash in His side, has acted upon me like unto a magnet. I have gazed at that opening with loving eye, never veiling my face before its ruby light. "There is my element," I would say to myself. Whilst in my meditation, focused upon the end of all Need and the gateway to our eternal homeland, I longed to fly through, to simply let go, abandon all volition and allow myself to be sucked in and drawn across. But like Moses, I have only been allowed to look upon, not enter, the Promised Land. I have knelt at many deathbeds—those of Children, Sisters, and Brothers. I have helped *sing* them over and afterwards I and the others grouped around those billets of final repose, each of us longing to be next called home, sang yet other verses—"You man of sorrows so beautiful," "*Oh Haupt voll Blut*," or "Pale Lips, kiss him on the heart," thinking the while of the Saviour receiving the fortunate departed into his open arms. And many a time, I have mounted the broad stairs of the Bethlehem and Nazareth *Gemeinhäuser* and stepped out on the balcony with the other three members of the trombone choir. Over the decades, in both settlements, I served the Lord in dual capacities, firstly as a teacher at the Day School in Bethlehem, and, later in my life after my wife's death, at Nazareth

Hall where boarding boys—the children of the Brothers and Sisters who attended the Lord as missionaries or *Pilger*—were correctly and fully instructed in the beliefs and practices of the *Unitas Fratrum*, and secondly as an organist and trombonist. In both communities, I have taken each of the four horns out of the storage cabinet. At one time or the other, I have played all four parts, but the two instruments I loved best were the smallest and largest, the diminutive slide trumpet or soprano *Posaune* and the nearly seven-foot long F-*Baßposaune* which has the capacity of playing a chromatic scale in the range of the human voice, and which the Indian at Gnadenhütten known to the Brothers and Sisters as Paxnous, upon hearing for the first time as he came running through the woods, in his ravishment mistook for the voice of the Great Spirit or Manitou as he stumbled over his feet and came crashing to the ground. Yes, during the course of those years, I have taken each of the four cards—*Sopran, Alt, Tenor,* and *Baß*—with their beautifully drawn semibreves, minims, crotchets, and quavers from the cupboards at the top of the stairs of both *Gemeinhäuser* and affixed the card in question to the appropriate instrument, whichever of the four was assigned to me at the time, and have taken my place behind the railing. Often as I glanced below at the cobbled square in front of the *Gemeinhaus* and at the beautiful buildings situated around it, I would grow dizzy and weak-kneed (heights, how I always grew sick and dreaded casting my eyes down from them but invariably always would as if I were the Lord and Satan offered me all the Kingdoms of the World and dared me to plunge through the sky saying that God's Angels would surely uplift me). I'd always have to look out into the distance in order to gain my poise and equanimity—to stop the sensation of whirling and falling. At Nazareth, where my two boys are now students in the Hall, the sweat beading from my brow, I could see furrowed fields and green pastures and further to the south outlined against the sky undulating hills marking the end of the broad river valley. I took a deep breath, nodded to the other three, and the four of us began playing the first chorale which announced to the settlement that one of our fold had ended his or her earthly journey and was now asleep in Jesus, or, in other words, had entered into that desired state which was the goal of all. A subsequent chorale would identify the choir wherein the death occurred. As we stood there repeating the final chorus, I, too, yearned to be perfected but so far the Lord has not vouchsafed me his loving kiss and for that there must be a reason. From the time I arrived at Bethlehem as a mere stripling, one of two hundred refugees displaced from Herrnhaag after the latter community's dissolution in 1750 after the death of the aged Count of Yesenburg-Büdingen, who in the 1730s had given permission to Papa Zinzendorf to purchase land in Wetteravia and establish a congregation there at a time when Papa feared that the Moravians in Herrnhut might be expelled from Saxony, when the new Count of Yesenburg-Büdingen, who had a strong personal dislike for Zinzendorf, his father's trusted and revered friend, demanded that the community drop its allegiance to our spiritual leader and head as well as other religious and financial accommodations all of which we were unwilling to consider or agree to even though it meant abandoning our beautiful homes there and the relocation of a number of us to the wilds of Pennsylvania where life on the frontier came as quite a shock accustomed as we were to the more opulent mode of existence prevailing at Herrnhaag, my most fervent wish has been to join the *Pilgergemeine*. Though raised in Wetteravia, I never belonged to the order of Little Fools, those misguided youth from the single men's choir who congregated about the person of Christian Renatus, Zinzendorf's charismatic son and Pastor of Herrnhaag, who each and every one affected a childlike dependence on Christ and saw no end or goal to our life's journey other than that of entering into and maintaining a state of infantile or cherubic bliss. Those scatterbrains and empty-heads given to lighthearted silliness considered any activity other than their "child's play" at the foot of the cross—even our mission work, our task of winning souls to the Lord—empty and frivolous as they believed good works were of no avail, that only Christ's grace got one into heaven. If He desired little children about Him, they would suffer themselves to become, would turn themselves into, what He desired and do nothing but gambol and prank. Did not Papa himself write, Christian Renatus would argue, that children are little Royal Highnesses, that baptism is their anointing, and that from then on they should be treated as none other than kings by birth? Did he not say that children functioned as ambassadors from God carrying within them a spark of the divine and that their innate simplicity and humility could serve as an instructive model to their teachers? Indeed such had been Papa's words. Look to the children for your own edification, he said. They offer everyone a standard and ideal, a miniature, a small-scale representation, of what a good Christian should be. In all my pedagogical endeavors, I have kept the Count's comments in mind and often pupils of mine have opened my eyes and revealed to me wisdom from on high, truth beyond their years. The order of Little Fools went astray by taking things to excess, by going beyond the pale. At first Papa looked at their antics and horse-play indulgently. In the end, however, he saw the need for curb, whip and bridle—realized that the wheat needed sifting—and removed his son as Pastor of Herrnhaag. He did not mean for his followers to abdicate all responsibility and do nothing but frisk and trifle. Yes, we poor sinners remain totally dependent on Christ's mercy, our salvation contingent on him alone. Yes, one could call childhood the best time in life and one could learn much from observing the little ones in that blessed condition prior to their spinning their cocoons and entering that intermediary state: those awkward years of transformation when while more than child one is not yet fully adult, a sappy, syrupy time when your new body is very much in control of you and you are bridled by that which you yourself should bridle, and yet your Saviour stands never closer. He walks with you in all your ways. We are not meant to remain in our pupal state. Christ himself demands purposeful activity and energetic exertion from us. After all He has done for his butterflies and his buzzing bees, He asks us, in our turn, to do something for Him: to spread His gospel to the ends of the earth. Unlike the Little Fools, I avidly read the journals and gazettes of our church and learned all I could about the many aboriginal people around the globe whom our missionaries greeted as brothers. Since 1732, when the first of our *Pilger* departed for St. Thomas in the West Indies, to the present day, they have quit the *Vaterland* in a steady stream, traveling across the globe telling all people, no matter what the color of their skin, that the Lord of Earth and Heaven had become human and shed His blood for their deliverance, and I thrilled from afar at the accounts of Papa's exploits in America among the Shawnee. Initially the occupants of the six lands regarded Papa's small party with great mistrust. Accompanied by his interpreter Martin Mack and a few others, Zinzendorf had penetrated the Pennsylvania wilderness as far as the Wyoming Valley, where he set up camp on the North Branch of the Susquehanna, resolved to prosecute a vigorous missionary work among the native people of the region. They had traveled part of the way on horseback and part of the way on foot. Papa came dressed in a plain single-breasted coat, a mantle partially drawn over his shoulder and wearing a white cravat gathered in a simple fold. The Indians had no appreciation of the pure and holy motives which had induced him to seek them out in their vast forests. They thought him a spy and believed that he had come at the behest of the Proprietaries of the Province—those very unfatherlike sons of Miquon or William Penn—whom they had come to see as enemies, as robbers of their lands and despoilers of their hunting grounds. Believing his intentions evil and his presence dangerous to the people, they determined that they would take his scalp of dark hair, smoothly parted on the left side and hanging in graceful ringlets down his neck and shoulders. Several braves silently sought the place under the dark trees beside the riverbank where Papa had pitched his rude tent and in which he sat deep in meditation. It was a chill night and the Count had lit a small fire to lessen the effects of the cold and damp. As the Indians cautiously approached the tent, the flickering of the flames revealed the Count in his abstracted state, serenely unconscious not only of their presence but also that of a huge rattlesnake, which seeking the warmth of the fire had slithered into the tent unbeknownst to Papa, and at the very moment the Indians crept up and looked inside, slowly drew its hideous length right across the foot of the pious Moravian. The Indians at once withdrew and left him unharmed, glad in their hearts not to have reddened their hands with the blood of one whom the Great Spirit so evidently held under his sheltering wing. And Papa, he never noticed the presence of the venomous reptile, that loathsome creature, our first father old Adam's ancient enemy. Not as it coiled over his foot toward the fire. Nor later, though no eyes witnessed it, as it slid out of the tent and back into the morning dew-of-June-wet grass. He only learned afterward of the dart Satan had cast at his heels from the very Indians who had sought his life when he met with a large assembly of Shawnee shortly thereafter and told them of the heavenly errand on which he had come to the people and one of the chiefs answered: "Brother, you have made a long journey over the seas to preach the Gospel to the white people and to the Indians. You did not know that we were here, and we knew nothing of you. This proceeds from above. Come, therefore, to us, both you and your brethren. We bid you welcome among us and take this belt of wampum in confirmation of our words. You whom the great serpent himself dared not sting." Jesus, his hand extended protectively, must have been in Papa's tent warding off and ready to smite dead that fanged and, no doubt, in the Saviour's presence, hissing reptile. And of course my own parents, too, had been missionaries. Although they were not among the refugees fleeing persecution in Bohemia and Moravia who took shelter and sanctuary on Papa's estate in 1722, but like the Pietist nobleman himself stood good Saxons and Lutherans, they numbered among the first Herrnhuttian *Pilger* to the Baltic, setting off to Urvaste in 1739. I was a mere boy at the time. When they took leave of the Count's wife Dorothea von Erdmuth, who, upon the Prince of Saxony banishing Papa from his own country for purportedly disseminating false religious doctrines, had assumed charge and control of the Zinzendorf family estates and therefore also the Herrnhut community, I found myself hard on the heels of father and mother and soon departed to the Moravian boarding school in Herrnhaag. Like the other Brothers and Sisters, my parents prided themselves on being lowly worms—manual laborers, blacksmiths, carpenters and farmers—and not ordained priests. The latter condemned the Estonian people as wicked pagans but our missionaries called the Baltic the "Land of the Good." They befriended the serfs and told them they were God's children and the equals of monarchs for which the Empress Elizabeth banned the Brotherhood from all the Russias and the knights of Estonia sought to root us from the land imprisoning any *Pilger* that fell into their hands, yet the Brothers and Sisters remained among their flock, outlaws of the realm, and what the priests could not do they accomplished—the serfs tore apart the former sacred groves and overturned the stones they once considered holy as they copied the Gospels into their native tongue and at the behest of the Herrnhuttians wrote their individual life stories and began composing hymns in their own language. So naturally when I arrived in Bethlehem, I wanted to follow my parents' footsteps and spread God's word among the Lenni-Lenape and the other tribes, to join the ranks of men such as Martin Mack, Christian Heinrich Rauch, and Johann Frederick Cammerhof, who died in the service a year after my arrival after the Oneida nation had adopted him into its ranks and bestowed on him the name Gallichwio or "Good Words" due to his fluency in native tongues. Despite my weak constitution, the question was prepared for the Lot. Christ, our chief Elder, spoke directly, as always when the right course of action was not clear. In my case, neither the yea or nay but the blank lot was drawn, the lot which means "wait," and I was assigned to the *Hausgemeine* instead of to the pilgrim community proper. As a member of the home congregation, my task was to support and afford sustenance to the missionaries and to keep the home fires burning as they went out into the forest to do their evangelical duties among the Mohawk and the Iroquois, the Algonquian and Delaware. I did not erect buildings or plow fields. My lot was to lead an indoor existence. For the same reason it had been thought that I would make a fine missionary, my proven ability to quickly learn languages (I had mastered Hebrew, Latin, Greek as well as French and English at Herrnhaag), as well as for my known musical abilities, Bishop Nitschmann decided that I would become a teacher and not an apprentice bound to serve a Master for a prescribed period with the view of learning a specific craft or trade. The Lord had a plan for my life and indeed it quickly appeared that I did not have the constitution fit for a *Pilger*. The air of the New World proved noxious or I should say stinging and itchy to me. A thousand little needles churned into my pink bloodshot eyes when the world about me suddenly blossomed, exploded, into renewed life after the March snows had given way to the blazing egg-yoke-yellow sun of April and downpours of spring rain alternated with clear bonny blue days, the temperature rising higher and higher until the first thunder boomed on high one sweltering afternoon and my oh-so-irritated nose tickled as if the Ideal or true Platonic Form of a blade of grass had been inserted in it by some malevolent deity and once I started sneezing I couldn't stop. I never had such problems in Germany, but in Pennsylvania especially during the spring and fall, my eyes would blear and redden. Vexatious eternal distraction! Itch that would never go away! The lids would become heavy and swollen. Rubbing the raw orbs with my knuckles or the palms of my hands to try to relieve the itching only made matters worse but nonetheless I would rub and rub away, the balls rolling up and down and from side to side behind the lowered lids—and simultaneously my mucous-filled nostrils would begin to spill. Clear strands of snot would dangle from my sore red snout (for I would excoriate and rub it constantly just like my poor eyes) until I wiped them off with my shirt sleeves shamefully soiling my garments and I could not help but recall the shameful rubbing of other parts of my damned dog's body and the telling stains those rubbings would produce. Eventually my nose would become so full so as to plug, and I would be forced to breathe through my mouth. Every year with the coming of spring, I would develop incessant catarrh and painful chest cramps and some years red splotches and wheals would appear and rise all over my skin. Bishop Spangenberg, the *Vicarius Generalis Episcoporum et per Americam in Presbyterio Vicarius* himself, would visit my bedside and try to comfort me, he whom we had christened Brother Joseph for his skillful and adept management of our *Gemeine* in memory of the Provider who governed all Egypt in Pharaoh's name. He taught me that my affliction was a mark of God's favor, that suffering was indeed holy because Jesus suffered, too. We could aspire to the divine because the divine itself had become human, and thus every side and facet of human life had thereby become sanctified. Jesus ate and drank, made water and moved his bowels just like us and by eating his flesh and drinking his blood we fallen and damned could grow Christ-like ourselves and become one with him. Nonetheless the Lot had not said No, merely Wait. Over the years and in spite of my infirmities, I again and again petitioned to serve with the *Pilger*. How I wanted, how I burned, to work alongside David Zeisberger and accompany him to live among the Lenape. I knew, given time, that I could learn the Delaware dialect. And how helpful I would be in the production of dictionaries and translation of religious works. But again the Lot said Wait, and John Heckewelder was chosen as his assistant. The Lot kept saying Wait—just as for years would also be the case whenever one of the elders proposed me as a candidate for marriage. All the time, the nearly five decades I remained in Bethlehem, I never left the *Hausgemeine*. Not until I returned to Herrnhut as an old man did my time finally come—two years into the new century. I thought I would end my days, that I would quietly round out my life, at home in Saxony. In America, I had lived through two terrible wars and saw the efforts our missionaries among the Indians come to naught. Both Gnadenhütten massacres tore at my heart—the first during the old, the so-styled French and Indian War when frenzied hatchet-wielding natives in war paint, renegade Lenape who sided with the Mingos and Maguas of the North, brown Hearts we called them, waylaid our missionary station of that name in Pennsylvania and ten or eleven of our *Pilger* burned alive in their houses as they folded their hands in prayer after which the Indians divided the spoil, soaked bread in milk and made a hearty meal. And the second in the American War for Independence when Pennsylvania militiamen laid low Zeisberger's Ohio settlement of the same name after David's arrest and subsequent imprisonment at Fort Detroit, slaughtering over a hundred of his Delaware converts who pleaded for their lives on bended knees to fellow Christians who remained stone-faced, deaf to all entreaty and supplication, or else smiled and laughed as they discharged their pieces in the crowd.... Yes, the call came at last. From the far north. From ultima Thule, a land of perpetual winter, of icy, crisp air and little or no pollen. The *Pilger* there wanted a musician, and, when I dared, old as I was, to put my name up in nomination, finally the Lot said Yes. So now I, Polycarp Schober, a worm, a maggot, a buzzing bee who has long battened and bathed in the slain Lamb's blood, I, who have knelt at the side wound and licked drops and drops of the precious liquid of our rescue and deliverance, who have nursed upon and guzzled the carcass Lamb's purest honey, I, Polycarp Schober, shall at last have the opportunity to toil in our-blessed-Spouse-the-Lord-our-Bridegroom's vineyard. For although the Directorium of our Church—those foolish and short-sighted old men who after the Count's death fixed and formalized our liturgies, formerly ever changing, ever in a state of becoming, and demanded that the church no longer ordain women and that they from now on keep to traditional roles—concerned about the opinion of the outside world and frightened of its condemnation, have forbidden us to make public reference to certain "suspect" teachings of our founder, Jesus remains the end-all and be-all, the sum and key, that Count Zinzendorf affirmed Him to be. For Jesus *is* the Heavenly Father. For it is only through Jesus' mediation that one can approach the Unfathomable One, who shrouded and hidden in a cloud of unknowing, reigns over the abyss of time, space, and eternity, A Sea of Stars Stretching Out in All directions, An Ocean Vast and Endless, before which men are as uncomprehending insects and creatures of an eye blink, a terrifying Medusa-like Presence, a Face thankfully ever veiled from us, but a Fact before which we shudder, reel, and go limp, a Bottomless Gulf and Chaos, a Torrential vortex, at whose lip we sway ever-so precariously, running the risk of losing our footing and falling in, Pillars of Salt in perpetual plummet. For the Divine Essence took human form in Jesus, became understandable as high wheeled into low and what was fallen dross, refuse thrown off—ejecta of the Divine—became sanctified. Jesus the Word created the world of forms and entered into it, became mortal, subject to time, change, and death. Therefore he is the true Father and Maker. As well as Mother, for the Holy Spirit, the Holy Ghost shows itself maternal and comforts Her children, and Jesus is the Holy Spirit as well as the Father. Through the side hole, we children of matter and time gain entry to eternity and the realm of the Spirit. And most importantly He is the bridegroom, *my* Saviour and bridegroom. For as the Count wrote, all souls stand sisters. Christ the Creator formed no *animos*, no manly souls, only *animas*, who are his Brides, candidates for rest in his arms in the eternal bedchamber that is Heaven. In this world, humanity has been split—bisected—into two genders, and we males stand especially blessed to have organs of generation like unto the Lord's. Christ's purpose in so dividing us is that husband and wife can enact the roles of Christ and his Church metaphorically. Men stand as mere proxies for Christ, for he remains the true consort of us all, and procreative, generative, congress between the married pair constitutes and amounts to worship, to liturgy and lovefeast of the most exalted order. In the hereafter, however, shed of the flesh, the vital principle, the animating force within living man, the seat of a person's innermost being will be uncased, and Christ's proxies will also serve as they were meant to serve—as spouses and playmates for the marriage bed of the blessed Creator and Husband of the human soul.

Yes, at last I have the opportunity to gather first fruits, bring the glorious tidings of our salvation to receptive ears. Ears which I will fill with sublime sounds, proclaiming the Lambkin's name with cymbal, tabor, and lyre. For wherever Moravians travel—be it

Egypt, Persia, or Surinam—be it Ceylon and the Nicobar group, SE of the Bay of Bengal, SW of Burma, or the Cape of Good Hope or the azure-sea-fronted white sand beaches of the Caribbean such as Antigua in the West Indies—we bring music, and I carry sheaves of it with me (not to mention the hymns I have committed to memory, that I carry in my head). But these sheaves remain very special, more than a hundred works of music for choir and orchestra, all handwritten with text in Inuit. At the mission center in Herrnhut, the Brother who had translated them, a former member of a mission to Greenland who could speak the tongue of the "Eaters of Souls," entrusted them to me. And I also bear a little harmonium as well as a slide trumpet into these northern wastes of Labrador, and the *Gemeine* in Herrnhut promise that other instruments will follow, that within a year I shall have violins, cellos, flutes, clarinets, and hautboys. Yes, music wins souls, directs them to the side hole through which all mankind can be reborn, and all people everywhere have a natural belief in God. When He is at last depicted to them, He is seen and recognized, and we *Pilger* accomplish our mission. We bring the scattered children of God into the arc of holy Christendom, and I, an organist and *Tonsetzer*, have an additional office of the Spirit, a gift (or should I say wound, affliction?) which must be governed and led by the Mother. If it is of the proper sort, it will be directed by the Mother in a blessed poor-sinner spirit, with a heart in Love with the Lamb and his side, according to the heart of and the joy of the Saviour and his angels, and it will be, it must become a warrant and a call, a justification and a testimony, in the living, beating, hearts of all men who hear and stand touched by the Lord through the agency and puissance of His songs.

Would my distant forebear—ole "Many Fishes" or "Manna for the Eskimos" as I jokingly like to call him—begin thusly? And indeed did not the Lord feed thousands—the entire Inuit people—from out his single small carcass? Aren't choristers in Nain on a Sunday morning still singing from his sheets of music—blackened at the edges by generations of thumbs and index fingers coated with seal oil—some one hundred and seventy years later? I learned this reading an obscure little music journal at our local university library, an interview with one Allison MacKay, a period instrument player with the Toronto Consort who had just returned from a trip from Nain where her group had been invited to a performance by Inuit choir and orchestra. What an incredible coincidence that I would happen to lay my hands on this pertinent and highly gratifying bit of information, that I would make such a serendipitous discovery. Although music has meant more to me than most, and, although for fun or to kill time, I might, if inside a temple of specialized learning, more than the average Joe, find myself thumbing through some obscure musical publication from north of the border—considering my interests and credentials this should not surprise or disturb anyone—still what incomparably good luck and what a sign of high favor that I should come across an article that concerned and bore on an antique relation and predecessor of mine that only I could ever know appertained to him, as long ago in the 1920s during my student days abroad I had scoured through the archives in Herrnhut and to my astonishment found the Lebenslauf *or "biography of the departed," as told by a friend of course, some Brother in the Faith, usually a close associate of the deceased, of great great how many greats exactly I always forget grampus Polycarp and therefore knew it had been he and not some other cetacean who brought those precious manuscripts to the Moravian mission in Labrador in eighteen ought two. For the Canadian article did not specify Polycarp by name. It only stated that late in the eighteenth or early in the nineteenth century (I already knew 1802 to be the correct date) Moravian missionaries had brought handwritten copies of these great works to the new world and that long before such music was performed elsewhere in Canada, the Inuit of Labrador worshipped and made a joyful noise—or is it sound? —unto the Lord by singing in their own language, Inukitut, hymns and cantatas by Mozart, Bach and that other Papa not Zinzendorf but Haydn. Again today I find myself in Stabley Library. I am here often now. Though I also spend many hours at the much smaller public facility near the new courthouse also researching my subject for although the collection is much smaller there* are a few old volumes, their spines long since cracked or broken, on Pennsylvania religious sects, discarded no doubt from the basements of one or another of the local churches that I find most helpful. After making that initial surprise find, I have been visiting one or the other of the two libraries on almost a daily basis, boning up on the early Moravian missions, a subject by no means new to me but one that I have not revisited since my days in seminary, preparatory to beginning the new work. I hope to outdo all that I have yet done. Yes, the course my life has taken since making that chance discovery has been determined by the fact that I did indeed make it. Had I not come across that academic journal, I don't know what I would be doing now. Composing no doubt but hardly contemplating a return to opera ... the genre I applied myself to in my salad days in Germany.

Though I see I pretend not to notice many taking a swift second glance at me. You might expect to encounter an Amish man (or someone whom you might take for an Amish man) in his field behind his team plowing furrows or traveling down the pike in his buggy with his prim sour-faced wife or at a barn raising with his burly blackhatted blackgarbed and yes as they were all married blackbearded neighbors, also members of the sect for often you do see them out in groups though some of course have blond, bright red, auburn, or silver, not to mention salt-and-pepper, beards. Only the souvenir ceramic dolls and the salt and pepper shakers made to look like Amishmen are all blackbearded, and invariably Amish males so appear in the illustrations of all the old books. In a worn volume on Pennsy folklore, say, you'll see one of our number so dourly and predictably depicted painting a hechs sign to ward away some spirit or devil conjured up at an Indian pow-wow by the savages and their cohorts the Chicanere or German gypsies whom the Amish also call Smutsers or Black Dutch but you would not—I say, you would not—expect to see one of us primitives alive and in the flesh in the periodical room of a university library. Especially on a Sunday, which today is. One would naturally do a doubletake. Yet here I sit, my black felt hat doffed and sitting on the table before me, with only hooks-and-eyes on my coat and vest, wearing trousers with a flap that buttons along the waist instead of one with fly-closings, my long hair cut in bangs and my beard—albeit mostly gray—as bushy as can be. But then again I scratch my ears and reflect that all sorts frequent this *library nowadays. Nobody's much of a novelty anymore. Everyone has seen everyone else by now. In the eighth decade of our troubled twentieth century, no human being is too* outré *or monkey-like. We have come to accept all racial attributes and facial features and all styles of dress. Even black broadcloth and a pilgrim's plain black hat. It is now impolite to stare even if it is at a Hottentot and how much less so at some disfigured old gent with what looks like a harelip. Actually a scar from the old car crash. Besides, although not in Lancaster but in Indiana, the home town of that star of the silver screen and U.S. Air Force Ker-nal Ji-Ji-Jim-my Stewart, we still remain geographically situated in the state of Pennsylvania, where the sight of an old-style Dutchman can't ever look too, too out of place. Even this far west, as a few of the tribe make their home now in Jefferson County, just across the Indiana line.*

It appears that I have survived another crossing. Paul braved Christ the Creator's seas as surely as did Ulysses bearded, triple-trined-trident-bearing Poseidon's and shortly when we put into port in Esquimaux Bay in this Newfoundland, I shall surely step on soil of the same sort which shall one day cover my earthy remains and bony remnants, for I doubt if I shall cross the Atlantic for a fourth time. Or even brave its waters on even a relatively short trip such as the one I took with Brother Joseph to the Carolinas. I made my first passage as a mere boy in the company of all the other Herrnhaagers. Traveling together on shipboard, we permitted our usual activities to be interrupted as little as possible. Thus, we organized as a Sea Congregation, maintaining services, discipline, physical care of individual travelers, and singing together as a group….

Richard turned from the excerpt reluctantly. He hoped that someday he would again take it up and proceed with it. He knew, however, that he would soon be at work at something much closer to his own heart, which would also encompass his present devastation. American Indians, however, would also play just as pivotal a part in it, as they did in the Moravian story. At his desk beside his computer lay the little piece of red quartzite he picked up at Devil's Lake during his second trip to Wisconsin, which had what looked like either a triangle, an arrowhead or a pointed horn incised or engraved into its one side. He lifted the stone up, turned it over in his palm and stared at the place where the missing triangular flake had chipped off. If one squinted, it looked like a fossil imprint or impression. His Wiccan friends had told him that we don't ever arbitrarily pick up a rock. The rock or stone selects or chooses us.

Lynn would pay him two calls in Pennsylvania before he would again visit her at the white farmhouse. Both her trips to her home state would occur in the summer, the first just seven months after Richard's Christmas vacation in July 2008, the second in July of 2009. They spent both of her visits camping. In 2008 she had come home to attend a girlfriend's wedding, a woman whom she had met in Chicago but who had grown up in Pennsylvania not at all that far from her. Erika had been married and divorced twice and soon she would be relocating from Chi to take up residence in Akron with her new husband. At the wedding, Lynn acted as maid of honor. She hadn't known how much time she would be able to squeeze in for Richard. The wedding was in Philly and she simply had to make time for her elderly parents—she only usually got to see them once a year. She managed to free herself up for three whole days just after the Fourth of July weekend. For years—since she first started revisiting him in Mercersdale in 1995—he had joked that he would someday kidnap her and take her to "his mountains," where they could stay hid where no one would ever find them for as long as they didn't want to be found. She had always replied that she would love him to abduct her but that she could not stay long in the wild, for she had her two young boys to return home to and care for. Well, after loading her Windstar with their gear, they at last headed out northward for what his grandfather Owen always called "Pennsylvania's wild country," a scenic, largely forested and increasingly mountainous stretch of isolated and deserted highways along which the West Branch of the Susquehanna looped and meandered (Richard pointed out numerous retired and semi-private swimming holes), former strip mines abounded, some of them growing scraggy conifers planted as part of a reclamation project, the newly constituted Pennsylvania Elk herd roamed, and in which one found the picturesque little communities of Frenchville, Keewaydin, Karthaus, Benezette, Keating and Renova. The story of Frenchville was a little bit like that of Wisconsin's New Glarus. Its early settlers, all Catholic immigrants from the Haute-Marne region of central France, had walked overland from the port of Baltimore to settle there around 1830. No one knew for sure why the early settlers left France, perhaps so the men could avoid conscription. Richard recalled that his grandfather had said that one hundred years later, when he had started out in business, the isolated town had the reputation of being a rough place. The insurance companies Owen worked for did not wish to issue homeowner's policies there as too many of the town's residents had the habit of solving financial difficulties by setting fires and that many of the houses hid stills which blew up again and again on the bootleggers. At that time the state police did not go to Frenchville except in pairs, and game wardens knew better than to show up. The people did not hide their poached deer but hung the slain animals in their backyards for all to see. Despite the warnings he had received from certain of the companies he represented, Owen worked the area and developed a select clientele. He found companies that would sell to the backwoods folk, and he eventually made many friends among the French people. He said that the men of the town were very protective of their women. No woman would ever be seen on the street without a male escort. The Frenchville of that time was now like the Frenchville of the 1830s a thing of the past. In the turbulent 1960s, linguists at Penn State became interested in the little town, because many of the town's older residents still spoke a classically pure French, without American accent and without the slang of the contemporary French. Lynn remembered hearing something about this while she had been a student at Penn State. Today Frenchville was known for its annual picnic and for its winter coyote hunt, sponsored by the local Mosquito Creek Sportsmen Club, which drew competitors from as far as two or three states away. Richard directed Lynn onto a dirt road which he said would loop back to the main highway in six or seven miles. He wanted to point two places out to her, first a log cabin erected in the 1840s, the second oldest in the region still intact and standing after the Heinrich Mercer House, now a hunting camp bearing a sign and nameplate—Camp Never Shut Off—and second, a haven and sanctuary for nuns in the middle of nowhere. He said the cabin situated in the middle of dense forest gave a better idea of what the Mercer House must have looked like in 1807 when there was still no town only six or seven log houses than the Mercer House of today surrounded by its many neighboring properties and commercial buildings and not a single tree. He wanted her to see Bethany Retreat because she had just read (at his suggestion) George Moore's *Héloïse and Abélard.* Shortly after they drove back out on the highway but before they reached the Keewaydin Fruit Farm, where each fall Richard drove for fresh cider, he had Lynn pull off the berm in front of a stone farmhouse. He wanted to point out the name on the mailbox: Lefebvre. He knew that her people came from further to the east, but perhaps she had a country cousin or two she did not know about. Lynn brightly answered that she just might. The Lefebvres were an awfully big family. Richard and Lynn pitched their tents at the campground at Sinnemahoning. The true-life protagonist of one of Richard's unpublished novels, the notorious Pennsylvania highwayman Robber Lewis, had been shot and wounded here by a sheriff's posse in 1820. He would die of gangrene in a Bellefonte jail cell twelve days later. Richard read poems by the fire, and the two hiked to see the elk amidst the rhododendron and honeysuckle. They sat for hours on a little bench beside the Sinnemahoning Creek. Two children running ahead of their parents on the trail caught them kissing. Like a woman, Richard closed his eyes when his lips met Lynn's. Lynn wanted some wine for their last night, so early in the day they drove the twenty or so miles to the state store in Renova, a little brick railroad town in the Pennsylvania hills that looked today almost exactly the same as it had in the 1930s. Richard had read somewhere that there were nearly twice as many women in Renova as men. A statistic in some magazine. A joke about where lonesome bachelors should head. The mountains along the narrow West Branch reminded Richard of those along the much broader Rhine. There was no prettier drive in all of Pennsylvania. Neither Richard nor Lynn received signal on their cell phones. They might as well have not brought them. They stopped at two of Richard's favorite places to swim. Two train bridges crossed the river at Keating—not a town really, only a cluster of three or four homes. Richard had swum once between the bridges as a freight train crossed in either direction. He and Lynn took a short walk hand in hand. Looking down from one of the two trestles, they saw the skeleton of an elk in the water below. Richard actually took a dip at Kettle Creek. Lynn took a seat on a park bench and read nearby, her face shaded by the brim of her straw boater. Fifty or sixty Canadian geese honked on the sandy beach. Two men pointed to a tree across the water. Richard would later fetch Lynn so that she also could see the bald eagle feeding its chicks. That afternoon she spoke to him about the many summers she had spent as a counselor at exclusive children's camps in Canada and elsewhere. She never spent a single summer at her parents after she turned seventeen. She spent the night in his tent. The following morning before they checked out, they had just broken down their campsite and stored all their gear in the trunk of the Windstar when it started to pour down rain.

The following July they again took a retreat in the woods, this time just outside of Mercersdale at Cold Mushroom State Park. This year Lynn's visit fell on the holiday weekend. She had again wanted to tent out, but, when Richard attempted to book, he discovered that all the camp sites had already been taken, so he decided to splurge and rented one of the still available cabins, all built by the Civilian Conservation Corps in the 1930s but since remodeled and equipped with modern amenities, for seven days—one could not hire one for any shorter period—even though Lynn's stay was again limited to only three days. He felt like celebrating. Not only had he just finished the proofs for his novella collection—the book would be out before he visited Lynn in October—he had also just received word that a grant he had written for a proposed Mercersdale Veterans' Memorial had received state funding.

A Romain Rolland pacifist and soon he hoped a member of the Wider Quaker Fellowship, Richard had nonetheless battled ferociously for the project for the past six years. The idea for the memorial had been Owen's. On Memorial Day 2000, the Amvets had invited Richard, a trustee of the Mercersdale Historical Foundation, to be their featured speaker, and he spoke on a subject he knew quite a lot about, Mercersdale's earliest veterans, those who had fought in the Revolution, the War of 1812, and the War between the States. After giving his speech in the park, he had to give it again at home. Battling his cancer, Owen had been too sick to attend. Although delighted that his grandson had been asked to speak—he himself had done so many times—he could not come to see him. After Richard had finished, Owen looked him in the eye and asked pointedly if Richard knew how many soldiers from World War Two, who had lived within a two-block radius of their apartment on Second Street, had not made it back home. Richard confessed that he had no idea. Owen told him that there had been five and spoke for a little about each. They were his contemporaries. He had known them all well. Despite all his community service over the years, he said that he should have done one thing more, seen to it that a memorial to the area's servicemen and women be built in Mercersdale. The town should have put it up years before. The recognition was long overdue. Owen was not a veteran. He tried to enlist three times and was drafted once, but on all four occasions the Army turned him down for health reasons. Ina and Rebecca had both prayed that the doctors would reject him because of the large scar that ran across his belly from the intestinal surgery he had as a boy. Arriving after the operation, Owen's grandfather had brought him the two items he craved most: Welch's grape juice and real toilet paper. The Lord listened to the petition of Owen's wife and daughter. Owen couldn't pass the physical. He became Mercersdale's air raid warden, and he chaired all the wartime Red Cross blood drives in the Cold Mushroom Valley. He knew all the men who had died and wanted to see them honored. He told Richard that he should take the project on. Richard had never carried through. He could never find anyone who would help do the research. That changed when his acquaintance from the Amvets Bill Hamlin retired in 2003. The two spent many hours reading all the obituaries in the Mercersdale *Courier* from the war years. Fortunately all the newspapers had been preserved on microfilm at the Mercersdale Historical Foundation. By the time the two started to work, Richard had forgotten the names of all the five men and only vaguely recalled the story. Owen had always chid Richard about his poor memory. Richard could almost hear him venting his frustration: "Richard, when God was passing out brains, you had your head in a woodpecker's nest looking for eggs." Richard knew the names of all five men now. Four they found quickly. The identity of the fifth had remained a mystery, but an elderly lady from the historical society at last revealed his identity. Mr. Humphry's parents resided in Nestor Hill. His obit gave the Nestor Hill address. During his high school years—the time Owen had remembered him from—he resided with his maternal grandparents on Second Street. All five boys had served as airmen. All five had perished when the enemy shot down their planes. All five had been the only sons in their families, and all five, if one counted Mr. Humphry as living on Second Street, resided within two blocks of each other. Richard wanted to see the memorial built, however belatedly. And now it looked like it would be.

Yes. He had much to celebrate. On the porch of the little cabin—in Richard's mind their honeymoon cottage, for the three days he spent with Lynn there came as close to a honeymoon as Richard would ever experience—the couple lit sparklers and firecrackers. They cooked outside on a grill all three days. Richard had to fill their five-gallon water container each morning and haul it back to their picnic table from a pump outside the shower area a quarter of a mile away so that they would have water to clean their dishes which they left dry in the sun stacked in a strainer on the picnic table. Their neighbors in the next cabin were a middle-aged Amish couple and their two grandchildren. Lynn had brought her bicycle with her and she spent hours pedaling down the mountain bike trails through the acres of pink and white mountain laurel. The two read each other poems and Richard rubbed and massaged Lynn's feet as she sat in her lawn chair and read. She wore the same straw boater she had at Kettle Creek the previous year. They hiked all eleven miles of the muddy bog trail round the peat-stained black waters of Cold Mushroom Lake. In 1984, they had started down the same trail their last day together before Lynn's marriage but had turned back after only one or two miles. They found the trail quite a bit dryer this time and made it all the way round. The two crossed the northern tip of the lake on a long pontoon bridge. That night they signed up for a full moon canoe paddle at the Park Office. A park ranger led forty canoers across the length of the lake. Richard looked up at the sky not only to see the great silver orb shining brightly but also several magnificent shooting stars. Lynn sang doggerel verse from her days as a lifeguard and children's camp counselor:

> Just a boy and a girl in a little canoe and the moon is shining all around.
> As he glided his paddle, he didn't even make a sound.

Well they talked and they talked until the moon went in
And he said you better kiss me or get out and swim.
Well you know what to do in a little canoe
When the moon is shining all a-, the moon is shining all a-, the
moon is shining all around.
Get out and swim? What the heck go and neck!

That night they both wrote long entries in the Cabin No.
9 Journal after reading the previous narratives of other camp-
ers who had stayed at the cabin over the years. Lynn had such
a splendid time at Richard's home lake that she determined
then and there that she would take him to Devil's Lake, her
favorite State Park and lake of all the many parks and lakes in
Wisconsin, when he came to visit her in the fall to celebrate
the publication of his new book.

The following morning before she headed out on the long
trip home, Richard borrowed her pocketknife and carved their
initials by the fireplace in the cabin wall. Lynn had forgotten
to turn off the dome light in the Windstar the previous night.
A park ranger had to give her a jump. Before departing, she
dropped Richard off at home. He returned to Cold Mushroom
State Park in his own car with a bottle of shoe polish. He used
it to paint over and camouflage the set of carved initials.

After disguising his vandalism and returning home, he
unpacked his suitcase—the same one he had taken to Wisconsin
two years before and which he would again pack in three
months when he would visit Lynn's home for the second time—
and discovered among his shirts, shorts, socks and swimming
trunks a pair of Lynn's black jeans. He felt certain that she had
as a joke purposely "packed her clothes with his," as one of the
many CDs they played on his boom box over the Fourth of July

weekend was Bob Dylan's *Together Through Life,* where Bob urged his love in one of the songs to do just that, as they journeyed together on the wheel of time and space. In order to return them to her, he laundered, pressed and folded the jeans and then tucked the pair of pants together with his own clothing in his already overstuffed suitcase when in October—his favorite time of all the year, when the trees let fall and drop their precious leaves now all changed in color—he made his second trip to Wisconsin. Ned again drove him to the Amtrak station in Altoona, where he again boarded the westbound *Pennsylvanian.* As before, he changed trains in Pittsburgh and then sped onward until the *Capitol Limited* reached its destination in Chicago. This time Lynn met him at Union Station. In September, Sean had started his first year in college. He had begun his coursework at the University of Wisconsin-Madison. Micah still lived at home, a junior now in high school.

As they had done at Christmas, Richard and Lynn took numerous day trips across Wisconsin sightseeing. In Spring Green, they visited Taliesin, Frank Lloyd Wright's great estate and workplace where he founded his famous Hillside Home School and stopped at the Visitor Center where they dined at the Riverview Terrace Café, where through the wide windows spanning the entire length of the building they looked out at the parti-colored hillsides rising above the Wisconsin River. They did not stop at the House on the Rock but drove through the grounds of the American Players Theatre, famous for its plays in the woods and its outdoor Shakespeare festival each summer. They also parked downtown and visited a number of little shops. Lynn snapped several shots of Richard standing in front of a small compact modern streamlined bank, designed and built by the great Frank Lloyd Wright for use in his own hometown, which would also later serve as the adopted residence of Joseph Stalin's daughter, the anticommunist Svetlana Alliluyeva.

Another day they returned to Mineral Point and New Glarus, and once more Richard feasted on *Wienerschnitzel* and *Spätzle* and later in the evening the two again waltzed and polkaed. He also accompanied Lynn twice to Quaker Meeting in Kenosha, and on a Saturday he met all the members of her sailboat racing crew as they towed their boat out of the water and placed it in dry-dock for the off season as a few first snowflakes skirled and danced in the crisp October air. With Micah, they attended a concert by a famous string quartet in downtown Chi and afterwards the three ate out at a gourmet Indian restaurant, Richard's treat. They ran with the dogs, and Richard spent the better part of one afternoon picking up and throwing into the garbage the endless fallen black walnuts scattered under the seven trees in Lynn's front lawn. Richard would take back to Pennsylvania lots of wonderful memories of sweet things he and Lynn had done together—including pumpkin carving. She carved a happyface pumpkin and he a fanged fiend. They toasted and ate the seeds after cleaning up all the pulpy mess. Richard treated Micah to his first rock concert. He asked his mother for the money to purchase a ticket. With the tuition and child support she currently had to pay, she said that she could not afford it. Richard thought of the money he had wasted on booze over the years and gave the elated boy the fifty dollars for the ticket. Once again in his life, he vowed to quit drinking.

Lynn saved the trip to Devil's Lake for the weekend before his departure. She told him this magical lake a holy place for the Ho-Chunk was perhaps her favorite place in all of

Wisconsin. Over the years she had come there again and again and often in the company of her two boys. On the long drive, they stopped at a country store for tea and cider. Hundreds and hundreds of pumpkins sat in the mown grass. Life-size ghosts, goblins, witches and scarecrows decorated the parking lot. Richard thrust his head through the aperture of a mock guillotine and stuck out his tongue. Lynn snapped a photo. A giant sign beside the convenience store advertised the "farmtastic experience" of the thirtieth annual Kalberth Country Farm Haunted Halloween Corn Maze. The sign proclaimed: "You'll never solve this labyrinth! Stride in and you will find yourself lost forever!" Richard saw the entrance to the maze in the field just beyond the store. *Abandon all hope.* The cornstalks looked frayed and dried. Lynn said how she and Shane loved to stop at such mazes when the boys were still small. There was always additional fun such as hayrides and farm animals for petting. You had to watch. If it had rained recently, you had to come prepared. A bit of muck was fine if you brought rubber boots and a big plastic bag to store all your dirty stuff. Richard thought of all he had missed out on in life. At one time, he would have loved to have children. He was too old to start a family now. Anaxagoras said to a man who was grieving because he lay dying in a foreign land, "The descent to hell is the same from every place."

Lynn told him as they drove along the river in the bright sunshine that the little town of Baraboo which they would soon enter was the county seat of Sauk County and the home of Circus World Museum, the largest collection of circus gear, circus wagons and other circus memorabilia in the United States. It had been only logical for the museum to locate here, as Baraboo had been the former headquarters and winter home of the famous Ringling Brothers circus. Every once in awhile the museum hosted an old-fashioned circus parade through the streets of the town after which the attendants set up the antique circus rings underneath the bright, tenderly cared for, century-old canvas tents. They could not have asked for a brighter fall day. The blue sky remained unspotted and cloudless. Richard saw the name Veolia painted on Baraboo's dumpsters and garbage cans. A huge company and conglomerate, Veolia Environmental Services provided waste disposal services in twelve states, the Bahamas and Canada. Richard knew this because the giant had just purchased Mercersdale's little mom-and-pop garbage company, John Glenn Sanitation, no relation to the astronaut and United States Senator. It made him snicker. The same curbside collectors picked up trash in both Mercersdale and Baraboo.

Lynn asked Richard if he ever read Aldo Leopold's *A Sand County Almanac,* and he replied that he had not. She said that Leopold was a famous Wisconsin naturalist whose writings many considered worthy of John Muir's and Henry David Thoreau's. She tried to paraphrase something she had read somewhere, as she couldn't remember the exact quote, something about a pinball machine. Yes. Aldo's shadow was like that of a great pine. It cast itself gigantically across the land and into all its remotest corners, the conscience opposing an evil scheme and monster ambition to make the world one giant pinball machine. His shack and farm along the Wisconsin River which he celebrated in that book and close to where he died in 1948 fighting a grass fire on a neighbor's farm, was located near Baraboo, the only chicken coop on the National Register of Historical Places. This region was well known for its celebrated naturalists and conservationists. Later in the day, they would visit Wisconsin's first designated State Natural Area, the beautiful Parfrey's Glen, a narrow canyon cut into the south slope of the South Baraboo Range just east of the Devil's Lake gorge and managed by Devil's Lake park staff. The trail there had been closed due to flooding but had recently reopened. Indeed in several hours' time, they would discover, as they walked through the canyon, which was formed when meltwater from the ice sheet cut in during the Pleistocene era, the fast cold mountain stream had jumped its bed and had begun to create a new path. Nature, as always, was forever rearranging the land. To reach the high walls, grand boulders and top waterfall, they had to continue past the sign saying End of Trail. As they passed through plantations of yellow birch, mountain maple and red elder, Richard marveled as he looked up at the glen's sandstone walls studded with pebbles and boulders of shiny red quartzite.

Before they proceeded on to Devil's Lake, they stopped in Baraboo to browse at a used bookstore and several antique shops. They had lunch at a restaurant beside the Al Ringling Theatre, a grand-scale movie palace designed in the style of a rococo French opera house, a city landmark and a fixture in downtown Baraboo for three-quarters of a century. Richard didn't think it any more grand than Mercersdale's Garland though it beat his home theater in one respect: its Barton theater organ still functioned.

Lynn had the required sticker on her windshield so they didn't have to pay any entry fee to visit the park. She commented that the stone buildings at Devil's Lake had all been built in the thirties by the local CCC—just as the cabins and cottages at Cold Mushroom State Park in Pennsylvania had been. Soon they were hiking the steep 1.7 mile long East Bluff Trail.

Perhaps because he had just eaten lunch but also no doubt due to his being out of shape and because of his frequent smoking, Richard huffed and puffed. He found the steep trail so hard going he had to frequently stop and pause for breath. Lynn had no such difficulty but she sat down with him on the frequent benches as the path continued its ascent. The quartzite rock cliffs rose upwards of a hundred feet. With its mellow toproping and its headpoint style leads, Devil's Lake offered some of the best rock climbing in the Midwest. The sport climbers that Richard and Lynn saw that day brought plenty of sling, as many of the anchors were a good way back from the cliff edges. They encountered many other hikers, some coming from the other direction. When they reached the crest, before heading back down the other side to the lakeshore, they stepped out onto a precipitous ledge and had their photo taken together with Lynn's camera. They asked a couple visiting from Ohio if one of the two would oblige. The woman took the snap. She said she caught in the frame a bit of the blue lake below, its water the same shade as Lynn's eyes. The gorge, plugged by Wisconsinan Moraine at each end and occupied now by the lake, was a most impressive sight. Lynn said that scientists believed that the Wisconsin River had flowed through where the gorge now lay prior to the last glaciation. Richard found even more amazing the maroon and purple boulder field below. It looked like a landscape from another planet. The pink, red and darkish purple indicated the presence of hematite and other colorants in the metamorphosed sandstone. At the boulder field, Richard reached to the ground for a little red stone and slipped it in his pocket.

Richard's fortnight in Wisconsin flew by all too quickly. He did not want to leave.

Two nights before he and Lynn said goodbye, he scanned the want ads in the Kenosha paper. In the jobs section, he saw a piano salesman position advertised. Perhaps he should have called that number and seen if he could have arranged an interview with the company representative before he departed. New pianos would be hard to sell in these difficult economic times. His ability as an amateur pianist, however, would have served him in good stead. He would have dazzled prospective customers with his playing. His skillful tickling of the ivories, the seeming ease and finesse of his playful improvising, might have so impressed the undecided customer, especially if he was contemplating making a purchase so that his child or grand-child could take lessons, that at last he would make the decision to take the plunge and buy, invest in an instrument that would bring his family and him years and years of pleasure. Lynn kissed him goodbye as he got out of the Windstar. He asked if he could finally call her his girlfriend—if he could finally tell his friends back home that he now had a girl in Wisconsin—and she said yes. Again he hesitated. He did not wish to leave.

He began to cross the parking lot with its many scattered and blowing leaves toward the waiting bus, which would drop him off in Chi at Union Station.

The full-length shadow that extended before him as dark as any inkblot slowly began to shrink and fade and then it disappeared all together as he stood in line with his ticket held out, as those in front of him began mounting up the steps into the coach.

Postlude in the Upper Circles

Richard did not die until many years later. Indeed Natalia went first. Richard would not follow her into the beyond until exactly seven years to the day of her passing. He was one of the fortunate lucky ones. He went to sleep and awoke dead. His soul had perished many years before his body. He dated his real death all the way back to the moment he boarded that bus in Kenosha. The last thirty years of his life, he devolved into nothing more than a *wanagi* or a ghost. No one would ever designate or call him a *worak*. He observed life from the sidelines with ironic detachment and a jaundiced eye. Yet at the same time he kept manufacturing his other ghost—the one made of words. The process was an excruciatingly slow one, but with the passage of fifty years he had succeeded in turning himself into dead print. The flesh became word. He read himself almost blind. He spent more time communing with the ghosts of authors past than with persons living and breathing and present. He knew his own achievement was but at best a humble one. Richard Mercer would live on as only a small all-but-unnoticed spook. He had not the vitality of, say, a Charles Dickens, whose collected works made up a very great ghost indeed, a green-robed jolly giant, glorious to see and bearing a glowing torch, in shape not unlike Plenty's horn. A veritable Yula *Alf*. However small a crumb, whether recognized or not, Richard did add his small something—his widow's mite—to the grand total of creation and thus aided honorably the Prime Mover and helped him in His ceaseless productive toil if only in a time-bound manner and for a span of three score and ten. Indeed in short order, he became an aged man, a virtual skeleton in his rocking chair looking with affection at his own death.

He awoke dead and blind. The funny thing was he did not see black but white. And for a long time he remained as lost as Polycarp Schober in a squall and whiteout in Labrador.

He felt still like Richard but also like something infinitely greater than Richard, something of which Richard constituted a part, but only the smallest fragment. At last he heard a gentle voice call out to him: "And I, Prince, consign myself to your ear and find that nest sufficient." He recognized the voice of his beloved. Her distinct voice. Yet he heard other muffled voices within hers. He had multiple Mes and so apparently had she.

"Yes, Richard, we both lived numerous lives, some parallel and some skew. Memories from all yours will soon start flooding back. My Baldr, we knew each other in not one but in all of our lives, and I daresay in each life we dearly and deeply loved each other. No one called as witness could possibly deny it. Yet, as Red Horn and Oma always said, in all the *worak* Beneath Worlds—even in the best of all the possible Beneath Worlds—things seldom if ever turned out rosily and well. Even in our best incarnations, all that we loved went away in the end. Yet the Prime Mover kept bringing us back, hiding our identities as if with a foliate mask. You will hardly recognize yourself in some of your avatars; the Prime Mover superimposed the false faces so well that the true one hardly ever shined and glimmered through. But I always recognized my beloved on first sight. I knew you not only when you were famous and great—when you were Milton, Henry James, and Thomas Wolfe—but also when you were unrecognized and obscure. I knew you in your unproductive and unliterary lives, as well. I loved you when you called yourself Billy Steiglitz. That was perhaps the sorriest of our incarnations, but we had our happy times, too. We leapt into many parallel lives all at once, but, among all the others, we did indeed lead the existence we had envisioned before we fell or rather leapt. You did become my Minnesinger, and in that life I bore you many children. Eventually you will encounter all the loved ones from your many, many lives in all the worlds below, for, although the journey may be long and dark, all souls in the end find their way home. Yes, my dear Tom, you can go home again! The splintered at last does become unsplintered. And we married not just in one life but in many. Richard and Natalia's near twins Michael and Elissa at long last did say their vows in the little Union Church in Rallingsburg built by Michael's forefathers. From the smile on your face, I see that you are remembering, my dear Baldr. They wrote their own vows. Hush, you need not recite them. I wrote them with you, remember. We had our children when you were Richard, too. No, not flesh-and-blood children. Richard's books. The above does reflect the below. You gave birth in that life, Baldr. You left Wisconsin pregnant. You may have written that beautiful little book all by yourself, but in a way she is just as much my child as she is yours! But enough. All those lives are over now. You have mastered all your lessons, made the grade and graduated. My fawn will never again leave my side. No longer will you only glimpse tantalizing intimations of the hereafter in the here. You have learned the meaning of transience. You now understand the insignificant and limited. Therefore you can now appreciate the perfect and unflawed. Regain paradise. The Summerlands beckon. Return now to the land of eternal ideas!" The fog began to lift, or the scales fell from Baldr-Richard's eyes. He first made out the fantastical outcroppings and the great cragged lopsided formations at the tops of the bluffs. He then saw the rippling waves of an otherworldly lake and a great field of purple, cascading boulders.

On the white beach stood his Beatrice wearing her shining crown.

Author's Note

In *Baldr and Beatrice*, a single voice speaks, that of the present raconteur. The careful reader will soon notice, however, that this voice recalls other voices—those of other beloved raconteurs—from all times and places in the human odyssey. Echoes and allusions proliferate and teem in *Baldr and Beatrice*. Quotations also abound and not all of them are marked. The present raconteur says along with Molière: *Je prends mon bien où je le trouve.* I take my property where I find it. Kipling sings a similar tune:

> When 'Omer smote 'is bloomin' lyre,
>   He'd 'eard men sing by land an' sea;
> An' what he thought 'e might require,
>   'E went an' took—the same as me!

My borrowings from Milton, the Brothers Grimm, and Adelbert von Chamisso are flagrant, but other raconteurs also smile and doff their hats—including George Meredith, Somerset Maugham, John Steinbeck, Ernst Jünger, and Rainer Maria Rilke, among others. To the reader who enjoys searching for texts behind texts—and I confess that ever since reading *The Wasteland* I am such a one—I wish a very merry chase.

I would also like to acknowledge one specific and special debt. In August 2010, I was fortunate to attend a Corn Moon Esbat in Shawville, Pennsylvania, conducted by James P. Leonard, Sr. (Reverend Golden Raven Hawk H.P.) and Scott D. Koenig, Sr. (Dragon Star). The Full Moon and healing rituals Beatrice performs in Chapter Nine owe much to the religious ceremonies they devised for that night.

I have also chosen Scott and his wife Mary (Morning Moon) as godparents—or as I prefer calling them godfather and goddessmother—for this little book.

I deeply thank them for befriending me when they did.

Mark Seinfelt is the author of several books. He holds a Bachelor of Arts degree in English from the Pennsylvania State University, where he received the Henry Sams Memorial Award for his thesis and where he studied under critically acclaimed author and Lannan Lifetime Achievement Award winner Paul West and novelist and screenwriter Robert C.S. Downs. He also holds a Master of Fine Arts in writing from Washington University in St. Louis, where he worked with the noted fiction writer, philosopher, and essayist William H. Gass, who served as chairman of his dissertation committee. In 2004, his study of famous author suicides *Final Drafts* was selected as an alternate selection of the Readers' Subscription Book Club. His novel *Henry Boulanger of Mushannon Town* won the 2010 Pinnacle Book Achievement Award in the category of Historical Fiction. The North American Bookdealers Exchange (NABE) Pinnacle Awards annually honor top genre books published by independent publishers. Seinfelt's fiction and non-fiction has been featured in numerous publications. Currently, he resides in Philipsburg, Pennsylvania.